THE EIGHTS

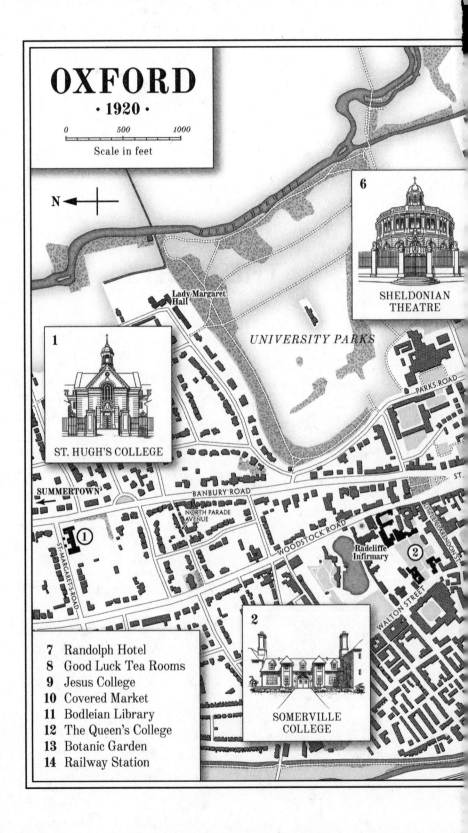

OXFORD
· 1920 ·

0   500   1000
Scale in feet

N

1 ST. HUGH'S COLLEGE

6 SHELDONIAN THEATRE

Lady Margaret Hall

UNIVERSITY PARKS

PARKS ROAD

SUMMERTOWN

BANBURY ROAD

NORTH PARADE AVENUE

ST. MARGARET'S ROAD

WOODSTOCK ROAD

Radcliffe Infirmary

WALTON STREET

2 SOMERVILLE COLLEGE

7   Randolph Hotel
8   Good Luck Tea Rooms
9   Jesus College
10 Covered Market
11 Bodleian Library
12 The Queen's College
13 Botanic Garden
14 Railway Station

RIVER CHERWELL

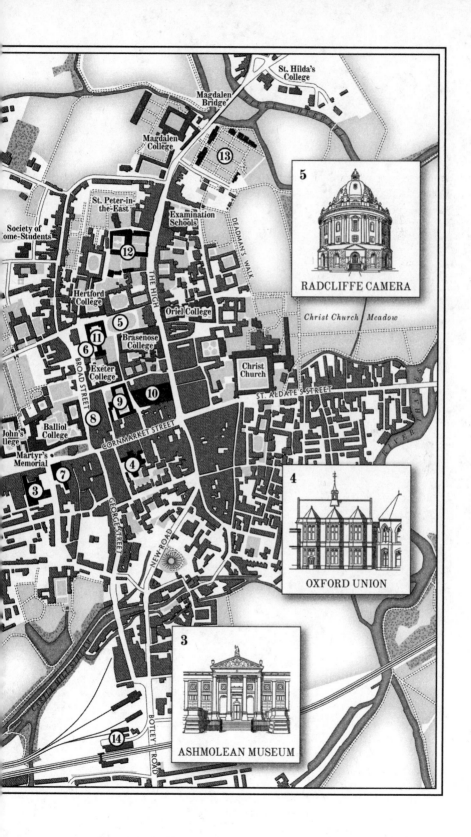

St. Hilda's College

Magdalen Bridge

Magdalen College

⑬

St. Peter-in-the-East

Society of Home-Students

Examination Schools

DEADMAN'S WALK

⑫

THE HIGH

Hertford College

Oriel College

⑤

Brasenose College

⑪

⑥

Exeter College

Christ Church

⑨ ⑩

ST. ALDATE'S STREET

BROAD STREET

⑧

John's College

Balliol College

CORNMARKET STREET

Martyr's Memorial

⑦

④

③

GEORGE STREET

NEW ROAD

RIVER THAMES

Christ Church Meadow

5

RADCLIFFE CAMERA

4

OXFORD UNION

3

ASHMOLEAN MUSEUM

CASTLE MILL STREAM

⑭

BOTLEY ROAD

THE
EIGHTS

JOANNA
MILLER

G. P. PUTNAM'S SONS
NEW YORK

PUTNAM
— EST. 1838 —

G. P. Putnam's Sons
Publishers Since 1838
An imprint of Penguin Random House LLC
1745 Broadway, New York, NY 10019
penguinrandomhouse.com

Map by Mike Hall

Book design by Shannon Nicole Plunkett

Library of Congress Cataloging-in-Publication Data

Names: Miller, Joanna, author.
Title: The eights / Joanna Miller.
Description: New York: G. P. Putnam's Sons, 2025.
Identifiers: LCCN 2024033366 (print) | LCCN 2024033367 (ebook) |
ISBN 9780593851418 (hardcover) | ISBN 9780593851425 (epub)
Subjects: LCGFT: Novels.
Classification: LCC PR6113.I5624 E34 2025 (print) |
LCC PR6113.I5624 (ebook) | DDC 823/.92—dc23/eng/20241004
LC record available at https://lccn.loc.gov/2024033366
LC ebook record available at https://lccn.loc.gov/2024033367

Printed in the United States of America
1st Printing

The authorized representative in the EU for product safety and compliance
is Penguin Random House Ireland, Morrison Chambers, 32 Nassau Street,
Dublin D02 YH68, Ireland, https://eu-contact.penguin.ie.

For Darcy, Jackson, and Archie

Any great change must expect opposition because it shakes the very foundation of privilege.

—Lucretia Mott (1793–1880)

Many would be cowards if they had courage enough.

—Thomas Fuller (1608–1661)

THE EIGHTS

DAUGHTERS OF THE UNIVERSITY

A memorable occasion in the history of university life at Oxford takes place tomorrow. For the first time in one thousand years, students from the five women's institutions will matriculate to become fully fledged undergraduates. At ten o'clock, the entrance to the Divinity School is expected to fill with trim figures in cap and gown, carrying the University statute book under their arms, proud of their newly won distinction.

While this historic event will be celebrated by many, it will be disappointing to those who believe Oxford should remain a "man's university." One unhappy don has stated that he plans to mark the occasion with a black armband.

OXFORD TIMES
WEDNESDAY, OCTOBER 6, 1920

MICHAELMAS TERM

1

Thursday, October 7, 1920 (0th Week)

ACADEMIC DRESS

Students are expected to wear the undergraduates'
gown and cap of the approved pattern for lectures
and tutorials and when they enter any university
building. This includes the university church and
the libraries.

They are also expected to wear academic dress
if they are out after dinner unless they are going
by invitation to a private house.

They are required to wear for their
examinations a special dress under the gown,
namely, a dark coat and skirt and a white blouse
with black tie. Shoes and stockings must be black.

On other occasions they are advised to wear
under the gown either a dark coat and skirt or a
dark coat frock. Bright and light colors are
inadmissible.

Caps are retained where the male
undergraduate removes his, for example in
university ceremonies.

Caps and gowns can be ordered from Oxford
tailors and from Messrs. Ede & Ravenscroft,

93 & 94 Chancery Road, London. Students with
the status of scholar should wear the scholars'
and not the commoners' gown.

MISS E. F. JOURDAIN
Principal

The square cap, made of wool, is an odd sort of thing.
Floppy, but pointed at four corners, it has no brim, just a
thick felt band secured by a button on either side. Does the
band go at the front or back? She cannot say. All she knows is
when she puts it on, she resembles a rotund Tudor courtier in a
Hans Holbein portrait, which is surely not the intended effect.

Strange little cap or no, Beatrice Sparks can hardly believe
that she has woken up somewhere other than the cluttered town
house in Bloomsbury that has been home for the last twenty-
one years. When she said goodbye to her father last night, she
felt like a sheet of paper folded in half and torn roughly along
the crease. Two smaller versions of herself exist now, each
with an edge that is undefined and feathery. Her first day at
St. Hugh's is an opportunity to rewrite one of these pages.

The mirror on the bedsitter wall is so small that she is
forced to back all the way across the room in order to get a
glimpse of herself in her commoners' gown. Sold by mail order,
the gown sits at her waist rather than the regulation hip and
cuts tightly into the shoulders of her jacket; she will simply
have to buy a man's size instead. But she is used to the accou-
trements of life being ill-fitting; last night, as she tried to sleep,
her feet tangled repeatedly with the cold metal rungs of the
bedstead. Nobody could ever label Beatrice an average woman;
she has inherited her six-foot stature from her father and her
hearty appetite for politics from her mother.

To be the daughter of a former student of the college is something, she supposes. A militant suffragette, disciple of Mrs. Pankhurst, and alumna of the hunger-strike brigade, Beatrice's mother is a woman of considerable renown, who believes in equality for women in education. Hence, there was never any doubt that Beatrice would apply for Oxford, regardless of whether matriculation was possible. Thankfully, to her mother's satisfaction, both those expectations have become a reality. Most women (and men) are intimidated by Edith Sparks, and, as Beatrice knows to her cost, she is a hard person to please. Fortunately, after more than twenty years of marriage, her husband is still besotted.

Today is unusual because Beatrice is not the sort of person that history happens to. She has certainly witnessed it in the making—her mother has seen to that—but usually from the sidelines. Beatrice may be fluent in ancient Greek, propagate orchids in her own greenhouse, attend debates in the House of Commons, and type begging letters on behalf of Serbian orphans, but she has never lived alongside other young women. An only child, she has the singular qualification of having absolutely no friends her own age. What she has discovered of friendship comes from observing her mother's relationships. It occurs to her that these are rather like cocoa; some are too strong, some too weak, and some spoil if left too long. Some even burn the tongue.

Glancing through her ground-floor window, she watches a lone wood pigeon pace the lawn, as if it has lost something, its purply-gray plumage distinct against the wet grass. As she swallows the cold egg on toast the scout has left in an approximation of breakfast, she hears muffled movement in neighboring rooms. She supposes the other occupants of Corridor Eight must also be forcing balls of toast down dry throats, buttoning too-tight white blouses, adjusting black ties, and shaking the creases out of academic gowns. Like Beatrice, they will walk to the Divinity School in the heart of the city, where at ten o'clock they will be among the first women to matriculate at Oxford University.

"Good morning. My name is Beatrice Sparks," she says to her reflection.

She takes a deep breath and reaches for her cap.

———◇———

IN THE ADJACENT ROOM, MARIANNE Grey is considering how to tell the principal of St. Hugh's that she intends to abandon her degree course after just one day.

Despite the fact that the college was built for purpose only four years ago, Marianne's corner room with its two exterior walls is undeniably drafty. As if resenting her presence, the mattress exhaled cool air last night as she tossed and turned, and an itchy patch of red scale threatens on her left index finger. Unfortunately, her exhibition of twenty pounds a year, while very welcome, will not stretch to extra buckets of coal, so she must make do with the twice-daily fires laid by the scout—if she decides to stay, that is. Her choice is this: remain at St. Hugh's to fulfill her life's ambition and continue to build lies upon lies, or give up the whole wretched scheme entirely and go home to the rectory, exercising her brain for the next three years teaching Sunday school and composing the parish newsletter.

She wonders what her father is doing right now. Preparing his sermon, perhaps, or eating a breakfast of crumpets loyally smothered with the appallingly tart gooseberry jam she made over the summer. Mrs. Ward, who has Thursdays off, will be taking her granddaughter to visit friends in Abingdon.

Marianne glances at the solitary postcard propped on the mantelpiece featuring Rossetti's *Proserpine* curved shyly around a bitten pomegranate. Like the goddess of the underworld, Marianne has given in to temptation (the lure of three years of study, in her case) and must pay the price of being separated from home for half the year, although that is where the similarity between them ends; Marianne is well aware she is no goddess or romantic heroine. She may have been christened after Jane Austen's Marianne, but she has none of her namesake's passion and energy. Sadly, she has far more in common with Tennyson's Mariana, a miserable woman shut in a tower, wishing and waiting until it drives her quite mad. Neither character, she is sure, was bothered by the price of coal—or by chilblains.

Glancing in the mirror, she sees an unremarkable woman with hooded eyes, flat chest, and hair the pallor of weak tea. A woman dressed in a secondhand academic gown and shoes that don't quite fit, trying out a life that isn't quite hers.

———◇———

IN THE ROOM OPPOSITE MARIANNE'S, Theodora Greenwood, known to her family and friends affectionately as Dora, is congratulating herself on meeting the simple dress code of sub fusc, although careful inspection of her attire will reveal an artfully tied black ribbon at her neck and a silver brooch with a diamond chip at her lapel. Her waist-length hair is tightly pinned, all strands accounted for.

How easy life would be, she muses, if she were as neat and tidy on the inside. If her brother could see her now, he would laugh at her square cap, call her an old maid, and pull it down over her eyes. Poor George, who ought to have graduated from Jesus College and be running the printworks with Father by now. But then, had George survived Cambrai and all the varied opportunities for death that followed, she would not be sitting here at all; their father would never have permitted it. A different version of Dora—provincial Dora—would most likely be spending her days pouring tea, playing whist, or being paraded at church (*Do not mention novels, Dora*).

But George did not survive Cambrai and Dora is the keeper of their childhood now, the curator of their childhood games, the silly notes, the selfish arguments. Even after three years, it is hard to accept that George and his restless bravado no longer exist. That, like thousands of others, he ran daily into a barrage of hot lead, blade, and shell until his flesh was blasted from his bones. How is it that her handsome, spoiled brother who smelled of grass and sweat and cigarettes, who swore her ball was out when it was plainly in, who only wrote her a single letter in his life, can no longer exist?

Unfortunately, she has letters enough to weep over: pages of crooked handwriting smudged with tears and refolded so many times the seams have given way to dust. All written by Charles, to whom, if life were not so despicably cruel, she would now be married. Charles who was to read Law at Queen's. The most popular cadet in the garrison who chose her (*her!*) from all the other girls in town. Charles who, when he led Dora into the bracken, made her feel so alive, so alert, so open to possibility that the plain, ordinary world she knew became a dizzying, shimmering place. Even now, she can conjure the sweet fruitiness of his mouth, the warm breath teasing her neck. Had Charles lived, she would never have wanted to study at Oxford. She would never even have considered it.

So why is she here? So many reasons: to become closer to George and Charles; to escape her mother's overbearing grief and reliance on her; to read and study and play sport as if she were back at school again before everything fell apart; and because she cannot sit at home and become a lonely old maid in a Hertfordshire market town without at least trying to meet somebody new—even if she cannot summon an ounce of interest in any man except the one she cannot have.

As grief knots in her temples and throat, Dora places the lid on the battered cigarette tin where she keeps her hairpins and busies herself rearranging her tennis shoes and hockey boots at the bottom of her wardrobe. She refolds her girdles, stockings, slips, drawers, and chemises in her dresser and removes the tissue-wrapped corset (her mother's parting gift) and places it under a blanket at the back of the wardrobe. Then she reorders the novels on the shelf into alphabetical order, recalling the pleasure she took in sorting, classifying, and reshelving the stock in the library where she volunteered during the war. Restoring order from chaos, as in a Shakespeare play.

Soon enough, it is eight o'clock, and through the window she notices that women are already assembling outside the lodge. Glancing at Charles and George on her exit, she walks briskly along the hallway and out onto the busy central corridor that links the west wing of the college to the east. Just ahead of her, a tall woman with broad shoulders is striding along humming to herself, pausing every so often to yank at the gown sliding down one arm. Dora cannot help but wonder if this woman's heart is drumming as furiously as her own and whether she, too, is here to make a fresh start.

———◇———

UNLIKE THE OTHERS, OTTOLINE WALLACE-KERR did not sleep in the college last night but stayed at her aunt's house, in the Norham area, with her sister Gertie. They dressed up for dinner, drank cocktails, played backgammon—a last blast before matriculation. Gertie is always keen to leave her children with Nanny, and that dereliction of duty is why Otto keeps having to pinch the spot between her eyes to stave off a headache. The family have absolutely no idea why she is seeing this through when she does not have to. Her mother, furious that Otto refused Teddy's proposal, has not asked once about Oxford. Her father calls her his "Bluestocking Bismarck" and has never taken her studies seriously. To her parents, Otto is the daughter most likely to laugh at a joke about herself and the first to say "Let's go out." What they do not appreciate is that there is a dead weight inside her that just will not budge in London. If she remains, Otto imagines it dragging her thrashing to the bottom of the Thames. Oxford is her life buoy.

The morning is misty, and Gertie insists on driving her over to St. Margaret's Road. It is a gesture kindly meant, but Gertie's driving is an acquired taste; even her husband Harry is terrified by it, and he made it through the Somme.

"Here we go, darling," says Gertie, pulling up to the gates. "Gosh, it looks rather like a prison. I've a mind to kidnap you and drive you straight back to Mayfair."

Some of the assembled women turn and stare.

"Oh, do shut up, Gert," says Otto, jumping out. "You're just jealous."

"Perfectly jealous. I'm spitting with envy over your delectable cap. Do buy me one for Christmas."

"See you later," says Otto, blowing her a kiss.

Otto enters the gates and looks about for the person in charge. Although she has attended dozens of parties alone, among these sober-looking virgins she is unaccountably jittery. She stands to one side, groping in her pocket for one of the several parting gifts Gertie has given her, a cigarette case engraved with a racing hound at full gallop. It alludes to their old headteacher who often described Otto as being in a perpetual state of motion. *Ottoline rarely sits for long, unless it is to complete complex calculations, something which she does with formidable ease and enviable accuracy* read her final report.

It is true that mathematics provides moments of absorption and calm for Otto that she cannot replicate by any other means. Even when sleeping, she has the sense that there is somewhere (or someone) else she ought to be. She adores the clarity of mathematics, the certainty of right and wrong. No droning on about different interpretations or writing essays that go around in circles. And of course, because she was born on the eighth day of the eighth month, eight is her favorite number.

And now, two years after the idea of studying at St. Hugh's first came to her, Otto has been allocated a room on Corridor Eight. An auspicious start indeed.

2

Thursday, October 7, 1920 (0th Week)

FIRST-YEARS—
ST. HUGH'S COLLEGE, 1920

Miss Florence Alderman   *Modern History*

Miss Josephine Bostwick   *English*

Miss Patricia Clough   *Modern Languages*

Miss Sylvia Dodds   *Modern History*

Miss Joan Evans   *Modern Languages*

Miss Elizabeth Fullerton-Summers   *Modern History*

Miss Theodora Greenwood   *English*

Miss Marianne Grey   *English*

Miss Yvonne Houghton-Smith   *Jurisprudence*

Miss Esther Johnson   *Modern Languages*

Miss Phyllis Knight   *English*

Miss Katherine Lloyd   *Modern Languages*

Miss Ivy Nightingale   *Lit. Hum.*

Miss Rosalind Otley-Burrows   *Modern Languages*

Miss Beatrice Sparks   *PPE*

Miss Norah Spurling   *Modern History*

Miss Celia Thompson-Salt   *English*

Miss Temperance Underhill   *English*

Miss Ottoline Wallace-Kerr *Mathematics*

Miss Ethel Wilkinson *Modern History*

MISS E. F. JOURDAIN
Principal

Dora glances at the women assembled alongside her in the courtyard. Although nobody looks particularly clever, the group is an eclectic mix of shabby coats, expensive tailoring, unbrushed hair, and carefully pinned curls. The air smells reassuringly of Pears soap and lavender water. She wonders how her brother George felt on the morning of his matriculation; no doubt he was already great pals with everyone and was nursing a headache from too much wine the night before.

"Congratulations to you all on this momentous occasion," says a watery-eyed tutor with a tremulous voice who introduces herself as Miss Lumb. "I will be your chaperone on the walk to the Divinity School. Our crocodile will depart early today. There may be crowds and press, so the principal, Miss Jourdain, wants us there in plenty of time."

Behind Miss Lumb, a gaggle of older students whisper like excited theatergoers.

"Please arrange yourselves according to corridor," says Miss Lumb, pointing to different corners of the courtyard. "Corridors Four and Five gather here, Six here, Seven here, and the Eights over there. Your corridors will provide your walking— and cycling—companions for the next few weeks while you orientate yourselves."

Dora finds herself standing between two young women who introduce themselves as Beatrice Sparks and Marianne Grey. Beatrice, the girl Dora followed down the main corridor, pumps Dora's hand enthusiastically. As well as being immensely tall,

Beatrice has an indistinct jaw, curious eyes, and ruddy cheeks. Her fingers are dappled blue with ink. Marianne, in contrast, has a long neck and a pale, freckled face. She looks fragile and insubstantial, like a handkerchief worn over time to a mesh of delicate threads. It is strange to think these are the people Dora will spend every day with for the next eight weeks.

A petite woman with skillfully drawn lips ambles over to join them. She has bobbed hair the color of wet terra-cotta and is at least a foot shorter than Beatrice. She could have stepped straight from the society pages of one of Dora's magazines.

"Hello, neighbors," says the redhead, offering a limp hand. A cigarette dangles from her mouth and Dora wonders at her audacity to smoke in public.

"Ottoline Wallace-Kerr," she says. "But you can call me Otto."

Dora recognizes the surname from the nameplate above the door next to hers, which means all four rooms on Corridor Eight are now accounted for.

"Good morning," says Beatrice cheerfully. "My name is Beatrice Sparks. Oh, and this is Dora and Marianne."

"Sparks, I like it. Good name for a brainy sort," says Otto, directing a plume of smoke over Beatrice's shoulder. She casts an appraising eye over the other women in the courtyard before raising a single penciled brow. "Well, tally ho, then."

And the procession is off, filing out of the gates and onto St. Margaret's Road, with the Eights bringing up the rear.

All about them, Oxford is rising. On Banbury Road, omnibuses snort their way toward Cornmarket, bicycles rattle past, and hotels shake out their guests and laundry. On St. Giles', male students emerge from sandstone walls to join the swell of movement southward. Dora is mesmerized by how their mortarboards dip and tilt, the silken tassels swinging. It occurs to her that the women, walking in pairs behind Miss Lumb in their floppy woolen caps, bear a striking resemblance to schoolchildren on an outing.

The crowd about them throngs with boisterous conversation and it is hard to make oneself heard. Some men smile and stand aside gallantly for them, while others shout greetings to each other across the women as if they were not there. Beatrice, walking beside Dora, frequently taps her on the arm to point out important sights, such as the Ashmolean (which Dora knows) and the Lamb and Flag (which she does not), where Hardy wrote parts of *Jude the Obscure*. In front of them, Otto's satin boots with their diamanté buckles trip along the pavement while Marianne appears to have newspaper caught in one of her heels. Neither of them says a word.

On the corner of Broad Street, Otto stops to light another cigarette and the four women pause while the rest of the crocodile continues without them. Dora takes the opportunity to reposition her cap, poking unwilling pins back into the resistant mound of hair beneath. A few of the men stare as they pass by, one venturing a "good morning" that causes her to blush and dip her head. When she finally looks up, her breath stalls in her throat, and she wonders if she is going mad. Not twenty feet in front of her is her fiancé, Charles, or a version of him, the same thick brown hair and rutted chin, laughing in the midst of a group of young men surging up Broad Street. Her vision blurs, and though she wants to call out, to cross the street and force her way through the mass of bodies, her shock is such that she cannot move. Then the man turns to speak to his friend and, with a plummeting sense of folly, she realizes that he looks nothing like Charles. This stranger is older, mustached, sallow-featured. Of course it is not him. Her Charles lies somewhere in France in an unmarked grave, perpetually eighteen—she knows that. And yet for some reason she cannot fathom, he insists on appearing everywhere she goes.

As if the morning were not strange enough. Three days ago, Dora was in a market town, batting balls at the tennis club with the twins, her mother bemoaning the defection of the scullery maid to a tinned-food factory. Now here she is, about to matriculate at Oxford University. Making history in a world where, Dora wonders, there has surely been enough history made already.

———◇———

OTTO TAKES A LONG DRAG of her cigarette, then nods in the direction of the Bodleian, and they set off again, absorbed back into the current. Marianne wonders if now is the moment to slip away to catch the late-morning train back to Culham, then reluctantly quashes the idea. It would cause an awful fuss if she simply disappeared, and she does not want to ruin such an important day for the others. There is nothing else for it; she will have to go through with the ceremony.

The rest of the crocodile is at least fifty yards ahead, but before the Eights can catch up, a large group of young men spill from the entrance to Balliol College into their path. It is a lively scene; from a window above the college lodge, two students provide witty commentary via a megaphone, mocking individuals below for their looks or lack of drinking prowess.

It is obvious to Marianne that the men milling about on the pavement ahead are freshmen. Not only are they wearing sub fusc, but most are too young to grow a decent mustache and cannot possibly have served in France. It is comforting to see this new, untarnished generation going out into the world. They remind her of the fledgling magpies that gather on the green at Culham: handsome, strutting, and clever, but not quite ready to leave the flock.

"Look out, chaps, the Amazons are here!" Without warning, the megaphone turns its attention to the Eights, and the Balliol men turn to stare curiously at the women. "What on earth are they wearing on their heads?" it continues.

The men laugh, delighted, and converge around Marianne and her companions, hungry for entertainment. As she glances about her, all Marianne can see are rows of leering faces and stark white bow ties. Suddenly she feels weak and giddy as if someone has dropped a pile of heavy books into her arms.

"Nobody will marry you now, ladies!" shouts one of the freshmen, and the crowd responds with wild applause.

A distant memory surfaces in Marianne's mind: village boys cornering a shuddering harvest mouse and poking it to death with sticks. She squeezes her fingernails into her palms to avoid grabbing at the locket concealed beneath her blouse.

"Anyone need a button sewn on?"

"They'll be in the Union next."

"It's enough to send a chap to Cambridge."

And on it goes, the men cheering, whistling, and jostling, pleased with themselves. Marianne looks about in vain for someone to step in and defend them—a proctor or a porter, perhaps—but nobody comes to their aid. Her companions appear equally stunned. Horns honk, bicycle brakes screech, and the earth spins away, regardless.

It is Beatrice who acts first. "Take no notice," she says, her round face flushed. She pushes through the crowd toward the edge of the pavement. Otto follows her.

"Let's go," whispers Dora to Marianne.

But before Marianne takes a single step, the megaphone starts up again. "Oh, please don't leave us," it calls after Beatrice. "We could do with a strapping girl like you in the boat race."

Otto halts. "Hold on just a minute," she says, and marches back into the center of the crowd. She turns a full circle, slowly scanning the men's faces, her eyes narrow and mocking. "Is this what the men of Balliol consider sport?" she says, gesturing toward the window. "Insulting women who probably beat you hands down in the Oxford Senior? What utter bores you are." She flicks her cigarette butt, crimson-kissed, at the men's feet. "I'll make sure I pass on your observations to the Master when I dine with his family next week. His daughters are particular pals of mine."

Otto, with her angular, painted face, is clearly aware of the impression she makes. Her gardenia scent hangs, like her words, in the air. The men titter uncomfortably and Marianne is taken aback by her boldness. Nobody speaks for a moment, and then Otto's spell is broken by a gawping freshman who staggers forward and trips on the lip of the pavement. He flails for a second, then topples to the ground, grabbing at Marianne's skirt on the way down. She is jolted forward with such force that stitches rip at her waistband. She lands hard on her knees, then pitches sideways, putting out her hands just in time to stop her head from hitting the curb.

"I think she's fallen for him," sings the megaphone.

The crowd begins to whoop. Marianne lies dazed on the filthy pavement among the cigarette butts and dead leaves, surrounded by a wall of trousered legs and polished brogues. She tries to right herself but her legs and skirt are tangled somehow and she cannot move. Then someone grasps her by the arm—Beatrice—and pulls her to her feet. Her hands are imprinted with grit from the gutter. The laughter continues and her cheeks burn with shame.

"You utter buffoon," says Otto, glaring down at the freshman.

"So terribly sorry," he stutters, before scrambling to his feet and disappearing into the crowd.

Dora steps forward. "It's Marianne, isn't it? Are you hurt?" She takes Marianne by the arm, brushing detritus from her gown. "I'm afraid your skirt needs washing. Here, I have your cap."

"I'm fine," Marianne says, although she can feel the sting of a graze on her palm and wishes she could lean on something. This is not how she imagined Oxford: not as a place where women are mocked and derided for wanting to learn. She tries to replace her cap, but part of her hair has escaped the pins and is hanging loose about her neck. Her knees are throbbing and her skirt is wet with what may well be horse dung. Thankfully, the megaphone has fallen silent, and the freshmen, now bored, wander off down the road, gowns flapping behind them.

"I'm so sorry, Marianne," says Beatrice. "Are you all right?"

Otto yawns. "Silly, silly little boys."

A bell tolls nine overhead. Thankfully, there is still an hour before the ceremony begins. In the melee, they have lost sight of Miss Lumb and the group from St. Hugh's. The others wait as Marianne attempts to brush herself down. She wonders if they can see her hands shaking.

"I have to ask, do you really know the Master of Balliol?" Beatrice says to Otto.

"Never met him," replies Otto with a grin.

"Well, it was a jolly good fib." Beatrice turns to Dora and Marianne. "The Master of Balliol is A. L. Smith." They look at her blankly. "The education reformist? He believes Oxford should be open to all."

Otto turns to Marianne. "If you don't mind me saying, you look almost transparent and I'm certain ghosts can't matriculate. You need tea. Sugary tea. My treat, and I simply won't be dissuaded."

Marianne tries to protest, but when Otto ignores her and takes her arm, she is grateful for it. All she wants to do is get off the street and have a moment to gather herself.

Otto pokes a finger under the rim of her cap and scratches about in her coppery bob. "One thing those boys got right," she says, "is that these caps are utterly hideous." She waits for a shoal of bicycles to pass and shepherds Marianne across Broad Street to a door leading to an upstairs tearoom, the others following.

The four women file up the narrow stairs to the Good Luck Tea Rooms, and the door jingles shut behind them.

3

Thursday, October 7, 1920 (0th Week)

In the flock-wallpapered WC of the café, Marianne rolls the gray cake of soap around her hands, taking as long as she can. Through the open window, she hears ill-matched bells tolling a quarter past nine. They sound like spoons hitting copper pans. For a moment, she is back in St. Mary's counting the hymn books for worship, inhaling the musty odor of the pages. The cool air settles on the nape of her neck; her fingertips brush the varnished pew tops. And then the nausea returns. That she fell in the street is not important; what matters is that she has left her father to manage alone. Mrs. Ward will ensure he has clean clothes, but who will type his letters and sermons, organize the flower rota, bank the offering now that she is gone? And what if he *can* cope without her? What does that say about her? Marianne has never lived away from the rectory or brushed out the tightly braided strands of her life that it holds secure. Although she is not hurt and no longer shaken, what happened just now merely reinforces that she does not belong here. She locates her locket through her blouse and presses it hard into her sternum, resolving that she will leave Oxford that very afternoon.

Taking a fresh piece of folded newspaper from her pocket, she replaces the torn piece at the back of one of her shoes. Bought secondhand from a market stall for special occasions, they have always been too loose, and after all the walking a blister is blooming on her heel. She returns to the table, greets the others with a nod, and takes the empty seat next to Dora, who keeps glancing out of the window. Otto and Beatrice act as if they frequent tea shops every day of the week. They talk and talk, as if there is a requirement that every lull in conversation must be crammed with words. *Londoners are exhausting*, she thinks.

Dora turns to her. "Do you think the others will be looking for us?"

"I expect so," replies Marianne. "I'm sorry, it's my fault we're here."

"It isn't. Not at all." Dora smiles. "I just wonder whether we should be such rebels on our very first day. It's the head girl in me, I'm afraid."

Together they watch an omnibus shudder past in the street below. A road sweeper pushes a steaming knot of manure into a heap, only for a delivery boy to cut through it on a bicycle. *How conspicuous we are*, Marianne thinks, *sitting here in sub fusc, among the elderly patrons ordering eggs and bacon.* She tries to swallow down the queer lump that has been lodged in her throat since she arrived last night.

When there is finally an opportunity, Dora says to the table, "I say, do you think Miss Lumb will be wondering—"

"Oh, we'll only be ten minutes," says Otto, dismissing Dora with a wave of the hand. "I'll order four teas—or would you prefer coffee? No? Four teas it is." She calls across the room to a waitress. "Hello there!"

Marianne has never frequented a tearoom for only "ten minutes" as if it is a mere convenience. Her father would be amazed. The waitress weaves between the tables, notebook bouncing on a string at her waist. Each table is set for four, with a pink carnation at the center. Nearby, a man is holding a copy of the *Daily Mail*. The headline reads "A Million Women Too Many, 1920 Husband Hunt."

"Oh, it's Miss Wallace-Kerr!" says the waitress, arriving in a waft of hot milk and carbolic soap, her expression bright with recognition. "You're a sight for sore eyes."

"Hello, Betty, how are you?" replies Otto.

"Can't complain. My eldest made it home, you won't know that. He's at the Morris factory."

"I'm delighted to hear it." Otto glances around the table. "I was a driver in Oxford during the war. Betty here looked after me."

"Miss Wallace-Kerr was very kind when I lost Ernest, my youngest," says Betty, her eyes filling with tears.

As they offer their condolences, it is hard not to notice that Betty's eyeballs are the color of mustard. *Jaundice*, thinks Marianne, and tries not to imagine poor Betty's liver twisted and bulging under her pristine apron.

"I often wondered about you, miss," says Betty. "When you stopped coming in, I thought the worst. I said to my friend, Miss Wallace-Kerr's gone to France or something."

There is a momentary tightening around Otto's lips. "The job was only for six months. The parents wanted me home. It was remiss of me not to say goodbye, do forgive me." She taps the menu with a varnished nail. "Anyhow, we're in a bit of a hurry. We have a ceremony to get to. I'm sure you understand. Four teas, please."

"Righto," says Betty, scribbling on her notepad.

"It really is very good to see you again," says Otto, softening, and Betty, dismissed, gives a little curtsy.

Marianne is fascinated by Otto's clipped vowels and the way she pronounces every syllable so cleanly, as if she is determined to suck every morsel from it. Beneath her gown, Otto wears a tight-fitting velvet jacket, her eyebrows plucked into high arches that accentuate the angles of her face. Marianne is reminded of her neighbor's sleek little dachshund, unpredictable and imperious.

They gulp down the tea that Betty brings, discussing the

subjects they are studying and how lucky they are that ancient Greek is no longer required. Beatrice is taking a new course known as PPE, Otto is one of a handful of women to read Mathematics, and Marianne and Dora will study English. Nobody mentions the taunting on the street. It is as if by not acknowledging it, they retain a little dignity.

As they depart, Otto promises to read their tea leaves another day. She slides a generous tip (a whole crown!) under her napkin and pops a teaspoon in her jacket pocket. "Souvenir," she says to Marianne, and winks.

Marianne is amused and horrified in equal measure. She cannot help but notice that Otto's teeth are all the same size, like a row of tiny ivory dominoes.

THE ODD LITTLE GROUP STEPS out of the café door onto Broad Street and heads toward the pleated pillars of the Clarendon Building. It is a road Otto has driven a thousand times before. When she was in the Voluntary Aid Detachment, she used to park outside Balliol and dash over to the Good Luck Tea Rooms for a cigarette and coffee, sometimes two or three times a day, always dressed in the same scratchy uniform, fishing in her pocket for lipstick as she crossed the road. For five months, she went back and forth driving medics and patients and forms and medicines between sites until she thought she would go insane. It kept the office well supplied with teaspoons, at least. Now she is in another uniform, even dowdier than before, being harangued on the street by boys whose defining feature is that they had the good fortune to be born a younger brother.

In many ways, little has changed. The same potholes, the same errant bicycles, omnibuses retching fumes, pigeons poking about in the gutter. B. H. Blackwell is open for business, cabbies idle at the shelter. But what is inescapable is that there are young men everywhere, gowns flapping, coughing, laughing, and taking up space. Even if some of them hop on crutches like locusts in a biblical plague.

The women pass the rear gates of Exeter College and the office of the *Oxford English Dictionary*. The flat-footed girl, Beatrice, a veritable giantess, is expounding about the dictionary to the other two, but Otto has heard it all before. One of the doctors she used to drive about—the odd-looking one who caught tuberculosis and went home to his mother—told her that the *OED* office is stuffed to the gills with words on slips of paper sent by contributors all over the world. Give her numbers any day. Words are flimsy things, easily manipulated, open to interpretation.

As they walk up the steps to the Clarendon Building, she glances back up Broad Street, seeking out her sister's lilac hat. Gertie is hosting a lunch after the ceremony with a few of her Oxford pals. Otto's current companions are terribly serious, and she could do with a drink before she attempts to unpack. At least Marianne has more color in her cheeks now, but she looks so miserable, Otto would put a guinea on her not lasting the week. She recognizes the signs: bags under the eyes, bitten nails, the disinclination to connect with the outside world. Rectors' children are bred to be sociable, so it is unlikely to be shyness. Marianne is out of her depth; she is homesick.

They pass straight through the Clarendon Building, cross a courtyard, and enter a damp stone passage that opens into the shadowy quadrangle of the Bod. The other first-years from St. Hugh's are standing waiting. Some look bemused at the return of the four missing women; others are plainly annoyed. Just as Beatrice opens her mouth to apologize, a flustered-looking Miss Lumb ushers them all into the building.

———◇———

"IT'S A FAN VAULT CEILING, fifteenth century," says Beatrice, turning to the others.

She has rehearsed this moment in her head many times and here she is at last, finally sitting among women her own age with whom she desperately wants to discuss the things that matter to her: politics, architecture, history, novels, languages, all of it. And though she longs to serve up her thoughts and observations on a platter right now, she shoves her hands under her thighs and clamps her lips shut. It is important she does not put her new friends off with what her mother describes as *Beatrice's infernal and wearying interest in everything.*

Above her, the structure is truly magnificent. Composed of a repeating pattern of creamy ribs that fan out from huge sandstone arches, it is as if the ceiling has been constructed with scallop shells. Gothic initials, fig leaves, and the insignia of long-forgotten benefactors are carved at every joint, each one perfect and unique. She wonders how it is possible for so much stone to balance overhead and remain there for five hundred years without coming crashing down on the students below. It must be thanks to geometry, she supposes.

It amuses Beatrice to think that Queen Elizabeth was bored half to death when she visited this room in 1566, when the Divinity School was the location for viva voces, and when examinations were not written but debated, often for days on end. Straining to see over the square caps in front of her, she catches a glimpse of the top of the famous Drake Chair, fashioned from remnants of the *Golden Hind*. It really is quite thrilling, she thinks—until she remembers that the men are undergoing matriculation in the Sheldonian Theatre, next door. In the traditional location. Without them.

After standing for the ceremony in Latin, which lasts no more than a few minutes, the matriculands huddle outside the Bod in the pale sunlight and pose awkwardly for photographs. An excited crowd of academics and students, mostly female, gathers around them. Dora and Marianne stand beside Beatrice, smiling and shaking hands with strangers, their university statute books wedged under their arms. A few of the men, having completed their own ceremony at the Sheldonian, come over to offer their good wishes. Beatrice holds back, suspicious after the episode outside Balliol, but Dora, with her athletic physique and dark eyes, causes quite a stir, and several of the men flush pink as they compete to congratulate her. Otto is nowhere to be seen.

"We've waited sixty years for this moment," says an elderly woman, seizing Beatrice's hand and shaking it vigorously.

Beatrice smiles and nods, feeling the dry heat of the woman's swollen knuckles. Despite her own pride in matriculating, she cannot help but imagine herself the winner of a relay race—being congratulated even though she only took the baton the last few feet over the line. As her mother often likes to point out, Beatrice's generation is benefiting from years of lobbying, militancy, suffering, and protest by women like her who refused to accept the status quo.

But having passed the entrance examination, Beatrice is here on her own merit, surely? At least she hopes so. Her father donated a large amount of money to the rebuilding of St. Hugh's and, despite what her mother might think, Beatrice knows how the world works. It only makes her more determined to prove to her mother and herself that she is worthy of her place. She will make the most of every opportunity Oxford affords her. She will persist.

She pats the inside of her jacket to check that her lucky penny is still there, tracing its familiar outline with her finger.

"This is the proudest day of my life," says one of the principals, extending her arms as if eager to embrace them all. "You are historic figures, never forget that. The first women to matriculate at Oxford, the greatest university in the world."

4

INTERCOLLEGIATE RULES
FOR WOMEN UNDERGRADUATES

1. A woman undergraduate may not reside in Oxford out of term except by permission of her principal.

2. A woman undergraduate may not enter men's rooms either in college or in lodgings without obtaining leave from her principal. She must have a chaperone approved by her principal. Conversation between men and women undergraduates before and after lectures is not encouraged.

3. A woman undergraduate must obtain leave from her principal before accepting invitations for the evening, or for mixed parties. She may not go out after dinner without permission and must always be back by 11 p.m. and must report her return.

4. A woman undergraduate may invite men friends to tea in the public rooms or grounds of the college or hall to which she belongs after obtaining permission from her principal, provided there are at least two women in the party. A woman undergraduate may receive her brother in her room but not other men.

5. A woman undergraduate may go to matinees with men friends if leave is obtained from her principal, provided there are two women in the party.

6. Mixed parties may not be held in cafés, restaurants, or hotels without a chaperone approved by the principal.

7. A woman undergraduate may not attend a public dance.

8. All joint societies must be approved by the principals, and such approval must be renewed annually. Meetings of such societies may not be held in undergraduate rooms and may only be held in men's colleges with written permission from the dean of the college, provided that a woman senior member is present.

9. A woman undergraduate may not go for walks, bicycle rides, or motor rides alone with a man undergraduate other than her brother. Permission for mixed parties may be given at the discretion of the principal.

10. A woman undergraduate may not boat with men other than her brother without a chaperone approved by her principal.

11. A woman undergraduate may only be present at football or cricket matches or boat races under conditions approved by her principal.

12. Woman undergraduates are not allowed to play mixed hockey.

When the dinner bell rings that evening, Dora and her companions hurry along the main corridor, having been warned that the principal will not tolerate tardiness at dinner.

Rumor has it that late arrivals are forced to stand blushing in front of the entire college until Miss Jourdain nods them in.

The dining hall, with its long, straight rows of tables, rings with conversation and the scraping of soup spoons. Dora is disappointed to find that the room smells of boiled cabbage, having expected something a little loftier: furniture polish and freshly cut flowers at the very least. One thing is clear from this morning: the modern building of St. Hugh's, with its three floors of regularly spaced windows and redbrick walls, bears little resemblance to the men's dreamy Gothic towers and crumbling sandstone.

"It looks like a home for lost governesses," whispers Otto.

They are seated with other freshers, and Dora is glad she suggested that the Eights, as Miss Lumb referred to them that morning, should go in to dinner together. First days are always so awkward, and having enjoyed school, she is sure she will be happy at St. Hugh's—as long as she does not allow herself to dwell too much on the war. Her bedsitting room is nothing like as grand as her brother's set was at Jesus, but it is reasonably private, being at the end of the corridor. She is next to Otto and opposite Marianne. Beatrice has the short straw, because her neighbor on one side is a severe-looking history tutor on crutches, whose door regularly opens and slams throughout the day. Fortunately, the tutor, Miss Bazeley, does not appear to sleep there and behaves as if they do not exist. On the other side of Otto is the lavatory and, beside that, a red-tiled scullery used by the scout, Maud.

"Have you read the rules? I wasn't expecting it to be *quite* this strict," says a scruffy woman sitting opposite Dora. She has a lopsided nose, and her gown is such a mass of creases it looks two sizes too small. "Patricia Clough, Modern Languages," she adds, as if introducing her rank in the army. Dora half expects her to salute.

"I was going to apply for Greats, but my brother said the classics are a terrible grind for a girl," Patricia continues. Then she lowers her voice. "I thought the year groups would mix a bit more, but the second- and third-years look disdainful, don't you think? They certainly don't want to sit with us."

"I'm sure they're eager to catch up after the long vac," says Dora, who is mesmerized by Patricia's furry upper lip. It does a little dance as it sips soup from her spoon.

"I bet they think we've had it easy. You know, being accepted from the off," says Patricia.

Beatrice nods. "I don't blame them. They've had to prove themselves more than the equal of men. And now they have to matriculate as an afterthought, while we get all the glory."

"Building colleges on next to no money, lurking at the back of lectures like lepers. What fun that must have been," says Otto.

Dora notices that Beatrice has spilled soup down her front, but apart from swatting vaguely at it with a napkin, she remains entirely unfazed.

"Some of them got stick for staying on during the war, I heard," says Patricia.

"Really? Why?" asks Dora.

"The majority remained here while all the chaps went to France. Carried on their studies as normal, had a ball riding bicycles around Oxford. In gangs," adds Patricia, savoring this information far more than the scanty onion soup.

"Well, that's rather simplistic," says Otto, tossing her spoon into her bowl with such a clatter that a few women at the next table turn around.

"What do you mean?" asks Patricia, furry lip wobbling.

"I mean that it is foolish to assume what anyone did in the war, don't you think?" says Otto, turning to her. "Were you in Oxford during the war, Miss—?"

"Clough. Patricia. Well, no, I wasn't, but—"

"So how could you possibly know what each of those women did?"

"I—I was just saying what I'd heard." Patricia looks around

at the others for support, but on this very first evening, nobody is willing to intercede.

Dora busies herself gathering the empty bowls.

"Well, I was here during the war," says Otto, "and I saw Somerville students with hands that were bleeding from pulling up flax for aircraft wings. The gloves they were given lasted three days before they were in shreds."

"I—"

"I saw students helping Belgian refugees to learn English and find places to live. Women picking fruit in the holidays, others working as translators in their spare time. I saw students reading to soldiers in hospital and putting on plays for them, digging vegetable plots on Port Meadow, running tea parties to raise funds for orphans. In my experience, the women who remained here were inventive, hardworking, and relentless."

"Oh, I didn't mean—"

"Bertrand Russell puts it quite well," says Otto. "He says it's a shame that gossips are obsessed with people's hidden vices when what they ought to be looking out for are their hidden virtues." She leans forward so that her beads crunch against the edge of the table. "Don't you agree, Patricia?"

Otto turns to Beatrice and changes the subject. Patricia looks momentarily confused, then attempts to smooth the multiple folds in her wrinkled gown. A poppy-red rash creeps up from beneath her collar. Dora, having assumed Otto would relish gossip of this kind, resolves never to underestimate her new neighbor again.

———◇———

AFTER FURTHER COURSES OF WATERY rabbit stew and bread pudding, there is a tap on Marianne's arm. "What about you, Miss Grey?"

Marianne looks up at the expectant face turned toward her.

"I asked, why did you apply to St. Hugh's?" says Patricia

Clough, apparently undaunted by her altercation with Otto. When Marianne doesn't answer immediately, Patricia continues, "I chose it because of Miss Jourdain. She's an immensely talented modern linguist. And, more excitingly, she sees ghosts."

"Ghosts," says Marianne politely. "My goodness."

Marianne is aware that their principal is also the daughter of a clergyman, although one of ten children. Marianne is an only child, having unwittingly killed her mother at birth. Growing up next to a churchyard is to know the presence of the dead, she can attest to that.

"Miss Jourdain is a spiritualist. Always wears black. Lots of women at Oxford experiment with such things. Do meditation and whatnot. Communicate with the divine," says Patricia, who appears to be gifted not only with interesting details about college life but also an overwhelming desire to share them.

"Mother says she watches everyone like a hawk and that she wanders about at night checking on things," says Beatrice, chewing on a piece of bread. "That's why she had the college built in corridors, not staircases, so she can better monitor students. She worked as a translator during the war and had the building searched for German spies on more than one occasion. Apparently, she's not to be crossed."

Marianne glances toward the staff table. Miss Jourdain, seated among her less elegant colleagues, wears a ruby pendant over a lace-necked black dress, her fine wheaten hair swept up into a chignon. She looks more like a milliner than someone who might commune with the afterlife. The principal lifts her eyes from her notes and meets Marianne's gaze. The older woman's violet irises are discomforting. The interaction lasts a fraction of a second, and then Miss Jourdain raps on her water glass with a spoon and the room falls quiet. She rises, and after a preparatory cough, she begins.

"This term, the undergraduate body of the university will consist of over five hundred women and four thousand men. Although we celebrate our victory, we still have much to strive for. Until we have a Royal Charter, we do not have the full rights of the men's colleges and cannot participate in decision making at the highest level. Many clubs and publications remain closed to us. Although we have a good deal of support from male academics, there remain many who adhere to the notion that women students are—and I quote—*second-rate simpletons*."

Miss Jourdain's voice is light and feminine, but Marianne is certain it could engrave metal.

"We live in a time of great change, in the shadow of a war many of us are still fighting. It is imperative that, at this key moment for women at Oxford, we maintain standards. We must not let our doubters find us wanting in matters of decorum or intellect."

Beatrice nods eagerly.

"Let us show the world the valuable contribution that women—and St. Hugh's—can make to learning and to society. Let us go forward together in curiosity, bravery, diligence, and dignity." She raises her water glass as if to toast them. "*Ubi concordia, ibi victoria*, ladies. Where there is unity, there is victory."

There is prolonged applause. A few of the women at the far tables dab their eyes. Despite herself, Marianne feels hope nudging her ankles like a cat. If she can adapt to this life twenty-four weeks a year for three years, then she can secure her future by eventually becoming a teacher or an academic. She must be firm of purpose. Her father will not live forever, and she can hardly expect to marry. To prove that women are the intellectual equal of men, to pursue a life of the mind? Well, that is a bonus.

"Will the food be like this every evening, do you think?" says Otto as the four women make their way out. "Two soups and a pudding so robust it could sink an ocean liner?"

Marianne does not know what to say. It is a vast improvement on her usual diet.

"Let's go back to my room," says Otto as they reach Corridor Eight. "I have ginger biscuits and a gramophone."

OTTO'S ROOM IS SO CRAMMED with paraphernalia, it appears half the size of the others on the corridor. Marianne was unaware until now that a person could casually own so many beautiful objects. Rolled rugs tied with string, embroidered cushions in heaps, oil paintings stacked against the wall. Magazines and gramophone records sliding about on top of one another, a jar of incense sticks, a child's abacus, a cut-glass ashtray, a potted plant with enormous splayed hands for leaves.

"Do you type?" Beatrice is asking.

"Oh God, yes, who has time for anything else these days? Although where the damn machine is right now, I couldn't possibly say," says Otto, vigorously winding up the gramophone. "Do tell us, Sparks, what on earth is PPE?"

"It stands for Philosophy, Politics, and Economics. It's the study of the structure and principles of modern society. We also learn French, German, and Italian. The idea is to create a batch of graduates ready to excel in the civil service, business, public life, and so on."

"That sounds like an awful lot of work," says Otto. "But terribly noble."

Marianne cannot help but ask, "Are you the only woman?"

"There are three of us; the other two are at Lady Margaret Hall and Somerville," replies Beatrice. "It'll catch on in a few years."

"I daresay," says Otto, handing her a pile of gramophone records. "You choose."

"Such a beautiful shade of blue," says Dora, stroking a silk scarf draped over the sofa.

Marianne tries not to stare at Dora's face, but it is hard not to. With her mournful dark eyes and tiny pink mouth, Dora could easily be a Pre-Raphaelite muse: a Jane Morris or a Fanny Cornforth, perhaps.

Otto tosses the scarf at Dora. "That old thing? Here, have it; I have a dozen just like it."

"Thank you but I couldn't possibly," Dora says, flushing. She repositions the scarf carefully over the back of the sofa. "Your name is such fun. I've never met a girl called Otto."

Otto shrugs. "Mother hates it and will only call me Ottoline, which is probably why I like it so much." She laughs, then drags on her cigarette so fiercely that half of it turns to ash and falls to the floor. Marianne resists the urge to jump forward and scoop it up as Otto kicks it vaguely toward the fireplace.

"Was it a problem during the war?" asks Beatrice, handing Otto a gramophone record. "You know, it sounding German."

"Oh, I was told to ditch it dozens of times, that I sounded like a Hun-lover and a traitor, but I didn't care. Otto means 'prosperity in battle,' you know. My father always wanted a boy, and I was the youngest, so that's why the nickname stuck. He used to call me his Little Bismarck because I could engineer situations to my advantage. A skill that arose from being one of four sisters."

"Four? Goodness. I'm an only child and so is Marianne here," says Beatrice. "That's right, isn't it?"

Marianne nods.

"Of course, the best thing about the name Otto is that it's symmetrical," says Otto. "In the upper case."

"And it's a palindrome," adds Beatrice.

"Did you notice all of our Christian names have eight letters?" says Otto. "Theodora, Marianne, Beatrice, and Ottoline. On Corridor Eight. I'd say that's a very good sign. Ginger biscuit, anyone?"

Beatrice takes two. "So you're a numerologist?"

"I don't count letters, if that's what you mean, but I do have rather a thing for the number eight. My family think I'm mad.

It's a lucky number in China because it sounds like the word for gaining wealth. Four is considered unlucky."

"Present company excepted," says Dora, and they laugh.

"Why are you going home at the weekends, Marianne?" asks Beatrice. "I heard you telling Dora at dinner."

All eyes are on Marianne and heat rises in her cheeks. "It's only once a fortnight. My father isn't well," she says. "I'm allowed to go, as long as I don't get behind. It's not far, just a short train ride."

"That's tough. Won't you miss out on fun at the weekends?" says Dora. "I hear everyone goes to the theater or to concerts on Fridays and Saturdays."

"What about your studies?" asks Beatrice.

Lies based on truths are the most convincing, Marianne has heard. "I can study at home on Saturdays and read on the train," she says. "My father is a rector and needs my help with his Sunday services. We haven't got a verger at the moment."

"You'll go on weeks two, four, and six, then?" asks Otto.

"Yes," replies Marianne.

"Well, that's something," says Otto. "I'm not a fan of odd numbers. Do say a prayer for me. I need all the help I can get."

The women do not probe Marianne further, but she can tell they are baffled by the arrangement. Whether she will be able to keep up with her studies is unclear. There is no point taking work home to the rectory when she won't have a moment to spare.

And in thinking this, she realizes that she has given herself permission to stay. A peculiar warmth floods into her limbs. Around her, the others are smiling and chatting. She leans forward and takes a biscuit from the plate.

Yes, the arrangement can work.

Yes, she will stay.

Otto is talking. "Miss Lumb stopped me after dinner and warned me that Miss Jourdain takes exception to bobbed hair. She insisted a girl grow it out last year."

"Gosh," says Dora. "What if she asks you to do the same?"

"Oh, I'm not worried," says Otto. "Prosperity in battle, remember. But have you read this ridiculous thing?" She seizes the *Intercollegiate Rules for Women Undergraduates* from her desk and waves it about. A copy has been placed in all their pigeonholes.

"Apart from the ban on alcohol in college, which I understand is Miss Jourdain's own decision and not the fault of the proctors, this is my particular favorite." Otto reads from the list in a pompous voice. "She may not go out after dinner without permission and must always be back by eleven p.m. and must report her return." She tosses the document onto Marianne's lap. "I'm an adult, for goodness' sake. I live in London. I often don't go *out* until eleven. It seems the idea of a daring night out here is a cocoa party by candlelight."

"Oh dear, it's very long," says Marianne, glancing down the list. "I haven't read it yet."

"In summary," says Dora, "if we want to do anything remotely exciting, we have to get permission and pay for a chaperone. We can't go anywhere without them knowing and we can't even chat with men after lectures. It's terribly strict."

"Mother says the new vice chancellor, Farnell, is behind it all," says Beatrice. "He describes the rules as 'equality with separation.' It will make Oxford a laughingstock."

"It's worse than school," says Dora. "And that ended two years ago."

"I never went to school," offers Beatrice. "I had tutors."

"Well, this must be a bit of a shock for you," laughs Dora.

"Not really, I'm used to big gatherings of women, but I longed to attend school as a child."

"I longed to *leave* school as a child," snorts Otto. "What about you, Marianne?"

"I went to the village school, and then my father taught me," says Marianne. "But I was free to wander all over the parish from an early age."

"Gosh, I can't imagine Papa teaching me," says Otto with a grimace. "He'd have killed us both." She looks over at Dora. "Where did you go to school, Greenwood?"

"Cheltenham Ladies'," replies Dora. "It seems an age ago now. I know the war mixed things up and we are older than usual, but I do resent being treated like a child at twenty."

Otto moves a box from the bed and flops onto it, yawning. "I'm twenty-four. Ancient and on the shelf compared to you lot. I'm quite happy about that, as it happens, which is just as well, seeing as we are rather short of suitors."

"I wonder if the men have the same rules as us?" asks Beatrice.

"Chaperones trailing after them and no alcohol in college? I very much doubt it," replies Otto. "But I do know they are forbidden to go into pubs. The proctors go in and turf them out."

They chat a little more about their reading lists (lengthy) and what they did during the war. Otto does not expand much on her time driving in Oxford, but Beatrice gives a colorful account of her role as a typist with the Women's Volunteer Reserve. Dora worked at a library for officer cadets until she lost both her brother and fiancé in France. These events, she intimates, are still very painful to discuss.

For a time, Dora's revelation and the accompanying condolences banish all gaiety from the room. Marianne wishes she could tell Dora that she carries the weight of loss too, how an encounter on Armistice night almost destroyed her. But she must not confide in these women. Not on her first day. Not ever.

"Life goes on," says Dora. She looks around absently, then gives a little cough. "Would you like some help, Otto? With your boxes, I mean, since we are all here. I rather like unpacking."

The others nod, the gramophone bursts into life, and energy is restored to the room.

"What a splendid idea," says Otto. She jumps to her feet and seizes an expensive-looking gray vase with an archer etched on it. "Apparently, the electricity goes off every night at eleven, so we'd better get a move on." She takes a step back and appraises Beatrice.

"Exactly how tall are you, Sparks?"

"Just over six feet," says Beatrice, smiling.

"An Amazon, indeed. Well, Miss Sparks, you can hang the pictures."

5

*I hereby undertake not to remove from the library, nor
to mark, deface, or injure in any way, any volume,
document, or other object belonging to it or in its cus-
tody; not to bring into the library, or kindle therein,
any fire or flame, and not to smoke in the library; and
I promise to obey all rules of the library.*

 My mother is coming to get her degree this week," says Beatrice over breakfast.

Now that matriculation is complete, the whole college is
talking about an even more important ceremony to be held on
Thursday. Women of all ages, from across the country, will return to Oxford to collect degrees they earned as students but
were not permitted to receive.

"Mother was at St. Hugh's," says Beatrice. "So afterward
she's coming here for tea and making a speech. She's pally with
Miss Jourdain."

"Hopefully you'll get a proper dinner out of it," says Otto,
eyeing her thin porridge. "I can't imagine why St. Hugh's is said
to serve the best meals. This is ghastly."

Beatrice pushes her father's letter into her jacket pocket
and takes toast from the rack, applying self-conscious restraint

in her scrapings of both butter and marmalade. She would apply twice as much if she were at home, but she has noticed how some of the girls here pay heed to such things. "Mother will be busy with important people, but Papa says he'll take me out for supper."

"I've always wanted to meet a real suffragette," says Dora. "Did she get arrested?"

Beatrice nods. "Oh, Mother was arrested eight times, and went to Holloway twice. The first time she threw a brick through the window of a fine-art dealer in Regent Street and was in for a week. Second time she climbed on a roof. Threw slate tiles at Asquith's train. She got five weeks for that."

The women breakfasting around them stop to listen; spoons cease their clattering, teacups hover in midair. Suffragettes are public property in a women's college, and Beatrice is used to the adulation that surrounds Edith Sparks.

"She went on hunger strike the second time and was force-fed. Vomited blood and said it was the worst indignity of her life. Worse than giving birth. She fainted, banged her head, and woke up in the hospital wing. They didn't want a martyr on their hands, so they let her out early."

"How terrible," says Marianne, looking pale but far less haunted than she did four days earlier.

"Oh, she was delighted at all the attention," says Beatrice, pouring another cup of tea and clamping down a yawn. "She is terribly proud of her hunger-strike medal; says it is her greatest achievement in life."

"Still. It must have been tough on you," says Marianne. "Were you terribly lonely?"

"I was used to it. She wasn't at home much. I had a nanny, of course, and tutors. Mother is incredibly open about not being the maternal type. She often says she never wanted children."

For a moment nobody speaks.

"Gosh," says Dora, eventually.

"Is your father in favor of suffrage?" asks Marianne.

"Oh yes, absolutely. He adores Mother, although he did worry when it became all about 'deeds not words.' Trailed about after her. She's his second wife, you see. He's much older than her. They met in an art gallery when she was dabbling in sculpture."

"My mother only gets excited when the milk is warm at afternoon tea," says Dora. "She thinks women's suffrage is appalling."

"Mine likes the principle but hasn't got the slightest inclination to do anything about it," says Otto. "Hats off to your mama."

Two first-years, Norah Spurling and Ivy Nightingale, entertain the table with how their mothers, once best friends, had a falling-out over the question of militant suffrage and have not spoken since. Apparently, their fathers have to dine in secret at their club.

Otto is delighted. "Oh, this is wonderful, do tell us more."

As Marianne laughs along with the others, her facial features momentarily relaxed, Beatrice remembers that Marianne's mother is dead. Should she have been more tactful and not brought up the subject of mothers at all? From what she knows so far of Marianne's generous good sense, she does not think so, but still, she would hate to upset her new friend. If only the Bod contained a book on the etiquette of friendship—a leather-bound copy, annotated and well-thumbed, page corners turned down at key sections like "Dead Parents"—she would be up to speed in no time.

ON THE WAY BACK TO her room, Beatrice stops to peruse the framed photographs that line the walls of the main corridor. She soon spots her mother standing with an ill-matched band of contemporaries. Together, they wield a curious array of items from violins to hockey sticks. One moon-faced woman—the only one smiling—is nuzzling a pug. Edith Sparks looks young, her waist narrow, her brow unlined. She is standing next to her friends Miss Davison and Miss Rix. Despite her quick temper, her mother has never been short of companions, which is something Beatrice has always envied. She never imagined, though, that friendship involved so much mundanity: arranging to enter rooms together, sharing one's daily timetable, lending and borrowing items. Not that she does not enjoy it, but mutual reliance and constant company are new concepts to her, and sometimes she finds herself in desperate need of a moment alone—no doubt something her mother would consider a weakness.

"That's all a bit P. T. Barnum, isn't it?" says Otto, appearing next to her and scrutinizing the image. "You know what? We should take our own photograph. A portrait of the Eights about to venture out on their first lecture. I have a Brownie in my room. What do you say?"

"Capital idea," says Beatrice.

ON THE WAY OUT OF the college, they divert to the garden for the photograph. The flower beds, past their best, are wilting to stalks, and yellowing oak leaves litter the lawn.

"Stand over there," says Otto, directing the other three. She is rather pleased with the Kodak Brownie No. 2 Autographic, another parting gift from Gertie. The perfect size for a bicycle basket, it is the latest model, with black-leather casing, silver-plated fixings, and gold-leaf settings.

Otto settles the Brownie on a sundial, looking down the viewfinder on top. After persuading a passing scout to press the shutter, Otto flicks a catch at the side and the lens extends in squares of folded canvas like a cuckoo clock. She nudges the silver arrows around the aperture, selecting *cloudy* and *middle distance,* then hops into line next to Marianne.

"Smile," she says, nudging with her elbows. "That includes you, Marianne."

Otto puts a hand on her hip, raises her eyebrows half an inch, and tilts her head. Marianne, hovering behind Otto's left shoulder, is holding one limp hand in the other. She smells of soap and coffee. To Marianne's left is Dora, looking absurdly healthy with her dark lashes and unblemished skin, hands clasped behind her back. On the far side is Beatrice, hair a wilderness, waistband slicing into her middle, and a jacket that does not want to meet. She looks like a jolly cook in a children's story. A couple of weeks ago Otto could never have imagined herself part of a strange little gang like this, but the situation, though unexpected, is becoming increasingly welcome.

There is a satisfying *clunk* as the shutter descends. Otto returns to the camera, opens the back, and, as her sister showed her, inscribes the date onto the red paper with the stylus: *October 11, 1920.*

"Are you going to join any clubs?" asks Dora as they pick up their satchels and make their way toward the lodge to sign out. "I'll definitely play hockey and tennis but I can't decide about lacrosse."

"I'm thinking about the Bach Choir," says Marianne.

"Hmm, Bach Choir." Otto lights a cigarette, dropping the match into a trough of purple cyclamen.

"It's mixed," adds Marianne. "One of the only societies that is."

"Even so, I can't see me in a choir, darling, can you?" Otto points at the racks of bicycles along the wall of the building. "That reminds me, we need to get you and Beatrice cycling. I hate walking almost as much as I hate omnibuses."

"I've ridden my father's," says Marianne, "but it's been a while. Miss Jourdain says I can borrow one from college."

"Mine arrives next week," says Beatrice.

Otto yawns. "We could go to the Parks and practice, take a picnic."

"Good idea," says Dora. "I've been feeling rather cooped up lately. I play tennis most days at home."

"Mother says I must take up a sport," says Beatrice with a doubtful expression. "She says it's improving."

"Women won a fifth of our medals at the Olympics this year," says Dora. "Most of them for tennis. I can recommend it."

"I think I'll start with the War and Peace and Debating Societies," says Beatrice. "Although the Essay Writing Club is jolly good too, I've heard."

Otto gives a derisory snort. "I'm really not a club sort of girl—unless the club is in London and flouts licensing laws." She offers the camera to Dora. "But seeing as you are all for being active, do you fancy a detour back inside?"

Dora rolls her eyes, then nods and dashes off toward Corridor Eight. Otto calls out after her, "Meet us at the lodge." Dora really does have the most excellent posture, she thinks, pulling back her own shoulders.

At the main gates, two third-years are leaving ahead of them. They are identical twins, painfully thin like a pair of hatstands, with matching Roman noses. Both wear trench coats under their academic gowns, and one is pushing a battered black motorcycle.

"I heard about these two," whispers Beatrice. "They worked as messengers in London during the war."

"Oh, I want one of those," says Otto. "Much faster than pedaling."

One of the twins props the machine against a tree and buckles first her own helmet, then her sister's. The first-years watch, captivated as the twins climb on, one behind the other, lifting their skirts to reveal matching leggings and brogues. Then the driver leans forward to grasp the handlebars, and her sister leans in too, until they are perfectly parallel at forty-five degrees.

"How wonderful that they never have to be apart," says Marianne, as the motorbike chunters up the road, spitting ferrous fumes in its wake.

"That's precisely why I came here," says Otto, nostrils flaring. "To get away from my sisters."

THE FIRST LECTURE OF THE year, an introduction to the Bodleian Library, takes place in the dining hall at Exeter College.

"Women enter here," says the porter, directing them through the farthest of two oak doors and indicating that they should sit together at one of the long narrow tables.

The heavy benches were not made with skirts in mind, and even Dora fails to look elegant as she takes her seat. Breakfast crumbs and blobs of milk linger on the sticky dark surfaces. Although Otto is relieved that chaperones are no longer mandatory at lectures, there were plentiful reminders at supper last night that speaking to male students before or afterward is forbidden. One must not pollute the education of young men, after all.

Male students stream in through the first door. Some notice the women, color, straighten their collars, smooth their hair nervously; others nudge their neighbors and whisper. Otto can identify the recently demobilized by the deep lines on their faces. The younger ones, probably fresh from Eton, Charterhouse, or Rugby, will have little understanding of the nightmares that plague their older colleagues. Otto spots a veteran she recognizes—a friend of Gertie's or her middle sister Vita's, perhaps. A fellow redhead, he sits at the end of the central row facing the women. As if reading Otto's mind, he lifts his head from his notebook and meets her gaze, but she still cannot place him. She wonders where they have met before, the thought scraping away at her. She hates not to have the upper hand.

She is aware she looks ridiculous in her academic dress. Which genius decided that women should wear the floppy cap sported by students four hundred years ago? It is impossibly itchy. She has tried a jaunty angle, pulling it down around her ears or wearing it at the back of her head. Nothing works. Oddly enough, Marianne, long-necked like a goose, looks as if she was born wearing one. The last few days have revealed that Marianne exhibits both empathy and a dry wit, a surprisingly appealing combination to Otto, but today Marianne seems anxious again, wringing her hands until her knuckles glow like pearls.

"It's just a talk, we're not going down with the *Titanic*," Otto whispers in her ear.

Marianne turns to look at her. "I've never seen anything like it. William Morris and Burne-Jones probably sat here." She gestures at the bench beside her. "Right here."

Otto follows her gaze across the hall with its high beams and paneled walls. Rectors in curly wigs glare out from within gilt frames, and above them is a fretwork gallery where someone ought to be strumming a lute. The black and white tiles of the floor look newly laid. Electric lights with pleated crimson lampshades are wired at regular intervals along the tables. She supposes it is rather impressive.

"What you need to remember is that William Morris was just a man," she whispers to Marianne. "A man with a terrible beard."

WHEN HE REACHES THE LECTERN at the far end of the hall, Bodley's librarian, Mr. Arthur Cowley, acknowledges the presence of women undergraduates, greeting the room as "gentlemen—and ladies," a gesture that results in a wave of murmurs and halfhearted applause. Not at all the skeletal hermit Dora had imagined, Mr. Cowley is ruddy-faced and genial. Although he does not call upon Beatrice to answer a question despite her raised hand, he readily shares a joke with some of the young men at the front.

As Cowley describes the library's history, its locations and traditions, and how every book that is published in Britain is stored there, Dora's mind drifts back to the extraordinary conversation the Eights had last night. After supper, they gathered in Otto's room again and Beatrice talked about Marie Stopes and her book *Married Love*, which gives advice on conception and how to avoid it. *A cap a woman might actually enjoy wearing*, said Otto, shrieking with laughter. They agreed modern women should talk of such things and not learn from watching animals copulate, like their parents did. Otto revealed that some Oxford men travel up to London to sleep with prostitutes. They return on the late train from Paddington, which has become known as the *Fornicator*. The conversation was both shocking and irresistible. In bed that night, thinking of doing these things with Charles made Dora's pulse thud hard between her legs. She would have made an utter fool of herself, no doubt.

She has thought about him a lot today. She assumes it is Oxford that is unsettling her. She thinks of the cleft in his chin and his clumsy proposal in the hallway. Of how he ought to be sitting in a lecture right now—this one, perhaps. Of the downright unfairness of it all. Even when after the lecture they walk over to the Bodleian to swear the library oath, she cannot help but compare the protection given to books at Oxford to the lives lost in France. Here books are housed in hallowed buildings and guarded zealously. They are not loaned out for fear they will be marked, defaced, or injured. Vows are sworn to ensure that they never encounter "fire or flame."

If only Charles and George had been afforded such value.

ON TUESDAY, DORA SITS RESPONSIONS, tests to check that her mathematics and Latin are up to scratch because she does not have the Oxford Senior qualification like the other girls on Corridor Eight. The mathematics is tougher than she is expecting, but certainly not a disaster. On Wednesday, she has her first tutorial. Although Anglo-Saxon will be taught in a group with Marianne and two girls called Temperance and Josephine, Dora will study Early and Middle English Literature with Miss Finch this year, just the two of them. Strangely, Dora finds herself unfazed about learning a new language, but the thought of being alone in a room with an Oxford don is utterly terrifying. Her hands shake as she knocks on the door of the tutor's office.

Miss Finch is a stocky woman with mannish gray hair and the air of someone who believes that brutal honesty is a kindness. She strides about in front of Dora, hands in the pockets of her tweed jacket. "We will focus on *Beowulf* for the next few weeks. You'll need to read it before next week and attempt a translation. What do you know about alliterative verse, Miss Greenwood?"

When Dora is not in Miss Finch's shadow, the sun threads through the windowpanes and settles on the crown of her head. It is hard to focus and she does not know what Miss Finch wants her to say. Is it a test or a discussion or both? It is not at all like school.

"It is an oral tradition," says Dora eventually, searching her tutor's face for a reaction. It seems like the right point to make. "And therefore needs to be easy to remember and entertaining."

"Tell me more," says Miss Finch. Prodding, poking.

Dora fumbles about for something to say. "There may have been many versions of a poem. It could have changed a little bit each time it was told."

Miss Finch's eyes narrow. "So how can we trust what we read?"

"I suppose we have to trust the text that remains," says Dora. "Although perhaps it might tell us something about the scribe too."

"Good, good," murmurs Miss Finch, passing Dora a worn book of Anglo-Saxon grammar. "First, we'd better go over the basics. Then we'll have a group discussion tomorrow. Did you know the first recorded use of the word 'friend'—freond—is in *Beowulf*?"

At the end of the hour, Dora concludes that Miss Finch is not quite as intimidating as she first thought, even if she cannot shake the idea that she has failed to impress her tutor. Though Dora knows how fortunate she is to be here, how many women long to take her place at Oxford, she is keenly aware that she would give it all up to have Charles back, or George. She would give all of this up in a second.

"Do you think it's normal to see the war in everything one reads?" she asks, before she can stop herself.

For the first time that afternoon, Miss Finch regards her with genuine interest.

"Because I can't seem to look at books and plays and poems without thinking of it," Dora adds.

Miss Finch does not scoff or laugh but gazes at her with an impenetrable expression. What Dora does not mention is that she thought of Charles during her first lecture that morning. That she thinks she sees him everywhere, even after three years. She fails to tell her tutor the whole truth, which is that she sees the world through the lens of war most of the time.

"I know of people who couldn't read fiction at all during the war," says Miss Finch, swatting at a fly on the windowsill. "I think it's very personal but entirely normal." She crushes the insect on the windowpane with her finger and sighs. "I can only speak for myself. The war has changed the way I interpret Shakespeare, undoubtedly. Two years of peacetime, and comedies where people come back from the dead or are in disguise still look ridiculous to me. But I can relate to the chaos created by 'vaulting ambition' in the histories and tragedies. Perhaps being able to watch a Shakespearean comedy is what we should aspire to—the ultimate indication of peacetime."

How wonderful it would be if life were a comedy and not a tragedy, thinks Dora. They could all walk out of Ashridge Forest: her, Charles, and George. People would come back from the dead or as a twin, and matters would conclude tidily with a wedding breakfast at the golf club.

"What do you like to read, Miss Greenwood?"

"I enjoy crime novels when I'm relaxing or on the train, but my favorite authors are Charlotte Brontë and Jane Austen. I like poetry too—Hardy, Wordsworth, Browning."

Miss Finch flicks the remains of the insect into the wastepaper basket. "I often wonder why crime fiction is so popular at the moment. It has all the components of a Shakespearean tragedy, if you think about it. When you meet Miss Cox, one of the chaperones, ask her for recommendations. She's a huge fan."

As Dora stands up, Miss Finch waves a piece of paper at her.

"Oh, I forgot to say, you passed the Latin Responsion, but you will need to resit the mathematics, I'm afraid."

"I failed?" asks Dora. She has never failed an examination in her life. She sits back down in the armchair, deflated. Either she made some awfully careless mistakes or her patchy algebra is to blame. Her last year at Cheltenham was a mess. She spent so much time either at home or sitting numb in her dorm that the school suggested the deputy take over as head girl. Why did she not sit the Oxford Senior before she left? Then she would never have had to sit the blasted Responsions in the first place.

"No need to worry, you can try again." Miss Finch smiles briskly. "There is no time limit as such, but you need to have passed by the end of the academic year. I suggest you mug up a bit, get a coach perhaps, then try again next term."

6

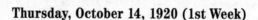

Thursday, October 14, 1920 (1st Week)

St. Hugh's College
Oxford

Dearest Gert,
You were an utter brick moving me in last week. What would
I do without you? Thank you for the gifts. Father sent a
hamper, Vita a scarf, Teddy flowers. Nothing from Mother or
Caro, as expected.

I'm sorry to say, you weren't entirely off the mark when
you compared St. Hugh's to prison. Infernal bells ring all day
long and, like bleary-eyed prisoners, we are required to
attend chapel EVERY MORNING for roll call. The other day I
suggested breakfast on a tray to the scout and she curled her
lip at me in the style of a stray dog backed into an alley.
Apparently, trays are only permitted on special occasions;
the principal believes we must eat together like a "Christian
family." Quelle horreur.

Maud (the scout) and I have come to a private
arrangement. She will wake me at seven with a milky
coffee every morning and I shall pay her two shillings a
term. Despite her gruff demeanor, Maud understands the
value of discretion and was quick to impart that the wine
merchant on the High will deliver their goods in unmarked

packages to women's colleges. I think she and I will rub along very well.

This morning we gathered in the college library for a talk on examinations and I raised a few unplucked eyebrows with my new lipstick from Max Factor. The library overlooks the garden and right in the center of the lawn is a spindly little tree that seems entirely out of place. We were informed that this bundle of twigs is an object of great reverence known as the Armistice Magnolia. This honorable status did not deter a local cat from squatting down next to it and doing its business.

It appears our entire first year will be devoted to passing examinations which prove we are bright enough to be here. Fail and you're out. I have no mathematics examinations at all. Instead, we are all to be tested on Latin and Logic at Pass Mods in June, and on the New Testament (the famous Divvers) next term. PLEASE don't tell Caro I shall be studying the Bible. She will dine out on it for months.

Apparently, when I leave with my pass degree, I will be amply qualified to become a secretary or a teacher. Should you tell Mother, or shall I?

Otto xxx

———◇———

ON THE ANNIVERSARY OF HER first week away from home, Marianne wakes at dawn. Stripes of greasy light fall on the covers. Layers of oil paint.

Outside, robins and blackbirds warble in the yellowing cherry trees, but inside, it is Maud's footsteps that herald the morning. Marianne knows how the scout's day begins. Buckets of coal to carry, fires to lay, laundry to collect, bins to empty. The morning coffee for Otto. Later there will be beds to strip, clothes to iron, floors to clean, errands to run. Luckily, Marianne does fewer of these tasks at home since the arrival of Mrs. Ward last year.

Maud works efficiently and avoids interaction with the inhabitants of her corridor. When concentrating, she often makes a funny little snort, which Otto has begun to mimic. Skinny and flat-chested, Maud has a nasal voice and muscular forearms like a boy. Marianne is a little afraid of her.

Maud always begins with Miss Bazeley's study, which takes her less than ten minutes. Then she moves to Otto's room, where she picks up objects underfoot: tortoiseshell hair combs, a cigarette holder, handkerchiefs smeared with coral lipstick that will need to be boiled off. In Beatrice's room, she will quietly retrieve teacups, pile up old newspapers, and remove the soiled garments from the laundry basket. It may be that, as she tucks a greasy hair behind her ear, Maud glances at the sleeping figure and wonders why women her own age get to talk all day and call it learning, whereas she must clear up after them. Next, she moves to Dora's room to lay the fire, but not for long. Dora is neatness personified; nothing is ever out of place there.

Marianne had planned to keep to herself this term, to find buttons to reattach, boots to clean, reading to do. She had planned to avoid distractions, to abstain from making too many friends to whom she would tell too many lies. But the others keep knocking on her door, inviting her to accompany them to meals, introductory talks, tea parties in the Junior Common Room. They ask her to join societies with them, visit the library, go for a walk. Sometimes they knock simply because they have left their rooms to use the lavatory and might as well chat. She has never lived close to other women, heard their snoring through the wall. Already, she knows their different treads: Beatrice flat-footed in men's boots, Dora's light trip, Otto's drag and scuff. They have threaded squares of paper onto a string and hung them with a pencil stub on each door so that they can leave each other notes about their plans: *Gone to the Bod with Otto*; *Meet in the lodge at 11 a.m.*; *We are in the JCR.* So often seen together, they are already known about college as the Eights.

Last night, they made cocoa in the kitchen and drank it in the garden after dark. The sky was sable, paint-spattered with stars. They found Pegasus (upside down) and long-legged Aquarius. Dora swore she could see a hatstand and Otto insisted she could see a pair of breasts (*So enormous they could be yours, Beatrice*), and they made up horoscopes. Childish stuff: *Hatstands, try not to be so rigid. Breasts, be careful not to attract the wrong kind of attention.* She found herself laughing, truly laughing, in the way one does when one feels free, for the first time in a very long while.

Finally, Maud enters Marianne's room, and to save them both embarrassment Marianne feigns sleep. She visualizes her notes, books, and fountain pen sitting on the desk, where she left them yesterday after her first tutorial with Miss Finch, her mind charged with the tutor's insightful theories on Grendel and Grendel's mother. Afterward, she had returned to her room and removed her locket in order to wash before dinner, placing it on the desk with the chain neatly spiraled. Maud will surely have seen it by now, perhaps wondered at its value. She may even be holding it, unable to resist a closer look. Perhaps she is picking up the laundry basket beside the desk and stealthily nudging the locket in with her elbow, watching it slither down beneath the soiled garments.

Marianne sits up too fast, then fishes for her slippers on the cold floor. Maud is kneeling at the fireplace before her, stacking kindling into a pyramid. She makes her little snort and wipes her fingers on her skirt, leaving comet-shaped smears in their wake. The locket lies as Marianne left it on the desk, its precious contents curled safely inside.

———◇———

St. Hugh's College
October 14, 1920

Dear Hilda,
Your letters are such a comfort, thank you. I am surrounded
by so many new and strident personalities here that a
familiar voice from school is very welcome. I would dearly
love to hear more about undergraduate life at Girton and how
you are finding Cambridge.

Today, Oxford awarded women degrees for the first time!
The entire college departed en masse for the Sheldonian
Theatre straight after breakfast. Our chaperone was Miss
Cox, a retired matron who shares our admiration for crime
fiction. On the walk into town she recommended a new
author, Agatha Christie, whose first novel, The Mysterious
Affair at Styles, has been serialized in the Times. Do you
know it? Apparently, Mrs. Christie was set the challenge to
write a novel where it was impossible to guess the perpetrator
of the crime, and the result is terribly good. To quote Miss
Cox, "The whole story is maddeningly complicated and
solved by a little man from Belgium."

Then Miss Cox let slip that she once chaperoned women
from Oxford all the way to Dublin where they were awarded
degrees by Trinity College! They were known as the
"Steamboat Ladies" because they took the early boat to
Dublin, hired robes in the afternoon, attended the ceremony
the next morning, and sailed home that evening. Naturally,
we made a big fuss of Miss Cox at this revelation. She was
rosy with delight when Otto called her a heroine. Then I
made the mistake of wondering aloud why so many women
studied at Oxford knowing they wouldn't get a degree.
Beatrice got terribly animated about how Oxford is the seat
of learning in the Empire, and how "If we want equality of
representation then we need to show we can compete at the
highest levels." Thankfully, Otto saved the day as usual, by

changing the subject to Patricia Clough (a garrulous first-year linguist) and how much she dislikes her.

When we arrived at the Broad, the place was thronging with women spanning eighteen to eighty years. I wish you could have seen it, Hilda. It was such fun to see men in the minority for a change, and watch well-wishers from the four colleges and the Home Learning Association halt the traffic. My thoughts drifted to Mother and what a pity it is she will never understand why this sort of thing matters. As maddening and shortsighted as she can be, I still find myself needing her approval.

As we joined the crowds gathered on the cobbled area, there was a carnival atmosphere. The chorus of women's voices was so loud it muffled even the college bells, and well-wishers handed out red carnations. They smelled like wet coins, but we pinned them on our lapels all the same. Otto steered us toward the Sheldonian, hissing that we must save her from Patricia "and her furry lip." As we stood contemplating the thirteen huge stone heads on top of the wall, Miss Cox explained that these limestone "emperors" once had unique faces and beards. Now the rain has eroded them to ghouls with flattened noses and deep eye sockets. All I could think of was mustard-gas burns. Men whose skin is so shiny and taut they can no longer blink.

"We'll all look like that in fifty years," Otto said, nudging me. "But Patricia will have the best mustache."

I couldn't help but laugh. Otto really is rather terrific.

The men came out first and later we discovered this was because they received their degrees before the women, which was a little disappointing. When the women finally emerged to cheering, we spotted Beatrice's mother and our principal, Miss Jourdain. The graduates posed soberly for photographs, a dignified group despite their square caps. It is strange to think that after so many years of fighting for degrees, women can now simply turn up and pay seven pounds and ten shillings for the privilege!

It has been, as Miss Jourdain put it, "A woman's day, and a day for women to remember." We have a reception and tea this afternoon and I am off there in a minute.

Trying out for hockey went well. Matches start next week. I am mortified that, being hopelessly out of practice, I have to resit a mathematics test next term. There is already so much to do, what with Latin, Logic, Divinity, and Anglo-Saxon, it is quite overwhelming. However, keeping busy holds the wretched dark thoughts at bay.

Do write and tell me how your brothers are faring. Is David out of the wheelchair yet? I think of them both often.

Yours affectionately,
Dora

LATER THAT AFTERNOON, THE WOMEN of St. Hugh's gather at a modest reception in college. The dining hall smells of the inside of a teapot and the windows are dull with steam. Maud, looking awkward in a starched apron and headband, is serving fish-paste sandwiches and jam tarts. Teacups clink, and conversation roars and abates like waves on a pebble beach.

Beatrice has received a good deal of flattering attention from other students now that her mother's identity is known, especially at the first meeting of the War and Peace Society (subscription two shillings and sixpence), where Josephine Bostwick insisted that Beatrice have the last fig roll. Despite this, her mother's presence in college leaves Beatrice's stomach churning uncomfortably, just as it did when Edith Sparks returned home from campaigning or a spell in Holloway. Beatrice would take refuge from her mother's capricious moods in her bedroom, rereading *The Adventures of Tom Sawyer* and imagining herself on thrilling adventures with Huckleberry Finn.

Although she will probably downplay it, Beatrice knows how much this day will mean to her mother. Beatrice is also aware, though, that outside St. Hugh's life goes on as usual. Mothers give birth, maids clean, widows weep, wives shop for groceries, waitresses serve customers, and daughters are told to sit still. Most girls her age are none the wiser as to what this day means. It is another tiny grain of sand added to the bucket of progress. The bottom of the bucket is almost covered.

As her mother steps forward, a hush filters through the crowd. Edith Sparks begins her speech only when she has the attention of the entire room. She knows exactly how to command an audience.

"I often ask myself," she begins, "if women had always been taught to paint, sculpt, publish, report, write, calculate, translate, and experiment, what kind of world would we live in now?

"And how will we ever know the contribution of women to the great scientific and cultural achievements of the past? What about the women who were instrumental in listening, editing, advising, inspiring, recording, and assisting famous men? Women who have been written out of history, their contributions unrecorded and unvalued.

"I put it to you that a country is only truly democratic if opportunity is not withheld from *all* its citizens at the highest level."

The dining hall bursts into applause. Dora nudges Beatrice with her elbow and Marianne catches Beatrice's eye and smiles sympathetically. Edith is a formidable figure, there is no denying it, and she can rouse a roomful of women with ease. She addresses the tea party as passionately as she might working women at Hyde Park Corner.

"For the first time we have a woman MP, a divorcée to boot.

A woman has won the Nobel Prize, twice. Yet there are still men—respected physicians—who argue that women are too emotional for rational thought, that their internal organs will spontaneously combust if they dare to think too hard about an equation."

The hall erupts in laughter. Otto, leaning on the doorframe with her arms folded, winks at Beatrice and mimes her stomach exploding.

"This country has progressed, yes, but it is shameful it took a war to make that happen. The fact is clear, men—most men—want us to remain subjugated." Edith pauses as the audience nods. "Women of your age still cannot vote. And now working women must give up their jobs for returning servicemen. Jobs they are paid less to do than their male counterparts."

Beatrice has heard this speech before, several times. She knows that any minute, spittle will begin to fly as her mother becomes increasingly agitated. She studies Edith's chin. It reclines on a pouch of flesh that hangs underneath her jaw and wobbles as she speaks. Her top lip has drooped a little to cover the upper teeth. Twists of hair, white and gray, creep along the temples. She still wears a corset out of habit and vanity, although she says it is to benefit her spine. Beatrice respects her mother's politics but does not see the shiny version of her she once worshipped as a child, the version that is now enthralling rows of hopeful, upturned faces. They do not see a woman who slaps or spoils servants depending on how much sleep she has had. A woman who talks so loudly all the time, you'd think she has a hearing impediment. A woman who at breakfast will not let you eat your toast quietly without asking you, *Why eat two pieces, Beatrice, WHY?* Who says she is surprised Oxford accepted you and demands to see the letter. Whom you love but you loathe, admire, deny, and celebrate in equal measure. To be born of such a woman as Edith Sparks is to be permanently exhausted. So powerful a presence in any room, there is no air for you. So lacking in physical affection that you flinch when she touches you.

Even though Beatrice was tutored at home, boarding school being *unconducive to freethinking*, it is normal for her not to see her mother for weeks at a time. When she thinks of the drawing room in Bloomsbury, it is her father she imagines, reading the newspaper and quoting bits to her. She looks up now, and there he is. His face rapt as if hearing the speech for the very first time.

7

NATIONAL UNION OF WOMEN'S SUFFRAGE SOCIETIES
OXFORD BRANCH
MARTYRS' MEMORIAL, JUNE 21, 1912, 2 P.M.

The order of this meeting can be kept by ABSOLUTE QUIET
on the part of the MAIN BODY of the AUDIENCE.

If anyone interrupts, do not turn round.
TAKE NO NOTICE.

Beatrice is thrilled that her mother wants her at today's rally, where Sylvia Pankhurst, Dorothy Pethick, and Maude Royden are speaking. It is an important day for Oxford women, and the London contingent must show their support—children too. Beatrice, thirteen last week, is proud to be seen entering Paddington at her mother's side. It hardly matters that she is pinched on the back of the hand and told—in a hiss—to close her mouth *unless she wants to look like a half-wit.*

Although the party comprises three other daughters, Beatrice is the only one traveling in the leather-studded privacy of first class. She is not seated with her mother but hears the reedy clarinet of her laugh along the carriage from time to time. There are two volunteers from the Women's Social and Political Union in her own compartment in animated discussion. They have been tasked with looking after Beatrice but completely ignore her. The man opposite tuts pointedly from behind his newspaper each time the women are shrill. Beatrice tugs at her new dress in its exhausting shade of aquamarine. The flouncy trim along the hem and sleeves is so bulky it might as well be fashioned from lead.

Because the weather is unusually hot, they take a cab from the station to the center of Oxford. It is Midsummer Day, which her mother says is very fitting.

"We need all women to see the light. To open their eyes and act. If we are bystanders, nothing will change. Do you understand?"

"I do," says Beatrice, determined to prove herself a girl—a woman—of action.

Huge crowds have gathered where a wide road narrows and splits around a Gothic-style monument. Raised on a hexagonal base of eight steps, it looks like a church steeple sticking out of the ground and offers an elevated position for the speakers. The London group makes camp at the railings of the Randolph Hotel, opposite. Beatrice takes out the guidebook her father has given her. She learns that Martyrs' Memorial is dedicated to the Protestants Cranmer, Ridley, and Latimer, who were burned at the stake nearby.

"It's a pertinent example of how fear and prejudice can divide what ought to be a unified cause," says Miss Davison, gently pinning a WSPU rosette onto Beatrice's lapel. "And also, handily close to the taxicabs."

Miss Davison, her mother's friend from St. Hugh's, has traveled down with them. Tall with frizzy hair that is barely restrained by pins, she has bushy brows and sorrowful eyes. She is always kind, but her lips are so thin they are hard to distinguish, and Beatrice has never seen her smile. Every time Miss

Davison speaks to her, it is as if she is thinking of something else entirely.

"I've been telling your mother: every cause needs a martyr," says Miss Davison, over the din of the crowd. "Someone who will be remembered three hundred years later. It's the only way to be taken seriously."

"Emily, do not put ideas in her head, she's only thirteen," says her mother, turning to Beatrice. "Miss Davison decided she'd put martyrdom to the test by jumping off a railing in prison, but she got caught in the netting and came away with a nasty bump to the head. Very silly." She strokes Miss Davison's cheek with the back of her hand. "We must be militant, yes. But suicidal? Absolutely not."

Beatrice is aware that Miss Davison has just completed a six-month sentence at Holloway Prison for setting fire to a pillar box and that she hid in a broom cupboard in Parliament on census night. Miss Davison worked as a teacher to save the money to attend St. Hugh's for a term, where she got a first in English Literature, although there was no degree at the end, of course. The odd thing is that other English universities give women degrees—perhaps because it is older than the Church of England, Oxford University thinks it can do as it likes. But Beatrice knows today is not about degrees. They are here because all women deserve a say on things that affect them and their families. Her mother says that their job is to stand up for women who cannot stand up for themselves. To do nothing is cowardly.

"Miss Jourdain is here in her robes, and Miss Rogers too. How splendid," says her mother, lured as ever by the crowd. She grasps Miss Davison's thin white hand and gives it a squeeze. Then she glances at Beatrice. "Wait here and look after Miss Davison, she needs to rest. I'll be back in a minute," she says, then inserts herself sideways between two spectators and disappears.

Beatrice wonders whether if she were a more interesting

person, her mother might disappear less. Then she might treat Beatrice as she does Miss Davison: ask her how she is, what she thinks; squeeze her hand.

There are hundreds of people on the roads and pavements now. One thousand at least, according to Miss Davison. The crowd begins singing "The March of the Women" and, despite Beatrice's disappointment that she is not enough for her mother, it is hard not to be uplifted. The militant women, "suffragettes," wear white blouses and skirts, and summer hats decorated as if they are going to a garden party. Some have arms filled with flowers; the scent of Chinese lilies, peonies, and mock orange lingers in their wake. They wear sashes, rosettes, medals, and some wave flags in purple, white, and green. Other groups sport academic dress or the nonmilitant red and green of the "suffragists." A mother and daughter wear loose cotton bags across their bodies from which they hand out leaflets encouraging the audience to *Take No Notice* if the meeting is disturbed, although Beatrice finds this very unlikely—the atmosphere is so convivial. Mustached bobbies in helmets and thick-soled boots stroll along the perimeter, buttons glinting in the sunshine. They nod genially, flushed from the midday sun.

Huge banners with golden tassels are held aloft by pairs of men wearing leather belts on their hips. Beatrice is familiar with the abbreviations on them; they are served with every meal at home. Her favorite is the banner of the Oxford branch of the WSPU, which features the embroidered head and shoulders of Emmeline Pankhurst. Her face looms, three feet tall, above the words *The Savior of Womanhood*. Some of the simpler placards are handheld, painted roughly on squares of whitewashed wood. *Votes for Women, Deeds Not Words*, the usual. One has been discarded against the railings beside her. From upside down, it reads *Fortune Favors the Brave*. She is half tempted to pick it up, but her mother often complains that placards give her splinters.

Among the throng of female heads are boaters, bowler hats,

and caps. Beatrice thinks sadly of her father, who was instructed to absent himself today. He had suggested they take a room at the Randolph so that Beatrice could watch from a window, and her mother was not best pleased.

AS THE AFTERNOON PROGRESSES, FLOWERS start to brown and wilt and tempers fray in the June sun. Miss Davison goes into the hotel in search of water and the WC. Beatrice tries to sit on the lip of the pavement but is buffeted by bags, skirts, and on one occasion what feels like a swinging fist. A grubby heat rises from the ground—hot leather, dung, petrol. She returns to the safety of the railing and stands with her back to it. Her feet ache and she has not seen her mother for hours. For the first time, she wishes she had not come.

She watches, astonished, as members of Balliol College try to disrupt the speakers. From a window on the other side of the road, students blast gramophone music and lob sugar cubes into the crowd. Someone blows wavering notes from a trumpet poked through curtains, and a group converge at the memorial steps to "smoke out" the speakers with pipes. Miss Davison does not return from the hotel, and Beatrice glimpses her in the crowd, linking arms with her mother. The women are closing ranks. She hopes they can go home soon.

By the time Sylvia Pankhurst takes to the steps of the memorial, the tension is palpable. Beatrice cringes as small stones fly from the outer edge of the crowd, spinning into the backs of women listening at the center. At first they stand firm. Beatrice, anxious, looks about for her mother and Miss Davison, but they are nowhere to be seen. A group of older men, brawny in open shirts and braces, push their way into the crowd, elbowing between the rows of women so that they totter like skittles. They are workingmen returning from an early shift, perhaps on the railway. They spit and boil with unconcealed rage. Scuffles break out where women or men push back at them. The policemen watch but do nothing. She looks around again with increasing panic. There is a twisting and tightening low in her abdomen. She is quite alone at the railing. She wonders if she should go into the hotel like her father wanted her to, but she cannot bring her feet to lift from the pavement.

"Why should a woman working in a factory be paid less for doing the same job as her husband, come home, and begin another job as a domestic drudge while his working day is over?" says Mrs. Pankhurst. "Why should she not be able to vote for people who will make life better for her and her children?"

She is calm and earnest, a seasoned speaker. Beatrice has heard her many times. There is a gentleness and civility about Mrs. Pankhurst that Beatrice usually finds comforting, but not today.

The heckling intensifies. "What would you know about hard work?"

"Go home to your married man, you whore!"

"Go home, bitch!"

From the pavement, Beatrice sees arms flailing and hears muffled shouts and shrieks. Her heart is drumming in her ears. She looks about for Miss Davison or her mother again but cannot see anyone she knows from the train, so she presses herself further into the hotel railings, gripping them behind her as if she is in handcuffs. The crowd begins to panic, and people peel off in random directions. Two men climb the memorial steps and rip rosettes from the chests of open-mouthed women as if plucking out their hearts. They grab wooden placards and toss them into the crowd. At least two women are knocked to the ground bleeding. There is screaming and women turn and flood toward Beatrice, mouths slack, hands thrown up to catch falling hats, knees rising through long skirts. Beatrice shuts her eyes tightly and waits for the barrage to hit.

A shadow bears down on her. The heat of another body in intimate proximity. Tobacco, grease, a meaty kind of scent. A cat sniffing at a mouse in a trap. She cowers, drawing herself in as small as possible. Invisible.

"This is what dirty little girls get," says a hot voice in her ear. She opens her lips to cry for help and a wet breathy mouth presses over hers, tongue forcing itself inside, pushing into her throat, licking her teeth. Bristles rake her upper lip and chin. She cannot breathe, gags. A hand scrabbles over the front of her dress as if looking for a handle, then pinches hard between her legs.

And suddenly it is over as quickly as it began. She opens her eyes, trembling. There are people pushing past, some shouting, some weeping, some sobbing, some bleeding from the head or nose. Policemen blowing whistles, flowers decapitated underfoot. She stands there for what could be a second or a minute or an hour. Somebody grabs her by the hand and says, "Let's go, Beatrice," and then she is in a taxicab and a horse is clip-clopping to the beat of her heart.

Inside the cab, Miss Davison leans against Beatrice's mother with her eyes closed. Edith Sparks fans herself in an agitated fashion, her cheeks blotchy and red. She mutters angrily to herself, then looks up at Beatrice. "Why are *you* crying?"

"I—" says Beatrice. She wants to tell her mother what has happened, but she fears that if she does it will somehow become her own fault. She dries her tears on the pollen-stained hem of her dress.

"There was a man—"

Her mother sighs. "There were lots of men, Beatrice. We all saw them."

"He said bad things—"

"And?" The fan moves faster.

"I don't know—"

Beatrice stares at her feet. Brown-tinged petals dangle limply from her shoes. Then the cab lurches and her mother is jolted forward. Their knees smash together.

"For goodness' sake," snaps her mother, her face pinched into a snarl. "Do you know what a burden you've been today? I wish I'd never brought you." Then she turns to Miss Davison and begins talking to her in a low and soothing voice.

AFTERWARD, BEATRICE WONDERS IF SHE imagined the whole episode, but as she looks in the mirror in her bedroom at Bloomsbury, her grazed lip and chin suggest otherwise. She never speaks of the incident to anyone. Her mother, she realizes, would dismiss it as nothing, or perhaps not even believe her. Or she would blame Beatrice because she stood at the railings of the Randolph Hotel, like the half-wit she is, and let a man assault her.

After all, to do nothing is cowardly.

8

Saturday, October 30, 1920 (3rd Week)

UNDERGRADUETTES

OXFORD HAT AND GOWN OF CHARMING DIGNITY

"At Cambridge they are fighting this term for the rights of women," writes a correspondent, but in Oxford the "undergraduette" is an accomplished fact. You can see the undergraduettes any day in the High in their academic dress. Not only the long gown of the scholar, but even the short commoners' gown confers an air of charming dignity on a woman. But the work of genius is the hat. It is not the cardboard square that the men have, but a flat pointed woolen "tam." They say it is exactly like the hat which every undergraduate wore in the days before powdered wigs were known. It may be; but in Oxford we have our suspicions that the learned dons were not entirely guided by antiquarian interests! There is a band at the back too, reminiscent of wartime uniforms—which all the world admitted to be charming.

DAILY MAIL
MONDAY, OCTOBER 25, 1920

Otto keeps her promise about a picnic in the park, but Marianne's commitments at home mean that the trip must wait until Saturday of third week.

The bicycle Marianne has borrowed from St. Hugh's is heavy, with long curved handlebars that require her to sit with her back straight and her arms at neat right angles. The seat is too high and the handlebars judder and vibrate, which makes her shoulders do the same. She has half fallen a few times, putting one foot down, which is frustrating; she has ridden her father's bicycle about the village on plenty of occasions albeit not for over two years. There is oil on her hem and, where the pedal has dug in, her stockings are ripped. She will have a job repairing them tonight.

"Come on, Marianne, everyone cycles in Oxford."

"Look forward. Pedal. Steer. Steer!"

The University Parks is a vast field bounded on the longest side by a tributary of the Thames, the River Cherwell. In the shade of mature elm and willow trees, chalky paths mark the perimeter, and she has already walked them several times on early-morning outings with Dora. A favorite haunt of both town and gown, the Parks are dominated by football and cricket pitches; matches are lost and won above the remains of Bronze Age farmers, long since turned to sod. War lingers in the corners where vegetable patches return to rose beds, airplane hangars house lawn mowers, and rectangles of flattened meadow revive.

Dora runs alongside her, the fittest among them—all those hours at the tennis club—and Otto stands facing them, hands on hips, leaning forward to suck in air. Otto and Dora are already proficient, of course, and Beatrice, on the other bicycle, is whooping as she rides in big circles on the grass. She carries a green plaid blanket in her wicker basket and has found learning to ride "a breeze." Marianne's torso is sweaty. Her coccyx aches. In order to find a rhythm she conjures a short poem by

Tennyson, the only thing she can think of in iambic meter. She pushes down with the flat of her foot with each stressed syllable.

> He clasps the crag with crooked hands;
> Close to the sun in lonely lands,
> Ring'd with the azure world, he stands.
>
> The wrinkled sea beneath him crawls;
> He watches from his mountain walls,
> And like a thunderbolt he falls.

She is propelled forward, and cool air gives way to her as it brushes her cheeks.

"Sit up, Marianne," shouts Otto. "Sit up!"

WHEN SHE HAS MASTERED THIS particularly awkward bicycle, Marianne waits for the others to catch up. October's sun is ineffective but welcome. The scent of cut grass waxes and wanes, giving off a moist, metallic tang. Small crowds cheer on footballers in unsullied kit, and in the bandstand, brass instruments tune up with squeaks and *parp*s. Families stroll with perambulators and, for the first time since she left home, Marianne sees small children at play.

One little girl stands out. Around ten years old, she sits reading on a bench, while her parents stand behind her whispering excitedly. Even from a distance, Marianne can see that the mother is expecting a baby. Despite appearing completely absorbed, the little girl does not turn a single page of the book she is studying. When she occasionally lifts her head, the look on her chubby pink face is one of impotent fury.

The scene reminds Marianne of the October, a decade ago, when her father contemplated remarrying. While he was taking tea with an articulate young widow called Mrs. Cresswell, Marianne was seeking kinship with other motherless children like Pip Pirrip and Oliver Twist. Looking back, Mrs. Cresswell, who had been educated at Girton, would have made an excellent wife for a rector, but Marianne was all fury and resentment. In her mind, the widow was lifted from the pages of Dickens: an evil interloper, a sharp-nosed dictator, a likely advocate of boarding school. Once, Marianne brought a maggoty rabbit skull to the table in an attempt to revolt their guest, but it only made Mrs. Cresswell more interested. After that, Marianne resorted to pointedly reading beside her mother's grave and refused to drink tea with the two gentle, lonely adults indoors.

By Christmas, her father had given up. His heart wasn't really in it, or so Marianne liked to think, and Mrs. Cresswell visited them no more. She wrote to them at first, but communication ceased when she married a missionary and went to India. Had Marianne not been so selfish then, things might have been different, and her father would not be alone. Because now the only thing the Reverend Grey is wedded to is his daughter's secret.

Eventually, the little girl is required to shut her book and trudges off behind her parents toward the bandstand. Marianne tears her gaze away to watch a group of convalescent officers in wheelchairs advance across the Parks, presumably on an outing from the nearby Radcliffe Infirmary. The men wear hospital blues: single-breasted suit, red tie, white shirt, polished shoes (or shoe), regimental cap, and medals. As the party approaches, Marianne notices one fellow with pimples on his brow and the soft whisper of a mustache. He looks like a tiny child in school uniform; the legs of his trousers are neatly folded and pinned beneath his short stumps. Another has no arms to speak of; medals extend like piano keys across his heart. Some of the men appear physically intact but stare listlessly ahead, and it is these silent figures with dull eyes that move her most. The nurses, youthful in starched veils and twill capes, maintain a cheerfully inane commentary. Marianne cannot help but wonder why wives or mothers are not caring for these men at home. Then she reminds herself she is hardly qualified to judge.

Miss Stroud the chaperone is also crossing the Parks. Her presence is required by the principal, who has given permission for this outing. A stout, humorless woman of around sixty years of age, Miss Stroud reminds Marianne of a battleship coming into port, grindingly tedious but indefatigable. The girls regroup and continue toward the river without waiting for the dark bulk of Miss Stroud to catch up. They find a spot midway along the bank, a respectable distance from Parson's Pleasure, the nude bathing area for dons. Marianne's father would approve of the concept. St. Mary's sits on a bend of the Thames, and he has swum naked many times in the twenty-five years he has been rector.

Laying down the bikes, they shake out the blanket and sit facing the river. Maud has made the lunch. The scout, despite her glum exterior, remains happy to do extra tasks for Otto and is paid handsomely for it. They eat boiled eggs and ham sandwiches (fresh ham!) and drink bottled spring water all the way from Derbyshire. They watch the punts, laughing at the boys who cannot get the hang of it. The trick seems to be to pull the pole up quickly, then drop it back in and push away. Marianne can row, having grown up by the river, but punting is a different matter. It is not simply a form of boating, it is one of Oxford's unique rhythms. Students have been propelling boats with sticks and smiling at pretty girls for hundreds of years.

To prove her point, the next punt to pass almost capsizes after the men leap up and bow comically to Otto and Dora. *What is it like to have a face that other people are drawn to?* she wonders. Life must contain many more opportunities if one is beautiful.

The entertainment provided by the punters is disturbed by

ragged shouting behind them. As she turns, Marianne spots Miss Stroud hovering a few feet away from the officers in wheelchairs. One of the men has staggered from his chair and is holding his head, groaning, and crying out. Miss Stroud is pale, her mouth slack. A nurse raises a flat palm and signals to the chaperone to keep still. The man wrenches off his tie, sawing it back and forth until it comes away. Then he starts on his jacket. Buttons fly as he opens the flaps of his shirt like wings. The girls watch in horrified silence. Some of the patients laugh and jeer. The nurses plead for him to stop, their voices dissolving into echoes before they reach the riverbank. They try to take him by the arm, but his strength is evident, as is his resolve. Spittle sprays from his mouth as he shouts inarticulate curses to the sky. He removes his trousers, hopping out of them and swinging them away over his head, followed by his undergarments. Then the shoes, which land with a *doof* on the grass. His body is lean but perfect. He is hairless except for a wad of dark fuzz around his genitals. The shouting gives way to a song, but the words are gibberish. Still wearing his officers' cap and socks, he scratches his belly and looks down at his pale penis. It hangs flaccid for a moment, then stiffens. He urinates in a perfectly formed arc, the fluid pulsing dark and warm like tea from a pot. There is quite an audience now. Some of the nurses are in tears, some of the men in the chairs applaud. The neat stream of amber explodes at the feet of Miss Stroud.

For a moment, Marianne cannot remember where she is. She thinks of King Lear tearing off his clothes in the middle of a storm: *off, off, you lendings*. Then she recalls Armistice night: the puckered sliver of moon reflected on the water, her hands struggling against rough cloth, buttons pressed into her cheek.

"Head injury," says Otto, turning away, but Marianne hears the brittleness in her voice, sees the glassy wetness of her eyes.

"Oh God, it's never going to end, is it?" says Dora. She stuffs her knuckles into her mouth. Her shoulders begin to heave.

"Don't look, old girl," says Otto, and she pats Dora's arm.

"Should we go and help?" says Beatrice, getting to her feet. Marianne joins her but there is nothing to be done.

They watch as two young men—students—come to the aid of the nurses and restrain the man, who flails, hitting one of them in the face, bloodying his nose. The students shout to their friends, who run over, and the patient eventually flops back into his wheelchair exhausted. He is manhandled into his jacket and a blanket covers his lower body. Order is restored and the day, sanitized, recovers its equilibrium. The invalids depart, pushed by the nurses. Punts, oblivious, continue to potter along the river. Crows continue to circle in the canopy above.

Nobody speaks for a minute.

"Well, Jourdain isn't going to like it," says Otto eventually. "*I am most disappointed, ladies. I did not give any of you permission to see a penis today.*"

"Now I've seen one, I think I prefer the marble type," says Beatrice.

Otto is highly amused and claps her hands. "You are a hoot, Sparks. Really? Never seen one?" She turns to the others. "What about you two?"

Dora blows her nose. "Of course. I've got little brothers."

"Not a first for me, either," says Marianne. "But please don't ask me a thing about it."

The three women look at each other in surprise. Marianne feels strangely elated.

"Surely I'm not the only one?" asks Beatrice.

"For once, Beatrice knows less than the rest of us. Tough luck, Sparks," says Otto.

"Poor Miss Stroud, I should go to her," says Marianne, but despite herself, she begins to laugh. It is an instinct quite beyond her control, as if her body has caught a dose of the madness she has just witnessed. The others stare at her as if she is a lunatic and then join her. And together they lose themselves in uninhibited, hysterical, choking, racking, throbbing laughter.

———◇———

BY THE TIME MISS STROUD reaches the picnic blanket, they are sated. Remorseful at not going to meet her, they make a fuss, blundering and apologetic. Dora watches as the chaperone struggles to lower herself onto the ground in her corset and old-fashioned skirts and is ashamed that they have not thought to bring something for her to sit on. The front of Miss Stroud's dress is dotted with dark, wet spots of urine. There is a faint odor of ammonia about her.

"Miss Stroud, can I help you to some water?" says Dora.

Miss Stroud's hands are shaking. A silver hatpin tipped with a periwinkle bead bounces off the chaperone's shoulder and spins onto the blanket. It looks like an exotic ant.

"I'm sorry if we—" says Beatrice.

"I was young once. I thought my view of the world was the only one that counted. That I was special," sniffs Miss Stroud.

Dora glances at Otto, who rolls her eyes.

"You may look pitifully at me, but I look pitifully at you. A generation that is guilt-ridden and damaged." Miss Stroud takes a handkerchief from her satchel and blows her nose. "It is sad, sad indeed."

"I'm so sorry about your dress," says Dora.

"We were not laughing at you, Miss Stroud, I can assure you," adds Beatrice hurriedly.

"Can I get you something to eat?" asks Marianne.

Beads of perspiration have gathered between Miss Stroud's scanty eyebrows. "I don't want anything," she says.

"Perhaps we should leave," suggests Marianne, turning to Dora, who shrugs.

Otto kicks at the blanket. "Surely not?" she says. "We've only been here an hour."

"Indeed, we should. Help me up." Miss Stroud holds out her arms stiffly like a shopwindow mannequin.

Between them, Dora and Marianne haul her back up. She dabs her eyes and forehead with the handkerchief, fumbles for her bag, and resumes her shuffling walk across the Parks.

"She's upset. We'd better follow her," says Dora, packing away the food. What Miss Stroud has said is true, is it not? They are all blighted. But she can't afford to think that way, or she would go mad. Besides, there is always somebody who has had it worse; what right has she to self-pity? She should be grateful she is not the man in the wheelchair. Still, it would be nice to look at the sky, a painting, or a flower one day and admire it just for itself, to feel no dread, no shame. But in this brave new world, she has come to learn, guilt is as prevalent, invasive, and necessary as the air.

"She's a jealous old witch," says Otto, seizing the blanket at one corner. The silver hatpin spins off toward the water's edge.

"The pin—" says Dora.

"Just leave it," snaps Otto, her jaw set so tight, the muscles in her cheeks quiver. She picks up one of the bicycles, stuffs the rug in the basket, and stalks off. Dora quickly rakes through the long grass looking for the pin, but she cannot find it. Why Otto is quite so upset over the premature end to their outing, she cannot say, but she grabs her belongings and hurries after her.

AFTER SUPPER, THEY RECONVENE AS usual in Otto's room.

"I think we all deserve a drink," says Otto, presenting them with champagne in delicate glass saucers. Although it is against the rules, no one refuses. They have one glass, and then another. They seem to be drinking rather a lot without saying very much and there is a delicious heaviness in Dora's tongue and jaw.

It is Marianne who breaks the silence. "I can't stop thinking about that poor man." She pulls a face as she sips but keeps sipping just the same.

"He looked perfectly normal from the outside," says Beatrice. She is sitting on the floor, leafing through a copy of *Pan* magazine. "Brains are such funny, vulnerable things. My father read a study on a man who has developed an aversion to newspapers since the war. He cannot touch or smell one without shaking in fear."

"I'm sure the same can be said for telegrams," says Dora, and although she is confronted with the image of her mother in the hall at Fairview clutching a telegram to her chest, for once she feels nothing. It is such a relief to be away from home after two years, to spend time with women who really listen, who view the world through an entirely different lens than her mother. "Life is terribly short and the body so fragile. It's a wonder we are here at all," she says, tracing the Greek meander on the glass with her index finger. The tip of it is buzzing.

Otto turns toward her, eyes narrow. "What's going on in that absurdly good-looking head of yours, Greenwood?"

"Do you worry about not getting married?" asks Dora. "That's why my mother agreed to me coming here, because the men outnumber the women. She said it was my last chance." It has been weighing on her, this unspoken question between them, and the champagne seems to have shaken it loose.

"I don't," says Marianne, "not anymore."

"I'd rather not marry than marry an idiot," says Otto, tucked in an armchair, head tipped back, eyes shut.

"If I don't marry, I'll have to live with my parents, and when they die, the twins won't want me," says Dora.

Otto strokes her chin. "You'll have whiskers by then."

"I can't live with my mother, I just can't," says Dora.

"Statistically speaking, two of us will be old maids. But I can't see it being you, Dora," says Beatrice earnestly. "You're too—fragrant."

The others burst into laughter.

"Fragrant or not, I'll have to go to the colonies like the papers say," says Dora.

"Canada," adds Marianne, with a little hiccup.

"You don't have to live with your parents, you can do anything you want. You can work, rent a room, pay your own bills," says Beatrice. She stretches out on the floor and pulls a fringed velvet cushion under her head. "In London, a lot of women—"

"I don't want to be a latchkey lady," interrupts Dora. "I want to be a mother and a wife and have a nice big house."

"A teacher," says Marianne. "That's my plan. We won't always have the rectory."

"Dora, you can live with me," says Otto. "In a spinsters' cottage in the woods, scaring children with our dowdy looks."

"Yes, Otto, you are so very dowdy, I pity you," says Dora.

Otto blows her a kiss.

"It's women like Maud we ought to worry about," says Beatrice.

"Maud can come to the cottage too." Otto makes a snorting noise.

Dora gets to her feet and reaches for the bottle on the mantelpiece. "You know, I wouldn't be here if my brother were alive. Papa would never have considered it, but losing George knocked the stuffing out of him," she says, clumsily pouring champagne into her glass. "What makes me mad are the rules about only brothers being allowed in rooms, or only brothers taking a girl boating. There are no bloody brothers left, and even if mine had wanted to visit my room or take me boating, I wouldn't be here to do it."

"All right, sit down, Greenwood, before you fall over," says Otto, pulling her onto the rug.

"We have to make the most of it. That's all we can do," says Marianne.

Otto reaches into a Selfridges box lined with black tissue paper and shakes out a beaded green dress, sleeveless with a deep V-neck and dropped waist. "What do you think of this?"

Dora reaches out to stroke the layers of emerald silk and chiffon. "A dress for a flapper," she says, pressing her face into the fabric. It smells of sandalwood, vanilla, and money.

"Take it, try it on, bring it back tomorrow," says Otto, tossing it at her.

Dora knows her mother would be horrified at her putting on another girl's clothes, but she is tired of following dull, provincial rules. Increasingly, she finds herself thinking, what would Otto say, what would Otto do? Otto is the measure of what the new Dora is capable of. Otto is not making the past her present.

"I'll do it now." Dora empties her glass with a grimace, walks next door into her own room, pulls off her skirt and blouse in a heap, and slips the dress over her head. It slithers down until it hits the hips. She tries to pull it back over her head, but the layers become confused, and the beads scratch her chin and nose. Pinned in the darkness, she cannot locate the buttons. One seems to be tugging on her hair? She staggers about and falls with a cry onto the bed. She lies there, breathing through cloth, until the room stops swaying.

She is a bright green butterfly in a cocoon, metamorphosing. But where are the bloody buttons?

"Come on, Greenwood, let's see it," says Otto from a long way away.

"You've been an age," echoes Beatrice.

"Stuck, stuck, stuck," Dora sings to herself. A few moments later, her reverie is broken by hands gently prodding the surface of her cocoon.

"Keep still," says Marianne. "This is going to take a while."

9

Friday, November 5, 1920 (4th Week)

GUY FAWKES DAY
SCENES IN OXFORD

For the first time since 1914, an attempt was made on November 5 to revive the traditional meeting of town and gown. Soon after seven o'clock, crowds began to assemble at Carfax, in Cornmarket Street, and in St. Giles'. Scenes of a tumultuous description were witnessed in the High Street where a bonfire was made and "Guy" was burned.

Fireworks were thrown from the houses on both sides of the High Street and traffic was, for a time, almost at a standstill. An armchair was taken from a college room and burned in the presence of a large crowd. Undergraduates filled the restaurants. A young lady in a pink scarf at the balcony of a Cornmarket hotel attracted a good deal of attention and was invited to make a speech on degrees for women.

The German gun that was presented to the city and placed in the Botanic Garden was removed and taken in triumph up the High Street. The police then appealed to the undergraduates "to be sportsmen" and to give up the gun. They complied, and assisted the police to drag

it down the High Street where it was taken into Magdalen College quad. There it remains.

OXFORD CHRONICLE
MONDAY, NOVEMBER 8, 1920

O n Friday of fourth week, Otto wakes with a whistling in
her ear. The pain begins soon after, lashing out from a
back tooth into her gum, jaw, and neck. She remembers feeling
something crack the day before, on a piece of nougat Beatrice
offered her at the pictures. Monthly cramps are nothing compared to this agony; she will never complain about her menses
again. She gathers yesterday's clothes from the floor and steps
into them. On her desk is an unsealed envelope bearing her
name. She shakes out the contents. It is a note from Miss Jourdain requesting that Otto's friends and relations refrain from
telephoning college so often. Otto cannot even be bothered to
screw it up.

A local dentist is the only answer, but the thought terrifies
her; she might end up looking like the head porter, Miss Jenkins, who has more mysterious gaps in her mouth than Stone-
henge. She wishes one of her sisters—Gertie, preferably—would
take charge and drag her off to some expensive chap in Harley
Street. She even has a pang of longing for Mama, although it's
been over a year since she last saw her at her eldest sister's
wedding. Mama is in New York helping Caro set up home on
Fifth Avenue. According to Gertie, this involves spending an
obscene amount of Warren's dollars at R.H. Macy and having
their photographs taken at charitable luncheons. Apparently,
Caro, with her sandy curls and flamboyant wardrobe, is the
toast of Manhattan. The same Caro who simpered and smiled
at family meals while kicking flinty bruises into Otto's shins

under the table. The Caro who held Otto's dolls over the fire until their faces dripped into the grate. The Caro who rarely acknowledges Otto and, when she does, calls her "Ratty." America is welcome to Caro.

Marianne takes one look at Otto and sends Maud for aspirin and a hot-water bottle.

"I just need to rest," says Otto, but neither of them is convinced.

"What you need is a dentist," replies Marianne, and when she puts her arm around Otto and leads her back to her room, Otto fears she will cry. She has not shed a single tear since she left voluntary service and it ought to take more than this to set her off, but there is something so gentle about Marianne's ministering, she is quite helpless.

Maud brings the news that Miss Stroud is to accompany them to the dentist. Otto has not seen her since the incident in the Parks, nor forgiven her for shortening the picnic, although if she is honest with herself, the anger she felt that day was probably a manifestation of something else. All things medical affect her differently since she hung up her VAD uniform. It is hard to explain, even to herself.

Wearing an odd brown hat reminiscent of a dead pheasant, Miss Stroud waddles along Banbury Road so slowly that Marianne suggests they catch an omnibus. When it arrives, they are motioned up the stairs by the conductor, which is a trial for Miss Stroud as the bus pulls off immediately, juddering through the gears. It is clear why the lower level is full; drips from overhanging trees splatter onto their heads and Marianne has to brush wet leaves off the bench. The conductor shrugs, tosses their coins into his waist pouch, and punches a hole in their tickets. Otto loathes omnibuses. All the decent ones went to France and came back as wrecks—just like the men. And who wants to travel down Banbury Road in an old ambulance or pigeon loft crammed together with strangers, the taint of war passing between them like influenza? The fierce ache in her jaw combined with the engine fumes makes her nauseous, and she pinches her thigh hard in an attempt to distract herself.

The journey to Summertown is less than a mile, but her legs quiver as she descends the stairs and stumbles onto the pavement. Marianne takes her arm. Miss Stroud puffs and sighs, tediously slow to dismount. Otto resists the urge to push her finger deep into the doughy flesh of the old woman's cheeks.

Finally, they reach the surgery. Marianne raps the knocker on the narrow three-story town house, and they are ushered in by a nurse in an obscenely white apron. The sight of her and the smell of the Lysol is enough. Otto's instinct is to turn and claw at the door, but before she knows it, she is standing in a dingy consulting room with a green linoleum floor. The nurse takes her coat from her shoulders. She is not entirely sure where she is, the place does not seem real, it is as if the paper on the walls is lifting off and rotating around her. Marianne speaks to her softly, but she cannot make out the words. Then she is lying back, gripping the arms of a chair, finding nicks in the leather that seem to be made for her fingers. The bad thoughts come—the ones that visit her sometimes at night. Flashes of blue uniform, rusty dressings in kidney bowls, warm bedpans. Water spilling onto a pillow. Lips on the rim of a tin cup.

"No, no," she says, struggling to get out of the chair.

"Don't be a silly girl," says the nurse, pushing her down.

"Open up," says the dentist. He puts his fingers between her teeth and prizes her jaws apart. It is such a liberty that she is astonished. He rummages about as if looking for a fork in a drawer. She smells carbolic soap as the hairs on his hands brush her lips.

"Hmm, this one? Cracked right in two. I'll need to pull it. Nitrous oxide, please."

There is bustling behind her, and she hears the dentist whistling, jovial. Her throat is dry, her scalp prickly and tight. She wants to jump up, to flee, yet she cannot move.

"Hold on to me," says Marianne, forcing her warm palm into Otto's clenched fist.

A rubber mask descends over her face, and she welcomes it. She breathes in deeply. Her mouth is metallic and dry, her fingertips tingle as if they are swelling. As the mask is removed, there is probing inside her, knuckles graze her teeth, and her head and shoulders are pulled off the back of the chair as more hands push her down. She might be choking but she doesn't seem to care as much as she should. There is a twang of fibers, a twisting pop. And then the hot flood of pain. In the corner of the room, Miss Stroud's pheasant is sitting up and flapping its wings. Marianne, with her long, white neck, is a swan.

———◇———

ON SUNDAY EVENING, WHEN MARIANNE returns exhausted from her second weekend at home, she finds a note from Beatrice on her desk. It is accompanied by a currant bun in a paper bag and a can of condensed milk.

We missed you! Rations left in case you are hungry. If you get back before nine, come to Otto's room for whist. She is feeling much better and says to tell you that she has some new magazines including Picture Show and Punch. If those do not whet your appetite, or you cannot wrestle them from Dora, I have finished The Age of Innocence (marvelous) and it is all yours.
B. S. x

Marianne is touched by Beatrice's kindness, and although she can hear her friends talking and laughing across the corridor, she does not join them. Not only has she too much to catch up on in terms of work and sleep, but she needs an hour or two of quiet contemplation to manage the transition between her two very different lives.

The next morning, she meets them for breakfast expecting to fend off questions about why she is so tired and why she failed to read a single page all weekend. However, they are in high spirits, even Otto, who is normally irritable first thing. Miss Bazeley has moved into a more accessible study near the dining hall, leaving her room empty, and they cannot wait to regale Marianne about how the lavatory got blocked on Saturday.

"I blame Sparks," says Otto. "She put the system under too much pressure."

Beatrice snorts with laughter. "I told you; I was working on a debate with Norah in the JCR."

"We had to go to Corridor Seven to use the facilities," whispers Dora. "Awful."

"Ivy Nightingale goes in and out of her room all day *in a red gingham apron*," says Otto.

Dora leans forward. "Apparently, she organizes daily tea parties and makes her guests anchovies on toast in the student kitchen. You'd never think she's studying Lit. Hum., the hardest degree in the world."

"And Josephine Bostwick's room is an absolute tip," says Otto. "Worse than Sparks's is. Door wide open, sports paraphernalia everywhere, and a *very* peculiar smell emanating from inside."

"Definitely moldy kit," adds Dora, taking a gulp of tea.

Beatrice grimaces. "I'd say you had a lucky escape, Marianne. How was your weekend?"

"Yes, we want to hear every single detail of your father's sermon," says Otto, with a grin.

"Oh, do shut up, Wallace-Kerr," mimics Marianne, and the others howl in delight.

THE RADCLIFFE CAMERA HAS BECOME Marianne's favorite reading room in the Bodleian, with its circular galleries and elegant domed plaster ceiling. The college library has a limited supply of books, which are always in demand, and so the Eights have begun studying at the Radder on Monday afternoons. Marianne's life is full, her days busy. She has joined the Bach Choir and attends weekly rehearsals of Parry and Vaughan Williams surrounded by young men whose lifted chins and earnest performances move her to tears. Together with Dora, she sells advertisement space in the *Imp*, the termly magazine of St. Hugh's, and when she can, she types up leaflets for the Debating Society as a favor to Beatrice. However, on these precious afternoons in the Bodleian, Marianne relishes the communal silence. The atmosphere has an intensity that reminds her of prayer. Some of the men cast curious glances, but most barge past the women on the staircase or slide into the seat beside them as if they were of no interest at all, and this, in itself, is immensely gratifying.

At six p.m., in good time to dress for dinner, they exit the library and return to their bicycles, which are propped against the low metal railings that span the Radder. Tinny bells call the hour to one another across the square.

"Lord, I look a fright," says Otto into her compact, her jaw still swollen from Friday's trip to the dentist. It was a swift and bloody extraction and Otto, usually so self-assured, was terrified. Marianne had to put her to bed on their return, where Otto remained for the rest of the day. Otto's reaction to the procedure was so extreme that Marianne wonders if there is more to it, but she resolves not to ask. Until Marianne is prepared to offer up her own secrets, surely she has no right to anyone else's.

"I hold you and your nougat responsible, Sparks," says Otto over her shoulder.

"That reminds me, I'm starving," says Beatrice, doing up the buttons of her overcoat.

Just as Marianne is digging in a hairpin to secure her cap, a young man in a gown bursts from the door of Brasenose College, twenty feet or so away from them.

"Help," he shouts. "Please help!"

He turns, using his hands to propel himself back through the doorway. Shouts of distress echo inside. The women, led by Dora, drop their bicycles and run around the railings, caps flying. They dash past the ancient studded door into Brasenose lodge. Panting and disheveled, they look around, expectant. Ahead of them, the quadrangle is empty, the lawn neatly mown. All is still. A shuffling don carrying a teacup appears from a stairwell. He smiles affably and continues on his way.

"What can I do for you ladies?" says a bowler-hatted porter, lowering a crate of wine to the floor. A second porter steps out of an archway by the pigeonholes, his mouth barely distinguishable among the deep folds of his face. He looks at them wearily and goes back inside without saying a word.

"Someone shouted for help," says Beatrice, gesturing toward the quad. The others nod and look about. On the back wall, a vine ripples like bunting and russet leaves float to the ground. On the left wall, an incongruous blue sundial dwarfs the windows and even the doorways. A guffaw of laughter is heard from around a corner—or perhaps from a window, Marianne cannot tell. Dora hears it too and motions to the others to enter the quadrangle.

"Sorry, miss, can't let you go inside without an invitation. We have rules—no unaccompanied females." The porter presses his bowler hat further down onto his skull and extends his arms to shepherd them back outside. There is movement and whispering behind him, but the porter remains willfully ignorant. "Off you go, ladies."

The four women exit the lodge into the diminishing daylight.

"Yet again the butt of a joke," says Beatrice.

As Dora scoops their caps from the cobbles, Marianne recalls the humiliation of matriculation day, when Dora held her cap as she knelt in the gutter, an anecdote in the making.

"And to think Edward VII was a Brasenose man," says Otto, rubbing her jaw.

Dora has told them stories about the ragging her brother got up to when he was at Jesus. This is what students do, Marianne assumes. Young men must let off steam. But when she returns to her bicycle and looks down into her basket, she finds her bag is gone. It contains her purse, her comb, her fountain pen, her essay notes from this afternoon. The dread she has subdued these last few weeks slips its reins and careers off.

"Toerags," says Otto. "My best cigarette case as well. The one with the doggy."

"They can't have got far," says Dora, looking around.

The cobbled square is dim, with only a small wedge of sunlight backed into a corner.

"They could be anywhere," Beatrice says.

"They'll be in college. There's another entrance on the High," says Otto.

While the others debate, Marianne clings to the railings. Her purse, her pen, her bag even. The loss will mean nothing to her companions, they are roommates with abundance, but she cannot replace these items without forgoing something more precious—her next train ticket home.

As they set off toward the High, a student in boat-club flannels jogs around the corner toward them. He is the sort of man that terrifies Marianne: newly cut hair, artfully draped scarf, waxed mustache. He smiles as he stops a few feet in front of them. Beatrice gives a loud sigh, Dora's soft mouth hangs slightly open, and Otto looks positively hungry.

"Sorry to bother you ladies, but have you by any chance lost your bags?"

Marianne's first impression is that the man is young, younger than her at least. He is undeniably handsome and, she would hazard a guess, very wealthy. He explains that the Brasenose bag theft is an old trick. The perpetrators climb in and out of a window while their hapless victims run into the lodge. It's a college tradition, required to join a prestigious dining society.

"Please let me apologize on behalf of Brasenose," he says,

with a bow. "Arthur Motson-Brown. At your service." They introduce themselves, one by one, shaking hands.

"How do we know this isn't part of the trick, Mr. Motson-Brown?" says Otto, who has recovered some postdental joie de vivre. Marianne cannot help but admire her. She has what Marianne's father would call *bottle*.

"Gosh, that would be elaborate but I'm afraid I'm just not that clever," he says, laughing. "Wait here and I'll see what I can find." He jogs into the lodge, his polished shoes tapping over the flagstones.

They stand around awkwardly a short distance from the doorway. The balls of Marianne's feet begin to thrum against the cobbles, and she remembers that they will have to ride back in the dark after all this.

As the gas lamps begin to fill yellow puddles on the pavement, the remnants from Friday's Guy Fawkes chaos are still visible. There is a singed patch on the lawn outside the entrance to the Radder where an armchair was set alight by a student mob.

"It's true, then," says Dora, pointing at it.

The *Oxford Chronicle* that morning had reported how a group of revelers, determined to restore a prewar tradition, had run amok down the High on Friday night and that women undergraduates were seen taking part. It was all anyone could talk about at breakfast. Marianne would certainly have suspected Otto if she had not seen her tucked up in bed that evening.

After what seems an age, Motson-Brown returns with their satchels piled in his arms like Christmas gifts. He hands over the bags, explaining he found the culprits in the JCR. Idiotic first-years on a mission to prove themselves. Marianne looks for her purse and bites back tears. Nothing is missing.

"No harm done," says Otto, tossing her bag into her bicycle basket.

"Thank you so much for rescuing us," says Dora. Beatrice and Marianne murmur their agreement.

Motson-Brown smiles. "I would ask you in for tea, but alas, rules are rules."

The square is in darkness by now but has grown busy with men in gowns returning to All Souls, Hertford, Exeter, Lincoln, Wadham, and the other nearby colleges.

"We should be off," says Beatrice, but Motson-Brown does not seem to hear her. He turns, instead, to Otto.

"How do you find Oxford? I hope it has been welcoming to you."

"Oh, it's been an education all right," replies Otto, looking up at him.

"You're rather familiar to me," he says. "Have we met before?"

"You'll have met one of my sisters. There are four of us." She offers a limp hand. "I'm Otto Wallace-Kerr."

"You are Vita's sister!" he exclaims. "Oh, she's such marvelous fun." He turns to the others. "The Wallace-Kerr sisters break hearts all over London."

He and Otto discuss London clubs and the people they know in common, exchanging names and locations in a seasoned game of one-upmanship.

"We really should be off now," repeats Beatrice firmly.

Suddenly, a bicycle rattles over the cobbles toward them, bell ringing, brakes whingeing. The rider jumps off while he is still moving and flings the bicycle against the wall.

"Returning bags again, are we, Motters?" the man says. There is a pause as the women look at each other. "Don't listen to any of his flannel, ladies, he's in on the whole plot." He punches Motson-Brown hard on the arm and strolls into Brasenose.

They stare at Motson-Brown, who gives a diffident shrug and puts his hands up. He smiles what he must consider to be his most charming smile. Marianne wonders why she did not see through him.

"What can I say? Some of us will do anything to meet the most beautiful ladies in the university," he says, unabashed.

"Oh my God, I knew it," says Otto, and she throws her head back in laughter. Marianne imagines she can see the bloody chasm in her mouth.

"I don't think it is funny in the slightest," says Beatrice. She goes over to her bicycle, lobs her bag in the basket, and rides off without another word. Her basket jiggles up and down as she bounces over the cobbles.

"Oh dear." Otto mimics a grumpy face. "Beatrice hates to miss dinner."

"Don't be angry," says Motson-Brown. "Let's have tea sometime. We're dying for some female company."

"You're a bad boy and a bad advertisement for Brasenose," says Otto, taking a cigarette out of her case. She offers him one.

"At least admit you were a little amused," he says, lighting their cigarettes. "Do come."

Motson-Brown hands Otto his card, and as she puts it in her coat pocket, his eyes flick briefly over to meet Marianne's. He nods politely at her and then offers his card to Dora.

10

Saturday, November 13, 1920 (5th Week)

NOTICE

Bells for the Michaelmas term will ring as follows:

BREAKFAST: 7 a.m. & 7:30 a.m.
  (Sunday 8 a.m. & 8:30 a.m.)

MORNING CHAPEL: 7:55 a.m.
  (Sunday 8:55 a.m.)

LUNCH: 1:15 p.m.

TEA: 3:45 p.m.

DRESSING BELL: 7:15 p.m.

DINNER: 7:25 p.m.

EVENING CHAPEL: 8:15 p.m.

WARNING BELL: 10 p.m.
  (Visitors must leave the building by last bell.)

LAST BELL: 10:10 p.m.
  *(Students must be in their rooms by 10:15 p.m. unless late
  leave of 11 p.m. has been given.)*

Attendance at morning chapel and dinner is compulsory.

MISS E. F. JOURDAIN

Principal

The Armistice commemorations dominate fifth week. The Scala Picture House on Walton Street is showing the Pathé newsreel of *The Unknown Warrior* on the hour and half hour. After six or seven viewings, Beatrice can shut her eyes and replay the images: the outline of the coffin beneath the Union flag; wreaths so enormous it takes two soldiers to carry them; women climbing the mound of flowers engulfing the Cenotaph; thousands of men outside Westminster Abbey replacing their hats in a single unified gesture.

Beatrice's mother has written saying the commemorations are nothing but a smoke screen to allay public discontent. Although Beatrice agrees with Edith Sparks that a state burial and a memorial by Lutyens will hardly atone for the fact that seven hundred and fifty thousand men are dead, one in ten still not accounted for, she is surprised to find that she does not agree with her mother entirely. The first time Beatrice watched the newsreel she cried as she recalled walking with her mother behind Emily Davison's coffin, throat tight, spectators throwing flowers under the muffled hooves of the horses. The second time she watched it, she cried for her first Classics tutor Mr. Lloyd-Brown, a gentle fellow who liked plum cake and chess and was killed working as a stretcher-bearer. It is clear the spectacle brings comfort to many people, and Beatrice cannot help but be moved by it.

On Saturday, the Eights leave the Scala in companionable silence and walk along Walton Street in the direction of Worcester College. The air has a fresh snap about it and russet leaves cling to their boots like stowaways. At Beatrice's request, they turn up Little Clarendon Street; she needs to collect some pamphlets from Somerville for the War and Peace Society. It is a narrow, bustling road lined with every shop one could think of and provides a welcome distraction from the newsreel. Outside the Duke of Cambridge public house, they are greeted by some of Otto's friends from Oriel College. Beatrice has never met them before, but like many Oxford men, they behave as if the whole street must be enthralled by every word they utter. However, today it is Otto who holds court. She is sporting her latest purchase from Webber's on the High: a blue velvet coat with glossy sable collar.

Otto makes introductions and the men's eyes slide over the women until, as usual, they settle on Dora, who smiles politely. One tips his boater to her. To Beatrice he looks like a pinstripe booby, but Dora, she has observed, always rises to male attention, however witless it might be. Another of the men has dense black eyebrows and a chin like Mr. Punch. He winks at his friend and looks Beatrice up and down with exaggerated effort. The friend smirks back. She will *take no notice*.

Across the road, a shoeshiner with one leg has set up a temporary stand next to a grocery shop. His ramshackle structure blocks the pavement, and the grocer, rotund in gray overalls, is remonstrating with him from the doorway. Inside the shop, a young woman waiting to pay picks through the coins in her purse. She has the look of someone who is tired of trying. Beatrice watches as the woman glances about, seizes a tin from the pile of goods on the counter, and stuffs it into her pocket. Then, in a more leisurely fashion, she takes a second item and inspects the label before returning it to the shelf. A child tugs at the woman's arm. The little girl's hair is matted at the back and she wears a man's jacket with the sleeves rolled up. Both of them are terribly thin. Beatrice, discomforted, looks about her to see if anyone else has noticed, but Otto is telling an anecdote about her sister Vita and the others are laughing. The shoeshiner is buffing the boots of a student, his face so close to the leather he could lick it. The woman pays for her goods and moves off up the street, her daughter trailing behind her.

Otto says Beatrice rattles on about politics too much, but it is hardly surprising there has been rioting and discontent in towns like Luton. People are going hungry. According to her mother, there was trouble at the unveiling of the Cenotaph that went entirely unreported by the newsreel, the protesters claiming that the government's time and money should be spent on the living, not the dead. If only Beatrice could make her peers understand that the war has not ended for the widowed, unemployed, and disabled. It frustrates her that most students are more concerned with enjoying themselves than addressing society's ills. But, as Otto says, it is not unreasonable that after years of being used as cannon fodder, young people want to live for the moment.

A dragging sense of failure accompanies Beatrice as she collects the pamphlets from Somerville and the women make their way slowly back to college. As they dawdle up Woodstock Road, she falls in step behind the other three while Otto speculates about the men she just met.

"Vita has probably slept with them all—she isn't fussy," she says. "My friend Teddy was meant to return to Oriel this term, but he simply can't face it. Badly injured"—she gestures below the waist—"down there."

"My brother was supposed to return to Jesus," says Dora, matter-of-fact.

"Your older brother?" asks Otto.

"Yes," says Dora. "George. He joined the Oxfordshires in 1915 at the end of his first year. He died of his wounds at Cambrai, two weeks after my fiancé."

There is a moment of stunned silence. Dora has alluded to her losses before but has never been so explicit. Two weeks! Beatrice cranes her head forward to steal a glance at her, but Dora is unreadable. Beatrice wonders how she should respond but cannot think of a thing to say.

"I'm so sorry," says Marianne, taking Dora's arm. "What was your brother like?"

"George was a lot of fun, very noisy, a bit of a rogue sometimes. We often played tennis together. Nothing ever seemed to bother him." She pauses as they cross the road. "My parents will never get over it."

"And so soon after your fiancé?" asks Otto. "How bloody awful."

"Yes, well, Charles ought to be here too, studying Law at Queen's. He was in the Devil's Own. He also fell at Cambrai. I met him when he was an officer cadet. His dog mauled our rabbit." She smiles at their horrified faces. "He was always smartly turned out and had a beautiful singing voice. Charmed the socks off everyone."

"He sounds wonderful," says Marianne.

"Oh yes, he does," adds Beatrice.

They walk on in silence, turning up St. Margaret's Road.

"Charles was all for women attending university," says Dora when they reach the gates. "He was very modern about all sorts of things. You would have had some good talks with him, Beatrice."

"I'm sure I would," Beatrice replies, surprised and gratified to be included in Dora's narrative.

"My father liked him, and he doesn't like many people," says Dora, and then halts. "Oh hell, I completely forgot," she says, her face pale and immobile. "Hockey practice before supper. I'd better run."

"Well," says Otto as Dora hurries off. "It was about time."

◇

DORA LIKES TO IMAGINE THAT it is Charles in the Tomb of the Unknown Warrior, encased in the oak casket made from timber felled at Hampton Court. She has cut a photograph by Horace Nicholls from the front of the *Times*. It shows the lone coffin on an empty stone floor at Westminster Abbey, chairs stacked to one side, morning light falling from high windows. All is quiet, reverential. Inside, Charles (never George: he is buried in Flesquières Hill Cemetery with a headstone) is pink-cheeked with neatly combed hair; clean, ironed khakis; polished boots. He has been lifted intact from the broken fields of Bourlon Ridge, like a prize root vegetable pulled from the earth, slightly dusty but perfectly formed. The sword that King George has picked out from the Royal Collection rests on top of the casket. She takes solace that Charles has been chosen to lie not with her but with kings. She would never say this to the others, though. Otto would snort and quote statistics, Beatrice would launch into a speech about repatriation, Marianne would burn with empathy. Dora has read in the newspaper that some mourners wore poppies at the Cenotaph inspired by a poem by John McCrae. She has written out "In Flanders Fields" and tucked it with the newspaper cutting inside her copy of *Lyrical Ballads*. This is Dora keeping faith, holding high the torch.

————◇————

IN THE EARLY HOURS OF the following morning, Marianne wakes, disorientated. It takes a moment for her to realize that some-one is knocking at her window. She struggles to light a candle, fingers alien and clumsy.

"Darling, I'm in a fix." Otto wipes her mouth with the back of her hand. "Forgot to leave my window open."

Marianne's heart is beating in strange whooshes in her throat. She wonders if she is the one who should sit down. She forces up the window and drags Otto in by the armpits.

"Otto, you can just push up your own window. You never lock it. Are you very drunk?" asks Marianne.

"I think I am." Otto flops onto an armchair. "Do you think I'm going to hell?"

One of her penciled eyebrows is smudged across the bridge

of her nose. There is an earring hooked to the felt collar of her coat.

"I don't think hell would want you. Take off your shoes, they're filthy."

Otto leans forward and pulls randomly at her laces until Marianne gives up watching, kneels in front of her, and tugs off the heeled boots. The leather is inexplicably soft, like the sole of a baby's foot. "Did you climb over the fence?" she asks.

"Maybe I did," says Otto.

"You've got to stop. You'll get sent down." Marianne rises and deposits the mud-caked boots outside the door. She sighs. "Do these people know what you're risking? And are they worth it?"

Otto's stockinged feet hang over the arm of the chair, the shape of each toe outlined in dirt. Marianne sits opposite and listens to Otto breathing. Outside, the silence is so dense that it feels as if they are the only people alive. After a while, Marianne's head begins to nod, and she yearns for the cocooning warmth of her bed.

"Do you miss your mother?" says Otto.

Marianne looks up at her. "You can't miss someone you've never met."

"Cut a leg off, it still hurts. I've seen it."

Marianne rises wearily and goes to the desk, returning with a misty glass of water, which she hands to Otto.

Otto takes a gulp. "I have a mother. She's in America. She won't talk to me unless I leave here and marry Teddy. What do you make of that?" Otto starts to laugh and cry at the same time, wiping her nose on her expensive sleeve.

Marianne hovers over her. "Drink it. All of it."

"It tastes of pipe," says Otto, screwing up her face, but she obeys. Then she jerks her thumb toward the silver locket that has swung out of Marianne's nightgown. "Is that your mother's?"

Marianne tucks the locket back in. "You can sleep in the chair if you like, but you have a perfectly good bed yourself."

"It's so cold in here."

"I don't buy extra coal. You know that." Marianne places a blanket over Otto's legs, tucking it in as best she can.

"You are a very good person, you know," says Otto. "I'm not good like you."

"Just give me the glass and go to sleep." She pushes a cushion under Otto's head and turns with the candle toward the bed, washing the wooden paneling with amber light.

"I think—"

"Otto, I'm exhausted. I have an essay to write tomorrow."

"I think you do. Miss her."

Somewhere a bell chimes half past the hour. Marianne thinks about marching up to Otto and shouting in her face. *I feel sick every day. I'm jealous when I see mothers with daughters. I feel like I'm half-finished, that I'm always waiting for something to happen, that I'm all alone. So yes, you could say I miss her.*

But Marianne has no intention of exposing the muddy undersoles of her life to anyone outside Culham.

"Good night, Otto," she says, and climbs back into bed.

———◇———

THERE IS NOTHING MORE FUN than solving the problem of how to get in and out of St. Hugh's undetected. Despite her vague plan of living a more "meaningful" life at Oxford, Otto has begun to sneak out after dinner to meet up with some of Vita's pals, climbing the fence and scrabbling through her window in the early hours of the morning. Vita, a volatile combination of energy and caprice, has just ended her third engagement. According to the *Daily Mail*, Vita is a Bright Young Thing, gadding about London doing treasure hunts and attending outrageous parties in secret locations. Some of her gang have come up to Magdalen and Oriel, where they have invented a cheap form of party called "Bring a Bottle." Though it only offers temporary respite, Otto finds heavy drinking an effective means of taming the images that circle and snap in the dark corners of sleep. She has not let her work slip—she finds it satisfyingly hard—but when she next meets her tutor, she is confronted with a warning from Miss Jourdain.

"The principal wonders if your mind is on your work," says Miss Brockett, holding a paper at arm's length and squinting at it. She is around forty, with bushy auburn hair and a nose like a blade. Her hands are scarred around the knuckles; her blouse, presumably once white, has been dyed an uneven gray.

"I've told her you are a gifted mathematician, brilliant at times. But you seem restless. Have you thought about taking up a sport? College has a strong tradition of hockey and tennis."

Otto has a fleeting image of herself in a hockey team photograph next to Patricia Clough, cigarette dangling from her lips. She composes herself and nods.

"I've been asked to point out that alcohol is forbidden at St. Hugh's. As is going out without permission and climbing the garden fence." Miss Brockett pauses to stack a pile of logarithm books on the shelf. She takes a deep breath. "Don't make the mistake of thinking Miss Jourdain won't send you down because college needs your fees. She insists I reinforce that St. Hugh's is not a finishing school. Standards must be met."

Tough luck on Miss Brockett having to deliver a lecture, thinks Otto. She knows there is no actual proof of her nocturnal activities, and Jourdain can do nothing based on a hunch. She gazes about the room. It reminds her of a recently built nest. She likes the way the blackboard leans back nonchalantly on the easel and the thin layer of chalk dust that ices everything. At home, attic rooms are for servants.

Miss Brockett continues. "Women come here who want to learn and teach and enter professions. Serious-minded women who see a goal in life beyond marriage and children. Look at what Miss Noether has achieved in Germany; she has proven that women can excel at mathematics. She has shown that numbers are a language that men and women can understand on an equal footing." Miss Brockett looks down at her hands and rubs at the scars as if they are unfamiliar to her. "What I'm trying to say is that adjusting to Oxford can be hard, but it's worth it. I understand you have less freedom now than you did. Which must seem ridiculous after the world has been turned upside down in the pursuit of that very thing." She glances at a piece of paper on the desk and tosses it on top of the overflowing bin. "As mathematicians we think outside the original framing to solve problems. We must be able to deal with unknowns. It is important to have purpose in times of change. Don't let the unknowns overwhelm you. Hold on to your purpose."

Despite herself, Otto's throat tightens and her eyes sting. She calculates it is four steps to the door.

"If I could think about algebra all the time, I would," she says. "But I don't seem to be able to stop—"

"Don't seem to be able to stop what, dear?" asks Miss Brockett.

Otto can't answer. She looks out the window, onto pewter roof tiles streaked with pearly excrement. She is confounded by Miss Brockett's interest in her. She has never received a speech like it, certainly not from her own mother or any of her teachers. This talk of having purpose, of wanting more, is something her parents would find laughable. In their eyes, Otto's purpose, her having failed to be a boy, is to flit about amusing herself and then to marry in a way that is advantageous to the family. Is this all there is to her? Does she have the potential to be "more"?

Miss Brockett sighs. "You know I am a friend of Miss Rogers. She is still on the board and tutoring Pass Mods here. She told me how you met. I was a volunteer myself."

Otto's head snaps up.

"Oh yes, I was a VAD too, nursed at Guy's. Last two years of the war," says Miss Brockett.

She holds her hands up to display her scars. Hot-water burns. Of course. Otto has a few herself.

"Oh. Um, bravo. I didn't know that."

"I'm not going to say it was easy. It was—well, you know what it was. I find, for me, it's not healthy to dwell, but if you would like to talk about it, Miss Wallace-Kerr, then I am happy to have tea with you any time. If tea doesn't appeal, try hockey." She laughs at Otto's expression. "Don't look so horrified, I'm not going to push it. I've said my bit, now let's have a cigarette and tackle the rather beastly problem on the board."

AFTER THE TUTORIAL, OTTO POPS her head into the JCR, where a group of third-years are passing the time until tea by reading articles to one another from the *Fritillary* and the *Oxford Review*. Otto walks over to the noticeboard and adds her name to the crumpled list of students interested in hockey practice. Quite frankly, she cannot think of anything worse, but if Miss Brockett wants proof by contradiction, then that is what she shall have.

Just below the list, a sharp-edged square of white card has recently been pinned.

NOTICE

Students are asked to pay particular attention to the college regulations, and especially the rule against going into a man's rooms (whether in a college or elsewhere) unchaperoned and without leave, as I shall be obliged to send down at once any woman undergraduate who infringes it.

MISS E. F. JOURDAIN

Principal

11

Dora, June 1915

When Dora is fifteen, her parents take rooms at the Randolph Hotel in order to visit George at Jesus College. The twins, boys of six, are left at home with Nanny, but Dora has been given leave from school to accompany her mother while her father attends to business. He is negotiating with the Oxford University Press to print recruitment posters, ration books, telegrams, headed paper, and anything else the army requires. Business is booming, and as his profit grows, his temper worsens. It is a relief that Dora and her mother will visit George on their own today. He has promised to take them punting.

Dora's movements are clumsy and slow. At first, she thinks it must be the hotel, with its thick carpets, thin walls, and air that tastes like thirty people have breathed it in before you. Her white dress, with its full skirts and matching coat, is equally oppressive. It looks outdated in Oxford, where hems are rising, hats are simple and close-fitting, silhouettes are long and narrow. On the streets, women are doing the jobs of men: conducting omnibuses, delivering parcels on bicycles, driving cars. They are dressed in plain working clothes, but their faces are animated and their voices loud and unapologetic.

From her third-floor window, Dora watches students in

gowns and mortarboards riding bicycles along St. Giles'. Some are chatting and laughing, others pedaling furiously as if they are late, one hand steering, the other clutching a stack of books. One of these frantic cyclists turns left below her, darting in front of a delivery cart, his gown billowing behind him. She moves to another window and there he is, stashing his bike carelessly against the stone wall opposite and running up the steps, disappearing between the fluted gray pillars of the Ashmolean Museum. How she would love to visit it. George has told her about Guy Fawkes's lantern, a Grecian urn painted with a six-legged octopus, and sketches by Michelangelo and Raphael. These precious objects are a mere two or three hundred feet away from Dora right now, but her mother will not let her venture to the museum, saying it is inappropriate for a girl of fifteen to go out alone and that many of the exhibits may be "unsuitable." Dora boils with indignation. The unfairness of it. The stupidity. How can two people so closely related view the same thing so differently? These are antiquities!

When her mother is finally ready, they descend the main staircase to the hotel tearoom, where the ding of cutlery and the persistent talk of war is stifling. There is a dragging in her abdomen and her breasts are tender. Her waistband digs in. Her mother says they will fit her for a corset on their return. Dora imagines having it sewn into her skin in an appalling naked ritual.

Her mother is making her usual comments about other people under her breath. These murmured observations involve categorizing other women as better or worse than her in some way, as if she needs to settle herself in the hierarchy of the room before she can proceed. Dora smiles politely and nods. She aches to say, *Mother, everyone in this room is looking at us, judging me, loathing you. We are out of place here. We are not rich, educated, beautiful enough for this salon full of wealthy Americans and parents of Etonians.* If her mother feels any of this, she does not say so, but she is snappy. The whole tea is a dull and unsatisfactory experience. There is a gap where George or Dora's father would normally take charge, confident, thick-skinned, the leader.

It is a short walk over to Jesus College, and they do not speak. On Cornmarket and Ship Streets, young men in khaki uniform stroll along the sun-bleached pavements. Notices hang on railings and in shopwindows, encouraging students to enlist. Although her father may print them, these posters with their rallying cry are not intended for George. Father says it is pointless, George volunteering; officer training lasts three months, and it can take a year to get a posting. The war will be over by then, he insists. George better serves his country by getting an education.

But George told Dora the previous evening at dinner that he is making a hash of his first year. If he fails Divvers again, he will be sent down.

"It'll mean I'm out permanently. I don't think Jesus wants me, Dora," he said, grinning. "Never had brains like you. Should be you studying here, not me, except you are probably too pretty. We do get women in lectures if the dons allow it. Frightfully clever girls. Very plain, though." He leaned closer and murmured in her ear, "Don't tell Pater but I'm joining up before I resit. It won't matter if I make a hash of Divvers when I get back. They won't send down a war hero."

Dora has always wondered how it is that George seems to live on the outside of himself: if he has an inner life, he keeps it carefully concealed. One is never in any doubt as to what ails or enthuses him; George shares everything. He can be easily influenced by others, unimaginative, lazy. Lies slip off his tongue as easily as oysters and he barely recognizes them as untruths. But despite it all, she adores him. He can be charming and funny, and he is her brother.

He greets Dora and their mother on Turl Street outside the wooden door of the lodge. As they step inside the creamy stone walls of Jesus, Dora's head pounds and her hatpins drag across her scalp, weighed down by her hair. Apart from George's speech days or cricket matches, she has never seen so many young men in one place. They hover like flies in the heat in their black gowns. Many seek her eyes out from under the brim of her hat, some bashful, some pushy. It is hard to know what to do, so she looks at her feet, blushing, hot and bothered. She is supremely conscious of her body, her chest, her waist. A body that her mother implies will serve her well. She seems proud of Dora for her developing figure, as if her daughter has shown great ingenuity in growing it.

George leads them around the tidy quadrangle and up a narrow staircase to his set, which comprises a large, airy sitting room with a smaller bedroom off it. They are introduced to his best pal, Frank Collingham, who blushes from collar to crown and bows as Dora shakes hands with him. George appears popular and relaxed. The scout addresses him deferentially as Mr. Greenwood and she senses her mother swell with pride. Neither parent has been to university, and she can see that her mother is intimidated by this privileged world. Her discomfort is hard to watch—she is usually so sure of herself and her universal truths of God and upholstery. George's sitting room is paneled with oak and looks out on both the back quad and the wooden slatted roof of the Covered Market. Dora can hear the shouts of the market traders, the clap of hooves, the drone of motors. It is fascinating to see how this academic world, so remote from everyday life, is located so centrally within it.

To her mother's irritation, Dora needs to use the lavatory. George says he can hardly send her two flights up to the shared facilities, so he calls for the scout, Walters, a wizened old man who must be approaching seventy. He leads both women around the front quad to a staircase leading down to the medical room.

"Some of the dons are married, madam, and we do have mothers visiting, of course. We even have women working in the kitchens now, so many boys gone to war. We've already lost the head porter's son. Terrible people, them Germans," says Walters, nodding to people as he talks. They do not walk on the grass but take the longer route around it on the squared pavement. Dora's mother comments on the upkeep of the flawless lawn.

"Sometimes we do have problems. Night porter found a sheep grazing a few years ago. We had suffragettes come in too, papers all over the grass. They tried to light a fire right in the middle. The bursar was raging. But then war broke out and we don't get so much of that now."

"That's something to be said for the war, then," tuts her mother. "Dreadful women."

Walters unlocks the medical room and leaves them to it. The lavatory is dark and cool, with neatly laid cream and navy tiles. Dora is glad to be alone for a few moments, even though her mother is only a few paces away adjusting her hat in the mirror. As Dora pulls down her drawers to sit, she notices they are wet with what seems to be blood, although on closer inspection it is more of a rusty-brown mucus. She is glad she is seated as her legs have begun to wobble. So this is menstruation. Somehow, she thought she would be immune to this monthly indignity. In some cultures, she would have to hide away in a dark room with a veil over her head—at least that is what her games teacher said when she gathered them all down in the gymnasium one wet afternoon a few years ago and showed them, to great tittering and consternation, how to fit a sanitary belt and how to safety-pin the cotton napkin to it. How a rubber apron will protect your clothes. How it is best not to bathe or travel or be too active at that time of the month. How to protect your sheets at night, how to remain discreet from your husband. Most of the girls had not the slightest clue this was their lot in life until she started talking, Dora included. How could she possibly not know? She looked at every adult woman differently for a while after that, wondering, is blood trickling out of her right now?

She dabs herself with the hard glazed paper and wedges some between her legs. The soft skin is sore within seconds. She is wearing a white dress and will need to change before she goes punting. Mortified, she realizes she will have to tell her mother.

"You can't possibly go punting now. You'll have to stay in this afternoon. We'll drop you on the way. I'll send a servant from the hotel to buy what you need. Oh, Dora. Really. Such bad timing."

They return to the Randolph, where they bump into her father. She sees her mother whispering to him and the appalled look on his face. She is installed in her room and told to lie down if she feels unwell. From the window above, she watches her parents and George climb into a horse-drawn cab. They are laughing about something, and she notices that George is taller than her father now. She wonders what might happen if she walked out of the hotel lobby across the road into the museum and bought a ticket. Would anybody stop her?

There is a knock at the door. A bored-looking maid hands her a package from the pharmacist wrapped in brown paper. Inside is a box of six washable linen napkins, a tin of safety pins, a sanitary belt size small, a sanitary apron (*Junior Miss*), and a pair of sanitary night bloomers. Once the maid leaves, Dora opens the boxes, tipping the contents onto the bed, wrinkling her nose at the bitter odor, which reminds her of marzipan. The belt confuses her at first. It looks a little like a pair of braces. She has to step in and out of it to adjust the straps at the front before securing the napkin inside with the pins. Then she puts on the apron under a navy blue skirt and paces up and down the room, unable to forget for a second that there is a foreign body wedged between her legs. What is she supposed to do now? Sit and wait until her mother returns to this stuffy room, which may be hours and hours? She wonders if this is her lot. To stay inside one week a month, trussed up like a pony in a trap? Her eyes prickle hot and indignant and she kicks her shoes across the room. Then she gathers up the boxes and leaflets and rips them into a thousand tiny pieces, which float down to the floor like ash.

12

St. Hugh's College
Oxford

Dearest Tedders,
Thank you awfully for the champers. (Every noun must have
an -er on the end here at Oxford, it is the law.) I shall drink it
illicitly in my wardrobe and think of you.

You ask what my days are like? Surprisingly busy. And
the mathematics? Really rather beautiful.

Today, I was at a lecture on Fermat's Last Theorem at
Keble. When the don walked in and it transpired E. T.
Spooner was a Miss, not a Mister, two chaps made a point of
picking up their coats and stalking out. You should have seen
their faces, all piggy and self-righteous. Some of these poor
idiots have never been lectured by women before and assume
we can't possibly be as bright as men. Their stupidity is quite
staggering.

Miss Spooner took it jolly well, I have to say, and made a
rather amusing digression about Sophie Germain, who,
despite being a whiz at number theory and making huge
advances in understanding Mr. Fermat, was not permitted to
make a career out of mathematics. She didn't even get a
degree.

Afterward, I lurked about with another woman, a refreshingly sarcastic first-year from St. Hilda's, and we overheard a few of the men grudgingly praising the lecturer. A chap with teeth like a racehorse sidled over and asked me to dine with him at Mario's but he lost interest when I said I'd have to bring my chaperone and be tucked up in bed with Fermat by 10:15 p.m.

I saw Lazenby and Butler-Reese at a party over the weekend, still insufferably full of themselves. Blotto on absinthe, or dope, or something equally dull. They've joined the Bullingdon Club and spend their time pinning esthetes to the quad with croquet hoops, then trashing their sets. Apparently, they were gated last week. I'm rather glad you didn't come up to Oriel now and therefore I do not have to despise you.

Don't send any more gifts, dear one, you are spoiling me. Actually, do! I can't bear Dora getting more attention than me. Although her father owns a factory, she is terribly pretty and innocent and would enjoy spending your money on nice things. I should introduce you. How is the wife-hunt going, by the way? I can assure you, you would not want me anymore if you saw me getting off my bicycle in the rain today, hands red-raw, stockings splattered with mud, armpits pungent. I am officially an old maid.

Don't mope about at home, darling chum. That is an order.

Your spinster friend,
Otto x

———◇———

ONE OVERCAST MORNING IN SIXTH week, Dora receives an invitation for "Miss Greenwood and companions" to have tea at Jesus with one of her brother's friends, Frank Collingham. The letter, which she props on her mantelpiece, is beautifully exe-

cuted in looping script and cobalt-blue ink. Apparently, Mr.
Collingham recognized her walking along Turl Street. She remembers him as being a quiet fellow, with excellent manners,
a doctor's son—someone her mother approved of. He enlisted
with George and completed officers' training with him. George
often mentioned Frank in his brief letters to her parents, and
she is comforted (but also a fraction resentful) that Frank has
made it back to complete his medical degree.

Miss Jourdain gives permission for the women to attend as
long as a chaperone is present. Miss Cox agrees to come on the
proviso that they pop into Blackwell's on the way back to look
at the crime fiction together. She has taken a liking to Dora,
considering her "the most promising and well mannered of the
group," and has given her the gift of a hand-sewn lavender bag,
much to the amusement of the others.

Mr. Collingham has booked a private dining room on the
ground floor of the front quad. It is surprisingly cozy, the table
laid with polished silverware and a brace of green-leather armchairs positioned around the fire. Otto hands the scout her
coat and slides into one of the chairs with a squeak, while Dora
slips off her gloves and warms her hands.

"W-w-welcome to Jesus," Mr. Collingham greets them, making the odd little bow she remembers from before. He is a couple
of inches shorter than Beatrice, stocky with dark curly hair and
a pronounced stammer that has come on since they last met.

"Please c-c-call me Frank," he says, and introduces his two
friends.

When they shake hands, Frank grasps Dora's fingers a fraction too long. "I recognized you b-b-because you look so much
like your b-b-brother," he says quietly, news that makes Dora
both gratified and downcast.

"What he won't tell you is that he telephoned two other
women's colleges before he discovered you at St. Hugh's," says
his friend, which causes everyone to laugh and Frank to blush.

"How are you finding Oxford?" he asks. "I think most chaps

are d-d-delighted at the introduction of ladies. And the waverers are relieved to find you aren't all militant suffragettes wanting to b-b-burn down the Oxford Union."

"Oh, we will soon if it doesn't buck up its ideas and admit women," says Beatrice, delighted. "I'm desperate to join."

Frank hovers around his guests as they warm their feet by the fire. "I can g-g-get you tickets for the gallery. The Thursday chamber debates are always entertaining, even if one detests politics," he says, glancing at Dora.

Oars inscribed with rowers' names and dates of victories hang at head height on the walls. Beneath them are prewar photographs of football and cricket teams in immaculate kit, standing with arms folded in the front quad. Dora wonders how many of the players are still able to stand with arms folded, let alone play football.

"We'd love you to join the Jesus Dramatic Society if you were interested," says Frank. "If you could get p-p-permission?" He glances at Miss Cox, who is reading at the table.

"What are you performing?" says Miss Cox, without looking up.

"*The Speckled Band* by Conan Doyle," says one of the Jesus men.

"Oh, how splendid!" she replies, suddenly animated. "I do adore Conan Doyle but I'm afraid it's not possible. You'll have to hire your leading ladies locally."

Two scouts enter with an array of delicate cakes and neatly sliced sandwiches.

"Tea. How wonderful," exclaims Miss Cox. "Oh, girls, look, Battenberg squares. I haven't had one of those since 1914."

The young people look at each other and smile.

AFTER TEA, FRANK WRINGS HIS hands before standing up at the table and addressing Dora. "Miss Greenwood—D-D-Dora—I invited you here partly—only partly—because I wanted to show you something relating to George. But I d-d-don't wish to cause you any unhappiness." He makes the odd little bow again. "I was terribly fond of George, as you know."

"I'd like to see it, whatever it is," says Dora. There is a low ache in her abdomen, which reminds her of the last time she was here. One never forgets where one started menstruating, she supposes. It was the day George introduced her to Frank and now here she is again, in some kind of strange symmetry.

"Perhaps it would be b-b-better if your friends came too," he suggests.

He leads the five women around the front quad into an empty reception room which, he explains, is to be called the Memorial Room. The windows are open, and after the warmth of the fire, the air is cutting. On the far side, a man in gray cap and overalls is working on a section of oak paneling attached to the wall. He is sanding the grain in long downward movements as if he is brushing the legs of a horse. Beside him, clean brushes are set out in a row, alongside dented pots of varnish and turps. His breath appears in clouds and mingles with the dust from his work. Propped up along one of the walls is what looks like a large painting covered with a thin sheet. They gather around it, blowing into cupped hands, jittery with cold.

"It's g-g-going to be unveiled in January," Frank says. "But I thought you might like to see it first."

He pulls aside the flesh-colored cloth to reveal another section of paneling to be added to the wall. Almost as tall as Dora, it has six squares, three above, three below, each containing a raised panel engraved with names. The central section on the top row is inscribed: *Lest We Forget. To those members of Jesus College who gave their lives in the war 1914–1918, their successors dedicate these panels. January 1921.* At least sixty men are listed, five of them Jones. She had forgotten about the Welsh roots of the college. When George came up, half the Jesus men were Welsh, many destined to be clergymen. Her eyes flick over the names, avoiding the first three panels until she can put it off no longer. *It is just carved lettering,* she says to herself, *and lettering cannot hurt me.* She starts from the beginning, reading each one, Alderson, Allan, Anderson, Armstrong, until she reaches the twenty-fifth.

And there it is. G. P. Greenwood.

Dora senses an arm link into hers on either side as if bracing her for a fall. Her temples ache. It is either quite dreadful or quite wonderful, she cannot tell.

"Lots of chums of ours, I'm sorry to say," says Frank, looking at his feet.

"Such a terrible loss," says Beatrice.

Dora says nothing. She used to be jealous of her brother for being a man. These days she is utterly grateful not to be one.

"Thank you for showing us, Mr. Collingham, it is very thoughtful of you," says Marianne.

"It is most kind, isn't it, Dora?" says Otto, giving her a nudge.

"It is," says Dora eventually, turning and holding out her hand to him. As he takes it, Frank exhales a long white breath.

———◇———

THE COLLEGE CAT NEEDS A place to birth her kittens.

The last litter, found blind and stumbling in the toolshed, were drowned by the gardener. At the direction of the principal, he carried them, roiling in a coal sack, down to the river at the Parks and threw them into the weedy depths. An old brick at the bottom did the trick. He watched a few bubbles rise feebly to the surface, tutted over the loss of a perfectly good sack, and returned to St. Hugh's on his bicycle.

The cat treads lightly around men now, but she has a job to do. To feed herself, she must hunt the mice and rats that frequent the college outbuildings and cellars. Occasionally, she will take care of the vermin in the residential houses down the street too.

A few of the students are charmed by the way she scoots under their hems and rubs, vibrating, around their ankles. A common moggy with all the gloss of a black mink stole, she has taken to climbing into Marianne's room through the window and meows outside until granted access. She attempted it once with Dora but was given short shrift in the form of a glass of water. Dora may like fresh air, but she is not at all fond of pets.

When the cat is bulging with young and gamely struggling to hunt, Marianne allows it to nest in the cupboard at the base of her washstand. She donates an old towel and morsels of egg and rabbit from mealtimes. By skimping on the purchase of quality tea and borrowing darning wool, she is able to visit the butcher in North Parade Avenue and buy overpriced slivers of liver and kidney—good, she thinks, for their nutritional properties. It is worth it; the cat chews with yackety sounds and swallows the meat hungrily.

A few nights later, it gives birth to six snub-nosed blobs with skin for eyes. Marianne rubs the sleek wet fur with a flannel and offers the kittens to their mother's teats. Two are dead and she places their undeveloped bodies in the grate wrapped in newspaper, not knowing what else to do with them. While she makes a pyre, tiny paws open and close on their mother's swollen belly as they gorge on her milk.

Otto and Dora are revolted by the feral nature of the litter (*vermin, Marianne, vermin!*), but Beatrice is fascinated by the instinctive drive of the animal to nurture her young and that the young in turn expect it. She kneels in the doorway watching them feed, unfazed by the cat's suspicious glances. Marianne entrusts Beatrice with taking care of the litter when she is in Culham at the weekend, and decides as soon as they are weaned, she will—somehow—take them back to the rectory. St. Mary's needs a mouser and she knows a kitten would be so loved. Her father's parishioners will find homes for the others.

The kittens must stay with their mother for at least a month, so she asks Otto to negotiate with Maud. Otto has the most sway with the scout, being both a generous tipper and used to instructing servants. Maud is usually amenable if it is not her day to scrub the floors, and most likely Otto will pay her to keep quiet, a debt that Marianne, on this occasion, is prepared to overlook.

The first few weeks are hard work, but while the kittens remain in the box it is manageable. Marianne cannot resist pressing them to her face and burying her nose and mouth in their soft, puny rib cages. Sometimes they doze in her arms, creating a dizzying warmth in her breast. However, within a month, the kittens, all black and white, become mobile and are swinging off the curtains like drunken acrobats. Marianne dreads finding them dead in the courtyard, but the window must remain open. Although she has rolled back the rug, during the day they urinate—and defecate—under and on the bed. She is running out of both time and newspaper.

The following Monday, she returns from an afternoon making notes on *Pearl* at the Bod and opens the bedsitter door warily, only to find it empty. She cannot work out if the cat has carried the kittens through the window or they have been taken. There is no sign in the bicycle sheds, courtyard, or garden.

Maud says she knows nothing about it and turns back to attacking the floor, water slopping from the top of the pail as she plunges in the scrubbing brush. Marianne weeps angrily into her pillow, fine hairs sticking to her lips and cheeks, but dares not raise a fuss. The next morning, she sees the mother cat in the garden stalking a thrush. The cat is apparently unperturbed and refuses to come when she calls. In her pigeonhole, Marianne finds a letter from Miss Jourdain.

Dear Miss Grey,
Please accept this as a warning that keeping animals in
rooms is expressly forbidden. I am disappointed to hear that

this has been the case and expect more of an exhibitioner.
Any further transgressions of this nature will result in
punitive measures.

Miss E. F. Jourdain
Principal

Marianne uses the letter to light her fire that evening and nurses her bitterness and resentment in the privacy of her room.

At the end of sixth week, she leaves college for her fortnightly visit home. Miss Stroud chaperones her as usual, and after alighting from the crowded omnibus and queuing for a ticket, they stand in glum silence watching the two-fifteen to Didcot crawl into the station. Gritty smoke billows. At the beckoning of the conductor's whistle, the doors clatter open and there is chaos as the descending passengers dive between the waiting ones on the platform. The hot hiss of the engine and the grind of conversation make Marianne's head pound. A hand tugs on her sleeve and she turns to see a familiar face hovering behind her among the throng. Before Marianne can speak, Maud pushes a picnic basket at her and beckons her closer.

"This is all I could manage," she says, matter-of-fact, and retreats into the crowd. Marianne nods, confused, but Maud is already stalking away.

"Come along," says Miss Stroud. "I have other things to do today."

Safely in the third-class carriage with the basket on her lap, Marianne watches the station and canal blur into a picture postcard. Opposite her sit a mother and son. The boy looks around five or six, still young enough to be excited by the train. He leans into his mother as she points out interesting sights through the window, whispering a commentary in his ear.

Marianne holds the basket to her chest, feels a familiar

quickening within. She opens the wicker lid an inch and peers through the hole. There is a mew as shrill and pure as bird-song. The boy spins around, his eyes questioning and wide.

Together they watch as a paw reaches out and claws at the air.

13

The four women sit facing each other in semidarkness. It is just as Otto has envisaged, although in the days to come she will wonder why on earth she thought the game the slightest bit appropriate. Thanks to the candles positioned about the room, the potted palm throws fingers of shadow up the wall, and although the curtains are drawn, the window remains open to encourage dramatic billowing. In a nod to the ancient Greeks, the mirror is covered to prevent the accidental trapping of souls. She is serving the Bordeaux claret her father sent incognito last week and has purchased Elgar's *Spirit of England*, recorded for the gramophone. Otto is hosting "an evening of wine and spirits."

"Why are ghosts always people of status?" asks Beatrice, seated at the table and waving her glass about. "St. John's have an archbishop in the library who kicks his head at undergraduates. Charles I pulls books off shelves in the Bod. But you never see the woman who swills out the chamber pot."

"Miss Cox says she's heard Cavaliers riding down New College Lane," says Marianne. "Apparently, the sound is absorbed in the stone."

"Or imprinted on the air," says Beatrice, "if you read Babbage.

"Well, that's rather hard to believe," Otto snorts. "Miss Cox is as deaf as a post."

Marianne chuckles. Her long neck is flushed, and she has rolled up her blouse sleeves to reveal freckly forearms. She is normally restrained when it comes to alcohol, but tonight she has confessed to Otto that she would enjoy "a small glass of wine" after a busy week juggling two essays, an Anglo-Saxon translation, a tea party, and two performances of the Bach Choir. "I read that Glastonbury is the most haunted town in the country," she says as Otto tops up her glass for the third time. "And the Holy Grail was buried there by St. Paul."

Dora laughs. "Surely you don't believe that? You're a rector's daughter."

Dora's thick dark hair is loose tonight and fanned out over her shoulders. She reminds Otto of the woman with the pomegranate in the postcard on Marianne's mantelpiece. According to Marianne, the artist created a dozen versions of the same picture, all slightly different, none of them definitive. *That's Dora all right*, Otto thinks. Tonight, Dora is surprisingly practical and head-girlish. Having lost two loved ones, she is, in many ways, the most qualified of them to comment.

"No, I don't. Not really," slurs Marianne. "But don't you think there might be spirits and things floating about that we can't see, like diseases, or radio waves?"

"And electricity," offers Beatrice.

"Maybe spirits exist," says Marianne. "We just don't know how to reach them." She takes another gulp of wine and grimaces as if she's stubbed her toe.

Otto raps her knuckles on her head. "I don't like the idea of spirits in the air. Don't want to breathe anyone else in, it's confusing enough in here already."

But Marianne is persistent. "There's a book by a scientist who says his dead son communicated with him through a gas called ether."

"Yes, and the officers all had whiskey and cigars in heaven, I know that one," says Dora. "Mother read it and cried for a week. I wish it were true, I really do."

Beatrice sighs. "That's why those sorts of books are bestsellers, they peddle hope. I'm sorry, Marianne, call me a bore, but no one comes back from the dead."

"Except Jesus," says Otto, raising her glass in a toast.

Beatrice mirrors her. "Queen Victoria liked to chat with Albert, which is a bit odd if you ask me, as Head of the Church."

Marianne rolls her locket slowly over her lips. "Didn't Patricia say Miss Jourdain believes in ghosts? And she's very, very religious."

"Pff, Patricia," snorts Otto.

"Miss Jourdain's thing is mysticism. Higher states of consciousness, trances," says Beatrice.

"Perhaps that's how she knows exactly what's going on around here all of the time," laughs Otto. "Now, will you all please drink up."

Otto removes the empty glasses from the table and replaces them with the slim wooden board she had the housekeeper send up from home. The letters *A* to *M* and *N* to *Z* are painted in parallel arcs with the numbers 0 to 9 positioned left to right beneath them.

"Has it ever worked?" asks Marianne, running her fingers over the letters.

"We only used it once," says Otto. "Gertie's husband was messing about. Made it spell *KISS ME GERT.*"

She drops the wooden planchette on the board with a clatter and sits down on her chair. The candles have created a meandering haze over their heads, and in the grate the coals have sunk into white balls of ash. Positioned around the small table, they are squashed so tightly that Otto can smell Beatrice's sour breath and the coconut tang of Dora's newly washed hair.

"Someone restart Mr. Elgar," she says. "It's time to raise the dead."

BEATRICE HAS NEVER USED A Ouija board before; her parents are not partial to parlor games. Evenings in Bloomsbury were spent reading or sketching alone in her room, bar the occasional dinner or theater trip. Even when she turned eighteen and volunteered as a typist during the last year of the war, she was rarely included in their plans. Now here she is, squeezed up with her own group of friends, in a way that, seven weeks after the unexpected trip to the tea shop, no longer feels awkward. She is thrilled by how their mismatched fingertips—slender, inky, bitten, brittle—meet in the middle of the planchette and make all sorts of symbols: a plus sign, a compass star, a cross, a four-leafed clover. How their heads almost touch as they concentrate.

"Look," says Otto. "It's better if we all use the same hand. Marianne, use your right. Otherwise, we are jamming elbows."

They press elbows, shuffle, give amused sighs. Nothing happens.

"Concentrate. Don't press down. Relax your fingers," says Otto.

As the conversation ceases, Beatrice has a fleeting sense of disquiet, as if she is viewing the scene from the world of ether that Marianne has described. Then, just as swiftly, she is back in herself again, pressing fingertips with her friends and leaning over the board. It must be the Elgar; requiems always leave her horribly sad.

The planchette makes a few tiny juddering movements but remains firmly in position, as if they are all pushing it with equal force.

Without warning, there is a terrible clanging from the wardrobe, and they jump and shriek. But it is only Otto's alarm clock, set to go off and terrify them. Otto howls with laughter, having frightened herself as much as the others. Dora jumps up and lowers the window. The fire is dying and a draft creeps under the door, licking at their ankles.

"We'll need more coal soon," says Dora, sliding back into place.

"I can't feel my fingers *or* my toes," whispers Marianne.

When the planchette starts to slide across the board, it moves decisively. The tug on her finger frightens Beatrice for a moment, but then she realizes with a grin that Otto must be responsible. Their hostess has begun shouting mocking encouragement to the spirits and is rolling her head around like a medium.

"What letter is it? I can't see," says Beatrice when their fingers finally come to a standstill. From where she is the board is upside down.

"Sit back, Sparks. It's too dark," says Otto.

"Looks like *C*, don't you think, Marianne?" says Dora.

Marianne nods. "*C*."

"Not *C* for—Charles?" says Dora, amused.

Marianne looks at her. "Shall we stop? I think we should stop."

"Absolutely not," insists Dora.

They return their fingers to the planchette and begin again. The wooden marker moves swiftly and cleanly down to the lower row and settles on the second letter, *O*.

"Not Charles, then," says Dora, the corner of her mouth curling up. She sits back into her chair.

"Hello, Colin or Constance, are you there?" says Otto, holding her palms aloft.

"Constance was my mother's name," says Marianne.

Otto raises her eyebrows at Dora.

Beatrice pats Marianne lightly on her forearm. "*C-O* could stand for 'commissioned officer' or 'conscientious objector,'" she says.

"Or 'commanding officer'? It could be Miss Jourdain," says Otto, turning to the door and feigning concern. "Perhaps she's watching us right now."

"Come on. Another letter," says Dora.

They lower their heads and return their fingers to the planchette, the light so low now that the room is drained of color like a photograph. The next letter is a *W*.

"Cow. Is that meant to be an insult? That is very rude of you, spirit," says Otto.

"Cowley Road?" suggests Beatrice.

"Cowper the poet?" offers Dora, with a grin.

"I'm sure Cowper the poet has better things to do in the afterlife than visit us," says Otto.

Marianne says nothing. Beatrice can feel someone's leg jiggling under the table. Dora mouths to Marianne, *Are you all right?*, but Marianne merely nods and continues to stare at the board.

The final three letters come quickly.

"*A*," announces Dora. "I think we can see where this is going."

Immediately, there is another tug on the planchette. It is so firm this time, Beatrice feels her shoulders sway. The next letter is *R*. Then their arms are jerked up to the top row, where the planchette finally comes to rest on the letter *D*.

"*COWARD*," says Dora, triumphant. "Bravo, Otto, you do put on a good show."

"I saw a play over the summer by a new chap called Coward," says Beatrice, and Otto gives an odd little laugh. "*I'll Leave It to You*, it was called. Short run but terribly good."

The gramophone needle repeats its little death over and over at the center of the recording, but nobody moves.

"The word 'coward' comes from the Latin for 'tail,' *cauda*, did you know?" continues Beatrice. "Fleeing with your tail between your legs."

Marianne begins to cry, shoulders heaving against Beatrice. Tears fall onto random letters of the board below. The needle scratches like a trapped rat.

"It's all right, Marianne. There's a perfectly rational explanation," says Beatrice. "After *C-O-W-A* there was only one word it could be, we obviously spelt it ourselves."

"Oh, do shut up, Sparks," says Otto, jumping out of her seat and striding to the window, spitting a piece of fingernail from between her teeth. "It was a stupid idea and I blame myself."

They stare at her. She is rigid with fury. "Whoever made it spell that. I can tell you it isn't funny, not funny at all. This will teach me to give alcohol to nuns. For God's sake, Marianne, stop blubbering."

She wrenches the board from beneath their elbows and, realizing it is too thick to snap in half, forces it sideways into the grate. The varnish ignites, emitting a curious sapphire flame. The room is stuffy and cool at the same time and not quite the same room as before. It strikes Beatrice as ridiculous that a few minutes earlier she was congratulating herself on the closeness of the group; this game has proved how little they know about each other. She gets up and flicks on the electric lights and lifts the needle from the gramophone.

"I said, be quiet, Marianne, or get out," says Otto, her carefully painted Cupid's bow pinched into a tight V.

"Marianne—" says Dora, but Marianne stands up. She looks ghastly, as if she might vomit. Without speaking or looking at any of them, she sways to the door and leaves. They hear her footsteps slowly traverse the hallway.

Beatrice's head is thudding. She is not entirely sure what has happened. Why is Marianne so upset? Should she go after her? And why is Otto so angry?

"We should go," says Dora to Beatrice, who nods. As they get up to go, Otto blocks their route to the door.

"Oh, just sit down," she says. "Please."

And then Otto claims the word for her own.

"WHEN I WAS A VAD, I had a very bad time," says Otto. She fiddles to light a cigarette, although Beatrice can see another smoking in a glass ashtray on the mantelpiece. "I signed up to be a nurse, not a driver.

"I don't talk about it, but suffice to say, I wasn't any good at it. I was at Somerville looking after officers with only one day of leave a month. They gave me all the worst jobs. I emptied bedpans—me! And all because I imagined myself reading to good-looking boys who needed cheering up.

"I managed six weeks, went a bit crazy, failed the probation spectacularly. They put me on General Service instead, driving people up and down the High. I moved in with my aunt and counted down the weeks till I could leave. I still have terrible nightmares, and my eldest sister Caro revels in the fact that I proved myself a washout. So, you see, our spirit has a sense of humor. I'm the coward, all right, the coward of the CO Ward." She laughs miserably.

"I couldn't have nursed for a day, let alone a month," says Dora. "I think you're terribly brave to try at all."

Otto turns her back on them. "Tosh, the others were capable of it, why not me?"

"It's perfectly normal to be appalled by what you saw," says Beatrice.

Otto shrugs. Beatrice knows enough about Otto to understand that she hates to lose. Mediocrity appalls her.

As she watches the board, half-burnt, shuffle down into the base of the grate, Beatrice contemplates her own cowardice. Her failure to stand up to her mother. Her inability to be a martyr like Miss Davison. Letting a man fondle and kiss her in the street without so much as a rebuke. The Balliol men on matriculation day. The board hisses and gives off a bottle-green flame. "Dostoevsky says all decent men are cowards and slaves," she says at last. "It's the human condition."

"Thank you for the heartfelt words, Sparks," says Otto darkly.

They sit in silence. All Beatrice can hear is the ticking of the clock and shifting in the grate. She takes a deep breath. "Ignore and mock me if you want, Otto, but the word 'coward' is a weapon of war, of control. Think of the boys shot for desertion.

Most of them were terrified to the point of madness, yet they were called cowards for having a perfectly human reaction to what they saw. War can't afford soldiers—or nurses—to be fearful or sensitive, so they wrap it up in shame. We need to rethink words like 'coward.' We're not at war anymore."

"Well, the Irish might think otherwise," says Otto, sneering. "But of course, you're the expert."

Otto's rebuke stings. Beatrice is used to such barbs from her mother, has become numb to them over the years in fact, but this is her loyal friend Otto, who usually reserves her cutting remarks for people other than the Eights.

Dora gets to her feet. "Beatrice is right. We knew which letters should come next and we made it happen. 'Coward' can never apply to Otto, or any of us for that matter. If anything, we are brave because we keep on going, despite it all, don't you see?"

Beatrice cannot stay a moment longer. She was an idiot to speak out—who is she to talk of cowardice and war, she who sat behind a typewriter while others were dying? Now Otto will hate her. She has ruined everything. Her head is pounding with the effort of not crying. She needs to be alone, to unclip her stockings and recalibrate herself with silence and a book. It takes all her self-control not to run out of the room.

"I'm sorry," she says. "I have to go to bed." She does not wait for a reply.

When she steps into the hallway, the light is on, and Marianne is sitting on the floor outside Maud's scullery holding a glass of water. There is a sour smell that reminds Beatrice of a sickroom.

"Are you all right?" she asks.

But Marianne looks happy. Her eyes are shining, and her face is radiant.

"She sent me a message," says Marianne, and retches into the glass.

Before Beatrice can ask what Marianne means, she hears the tap of footsteps. Someone is opening the door from the main corridor, a figure dressed in black with inscrutable lilac eyes.

"Do we have a problem here?" says Miss Jourdain.

14

Otto, January 1918

The soldier splutters something incomprehensible, his spit forming iridescent bubbles at the crease of his mouth. As Otto bends, the collar of her uniform rubs against her neck like sandpaper. She lowers her ear toward him, and he lifts his chin to meet her, breath sour with the wet stink of decay. She cannot make out what he wants, water perhaps. She turns her head to inhale, not wanting any particle of him to penetrate her, and offers him the enamel mug. He raises his head again, and this time she slips her hand to the base of his scalp, the hair damp and soft. She tips a little water between his lips. They are peeling in layers as if sunburnt. Most of the liquid runs down his neck and into the sheets. He heaves out a breath, and she slides out her hand. They are released from their embrace, spent.

"Wallace-Kerr, you're needed in the sluice," shouts a nurse from the doorway.

Otto lifts the pail and washcloths from the bedside and, ignoring feeble calls from other patients, weaves her way through the closely packed bed frames, tucking in a few blankets as she passes. The room is cold, the high ceiling echoing with coughs and moans. A few of the beds have wooden folding tables beside them with neat piles of letters and illustrated newspapers. Most of the men on this ward are too ill to sit up.

The Third Southern General Hospital has three makeshift sites in Oxford, and this one was commandeered due to its proximity to the Radcliffe Infirmary. The buildings belong to Somerville, a college for women. The students and staff have been relocated to a small quad in one of the men's colleges, Oriel. To avoid any scandal, the quad has been bricked up from the Oriel side, and the Somerville librarian cycles back and forth along St. Giles' to exchange the women's library books. As a probationer, Otto is not allowed much interaction with the convalescent men. There have been a number of love affairs in the past, including a recent scandal regarding a nurse with a fiancé and her patient, the poet Robert Graves.

Otto's role is akin to that of a servant: cleaning, mopping, carrying, and fetching. Like other VADs, she does the jobs that allow career nurses to dress wounds, give medicines, monitor vital signs, and consult with doctors. The problem is, she is not at all competent at the most basic tasks. They have tried to teach her how to squeeze out a mop, how often to change the water, how to lift a body, wash a body, lay out a body, talk to people who are dying, touch people who are dying. Most of the work can only be described as thankless drudgery and she is useless at all of it. She is no longer under the illusion that voluntary nursing involves reading to the blind and knitting bedsocks in a French chateau.

The hospital, with over two hundred fifty beds, is for commissioned officers only. Most are convalescing but there are also serious, bedridden cases. Bedpans from these wards arrive in the sluice—formerly the Somerville laundry—on a layered metal trolley, the sort one would normally see in a restaurant laden with fanciful desserts.

"Another one, sorry."

"Rotten luck being the new girl."

"Come on, Wallace-Kerr, I need the trolley back."

When she tips the contents out, sometimes the metal is warm, the matter pulsing with life—froth or mucus—still part of the body that has ejected it. The urine varies in volume and is stunning shades of amber and gold. The feces have their own palette: brittle gray birds' nests, coiling brown shoelaces, wet black fir cones. No two pans are ever the same. She wears a mask that helps with the stench, but the steam from the sluice billows up and clings to the windows, her clothing, her hair. There is no avoiding it. She will change her clothes when she gets home and scrub her skin, careful not to raise any rough edges. Her hands must be gloved and well greased at night according to regulations. The sister berates her for many things: for wearing lipstick and earrings, for not trying hard enough (*think of what the men have gone through*), for not scrubbing with the grain of the table leg, for working too slowly, working too fast. Then there are the assorted general failings in tucking, polishing, drying, folding, sterilizing, asking, watching, listening, thinking. She loathes it. Loathes it all, but cannot allow herself to give in. She will not prove her family's doubts well-founded.

At night when she returns in the dark to the nurses' quarters in Jericho, she cannot sleep. Her pulse beats in her ears so hard, she thinks her heart must be damaged. Her dreams are lurid and terrifying: maggots, offal, pale-blue tiles smeared with blood. She wakes thirsty, bathed in sweat, alert for danger. Sometimes she cries out and wakes with her bewildered roommate looming over her. In the mirror, she looks so old, she hardly recognizes herself. She barely eats, cannot face the grind of her teeth on matter. By the fifth week, she is given a warning for not completing tasks to a satisfactory standard; in the sixth week she faints on the ward and cannot get out of bed for two days. She is put on indefinite sick leave ("mental collapse") and a few weeks later is told she has failed her probation. An achievement so rare, it has not happened at the hospital before.

The matron knows exactly who Otto's father is, thanks to the War Office. What Otto does not know is that there is a reason she has been posted to work among officers in a beautiful medieval city. Sir Robert Wallace-Kerr MP has connections. Otto is both relieved and ashamed when she is reassigned to a six-month role in the General Service section of the VAD. Still under the auspices of the military, it provides cover for civic positions in hospitals vacated by men gone to the front—porters, telephonists, clerks, and so on. Because she can drive and is familiar with telephones, she is given a role in logistics, chauffeuring doctors between the hospitals, to the station, even home to see their wives. Based in the Examination Schools on the High Street, she becomes a familiar sight around Oxford, motorcar crammed with doctors and matrons, her red hair poking from under her cap. The orderlies call her the Red Baroness, which she rather likes. She moves in with her aunt, who has a large home in the Norham Manor area near the Parks.

The months roll by. She starts to feel more herself, although the nightmares persist. She regains a little of her old flamboyance and energy, but she is diminished by the things she has seen: the wet meat inside a human body, the moment between breath and absence of breath that marks the end of a person. One does not easily recover from these things, she realizes, but she is ashamed all the same. She has failed.

Oxford, so small compared to London, is unlike anywhere she has known. With most omnibuses requisitioned, the streets are dominated by bicycles ridden by women, old men, and beardless boys. Pedestrians rub shoulders with soldiers in khaki, patients in hospital blues, and nurses with red crosses on their chests. Delivery carts toil up the High pulled by the scrawniest nags, unsuitable for service. She learns to negotiate and predict who will wobble in front of her and who will stop abruptly to unload their wares into the mouths of flat-fronted colleges. What she never gets used to are the mourning mothers and the widows with perambulators who step off the pavement, minds elsewhere. She avoids going onto wards unless she must, especially at Somerville. She spends her breaks in an upstairs café on Broad Street, parking outside Balliol and running in for coffee, eggs, and the WC. The Good Luck Tea Rooms is like a second home.

She meets Miss Rogers in May when spring has unfurled its lime-green leaves and the bluebells have retreated into the flower beds. Driving back from the station to the Radcliffe Infirmary, she sees an elderly woman knocked from her bicycle by a delivery boy who swerves to avoid a dog. The woman is angry and shaken and, all the worse, highly articulate, so Otto takes both her and her bicycle home in the back of the car, mostly for the sake of the mortified boy who cannot stop crying.

Miss Rogers, it transpires, is a Classics tutor at St. Hugh's College and a well-known figure on the streets of Oxford in her long skirts and outlandish hats. They lean the twisted bicycle against the low metal railings of Museum Road.

"They'll be melted down soon," says Miss Rogers with a sigh, and enters number 39, a narrow three-story terraced town house made of the same buff-colored stone as the men's colleges and backing onto St. John's. Her home smells leafy, damp, and papery, like a cross between a library and a greenhouse. The small drawing room is decorated with art prints, colored-glass ornaments, and potted plants. A statuette of a Greek goddess, a dark wood Napoleon clock, and faded postcards jostle for position on the mantelpiece. Framed pamphlets hang on the wall in the alcoves, one featuring the words *Take No Notice* in enormous letters.

"My hobbies are bicycling, sitting on committees, and, more lately, being obstreperous," Miss Rogers tells her proudly, pouring them jasmine tea. The whine of a distant violin can be heard from next door.

"I'm interested to hear how you find things now the men are gone. Are you getting a decent standard of education, do you think? Which college do you belong to?" The old woman hands her a chipped cup without a saucer. "If you hang on, you'll probably get a degree. The Representation of the People Act goes to vote in the Commons next month, and they can hardly ignore that."

Miss Rogers assumes she is a student and, at first, Otto doesn't correct her. She has seen them about, of course, in their dowdy skirts and coats, looking like impoverished teachers. She finds herself telling this strange and compelling woman how she has ended up in Oxford driving motorcars around the city. Miss Rogers, in turn, relates how her mother recently died in that very house and how much she misses her. How she has found solace in gardening but has been banned from removing cuttings from St. John's to replant at St. Hugh's. There was an altercation involving catmint. In the future she will hide cuttings in her umbrella.

"Women like you, doing these jobs and being seen to do them, are making more difference than any of us trying to change the rules from a desk. Don't underestimate your contribution, Miss Wallace-Kerr."

Miss Rogers is not at all the person Otto took her for. She is an independent woman, earning her own living, coming and going as she wishes, pursuing her interests. Otto admires Miss Rogers's vitality and the way she views life as something to be seized. It rarely happens that Otto cannot get a word in edgeways.

"Do you think the men's colleges will ever admit women?" asks Otto.

"Lord, no!" laughs Miss Rogers. "But we will get degrees eventually." She pours more tea. "It's dangerous to allow men and women to fraternize," she adds.

Otto looks up.

"I encourage my students to dress modestly and remain within college as much as possible. What's the point in fighting as hard as we are if it's all thrown away over a love affair?"

Otto has a sudden vision of secret liaisons, yearning glances. Surely not every woman who studies in this city wants to spend her life with potted plants and books.

"I am known to be quite a meddler, but I'm also a stickler for the rules. Don't mistake me for a rebel," says Miss Rogers.

Otto finds out later that Miss Rogers was Oxford's first female don. That she was the first student to pass the degree-equivalent exams created for women in 1875 and that she achieved a double first in Latin, Greek, and Ancient History. That in her youth, Miss Rogers came top in the entrance examinations and should have been offered an exhibition to Balliol or Worcester, but when A.M.A.H. Rogers was discovered to be a woman, all she received was a set of books. Balliol College gave her place to the boy who came sixth.

IN THE SUMMER OF 1918, after her six-month service is up, Otto decamps to London in order to prepare for the Oxford Senior the following July. Returning to Oxford seems like the right thing to do and, while she cannot face Somerville, she likes the area to the north of the town, so she applies to St. Hugh's to read Mathematics. Her family are bemused by the decision. Although she has always been stubborn, her spark has dimmed somewhat, they can tell. She should accept Teddy's offer of marriage, her mother insists, but her father says she is free to do as she pleases, as long as she does not embarrass him. Perhaps if she did not have three older sisters, the darlings of London society, it might have been harder to get his blessing, but he is happy to indulge her. She engages tutors in mathematics and Latin—both recommended by Miss Rogers, to whom she writes for advice. She passes both the Senior and the interview, refusing to visit—or think of—Oxford again until term begins. It does not matter to her that the Congregation grants full rights to women students in May 1919 or that women aged over thirty vote for the first time six months later. When she finally takes up her place at St. Hugh's in 1920, Otto is a world-weary socialite of twenty-four.

15

Friday, December 3, 1920 (8th Week)

O n the last Monday of term, instead of the usual trip to the Bod in the afternoon, Beatrice is summoned with the others to an uncomfortable meeting in the principal's study to discuss the "antics" of Friday night. Miss Jourdain is at her most terrifyingly calm and states that if they are caught drinking alcohol on the premises again, she will rusticate them. The Eights are jointly fined half a crown for rule-breaking and will not be allowed out after eight p.m. for the rest of term. Even Otto dons a penitent face, which Beatrice thinks is wise, given that a furious Miss Jourdain had to help Marianne to bed and wake Maud to mop the corridor.

"You got off very lightly," says Patricia, over dinner. "She sent down a fresher last term for returning from the theater five minutes late."

Beatrice is aware that Miss Jourdain is usually far more draconian in her discipline, and she can only suppose that the principal is in a generous mood, the term being very nearly over. What concerns her more is that normality will never resume on Corridor Eight. The atmosphere is odd, like the air after a thunderstorm; a little too quiet, a little too clear. Otto apologized the afternoon after the Ouija debacle, presenting them each with a bag of sugared almonds and a bunch of damson-colored chrysanthemums. Beatrice, fearing she might burst into clumsy tears, apologized back and said she was only too pleased to put the incident behind them. However, since then, Marianne has kept mostly to her room, venturing out only for meals and to borrow Beatrice's typewriter.

Otto is frustrated by Marianne's apparent withdrawal from the group. "I explained all about my VAD work. She said she understood, and that there was nothing to forgive."

"She has a lot of work to do," replies Beatrice. "Marianne doesn't hold grudges. I think it was the Ouija that upset her. Something to do with her mother. It wasn't you."

"Perhaps she's a bit shaken," adds Dora. "Give her time."

"Hmm," says Otto, lighting a cigarette. "One thing's for certain, she needs to stop reading books by crackpots."

It is the last week of term, and everyone is busy with final essays and preparations for Christmas. Father sends fruitcake, which he knows is Beatrice's favorite, and she cuts it into quarters to share with the others. The weather is appalling, their rooms draped with steaming, wet garments. On Tuesday, she suggests they visit the Electric on Castle Street to see *Wuthering Heights* starring Milton Rosmer. In the poster he sports a comically large pair of sideburns, and Beatrice hopes the outing will restore the group's bonhomie. However, Marianne refuses. Otto suspects she is out of money and buys all four tickets herself, but Marianne will not budge. The three of them go without her, but the picture is disappointing and the atmosphere flat.

Between tutes and matches and outings, everyone thrashes away at their own work. Dora wrangles with Anglo-Saxon grammar in the college library while Marianne continues to hide away in her room working on a magnum opus of some kind, the borrowed typewriter stamp-stamp-stamping across the hall late at night. Beatrice wrestles with an essay requiring her to "Discuss in detail any one argument for the existence of

God." She has to go and shiver in the Bod to write it; she finds the presence of her friends on the corridor far too distracting, and the thought that their precious foursome is beyond repair keeps her awake at night. The last two months have been the happiest time of her life and, though she would not admit it to the others, the thought that Marianne has broken with the Eights terrifies her.

Otto is occupied too, completing the term's final set of calculations for Miss Brockett to the accompaniment of Bach. The group are working through German composers at the moment—Beatrice's idea—in an act of solidarity related to the terms of the surrender.

"You know, Mr. Bach isn't entirely unpleasant," says Otto, over late-night cocoa. "Whoever said that there is geometry in the humming of the strings was right. But I draw the line at Wagner."

"I think you'll find it was Pythagoras," Beatrice says, draining her cup. "Isn't it comforting to think that numbers and musical notes unite so many people around the world, regardless of what language they speak?"

"I would be more comforted," Otto replies, "if their leaders weren't so eager to blow each other's heads off."

———◇———

ON WEDNESDAY DURING HOCKEY DRILLS, Frank Collingham calls at the lodge and asks for Dora. When she arrives, red-faced and panting and without hat or coat, he makes his nervous bow and offers her his arm. They step out of the gates onto the pavement to talk, watched closely by Miss Jenkins and a group of gawping third-years. Dora is not surprised by their interest; Frank is good-looking in a swarthy sort of way, but it is a shame he is not a little taller. They have met twice since the tea party at Jesus, once by accident outside the Radder, and also when he invited them all, Miss Cox in tow, to watch a debate about the rights of workingmen at the town hall. Beatrice enjoyed it immensely, but Dora found the seats hard and the speakers even more impenetrable. She felt obliged to smile and wave at Frank when he grinned at her from the other end of the row.

"I have a g-g-gift for you," he says now, running one hand through his dark curls.

"Oh, I'm so sorry, I never thought—" she says, glancing back at the lodge.

"It's n-n-nothing."

She accepts the small parcel wrapped neatly in brown paper and tucks it under her arm. A book.

He mumbles something about managing to get an American copy, that it is not available in England yet, that it was no trouble, and then he asks if he can write to her over Christmas. There is a plummeting sensation inside her, but she agrees. She would be a fool not to. Who knows how many chances she may have to secure her future? Not many, according to the newspapers. And the thought of the alternative—taking care of her parents and being reliant on the patronage of the twins—utterly horrifies her. Much as she tries, she cannot share the plucky attitude of her friends toward singledom.

Abandoning hockey practice, she returns to her room, where Maud is filling the tin bath. Once she leaves, Dora bolts the door and rips the paper and string from the parcel. It is a copy of the novel with the Belgian detective that Miss Cox was raving about: *The Mysterious Affair at Styles*. She tosses the book onto the bed, undresses, and slips into the water as quickly as she can, knowing it will not stay warm for long. Goose pimples rise on her arms as she slides back, neck against the metal rim. Her hair flares out under the water as if tentatively exploring its newfound freedom. It takes an age to dry by the fire and will still be damp on her pillow in the morning. If she brushes it and uses scalp tonic, she only needs to wash it twice a month using sparing amounts of the coconut-oil shampoo her mother orders from London.

Reaching for the shampoo, she looks down at her toes, knees, stomach, and breasts making dimpled islands in the water. There are marks of student life upon her: inky fingers, a callus on her middle finger from her fountain pen, bruised shins sliced with bicycle pedals, dry knuckles from cycling into the wind. *What would Frank make of this body?* she wonders; he is studying Medicine, after all. She has a fleeting image of him stammering and blushing as he pulls a bedsheet to uncover her naked form. She shivers and reaches again for the shampoo, hands too wet to properly grasp the glass bottle. It spins across the floor under the desk and far out of her reach.

That evening she helps Otto prepare to sneak out after their curfew, changing the gramophone records as they chat. As she finishes Otto's half-smoked cigarettes, Dora can taste the castor oil in her lipstick, inhaling a little bit of Otto into herself.

"Have one of your own," says Otto, waving the packet at her, but Dora does not dare.

After Otto climbs out of her window and dashes to a waiting car, Dora tidies the room whilst listening to gramophone recordings of Ivor Novello. Not only is it calming to potter about piling magazines and beating cushions, but it is the least she can do when they spend so much time there. She hangs up a heap of Otto's clothes flung over an armchair. The two dresses with the peacock feather and geometric patterns are her favorites, with their matching costume jewelry, cheaply made in brightly colored plastics, chunky but not at all heavy.

When the room is satisfyingly tidy, she sits in the armchair and opens the letter in her pocket that arrived from her mother that morning. It begins in the usual cheery fashion:

The servants have all been troublesome this week. It has given me one of my heads. Alice refuses to clean the oven, says it is

Cook's job, and the gardener has sent word that he and his
son are ill and neither of them will be in for a week. I have a
bridge party on Thursday and if the garden looks a mess I
shall have to cancel. It is all too inconvenient.

Dora's eyes drift down to the final—lengthy—paragraph.

Mrs. Palmer-Anderson has a nephew at Christ Church, and
he says there are women students at Oxford known as "gaiety
girls," so called because chaps have fun with them, but would
never marry them. Dora, please promise me you will not
become a gaiety girl!

Dora stops reading and stuffs her mother back in the envelope; she has heard quite enough for one day. She makes her
way down the main corridor to the student kitchen, where Ivy
Nightingale is boiling milk in her red gingham apron. They
chat about Christmas and make cocoa together, and then Dora
takes a cup each to Beatrice and Marianne, who are still battling through essays in their rooms. She resists the urge to kiss
the tops of their heads but afterward rather wishes she had.

The next morning, Dora learns from Miss Finch that she is
scheduled to resit the mathematics Responsion early next
term. She has been working through past papers and Otto has
been coaching her in geometry and algebra. It is curious how
easily mathematics comes to Otto, like flexing or bending a
limb without any thought. For Dora it's more like learning to
walk on a prosthetic: painful, slow, deliberate, which makes
her wonder if she really should be here at all. At school she
worked hard under the direction of her teachers and was considered ambitious, diligent, clever, but Oxford requires the
ability to be frightfully good at so many things, beyond one's
actual subject. Although she enjoys her Early and Middle English studies and is doing well according to Miss Finch, she
would much rather be playing hockey than wrestling with the

Latin and Logic required for Pass Mods. Otto, Beatrice, and Marianne, all so well informed, never seem to question whether they belong at Oxford. Learning is effortless for them. Information soaks into their skin as easily as cold cream. In one of Otto's magazines, there is a list of flapper slang, and the phrase to describe a very stupid girl stands out from the rest. Compared to her brilliant friends, Dora is a "Dumb Dora" indeed.

———◇———

ON THE LAST EVENING OF term, the Eights request permission to visit Otto's aunt for dinner. Miss Jourdain agrees on the condition that the curfew of eight p.m. stands. What she does not realize is that Otto's aunt is in Morocco for the winter, and that Otto has a key to her home and is free to come and go as she pleases. Although Marianne feels guilty at deceiving the principal, she overcomes her qualms quickly. They are not doing any harm and it is only a ten-minute walk from St. Hugh's. She has worked hard all week on both her essay and her special project, neglecting her friends. Now they deserve her full attention.

The house is cavernous and the air inside chill, but the housekeeper has filled the bar and prepared a fire for them in the sitting room, which Dora sets going. Otto drags up four armchairs, lighting the gas lamps and then returning a moment later to lower them.

"Much softer than the electric," she says, disappearing into the darkness.

From her bag, Marianne plucks some sprigs of holly and a candle tied with a scrap of purple ribbon, which she arranges on the vast mantelpiece. She is ashamed of her meager contribution to the festivities, especially when she thinks of the opulence of the chandelier in the hallway with its fat crystal droplets swaying in the moonlight. Tomorrow, when she returns home, she will make the advent wreath for St. Mary's as she always does: three candles wrapped at the base with purple ribbon, one with rose-pink and the central candle left pure white as befits the light of the world.

Beatrice has purchased a recording of Handel's *Messiah* and puts it on the gramophone. Dora sings along to the soprano part.

"Born in Germany, just so you know," says Beatrice, pulling her boots off.

"Shall I light the candle?" asks Dora. "The purple ribbon is pretty."

Marianne nods. "It represents penitence and fasting," she says. "My father wears purple vestments at Advent and Lent."

"Penitence and fasting? Hardly appropriate, considering what we are about to receive," says Otto. She drags an enormous hamper from the hallway and pushes it between the armchairs and the hearth. "Look what St. Nicholas delivered."

The basket opens in a waft of straw and smoked cheese.

Beatrice delves inside. "Good old Fortnum's. They sent Mother a parcel on her first release. She drank beef tea for a month."

"Look at this," says Marianne, admiring a gold-rimmed wooden box inlaid with jellied fruits. The box is even more enticing than the contents.

"Quail with foie gras," laughs Dora.

"Cheese. Biscuits. Piccalilli," adds Beatrice, with a flourish.

"Most importantly, port and champagne," says Otto, lifting out two bottles and waggling them. "Oh, don't look at me like that, we're not in college and nobody will ever know."

The others exchange smiles.

"Well, tuck in then, we only have two hours," she says.

MARIANNE IS DREADING THE EXCHANGE of gifts that will come after supper. She shared her quandary with her father on her last visit home, hoping he might be moved to spare her a little money. He suggested she embroider something, make a Christmas pudding, bottle fruit. Well-meant suggestions, but neither her needlework nor her gooseberry jam are fit for consumption outside Culham. In the end, she selected three poems and borrowed Beatrice's typewriter, experimenting with how she might set them out to best effect. Then she purchased three frames from a bric-a-brac shop in Jericho, removing the browning pencil sketches of grand houses and replacing them with poems. "'Hope' is the thing with feathers" for Beatrice, and for Dora "The Soldier" by Rupert Brooke. For Otto, she picked a poem that Miss Finch showed her during a tutorial. Recently published in the American magazine *Harper's*, it is called "Fire and Ice" and is by the writer Robert Frost. It was the day after Marianne's visit home at the end of sixth week when Miss Finch had made her a cup of tea because she looked tired and asked her what she had read at the weekend, which had of course been nothing.

It is the most peculiar supper Marianne has ever enjoyed, so rich that it brings on her acid indigestion. Afterward, they sit around the hearth sipping Fortnum's port from glasses etched with leaping reindeer, which Otto digs out from behind the bar. Dora presents Marianne with a pale-green woolen shawl, Beatrice with a new collection of stories by Katherine Mansfield, and Otto, so hard to buy for, a new toasting fork.

As Beatrice distributes her gifts, she releases an excited burp in the middle of a sentence, and they laugh like schoolchildren. "I've only ever bought presents for my parents," she says. "I hope I got it right."

Otto receives a gramophone recording of Mendelssohn, Dora a copy of *A Room with a View*, and Marianne a pair of sturdy leather gloves.

"Warmer than your woolen ones, I hope, Marianne—and more waterproof," says Beatrice, smiling.

Marianne knows how worried Beatrice has been about the episode with the Ouija board and how it might fracture the precious bond of the Eights; tonight her relief is palpable.

When Marianne hands out her own gifts, she is ashamed of the brown paper she has stamped by hand, using ink and a potato she bought from the grocer on North Parade. The blue-black stars are, she reflects, unevenly blotted like bruises.

"I'm sorry, it's not much," she says, studying the progress of the reindeer around her glass.

As her friends read their gifts there is an ominous silence.

Otto leaps up and hugs Marianne. "How on earth did you find a poem to suit an illiterate mathematician? No wonder you were typing all week long."

"I kept having to start again. I'm a terrible typist," laughs Marianne.

"It's beautiful, thank you so much," says Dora, eyes glassy with tears. "At the end, where it says, 'And laughter, learnt of friends,' it describes the Eights perfectly."

Beatrice holds her frame at arm's length to admire it. "Gosh, Marianne, I think you have won."

And then it is Otto's turn. Two of the gifts are shop-wrapped in brilliant crimson paper and bows. Lipstick and powder puff for an ecstatic Dora, bicycle panniers for an equally delighted Beatrice. Marianne's is an envelope that reads: *For use at Blackwell's bookshop.* Inside is a neatly folded one-pound note, significantly more than Otto has spent on the others. When Marianne looks up at her in wonder and embarrassment, Otto shakes her head sternly and they laugh and hug. Yes, Marianne is rather drunk, and is fearful and excited about going home, but these women! It is no surprise that the noun *friend* is derived from an ancient root word meaning *to love*, that it is etymologically bound to the word *free*. These marvelous women give her the confidence that what she is doing is right.

Looking across the room at their smiling faces, Marianne wonders if now is the time to tell her friends the truth, but it is only a very brief moment of temptation that—thankfully—snuffs itself out as soon as it flutters into life.

HILARY TERM

16

The first few weeks of Hilary are dreadfully cold and, for once, long skirts are useful. It is easy to conceal an extra pair of stockings or even double up on bloomers. Hems are on the rise but still rub heavily against the legs when wet, and beneath her thick cotton stockings Beatrice has chafing on her calves to prove it. The leather soles of her new shoes (championed by Otto) are damp and the T-bars bite unrelentingly into her ankle flesh. You can either *wear clothes* or you can't, according to her mother. Better off with a solid pair of oxfords next time.

Tickets for today's lecture, "Opportunities for the League of Nations" by Lord Robert Cecil, have been hard to procure but Beatrice has managed it, queuing doggedly the previous day until her nose resembled a misshapen plum. She spent most of the Christmas vac counting down the days until the start of term, writing long, meandering letters to each of the Eights listing her ideas for outings in Hilary term.

The Sheldonian Theatre provides welcome respite from the wind and they arrive early to ensure they are seated together. Designed by Christopher Wren in 1664, it is shaped like a D in homage to the open-air theaters of ancient Rome. A neoclassical wonder of golden eagles, thrones, and lions, it has a thirty-two-paneled painting on the ceiling. Beatrice considers it quite magnificent, and even though they were not permitted to matriculate inside the Sheldonian with the men, she is comforted by the fact that the Eights will receive their degrees there in three years' time.

"Each panel was painted in London and brought to Oxford by barge. The ceiling looks like a fresco, but it's hiding ugly crossbeams. So clever," says Miss Turbott, the chaperone. "Christ is the one with the halo. He's leading the triumph of learning over ignorance. That's represented by the fellow with the snakes in the, um, state of undress."

Beatrice agrees, the ceiling is remarkable indeed. Around the edge, a painted awning, lustrous in auburn satin folds, is drawn back by cherubim to reveal classical figures representing the arts and sciences—women and men—seated on a wreath of charcoal clouds. Inside this circle, the clouds are radiant hues of gold, and in the central panel, a winged angel holds aloft what appears to be a combusting star.

Miss Turbott is an eager tour guide, panting like an elderly dog at the end of a walk. A retired teacher, she is burdened with Victorian corsetry and equally constrictive morality. She is not the worst of the bunch, Beatrice admits, but it is irksome that she must be there at all when the men are free to come and go as they please. Miss Turbott sighs and fusses over who should sit at the far end and settles on Marianne, whom she considers the least likely to engage in *indecorous fraterniza- tion* with the enemy.

She lowers herself down, all lumpy folds, like a bulky quilt pressed into a small trunk. "Marianne dear, budge up. I do dislike benches. So lacking in boundaries."

"Perhaps she'll knit herself a blanket and fall asleep," Beatrice whispers.

"She's got the knitting out again?" replies Otto. "On the front row? Mortifying."

But Beatrice knows Otto doesn't care one jot what people think. She likes being looked at.

Otto yawns, with a flash of sharp little teeth. "Was it necessary to get here quite so early?"

"The circle seats are the best," says Beatrice. "This League is going to stop future wars. You never know, we might read this lecture in textbooks one day."

———◇———

MARIANNE WATCHES YOUNG MEN IN gowns surge down the aisles and file into the rows of wooden seats, stuffing winter coats and scarves beneath them as they sit. They light cigarettes and chat to friends in the row behind. Handshakes and names are lobbed about like tennis balls. Necks crane upward to steal glances at the women. The air is heavy and male—hair oil, stale smoke, damp tweed, leather, coal dust, the sweetly sour smell of warm bodies. The room heats up quickly.

They are seated in the center of the curve, facing the lectern and organ, a five-woman archipelago in a sea of men. Miss Turbott's knitting needles begin a regular *clickety-click*. Her puffy hands look unexpectedly elegant as her index finger reaches for the loose woolen thread before deftly trapping and entwining it in something greater than itself. Marianne envies her this distraction, wishing she, too, could conjure a little woolen barricade. It is possible that she will become a chaperone in the future. The thought is not so bad. She welcomes the time when she no longer cares if she is noticed.

It is strange, being back in Oxford after such a quiet Christmas at home, and Marianne's anxiety has returned. She has not drunk or eaten much for fear of needing the lavatory and now she is thirsty. It is never easy to find a convenience for women in a thousand-year-old institution built entirely for men. She is squashed awkwardly between Otto and a strapping sandy-haired fellow in a college scarf. Above their heads, naked babies with chubby thighs frolic with daisy chains in a dirty teal sky. She cannot look at them. To give him credit, the man appears equally flustered, drawing up his long legs in order not to touch her skirts until his knees almost hit his chin.

He must be about six foot four, Marianne estimates, and his cheeks are liver red.

He surprises her by turning courteously to face the group.

"Good afternoon to you all," he says. "It's splendid to see ladies represented here. My sister hopes to come up next year."

Miss Turbott, counting stitches at the other end of the row, is quite oblivious. Despite herself, Marianne can't help but glimpse sideways at her neighbor. His face has deeper lines than she expected, but these are familiar etchings: he is not blushing after all. It is red scale that snakes down the side of his face. He has no ear on one side and a fist-size patch of hair missing above the remaining gash.

"Tell her St. Hugh's is the place to be if you want to freeze to death," says Otto.

The man laughs with a hoot-hoot-honk that results in relieved smiles all round.

"My name is Hadley, Henry Hadley, of Christ Church," he says to the group, and, much to Marianne's horror, he looks at her expectantly.

When she doesn't say anything, Otto sighs in exasperation. "I'm Ottoline Wallace-Kerr, this is Marianne Grey. St. Hugh's."

"Miss Wallace-Kerr," repeats Henry Hadley, nodding. "Miss Grey. Is this your first year at Oxford?"

Marianne glances at Otto, but just when she needs her, Otto is leaning forward to answer a question from Miss Turbott.

Fortunately, Henry Hadley continues speaking. "I've had a few years out. Hence, I look like an old donkey compared to these young bucks. Had rather a long stint in hospital after the war. In London."

She meets his gaze for the first time. "I'm sorry to hear that," she says, flustered. "I mean, not about London."

"I hate London, Miss Grey. Apologies if you live there, but it's not for me."

"I don't know it very well," she says, noticing he has a book poking out of his pocket and wondering what it is. "I grew up near Abingdon."

"Oh, that's a beautiful part of the countryside," he says with warmth.

How strange, she thinks, that this conversation with Henry Hadley should feel so easy.

"What are you studying?" he asks, and seems genuinely interested.

"English Literature," she says, before Otto interrupts.

"Oh, Marianne is the cleverest girl at St. Hugh's. She has the only exhibition."

"Well, bravo, Miss Grey," says Henry Hadley.

Marianne flushes. "And yourself?"

"I was a chemist, but now I've changed to Law. I wanted something less—volatile." He laughs with a slightly more restrained hoot-hoot-honk.

Marianne is curious at how the inane little threads are already entwining into an acquaintance. Miss Turbott coughs, waggling her needles at them, and Henry Hadley grimaces apologetically and the introductions cease.

"There are more women on the ceiling than in the room," observes Beatrice.

"Forget the women, there's one of those idiots from Balliol in the stalls. He's going bald. Serves him right," says Otto.

"See that woman in the third row," says Beatrice. "That's Vera Brittain from Somerville. And her friend Holtby. Terribly bright. Both nursed in France in the war. Apparently, Brittain saved her own brother's life, only to lose him in Italy. And then her fiancé died of his wounds." Otto pinches her arm. "Ouch. Oh. I'm so sorry, Dora. I'm an idiot."

"Don't be silly," replies Dora. "It's fine. Really. I heard the fiancé was a poet. Terribly good. He was in the Fourth Oxfordshire like George."

"I adore her hair," says Otto. "That wave is called the Peter Pan shingle. It's all over *Pan* and *Vogue* right now."

Dora cranes her head for a look. "Somerville women are so intimidating."

"Well, they do have their own entrance exam," says Beatrice.

"Somerville is filled with terribly clever and resourceful types who protest about all sorts of things." Otto yawns. "They particularly loathe the Treaty of Versailles."

Beatrice looks indignant. "I protested against the Treaty of Versailles."

"We know, Beatrice, you protest about everything."

They nudge each other fondly and Marianne, careful to maintain her distance on the bench, allows herself another glance sideways. Henry Hadley is suppressing a smile.

IN THE SOPORIFIC AIR, DORA feels a little drunk. Otto lights a cigarette and Dora watches the smoke trail upward to the ceiling of the auditorium, where it mingles with hundreds of other little smoke trails into an oblivion of haze. Beatrice produces a small paper bag of humbugs. Marianne declines but their new acquaintance, Henry Hadley, takes one. Miss Turbott is dozing, her top lip reverberating gently on the exhale. Dora cannot help but conclude that to come to Oxford and be judged on one's brain and not looks, to make such friends, to be encouraged to think for oneself, to become immersed in poetry, architecture, beauty, and truth . . . it is simply perfect, is it not?

Her roaming gaze settles on the back of a head in the stalls. Even now, grief is a persistent, thorny bramble eager to snag and draw blood. She takes the path around it whenever possible. Still, her heart beats a little faster. She knows that close-up this boy will look nothing like Charles, but she enjoys exploring the feeling—the thrill—of it. Strangely, it is always Charles she imagines she sees, not her brother, which is odd as she knew one all her life and the other for merely a few months. Once she followed a chap from Blackwell's along St. Giles' all the way into the Taylorian. She simply had to go in after him and ask him the time, and of course he was nothing like Charles. They were standing right under the clock in the entrance, and he stared back at her as if she were mad. She desperately wanted to lean forward and trace the tiny undulations of his tweed jacket with her finger. Another time she thought she saw Charles in a group of students looking at shrunken heads in the Pitt Rivers Museum and laughing about which one they would resemble if they were dried out and hung on a string like a gruesome puppet. Her first thought was of engineering a meeting with him so that they might have the chance to fall in love. She smiles at the absurdity of it.

It intrigues her, the idea that there is a woman who is her double going earnestly about another life in another city or another country, or perhaps speaking another language. The world must contain many doppelgängers, she muses. Dumas, Collins, Twain, and Dickens certainly thought so.

As they wait for the speaker to arrive, the afternoon sun dips below the base of the tall windows that surround the entire upper level, with the exception of the marvelous organ and its long pipes standing to attention. The room darkens perceptibly, the paintwork a little less gloss, a little more matte. There is a pause, a moment between thoughts and heartbeats when Dora has a queer sinking feeling as if she has been pierced by a shard of hopelessness. But it passes in a second. It always does.

And then, something unexpected.

"Buns. I say, Buns, is that you?" Henry Hadley, next to Marianne, shouts down through cupped hands to the stalls below. Charles's double turns and stares up at their group, eyes swiveling for purchase. Dora is surprised by how much he does actually resemble Charles. Older, of course, and thinner, but the similarity is there.

He shouts back to Hadley, "Hadley, you old rogue, how's the ear? Are you at a women's college now? Meet me outside after." The man signals the door with a wave of the finger, smiles lazily up at them, and turns to face the front.

Lord Robert Cecil, the lecturer, is mounting the stage. Applause and hearty cheers reverberate around the theater, making the wooden benches vibrate. Dora's legs prickle.

"What a splendid coincidence. We were in the Devil's Own Regiment together," says Henry Hadley to the group. He raises his voice to be heard over the clapping.

"What did you say? The Devil's Own?" says Dora, her eyes clamped on the head below, where waves of dark hair circle clockwise around the crown. "Tell me, who is that?"

"Charles Baker. We used to call him Buns. A pal from the war. We met in Berkhamsted at officers' training—1917, that would have been. Do you know him?"

Her throat tightens, and she gasps for breath.

"Is this a joke?" she says, standing up.

"Dora, what is it?" says Marianne.

"I say, is your friend quite well?" says Hadley.

"Miss Greenwood, you should sit down," says Miss Turbott.

Dora is pushing past them, stumbling, treading on feet, books, coats. She moves instinctively, eyes pinging repeatedly to the stalls below until she finds herself at the top of the stairwell. Facing her is the head of a golden lion with a sheaf of rods protruding from his mouth. He looks as if he is choking. Her hands are shaking. They feel terribly cold. She leans on the metal stair rail, suddenly weak. The lecturer is unfolding his papers and a hush descends. From this angle, the paneled ceiling is distorted. The ring of cloud looks like a gaping sore fringed with dark flesh, yellow pus at its core. The awning, a scab that has been picked away by grotesque cherubim.

There is pain behind her left eye—not a stabbing as such, more a relentless pushing and pushing. When she shuts her eyes, she is in the hallway at her parents' house, her hands opening the letter. She retches.

The choking lion says, "He is dead. He is dead. He is dead."

The cherubs reply, "He lives. He lives. He lives."

17

France
November 22, 1917

Dear Miss Greenwood,
It is with deepest regret that I must inform you of the death of
Lieutenant Charles J. A. Baker of the 5th Battalion of the
Royal Berkshire Regiment.

Lt. Baker was killed yesterday after leading an attack
against the enemy. He died bravely defending his country
and was a credit to all who knew him.

Lt. Baker asked me to write to you in the event of his
death. Sadly, he had not yet informed his parents of your
engagement. It was his dear wish that you refrain from
contacting them should the worst occur. He was concerned
that his failure to impart the news might add greatly to their
suffering.

Charles was a loyal friend and his loss is a great blow to
us all. He spoke of you often and with great fondness.

Yours,
Captain L. P. Ferryman
5th Battalion of the Royal Berkshire Regiment

The next morning, Beatrice types a note to Mr. Charles Baker of Queen's College stating that she is trying to locate a Charles J. A. Baker from London, formerly of Rugby School and the Royal Berkshire Regiment. Beatrice asks that if she has the right person, please would he meet her at the Botanic Garden at ten a.m. the next day for news of "a most delicate and personal nature."

When they half carried Dora away from the Sheldonian the evening before, Beatrice could barely register what she was saying. She flailed and fought to be allowed to reenter the building and Otto had to slap her. Goodness knows what happened to Miss Turbott. When Dora started raving about the Ouija board bringing back the dead, Otto hailed a cab. Miss Kirby, the vice principal, had to call out the doctor, who administered a sedative.

"She's certain it's him," says Beatrice, drawing her hands into her coat sleeves. She is waiting with Marianne outside the little bakery in North Parade.

"It might not be him," replies Marianne. "It could all be a misunderstanding."

They shuffle toward each other and turn their backs on the icy needling of the wind, until Otto steps out of the doorway clutching a box of cakes with which to tempt Dora.

"He looks the same, has the same name, the same nickname, he was in Berkhamsted at the same time, he's in the same regiment, and he's at Oxford," Otto says. "I think that is evidence enough."

The others nod reluctantly and begin the short walk along Banbury Road back to college. The sky is drab and unpromising; the wind continues to badger them, relentless.

"But Dora has a letter from a captain, saying he'd been killed," says Marianne. "I've seen it."

Beatrice fishes in her bag for her gloves. "I've read it too, but he was Charles's close friend, apparently. Although she wrote back, she never heard from him again. I think she assumed they were *both* dead."

She shifts sideways to allow two expensively dressed matrons to pass. They appraise her with appalled expressions and mutter to each other. Something about her height, no doubt.

"Did she check the announcements?" asks Otto.

"She told me she never saw his death listed in the *Times*," says Marianne.

Beatrice sighs. "Her brother died shortly after. She could easily have missed it."

"Or it wasn't ever there." Otto withdraws her cigarette case from a pocket, its greyhound still engaged in an eternal gallop. They stand on the corner of St. Margaret's Road while she struggles to light a match. "So either he faked his death, or his death was mistakenly assumed."

"There could have been a ghastly mix-up," suggests Marianne. "He might not have any idea that Dora thinks he is dead."

Otto snorts. "I know you like to believe the best in people, Marianne, but I highly doubt it."

"Perhaps he thought she was better off without him. Or he's maimed in some way that we can't see." Marianne shrugs.

"You mean he got his bits blown off? If only."

"Memory loss?" offers Beatrice, but she does not believe it.

"Just out of hospital?" suggests Marianne.

"Or he is a selfish bastard who simply changed his mind. He would never have expected to see Dora in Oxford." Otto, shivering now, motions to suggest they keep walking.

They turn down St. Margaret's Road and pick up a brisker pace along the avenue of lime trees. Dozens of spidery legs sprout from the bases of swollen trunks.

Beatrice lowers her voice as a sallow-faced nanny passes with a perambulator. "But the chances of being found out are high. Why not just send a letter ending it?"

"That's the big question. Why allow your fiancée to grieve for you?" asks Otto.

"You'd only do that if you didn't care about the person or the consequences, I suppose," says Beatrice.

"From what Dora said, they were madly in love." Marianne steps through the gates into college and gestures toward the lodge. "I'll sign us back in. Won't be a moment."

Otto takes a step through the gates and pauses halfway. She turns back to Beatrice. "There's a mathematical term called 'degrees of freedom.' It refers to the numbers of variables possible in the final calculation of a statistic. What I'm saying is, we can theorize all we like about what happened, there are many different variables, but it doesn't change the fact that he is back."

Beatrice hovers on the pavement. She may have longed since girlhood to be trusted with other women's secrets, but she never understood until this moment what a responsibility it is. "I'll take the letter to Queen's myself," she says. "Right now."

——◇——

IT IS FIVE-THIRTY P.M. AND the twilight has dissolved into darkness. A handful of stars blink and falter, unable to compete with the smoking chimney pots. Even if Charles does return to Queen's, Dora may not be able to recognize him from her position in the narrow lane across the High Street. And what on earth would she do if he appeared anyway?

That morning, all she could think about was seeing him. The thought of waiting another day was incomprehensible, and her limbs ached with a twitching energy. Skipping Divvers class, she left college without telling the others because she did not want to hear their opinions, however well meant. The fuss over eating and cakes was just too much. But now she is stiff and exhausted and her head aches. After three hours, it is pointless to wait any longer.

Wearily, she deserts her post beneath the little windowed bridge over Logic Lane and turns left up the High, calculating it will take her around thirty-five minutes if she returns via the cobbled square of the Radder to Parks Road. The dinner bell won't ring until seven twenty-five p.m. but she regrets not having brought her bicycle; she is breaking the university statute by being out without permission and without a chaperone. Fearing being spotted and reported to the principal, she takes off her gown and cap and pushes them into her satchel, wondering why she has not thought of this earlier.

The entrance to Radcliffe Square is so busy that she fears she may be recognized. Panicking, she continues up the High until she reaches the Covered Market. It is a longer route but more "town" than "gown" and she could pass easily as a young woman going about her business, a seamstress perhaps, or a servant at one of the colleges. Her clothes will not betray her; it is hard to see the quality of dark academic wear at the best of times.

The tang of blood and sawdust is unmistakable as she enters the market through the half-closed gates. Stalls and shop fronts are closing, the quiet at odds with the usual vibrancy of the place. Men in filthy aprons heave crates onto metal trolleys, grunting instructions to each other. Some stare, hands on hips, dangling cigarettes from the corners of their mouths, but others ignore her, eager to get home out of the cold. Frightened of encouraging lewd comments, she walks faster, her heels rubbing on the lumpy seams of her boots. Carcasses of animals hang upside down in darkened windows, eyeballs white, tongues lolling. A door slams behind her. She tells herself it is nothing. Ahead of her, rats scoot under tarpaulins. She shudders, lowers her head, and presses on out of the market.

Turning into Turl Street, she passes Jesus on the left and Exeter on the right. The road is empty ahead but is lit by the glow of college rooms on either side. Perhaps Charles is in one of those sets right now, visiting a friend. Risen from the dead. She senses a pedestrian joining the pavement in her wake, thinking nothing of it at first, until she feels someone closing in on her as she crosses Broad Street. She stops and pretends to look in the windows of Blackwell's bookshop, trying to master herself. It is not even six o'clock, she says to herself, nothing bad happens at six o'clock. In the reflection, her face looks pale and distorted against a display of lurid yellow book jackets. *The Tragic Bride.* Behind her a dark figure is approaching. She turns around to defend herself, mouth opening to shout for help, but the man has already passed. He is entering the White Horse. The door to the pub swings shut, exhaling warm, beery air.

Wondering at her own stupidity, she turns left toward the Museum of Natural History. Parks Road is busy with bicycles and cars and her hips settle into a comforting rhythm. She recalls visiting the ammonites and dinosaur remains with Beatrice and seeing Mary Anning's ichthyosaur fossil with its supper of fish bones preserved in its rib cage, Beatrice telling her how important it is that women seek equal citizenship of the mind. But there is no equality of mind between her and Charles. Quite the opposite, in fact. Her reality for the last three years has been a fiction of his making.

But what if he has a twin brother?

Or he was injured and lost his memory?

Perhaps he was mistakenly reported dead and when she stopped writing he assumed she no longer loved him?

What if it is all her own fault?

Thoughts circle and dive like carrion crows.

And then, a few minutes from the safety of the lodge, she is assailed. From the shadows of the leafless trees that fringe the Parks, two figures block her path.

"Dora, is that you? For God's sake, we've been worried sick," says Otto.

Marianne opens her arms and Dora steps into them.

18

Overnight, the city is muffled with a heavy fall of snow. Marianne's dilemma about whether to catch the first train to Culham or remain to support Dora is resolved for her when Miss Jenkins, the head porter, announces that Oxford station is closed. Marianne prays for a thaw so that she can travel later in the afternoon.

At least she sleeps more easily now that a telephone has been installed at the rectory by the diocese. She is comforted that her father or Mrs. Ward can contact college in an emergency, and if she had to get home quickly, nine miles is not so bad. In decent weather she could cycle it in an hour, walk it in three.

Only twice has she glimpsed faces she recognizes from the village: a farmhand driving cattle to Oxpens and an elderly couple clinging to each other outside the Radcliffe Infirmary. On neither occasion did she need to drag the Eights away; there was no danger of being engaged in conversation by her father's parishioners, they would never recognize her cycling along in her cap and gown. The arrangement is working and, in many ways, she does not want it to end; she doubts she will ever know such freedom again.

After breakfast, the plan is to set off immediately for the

Botanic Garden. Whether Charles Baker will be there, they do not know, but Dora is jittery and keen to leave. She refuses to come to the dining hall for breakfast and the three go alone, sitting apart at the end of a table.

"I doubt she slept," says Marianne, regretting that she did not offer to bed down on Dora's floor.

"All this shaking and crying is a worry. She's usually so— composed," says Beatrice. "You know she has her Responsion on Monday? We should leave straightaway."

"It's going to be bloody hard work getting there," says Otto, looking out of the window. Marianne follows her gaze. It is as if the gods have tossed a white sheet over the terrace. She wonders if the children are playing on the village green, pelting snowballs at each other from behind the wall of the churchyard.

They swallow their cold toast and coffee quickly and take some back for Dora. Marianne gratefully accepts the loan of a sturdy pair of boots from Beatrice. She stuffs the ends with newspaper.

AT FIRST, THE NATURE OF their mission distracts from the cold, each woman wrapped in her thoughts. They walk carefully, slipping occasionally and grabbing at each other, sweating within their woolen layers. The streets are so quiet that Marianne half expects to encounter medieval scholars trudging along as they must have done when the university was no more than a cluster of monasteries and orchard gardens. They, too, would have looked up at bell towers rendered white and seen a skyline drawn on fresh paper with a single sweep of charcoal.

By the time they reach Broad Street the light is watery, and the warmth of the limestone has dulled to a cool gray. A few hardy locals skid around on bicycles, but the snow is four inches deep and falling. The city is in ceasefire.

After nearly an hour, they arrive at their destination, puffing and ruddy-cheeked. The Botanic Garden sits below Magdalen Bridge, butting up on the river. Marianne clings to the icy railings as she descends the path, wading through deeper cushions of drift blown off the street. Cold slices through her new gloves. In front of her, Otto is muttering to Beatrice, and Dora is picking her way through the snow.

The entrance is through an elaborate archway. Known as the Danby Gate, it is decorated with stripes of rusticated stone, statues, shields, and other trimmings of seventeenth-century pride. Marianne always finds it curious that on the garden side, the arch is so plain and unadorned, it looks like a different structure altogether.

"A thousand years ago this was a Jewish cemetery," says Beatrice, pointing at the ground.

"Not very helpful," hisses Otto.

Fortunately, Dora, staring through the archway into the garden, does not hear.

They pause in the shelter of the arch, stamping off snow from their boots and shaking off their skirts. The last time Marianne visited, the air was fragrant, even in November, but today there is nothing to smell, not even witch hazel. She recalls that the garden was established to grow medicinal herbs. Dora is badly in need of some chamomile or lavender right now; in fact, they all are.

Ahead of them, the beech trees are heavy with snow, in the way that flour is lifted on the flat of a knife. Firs hang low in white forked claws. To the left, the glass conservatory creates a striking contrast. Spiky palms, waxy citrus fruits, and portly orchids bask inside. Beyond, smaller hothouses of water lilies and ferns overlook the river. The Cherwell has ceased its usual chatter, the surface locked in an icy crust.

A single set of footprints leads from the entrance straight up the central pathway.

"I don't think those come from a gardener's boot," says Otto.

The prints indicate a smooth sole and a square heel.

Marianne takes Dora's gloved hand and squeezes it as best she can.

He is here.

———◇———

AS THEY FOLLOW THE FOOTPRINTS up the path, Dora shivers uncontrollably. Her teeth rattle so hard that her skull itches behind her ears.

A robin hops onto the back of a bench and watches as they make their way up the central avenue to the main pond. Apart from this one curious bird, all is still. The pond reminds Dora of an eye glazed with a cataract; it has a fat stone lip around the outside, and in the center, jets of water have frozen in a pale-blue blob.

The footprints lead through an opening in a brick wall to a rear garden with a smaller pond. A man is standing at the back of the plot, looking out onto Christ Church Meadow, where students are gathering for a snowball fight. Distant voices echo from behind the trees. He coughs and lights a cigarette, discarding the match on the ground. His head is uncovered, the tips of his ears pink beneath thick, dark hair. He wears a navy-and-white-striped college scarf.

Beatrice shifts uncomfortably. "Would you like me to speak to him?"

"No," replies Dora, although it comes out as a croak. She takes a few tentative steps toward the man, treading carefully alongside his footprints. All she can hear is the rasp of her breath and the squeak of her boots. Beneath her coat, though, her heart is pounding hard into her sternum.

"Charles."

He turns. The frozen skin of the pond lies between them. No-man's-land.

"Hello. Miss Sparks, I take it? I got your note." There is a gleeful shout behind him. He glances over his shoulder.

"Charles, don't you recognize me?" says Dora. She pulls the scarf from her chin and slides her hat down the side of her head.

"I'm sorry, I—" His handsome face twists as if he has been punched. "Dora? My God."

"I'm so glad you're alive," she says gently, as if to avoid startling him. It is him. Her Charles. Made in flesh; the same dimple carved in the chin, the same four limbs, intact.

"I'm sorry," he says, putting his hand to his temple. "I need a minute to think."

"Of course," she says politely, wishing she had something to lean on. While the garden sways about her, perfectly formed snowflakes drift down like confetti. She feels both terrified and euphoric.

"Let's walk over here," he says, collecting himself.

She cannot stop looking at him. He glances at Otto, Marianne, and Beatrice watching from the entrance, then walks away from the pond to the back of the garden, where a gravel path runs parallel with the fence. She follows.

"How did you find me?" he asks quietly as she joins him on the path. His eyes are not able to meet hers. She notices that one of his eyebrows is quivering.

"I'm a student at St. Hugh's," she says. "I saw you at a lecture."

"Oh—"

He seems far more bewildered than she is. His eyes flit back to her friends. For a moment, she wonders if he is about to bolt.

"I— How are you, Dora?"

"I am—well." What else can she say? Inside her a pressure is building, like a kettle on the hob. She cannot keep it from boiling. "I thought you were dead," she blurts out.

He looks at his feet, miserably. "Ah."

It disconcerts her that he has so little to say. She searches his face for clues. It has lost the roundness of youth; his features are harder, his skin papery. He is shaking with cold, or perhaps it is a tremor, she cannot tell. Yellowing nails, chipped front tooth, a thin mustache. Did he have a mustache in 1917?

"Are you well?" she asks eventually.

He nods.

"What have you been doing? I mean, since we last met."

"Didn't get out until 1919, then went to Italy for a spell to get my head straight. Wasn't sure Oxford was for me, but the parents wanted it."

"Italy," she says to herself.

"Yes. Florence mostly."

"Were you injured?"

He pauses. "Not seriously."

"I think there has been a terrible confusion—" she begins, but then she is back in the practice trench in her blush silk with the olive-green sash, kissing him for the first time. She takes a step toward him. "I'm so glad you are alive."

He smiles tightly and says nothing. They stand looking out over the frozen Cherwell and she waits.

Eventually, he speaks. "Dora, it's very hard for me to explain what happened. I'm not sure I even understand it myself."

"Please try."

"France." He dusts snow from the top of the fence. "It—changed my mind."

"About me?"

"About marriage. About the world. Everything."

"I don't understand," she says.

He takes a deep drag of his cigarette and tosses the butt away. "When we met, a lot of us chaps were making rash decisions. I thought you were a splendid girl, I really did, and at that moment I did want to marry you, but we only knew each other for a short while.

"We were very young, Dora, and the truth is, my parents would never have approved. But the letter my friend sent was—inexcusable, and I am truly sorry for it."

Pulling off one glove, she reaches into her inside coat pocket and holds out a crumpled piece of paper. "Are you saying this letter was not sent by mistake?"

He looks at the folded square as if it might explode and says nothing.

"You are saying you—you sanctioned it, you were not in a poor mental state?"

"A poor mental state?" He flushes and presses his lips together. He sets off walking again and she stumbles to keep up.

"I know it was hard out there—"

"I regret misleading you. It should never have happened," he says curtly.

"It should never have happened?" she repeats, horrified. She tries to suppress the tears; her throat is tight. "You wanted to end it? But you couldn't even write me a letter?"

He stops again. "You can't understand what it was like," he says, staring out over the river. His forehead is so furrowed that his eyebrows are almost touching. "Everything from before seemed irrelevant. I never expected to live, don't you see?"

She nods, though she does not see. Her feet are so cold now that her toes ache as if someone has stamped on them. The hem of her skirt is chipped with ice. She feels the weight of the darkening cloth.

"It was my friend's idea. We were drinking rum. I told him I wanted out, so he sent the letter. The next day he was blasted to bits. I expected to be next. I apologize if it caused you— unnecessary suffering."

She is aware of a thickening in her head; her fingers twitch, a heat beneath her ribs pressing outward.

"Unnecessary suffering?" she laughs, in a shrill voice she does not recognize. "I mourned for you and for the life we were to have. I was pitied and condoled, for God's sake. People sent me cards!" She tosses the letter toward him. It flutters feebly to the ground.

He kicks idly at the limp paper, then stops. More deliberately, he places his foot over it and grinds it into the snowy gravel below. "As time passed and I made it through, I regretted the deception. But what was the point in contacting you and saying, surprise, I'm still alive, but I can't marry you?"

Each word is a metal barb digging into her skin.

He looks straight at her, his voice cracking. She notices one eye is shot through with tiny red threads. "I'm so sorry, Dora, but I thought it was kinder to you to remain dead."

"Kinder?"

"No scandal, no embarrassment."

"What?"

"Look, what do you want from me, Dora? Because I can assure you, I don't have anything left to give."

"I have wasted three years mourning you. While you were— in Italy! Tell me why I should not report you to your college, or the army for fraud." She may be shouting, she cannot tell, she does not care. "If I told my father, I'm sure he would sue you."

"Whatever you went through was not as bad as what happened out there, so let's not compete on that score. There are plenty of other things that keep me awake at night, Dora, much worse than this."

She is stunned. This is not her Charles. There is a pause; he glances back toward the meadow and then speaks. His face is slack, his cheeks blotched red and white. It is as if he is reading aloud from the newspaper.

"You won't report me because it would subject you and your family to gossip and ridicule. People would say I faked my own death to escape an inappropriate liaison with a factory owner's daughter—from a market town."

"This is why?" She should have known.

She hears distant laughter. They are back at the pond where they started. Charles bends and picks up a pair of ice skates that she has not noticed before. He slings them over his shoulder.

"I'm sorry but I have to go. My friends are waiting for me."

"Is that it?" asks Dora.

He cannot meet her eye. He looks a decade older than his twenty-one years. "Look, I know it's jolly hard, but I think it's better for both of us if we don't meet again. I am sorry. Truly."

He nods at the others, climbs over the fence into the meadow, and jogs away.

"Coward!" she shouts. The syllables solidify into tiny crystals.

She looks at her friends and shakes her head. They rush to embrace her, Otto and Marianne at each shoulder, Beatrice at her back.

19

Beatrice, February 1918

In the last year of the war, having turned eighteen, Beatrice joins the Women's Volunteer Reserve. She had hoped to train as something thrilling like a motorbike rider, so the news of her deployment as a typist in the administrative section comes as somewhat of a disappointment. Still, she is proud to put on her uniform each morning, the khaki Norfolk jacket and felt hat denoting to her fellow Londoners (and more importantly, her mother) that she is doing her bit. She does not dwell on the fact that the boots and spats are strangling her feet or that it cost her four pounds to enlist. It is worth it.

On her first morning, she is so nervous and jittery that she sets off far too early and has to walk around Brunswick Square four times before the office is unlocked. When she finally enters the narrow town house on Ampton Street—a crumbling white building on three floors that juts out like a wanton tooth—she is forced to proffer a very sweaty handshake. She is introduced to two typists her own age, Miss Gowar and Miss Dixon, and the secretaries, suffragette sisters known as the Misses Higginbottom, who are notorious around Bloomsbury for forcing white feathers on unsuspecting young men. The office manager, Miss Spinnett, is a gaunt, restless woman who marches about the room smoking and tossing documents into in-trays. She sets Beatrice to work typing letters near the door, at a rickety table that is barely wide enough to hold a type-writer.

"Sorry," says Miss Spinnett, pulling a face. "Last in gets the drafty spot."

"Oh, I quite understand," Beatrice replies hastily, jamming her unwilling knees beneath the table.

"I highly recommend fingerless mittens and a flannel vest," advises the younger Miss Higginbottom. "And perhaps a scarf."

Beatrice's fingers are trembling and clumsy to begin with and two of her letters are returned for retyping: one asking a local congregation to fund a tea stand in Dover ("a last taste of home") and another seeking donations of clothes for Serbian orphans.

"Mistakes on stocklists and invoices can be corrected by hand," Miss Spinnett says as she breezes by. "But letters need to be as close to perfect as possible."

"I'm so sorry." Beatrice's face burns as she hunches over the typewriter and berates herself for not being more careful.

"You'll get the hang of it," says Miss Gowar cheerfully. "Cof-fee? I must warn you, though, it's ghastly stuff."

Miss Gowar is not wrong about the coffee, but Beatrice gulps down the warm liquid gratefully. She would drink poison if they asked her to and not question it, so determined is she to fit in. As she flicks through the swollen card-index box for the necessary addresses for her letters, a wiry mouse sprints across the floor. Beatrice gives a little gasp and looks about her to see who else has noticed.

"Oh, don't mind Herbert," says the older Miss Higginbottom. "He's a friendly fellow."

The air is soon thick with cigarette smoke, jasmine per-fume, shouted telephone conversations, and the hammering of typewriter keys. By midafternoon, Beatrice's head is thump-ing. Miss Dixon takes her to the floor above, which is a store-room run by four wisecracking women from the East End.

Their job is to receive, sort, fold, and pack the donations that arrive and depart all day long via the front door.

"Don't worry if they bite your head off," says Miss Dixon. "They're pussycats really."

"We won't do that to Miss Sparks," says one. "It's only you we don't like."

Miss Dixon sticks out her tongue and the women cackle.

"You need to watch your 'ead on the stairs," says another, nodding sagely at Beatrice. "The postman knocked himself out cold once." They all laugh uproariously and Beatrice is careful to join in.

She discovers that one of her jobs is to run up and down between the two rooms with messages, a task that is not unwelcome; her legs become stiff and numb if she sits at the typewriter too long. It is also her responsibility to lock up the office each night, turn off the gas lights, empty the wastepaper baskets, rinse the cups and teapot (without soaking her cuffs— lesson learned), and lock up the petty cash. Miss Spinnett shows her what to do the first night, but as the weeks go on, Beatrice enjoys performing these practical tasks, especially when the last person leaves and she has the place to herself. The soles of her feet burn by the end of the day and when she is alone she can take off her boots and put on the pair of fur-lined slippers she keeps in her bag. Although the job is often a dull slog, she enjoys interacting with the other women and sees the discipline of typing all day as good preparation for university. She passed the Oxford Senior last year, so she only has the entrance examination to cram for now, which she will sit as soon as the war ends. In the evenings, she practices writing essays that might impress the tutors at St. Hugh's. She sleeps like a horse that has keeled over in the street.

At lunchtimes, she returns home to eat whatever Cook has left out for her, pulling her chair up to the fire and roasting her toes like chestnuts. If there is time, she visits the lending library on the way back. Her co-workers are a decent bunch;

the Misses Higginbottom play a lot of bridge and take care of their elderly parents. Miss Gowar and Miss Dixon are excitable girls who do everything together, including walking out with a pair of student doctors from Guy's Hospital and wearing the same cloying French perfume. Occasionally, they invite Beatrice to the pictures or to a café and she gratefully accepts, imagining how pally the trio must look to others, strolling along in their matching uniforms. In return, she types letters for the pair when they want to leave early. However hard she tries, though, she cannot insert herself into the tightly bound pages of their friendship. She does not follow movie stars, or own a powder compact, or dream of marrying a doctor, hence she always feels on the outside of their conversations. When she overhears Miss Gower telling Miss Dixon that "Beatrice is a good old stick but far too clever for us," she is not surprised. She can only hope that if she gets into St. Hugh's, Oxford is the place where she will finally fit.

IN FEBRUARY 1918, WHEN BEATRICE has worked at the WVR for three months, the Representation of the People Act finally becomes law and eight million women in Britain get the vote. It is a day of reminiscences, relief, and jubilation and, although the office closes at noon in celebration, very little work is done that morning. Mrs. Pankhurst has declared there should be no marches or public displays of victory at a time when the nation is steeped in mourning, so Beatrice's mother, recently returned from America, holds a private luncheon at home. After the office shuts, everyone goes to a café together—a rare treat paid for by the WVR—toasting each other with tea and sardine sandwiches. Only the Misses Higginbottom and Miss Spinnett can actually vote, as they are over thirty and qualify for the electoral register, but all agree it is simply a matter of time before the age limit drops to that of men, twenty-one.

Although it is a wonderful day to be a woman and Beatrice

is grateful for the courage and tenacity of those who have led the campaign for suffrage, she is in no hurry to get home. She loathes her mother's riotous parties, and this is why, after lunch, she returns to the office, types all the remaining letters she can find, and then catches an omnibus to Piccadilly, where she roams about the bookshelves at Hatchards until the assistants begin glaring at her. As she plods home through the damp streets, she prays the guests will have left. She is not afraid to walk at night alone, her silhouette sufficient to put off any would-be attacker, but since the bombing of Long Acre a few weeks ago, Londoners are adhering strictly to the blackout, which means she keeps tripping on furtive curbs and doorsteps. When she finally opens the front door, harsh yellow light spills onto the pavement and she is hit by a sickly blend of hot wax, cigars, and incense. Piles of newspapers, coats, and bags litter the hall and animated conversation echoes from upstairs, where someone is bashing away at the piano. She feels a rush of annoyance. Why couldn't they have gone home by now? Will the house be full of strangers? The thought appalls her. She is so much easier with people once she gets to know them.

It is only after she enters the hallway that she notices a couple embracing in the corridor that leads to the kitchen. She treads quietly along the hall and begins climbing the stairs. Halfway up, she peeps over the banister and sees that it is not a man and a woman pressed together but two women kissing hungrily, mouths wide and searching. One, with cropped hair, is holding her companion against the wall by the neck. Her other hand is up her lover's skirt, moving backward and forward, causing the woman to buck and moan. Beatrice stares for a moment, finding the scene both frightening and intoxicating. Then, terrified she will be caught spying, she dashes to the top of the stairs, where she pauses in shock to catch her breath. What astounds her most is not the sexual act itself—her mother has many friends who share their beds with women—but the desire pulsing, unbidden, from between her legs into her belly.

Once Beatrice has splashed water on her face and gathered herself, she changes her clothes and joins the party. The rest of the evening is spent in the sitting room chatting awkwardly to her parents' friends, many of whom she has never met before. She tries not to think of the women in the hallway again, because every time she does, she feels unaccountably hot and self-conscious.

Her mother staggers about, teeth stained purple, hanging off her guests, barking at the servants, and making rambling toasts to Emily Davison. "Come over here," she says, dragging Beatrice by the wrist toward a group of guests by the fireplace. "Look, look, see how tall she is. Shocking, isn't it?"

"She's perfectly statuesque," says a woman with prominent front teeth and puffy amber bags beneath her eyes. She smiles and offers her hand. "Elizabeth Rix. I was at St. Hugh's with Emily and Edith. Part of the old gang."

So this is the notorious Elizabeth Rix who chained herself to the grille of the Ladies' Gallery in the House of Commons and heckled the prime minister until both she and the grille were forcibly removed. Beatrice has collected countless newspaper articles about Miss Rix and her exploits. In 1914 Miss Rix famously took an axe to a display of Japanese teapots at the British Museum, reducing it to a pile of glittering scree. She was dragged away shouting "Votes for Women," and after that, women were no longer permitted to enter the museum unaccompanied. Miss Rix was sent to Holloway for the sixth time but was released after war broke out as part of the suffragette amnesty.

"I'm so pleased to meet you," Beatrice says. Suffrage has formed the backdrop to her youth and she is as dazzled by Miss Rix as Miss Gowar and Miss Dixon might be if they met their favorite movie star.

"So how are you spending the war, Beatrice?" asks Miss Rix. "Traveling the world drumming up support for the Empire with your mother?"

But before Beatrice can reply, her mother steps in.

"No, no, no," says Edith. "Beatrice is in the Women's Volunteer Reserve. *Typing*." She drags out the syllables of *typing* and pulls a face.

"It's where they said they needed me," Beatrice mumbles, reddening.

"Hardly changing the world, is it, though, *typing*?" laughs her mother. "Women typed before the war and will continue to type after. It's not one of those jobs that belong to men, like ticket-collecting or driving ambulances, that helped to bring about the vote."

"Oh, I think that's a bit strong, Edith," says Miss Rix. "All war work is valid. Well done to you, Beatrice."

Beatrice nods and smiles politely, turns her back on her mother, runs upstairs to her bedroom, and slams the door. She stands there panting, arms hanging at her sides, jaw clenched. All her life she has tried to please Edith Sparks. All her life she has admired her and listened to her. It would be nice to think that one day, just once, the feeling might be reciprocated and that she might make her mother proud. And in front of Miss Rix too. Unbearable.

There is a gentle knock at the door, and when Beatrice opens it, to her astonishment, Elizabeth Rix is standing right before her.

"Oh, jolly good. I didn't know which room was yours," she says brightly. "Lucky guess, I suppose."

"Oh, um, please come in," says Beatrice, aware of her uniform lying crumpled on the floor behind her.

"Oh no, that's not necessary," says Miss Rix. "I just want to give you something. Your mother tells me you are applying to St. Hugh's next year and I have an item that I think could be of use to you. I've been wanting to bequeath this particular object to the right person for a while now, and, well, tonight my intuition tells me that the right person is you."

As Miss Rix fishes in her pocket, Beatrice does not have the slightest idea what is going on. She wonders if Miss Rix will pull out her famous axe.

"This is my good-luck charm," says Miss Rix, holding up a penny. "I keep it in my pocket everywhere I go." She holds her palm out flat and nods at Beatrice to take the coin. "But now that I have the vote—oh, how wonderful it is to be able to say that—it is time I passed my lucky charm on."

Beatrice picks up the coin. The rim is worn and, as she handles it, the familiar tang of copper alloy rises. It looks quite normal: Britannia sitting erect, accompanied by her shield and trident.

"Turn it over," says Miss Rix.

On the other side, the familiar profile of Edward VII has been stamped, crudely and unevenly, with the words *Votes for Women*. The word *Women* bisects the king's throat like a ruff.

"A suffragette penny," says Beatrice, thrilled. "I've heard of them but never seen one."

"It's yours now."

"Mine?"

Miss Rix nods again and smiles.

"I don't know what to say," stammers Beatrice, aware she must look a complete idiot.

"Say nothing, just look after it and let it inspire you to never give up. Persistence is the key to change, Beatrice. Persistence and ingenuity."

"Thank you, thank you."

Beatrice stares at the penny and then at Miss Rix, who opens her mouth as if to say something further, then turns and walks away purposefully as if she might change her mind. "I stamped that one myself," she says over her shoulder before disappearing down the stairs.

Beatrice is left standing in the doorway of her bedroom, feeling for the first time in a very long while that she matters.

She presses the coin to her lips. Persistence and ingenuity. She will not forget.

20

Monday, February 7, 1921 (4th Week)

OXFORD'S AMAZONS

Not content with having votes
And scribbling down lecture notes
They cycle up the High in packs
And hog the Bodder's desks and stacks.
Plain of gown and plain of face
They're keen to dominate the place.
Their goal? Not simply just degrees
But bringing Oxford to its knees!
They will not stop until us chaps
Are wearing their square woolen caps.
They'll move into our quads of stone
And force on us their chaperones.
Resist the onslaught, yes, we must,
Lest Oxford's reputation's bust!

ISIS
WEDNESDAY, FEBRUARY 9, 1921

O tto does not last long at the hockey club, but she gives it a try to lift Dora's dismal spirits. By the time she has purchased an appropriate skirt and blouse, studded boots, and a brand-new stick via mail order, she has missed the first three practices of term. The drills, held on the lawn on Wednesday afternoons, remind her of games lessons at school. The clack of the sticks, the flap and brush of skirts, the jarring sensation that shoots up the arms when the ball is struck. She is still light on her feet thanks to the cycling and dancing, and despite the odd coughing fit, she's pleasantly surprised by how she can hold her own with the sporty girls. The third-year captain's repeated whistle-blowing needles her, though, and she loathes the feeling afterward of flaming cheeks and itchy, muddy hands.

"The whole premise of hockey is so primitive," she complains to Marianne. "Basically, one chases a rock with a stick."

It also annoys her that Dora is such a good player, despite her lackluster approach of late. The future hockey captain of St. Hugh's, no doubt, Dora is the type that Otto mocked mercilessly at school. Mostly out of jealousy, she realizes now, because she had the queer notion that the sporty, provincial sort of girls had nice families and were truly happy. Her sister Vita says it's best not to think too hard about one's deeper motives, though: that way madness lies.

What Otto does do is throw herself into her studies. Like many of the mathematicians at Oxford, she has found herself drawn to New College of late. G. H. Hardy, the brilliant new Savilian Professor of Geometry, has begun a series of lectures in which he leads his audience to a thrilling denouement in the last few minutes. He is very popular, and it is lucky for Otto that she looks the way she does, or she would never get a seat at the front. The same is true of Professor Elliott's "Theory of Functions" lectures at Magdalen. Although he is the Waynflete Chair of Pure Mathematics, Elliott is softly spoken and approachable, only becoming at all fired up when offered evidence of sloppy thinking. Otto rarely leaves his lectures without receiving a note from a fellow student inviting her to dinner or a boating trip, but she barely gives them a second thought. As she cycles off up Mansfield Road, thanks to Professor Elliott her mind is a kaleidoscope of numbers and symbols and mathematical possibilities. On lecture days, she sleeps deeply, and wakes rested.

ON A WHIM, SHE SENDS Arthur Motson-Brown a note one afternoon when she has nothing better to do.

Dear Arthur M-B,
Would you like to entertain me for tea next week? I am
dying of boredom and need amusing. I shall have to bring
an elderly, whiskered friend with me though, chap rules
decree it.

Yours,
Otto W-K

He replies by pigeon post the next morning, asking her to come on Valentine's Day at four p.m. She is in the mood to be flattered and does not mention it to the others. After all, one is not required to share everything one does with the group.

Otto wonders why she so often loses respect for her romantic conquests. The thrill of the chase rarely culminates in anything more than a desire to experience the thrill of the chase again. The last time she kissed a chap, she had found him irresistibly attractive until he professed his undying love for her. Then all she could think of was how his probing tongue reminded her of a mussel. She was forced to close her eyes when he kissed her, not because of some ensuing ecstasy but because she was trying hard not to think about shellfish.

The idea of the body as fragile and functional is something that she has been unable to jettison since nursing. Mortality is an utter bore and she prefers to ignore it, but she is still plagued with dreams of the men she saw screaming in agony at Somerville, the water pooling in the sour mouth and spilling down the side of the face onto the pillow. Occasionally, her nightmares feature Teddy with a bloody groin or the redheaded veteran she saw at the library lecture at Exeter. She spots the latter from time to time on Turl Street, and once going down a narrow alleyway near New College. He has a slight limp, and one foot is turned out. He always seems to be alone but appears comfortable with it, and that is a talent she envies.

It is for this reason that she wonders privately whether Charles Baker has told Dora anything resembling the truth. The man will have suffered terribly and most likely lost his mind and cannot bring himself to say it. As soon as Otto saw him in the Botanic Garden that morning, there was something familiar about the tautness of his face and his refusal to engage with Dora's emotions. *He is not the same man you loved,* she wanted to say to Dora. *That man, most probably, is dead.*

When Miss Jourdain gives permission for the outing, Miss Stroud agrees to come with her to Brasenose. They have reached an understanding since the episode at the dentist last term when Otto bled—and wept—all over Miss Stroud on the omnibus home. Otto bought her a box of marzipan and a new hatpin for Christmas; she finds that gifts to those in impoverished circumstances are a wise investment. Maud is another recipient of her largesse, as is Betty at the tearoom. And now she has their loyalty.

As it happens, the afternoon, in fifth week, is a disaster. Motson-Brown is not as funny or charming as she remembers and talks about himself and his accomplishments for a considerable part of the meeting. He is interested in whom she knows in London (so dull!), in Caro's wedding, in Vita's latest adventure, but not actually in her. There is no war work to boast of—he was at Eton until 1918, and the war ended before his officers' training did. Her mother once told her that men like nothing more than the attentive ear of an attractive woman, no matter what age they are, and one must make them believe they are interesting, capable, adored, but once Motson-Brown begins asking after Dora, Otto realizes it is time to go. Even Miss Stroud, who seems very taken with him at first, gets out her knitting after a while, and leaves with her umbrella hanging dejectedly by her side. As they exchange goodbyes on the cobbles in front of the college, he smiles conspiratorially and presses a folded brown postcard into Otto's hand. For St. Valentine, he says. She looks down. It is a photograph of a woman sitting on a bed, stockinged legs parted, chest exposed. Otto looks over Motson-Brown's shoulder as she returns it to the breast pocket of his jacket. She is exhausted.

She will treat Miss Stroud to a hansom cab back to St. Hugh's. They both deserve it.

———◇———

EXACTLY ONE WEEK BEFORE St. Valentine's Day, Beatrice is late for a lecture on Russian politics at Hertford College. She has been following the dreadful news about the drought and famine in the Volga region and is considering taking Russia as a specialism. Having been directed to the wrong location by a couple of students as a prank (would that happen to Dora or Otto? she wonders), she enters the lecture room late and stands at the back, catching her breath and scrabbling in her bag for a notebook and pen. The elderly don at the lectern stares at her with unconcealed irritation. The audience falls silent.

"You are late, young lady." A flush of heat sweeps over her and the room seems to expand and contract. She should never have come alone.

"I won't accept tardiness in my lectures," he says. "Please leave."

Beatrice turns toward the door, red-faced, stunned. A young man in cap and gown enters, slips past her grinning, and takes a seat.

"Gentlemen," says the don. "We should pity these poor women who have been encouraged to believe they are the intellectual equal of men." There is a ripple of amusement. "As I have said time and again, Oxford is not a finishing school."

A couple of students titter on the front row.

The don shakes his head in bemusement. "Now let us begin."

Beatrice, stung, slips through the door and wonders if she might pass out. Afraid of heaping further humiliation on herself, she sits on a bench and counts the number of paintings on the wall and tiles on the floor until she no longer feels dizzy. She is furious with herself. Miss Jourdain has drummed into them that women students have no room for error, and this is why. This sort of man, who will have voted against the new statute and fought long and hard to resist degrees for women, will never accept the evidence that women have the intellectual capacity of men. No matter how virtuous, punctual, or erudite one is, it will make no difference.

By the time she returns to college, the focus of her fury is the don, a man renowned university-wide for his view that *a woman at a lecture is a hateful sight*.

"Maybe Nanny spanked him too hard?" says Otto over supper.

"Don't give him any reason to eject you next time. And don't give up," says Marianne.

THE FOLLOWING WEEK, BEATRICE ARRIVES early after a sleepless night. Her anxiety has been heightened by publication of a poem in the *Isis* lambasting women students—and the fact that it is St. Valentine's Day. Such a timely opportunity for vitriol and mockery. She is first into the room, and despite wanting to sit defiantly on the front row, she selects a seat at the back in the corner. Women are not supposed to talk to men before or after lectures, so she is wary that some idiot may try to trip her up just to please Teacher.

The men begin to file in. Their energy is palpable, an irrepressible force. Chairs scrape on the floorboards, feet stamp, windows are closed. In the melee, a dark-haired man stalks over and tosses a sheet of paper toward her. Automatically, she holds out her hand and takes it. He does not look her in the eye. A few minutes later, a second, younger man sidesteps along her row as if he is about to sit down. He wears a scholar's gown and coughs like he has a ghastly illness. He puts something on the empty chair next to her, nods, and retreats. She is too embarrassed to turn her head and look, assuming what he has placed there is either not for her or some kind of warning. A dead mouse, perhaps, to make her scream, put there for a bet. She looks at her knees and fishes for Miss Rix's coin in her pocket. She must persist.

The don enters, barking greetings. Her hands are shaking and she adopts the body language of meek submission. She will not ask any questions, she decides, and sits low and still in her chair. Thankfully, the lecturer seems not to notice her. He begins to talk about the Romanovs, and she has to admit he is, as reputed, first-rate. After a few minutes, she feels brave enough to retrieve her notebook and pencil. She recalls the paper already in her hand, expecting an anti-suffrage leaflet, perhaps, or a cartoon. She takes a deep breath and glances down, fist prepared to clench and crumple. To her astonishment, it is a set of notes written in impossibly neat handwriting: the contents of last week's lecture on the Mongol invasions. She turns in confusion to the chair beside her. There is a small piece of paper, roughly torn. In watery blue ink are written the words *Take No Notice*. Beside it lies a hastily plucked snowdrop, still wet with dew, crumbs of earth clinging to the base.

The most exquisite and unexpected acts of kindness. From strangers. From men.

She fills her lungs again with air, and hope fizzes from her chest to her fingertips. Remaining low, she opens her notebook and writes the date.

ON FRIDAY MORNING, AFTER DIVVERS class with the chaplain of Lincoln, Beatrice and Marianne brave the pelting rain and cycle down to the Sheldonian to watch Thomas Hardy receive his honorary DLitt. At eighty years old, he sports a vigorous white mustache, lively eyes, and boots so highly polished, they flash at the hem of his robe as he walks.

Despite the inhospitable weather, the theater is crammed with students clutching novels and volumes of poetry in the vain hope of getting them signed. As the ceremony proceeds, Beatrice considers the characters this humble-looking man has conjured so vividly in her head—Bathsheba, Jude, Henchard, Tess—and is overcome with gratitude and awe. To witness this occasion with a cherished friend beside her is all she could wish for. Hardy receives a five-minute standing ovation.

Afterward, she and Marianne spend an hour in the Radder making notes on Pliny, then meet Otto as arranged at the Scala. They watch the new Chaplin picture *The Kid*, which is just Marianne's sort of thing, the sentimental tale of a tramp who raises a child abandoned by its mother, and Marianne duly sobs all the way through. Thanks to the free tea and cake, the picture house is always crowded in the afternoons, and the foyer is a good place to bump into acquaintances from other colleges, especially when it is raining outside. Beatrice is pleased to find that her story about the Russian lecture captures the attention of the group gathered within.

"You know from the moment you enter if a don is going to be pleasant or not," says Ursula Singh, a third-year from Somerville. "The smile or sneer test, we call it."

"Some of them haven't taught a woman in forty years," says her companion, whose name Beatrice does not catch.

"Or seen one naked," says Otto, biting into a piece of fruit-cake.

Ursula laughs and then her friend laughs too. Ursula is the cousin of a Punjabi princess and is daringly outspoken on the subject of Indian independence. She is also captain of the Women's Debating Society. Beatrice has admired her since last term when she single-handedly demolished two chaps from Wadham in a debate on the future of the Empire. Afterward, they went for tea and Ursula declared Beatrice "one of the least boring people I have met in Oxford," and now, whenever they are in the same room, Beatrice cannot concentrate because she is tracking Ursula's whereabouts. When Ursula is nearby it creates such a rush of nervous excitement in Beatrice, she has to bite her tongue for fear of looking a fool.

"A bit of resentment is surmountable, but ignoring women who ask questions is simply not on," says Ursula.

Beatrice nods vigorously.

"It's only the minority of dons, surely?" says Marianne.

Ursula appears not to have heard her. "I've known of girls reduced to tears," she continues. "And the principals simply bite their tongues, too afraid to rock the boat."

Today, Ursula sports her usual lemon-yellow beret and man's double-breasted jacket, which she has recommended to Beatrice on account of the "wonderfully large pockets." She is an eccentric dresser and claims to "despise clothes that are designed to subjugate females," which Beatrice finds thrilling. Ursula says that since she is so often the subject of ignorant stares, she might as well make the most of it. These are the sorts of sensible conversations about clothes Beatrice has longed to have all her life, and sometimes, in bed at night, she wonders what it would be like to kiss Ursula in a darkened hallway.

Unfortunately, Otto does not seem to like Ursula very much. She says Ursula ignores Marianne, although Beatrice is not aware of it. Plus, she is certain Otto would ignore Marianne completely if she lived on a different corridor. And Otto never gives anyone from Somerville much of a chance.

"Where is the delectable Dora today?" asks Ursula. "You lot are never apart, and I haven't seen her all term."

"Not feeling well," says Otto, giving a tight smile and buttoning her coat.

Ursula frowns. "Oh dear, still? What on earth's the matter?"

There is an awkward silence. Otto seizes a random umbrella from the bucket by the door.

"Oh, should I not ask?" says Ursula, her left eyebrow arched. "I do love a mystery."

Beatrice opens her mouth to answer, but Otto gently places her boot over Beatrice's little toe before crunching down on it.

"I say," says Beatrice, rather too loudly.

"Goodbye," says Otto, shoving Beatrice toward the door. "We'll give Dora your regards. We really must be off."

"That woman is an insufferable gossip," she hisses when they step out onto Walton Street.

"I like her," says Beatrice, looking back over her shoulder.

Otto pulls a face.

"More importantly," says Marianne, putting up her umbrella, "what *are* we going to do about Dora?"

21

Friday, March 4, 1921 (7th Week)

In seventh week, the first-years sit Divvers and the Eights are invited by Ursula to a private view of Pre-Raphaelite artworks at the Ashmolean Museum. To their horror, Miss Jourdain, an amateur watercolorist, has also been invited and will accompany the group. Formal evening wear is required, much to Marianne's distress, so Otto insists on lending her something. After rejecting Otto's more outlandish options, Marianne settles on a simple turquoise cocktail dress. It is fashionably tubular, a little short on her, but has a high neck and three-quarter-length sleeves with buttoned cuffs. Marianne hopes the outing will cheer up Dora, who continues to be withdrawn and distracted. Unsurprisingly, Dora failed the mathematics Responsion for the second time and does not seem terribly bothered. She does not want to talk about Charles's deception, refuses to tell her parents, and is attempting to behave as if nothing is wrong.

"I'm glad I know the truth," she says, even though it convinces none of them. "But my parents have been through enough."

Dora still comes to Otto's room after supper to smoke cigarettes—a new habit—but she also sleeps a good deal and often misses breakfast. Some days she is confused and angry, and other days she is filled with self-loathing. Marianne, like Otto, suspects Charles's actions may have had little to do with

Dora at all, and that in her own way, Dora is a victim of war. Every time Marianne recalls the meeting at the Botanic Garden, she cannot help but compare it to her own encounter by the riverbank. That night the river was deafening in its urgent pounding. And she could barely remember the soldier's name.

Poor Frank Collingham continues to send flowers and invitations, but Dora rarely accepts and often cancels. He has taken them all to a piano recital on the High, and on a chilly walk around Christ Church Meadow to watch Torpids. The outing was not a success; the rowers shivered miserably at their oars, and Dora asked to leave after only two races.

This evening, Otto insists Dora wear the emerald-green silk dress she tried on last term, saying it is too long for her anyway. Dora has applied lipstick and looks terribly sophisticated, even a little dangerous.

The aim of the event is to raise funds for the museum's new Coin Room, and it features works donated by local benefactors of the Pre-Raphaelites, Thomas and Martha Combe. The collection was donated by Martha on her death, and much of it is locked away. Marianne is thrilled by the opportunity to see it. She is fascinated by the Brotherhood, but Oxford's Pre-Raphaelite history is not easily accessible. The library of the Oxford Union, a society that will never admit women, contains a set of murals she longs to view in person. Based on Tennyson's *Morte d'Arthur*, they were painted by a group of artists including Rossetti and Burne-Jones. The floral ceiling design is by William Morris. Ironically, the man who wrote the words "I do not want art for a few, any more than education for a few, or freedom for a few" has created beauty for some of the most exclusive institutions in England. On three occasions, Marianne has admired the *Adoration of the Magi* tapestry by Morris & Co. in Exeter College chapel, marveling at its romance, grace, and stunning depth of color until Beatrice opines too long about the Arts and Crafts movement, and Otto insists she will die without lunch.

"THERE'S URSULA," SAYS BEATRICE, WAVING eagerly as they reach the top of the stone steps that link Beaumont Street to the museum.

Ursula, holding court at the edge of the crowd, wears a quilted smoking jacket, bow tie, and straight black skirt that ends midshin. Her dark hair, partly obscured by a porkpie hat, has been cropped close to her skull. She could easily pass as a spunky heroine in a Douglas Fairbanks picture.

"Stop gawping, Sparks," says Otto, following Miss Jourdain toward the building. The enormous ostrich feather attached to Otto's headband no longer appears quite so large against the towering columns of the museum entrance, and for once, even to Marianne's inexperienced eye, Otto is not the most remarkable woman present.

By seven it is already dark and the courtyard, lit by electric lamps and a pair of flaming torches, is shadowy and damp. They push through a thicket of conversation into the vestibule of the museum, where they are invited to leave their coats. A museum attendant leads them up a flight of marble stairs and across a room in which every detail appears to be blood-red, including the flock wallpaper and sumptuous carpets. Towering wigged aristocrats in gold frames dominate the walls, and a pianist plays Chopin's nocturnes in the corner. The lid of the grand piano is so polished that within it Marianne can see the muscular legs of a horse reflected from the portrait above. A further flight of stairs takes them up to a pair of noisy galleries, one containing oil paintings from the Combe Collection on permanent display, and the other the more fragile sketches, watercolors, and unfinished pieces that usually reside in the safety of the Print Room.

Otto daringly hands each of them a glass of champagne from a tray, starting with Miss Jourdain, who opens her mouth to say something, then accepts one and walks away.

"Well," says Otto. "That went better than I'd anticipated."

"I suppose we are off the premises," says Dora, taking a large swig.

Marianne works her way around the permanent collection. She is quite bewitched by *The Return of the Dove to the Ark* by John Everett Millais. There is something about the rapt expressions of the two little girls—Noah's daughters—and the passivity of the dove that moves her. She wonders what it must have been like for Martha Combe to host these talented men in her home and to own this collection all to herself for twenty years after her husband's death.

"Two greasy-haired children fussing over a pigeon in a barn. Next!" says Otto in her ear, passing behind her with a miserable-looking Dora in tow. Beatrice is nowhere to be seen.

The painting is so vibrant, Marianne falls easily back into its world. The sea greens and purply blues of the girls' dresses make her feel heady. Why has Millais painted these auburn-haired children in such regal colors? They are living jewels. Why has the plump dove brought the olive branch to them and not to Noah? Looking closely, she sees the myriad hues within each dress and the variety of brushstrokes. The white smock on one of the girls is actually blue and gray, green and cream; the hay at their feet so realistic, she could reach out and scratch her hand on it. She basks in the glow of the light falling from the deck above, sees the girls' stunted shadows melting into the soft black interior of the ark walls.

And then she is roused by a tap on her elbow.

"I said, what do you think of this one, Miss Grey?" says Henry Hadley, from a few feet to her right. "I'm supposed to be the deaf one, you know."

He gives the hooting laugh she remembers from the disastrous lecture at the Sheldonian. She has not seen him since, although she has thought of him on more occasions than she would care to admit.

"Mr. Hadley, it's very pleasant to see you again." Marianne calculates how quickly she can excuse herself and glances about for Beatrice or even Miss Jourdain to rescue her. And yet she wonders, how on earth does Mr. Hadley remember her name? And she his?

"Likewise. Do call me Henry." He leans forward to read the exhibit label. "*Convent Thoughts.* By Charles Allston Collins. Apparently, he wasn't one of the Brotherhood, but he painted it in the Combes' back garden."

Marianne focuses on the painting.

He smiles. "I'm intrigued by the Pre-Raphaelites, but sometimes I find them rather too idealized, if I'm being perfectly honest." He turns his head as if looking over his left shoulder, and she realizes that she was on the other side of him the day they met. This is his damaged side.

"I'm deaf on the left," he says. "I do apologize if I make owlish head movements. It drives my sister mad."

"Let me swap places with you," says Marianne, and she skirts around him, suddenly aware she is in borrowed clothes.

She turns her gaze back to the painting. The vegetation is so vivid, so lush, she could be in the garden at Culham. She has read that closed gardens imply virginity, but she will not say that out loud. The nun has a book in one hand and a passionflower in the other. Love of learning and love of Christ. A rather accurate summary of the Marianne Grey she portrays in Oxford.

"And who are you flirting with, Marianne?" says Otto, appearing at her shoulder. "Oh, hello, it's the chap from Christ Church. When are you bringing your sister for tea? We haven't forgotten, you know." She gives Marianne a wink and sails on. Henry Hadley might be blushing, Marianne can't tell, she is too busy being aghast. There is a moment when the noise and heat of the room rush to fill the gap, and then Henry speaks into his champagne glass.

"I do wonder what these paintings have to do with life today? To a world recovering from war." There is a blend of playfulness and agony in his voice. "Legends and Bible stories, innocent women and children, radiant colors and mythical lives. Please enlighten me, because I feel rather wretched about not appreciating them."

"I suppose some people enjoy escaping into art and literature. I do it all the time. Too much, perhaps," she adds, smiling. "It reminds me there's still innocence and beauty and creativity in this world."

She glances at him. He is taller than she remembered, but his manner is just as open. He smells of Pears soap and beeswax.

"I'm willing to be led by you," he says. He gestures at the painting in front of him. "Tell me what you see here."

She leans a little closer to him and considers the image. "I'm transported to the garden, I suppose. I want to know where it is and what the nun is feeling. What she smells and hears." She sips at her glass, still full, and continues. "I think there are times when we need to be uplifted and transported, and sometimes we need to face up to reality. But I think the two can coexist." She takes another, larger sip. "The Unknown Warrior is a good example. It's a figure of heroism and mystery, and people have responded to it. Don't we all idealize things— people? The painters here are exploring that lens." She thinks of poor Dora, whose lens has been cracked. "Sorry, I'm talking too much," she says, embarrassed.

She looks up at him, sees something flicker in his hazel eyes. It reminds her of the golden-brown trout hovering in the river at Culham, unknowingly lit by the evening sun. He is nodding, and the little furrow on one side of his brow suggests he is thinking too.

He returns her gaze as if he understands her completely. As if he always has done.

"I like listening to you," he says.

Marianne stares at the painting, heat rising in her cheeks.

"Did you know the poet Robert Graves was here earlier?" he adds.

"Gosh," she says, looking around.

"He's a second-year at St. John's. Lives outside the city on Boars Hill with his wife—he's not over France, by all accounts."

He shifts toward her. She feels the momentary brush of his fingertips against hers. "I'm minded of his poem 'Last Day of Leave' written in 1917, do you know it?"

"Do you remember the lily lake? / We were all there, all five of us in love, / Not one yet killed, widowed or broken-hearted," she says. Her heart is bucking, and before she can prevent it, her eyes fill with tears.

When she looks up at him, the golden trout are swimming too.

"By the way, Charles Baker is here, if that matters," he says when at last he looks away.

"WHY ARE HER FEET SO clean when she is standing barefoot in mud? Look, she's holding that vase and a crate of birds above her head with absolutely no effort whatsoever. And the sky is green," says Otto, waving her glass about. The pale-gold liquid threatens to slosh over the parquet floor beneath *The After-glow in Egypt* by Holman Hunt.

"Oh, do shut up, Otto, you are such a philistine," laughs Beatrice.

"I admit I adore the dresses, but there are too many animals. I've seen cows, sheep, birds, fish, and a goat. Who needs to see a goat in a painting?"

"Yes, we all know," says Beatrice, "you'd prefer to wear them as a pair of gloves."

Otto sticks out her tongue and waltzes off.

"She's glorious, don't you think?" says Ursula, squeezing in at Beatrice's side.

Beatrice wonders whether she means the painting or Otto, but it does not really matter, as she is enjoying the feeling of Ursula's hip pressed against hers. She allows herself to be led about the room, and when Ursula talks, Beatrice cannot help but study the plump curve of her upper lip and how it expands and contracts like a beating heart. Ursula smells of cigarettes and hyacinths, and the heat of her makes Beatrice feel reckless and giddy. Her mind flits back to the scene in the stairwell at home, the day that women got the vote. The hand up the skirt, mouth on mouth. Is that what she wants from Ursula? Would Ursula want that from her? Or is this a crush—which is how some of the girls at St. Hugh's describe their feelings for Miss Jourdain. One thing is certain, she has decided that from tonight she, too, will buy shirts and ties, men's shoes and jackets, and plain straight skirts like Ursula. She will cut her hair short and wear plain hats with masculine brims. Perhaps she will buy two of everything, then she will never have to bother shopping again. Ursula might even come with her to choose.

Her reverie is broken by Marianne pulling at her other elbow.

"Where is Dora? Henry—Mr. Hadley—just told me that Charles Baker is here. Otto has gone to look downstairs. She isn't in the Print Room or the galleries. I'll go and check the lavatory. Can you hold the fort here? Keep an eye on Miss Jourdain."

Marianne disappears into the throng, and the delicious euphoria Beatrice was experiencing just a few moments ago evaporates. In fact, she feels a little foolish and gently unhooks herself from Ursula, who is arguing with a trio of men about a new poet called Ruth Pitter. Beatrice pushes through the crowd to the center of the room, where she pauses beside the marble bust of Thomas Combe. He is all eyebrows, hair, mustache, with a beard that flows into his chest. Why is it all about hair with these Pre-Raphaelites? She scans bobbing heads for the emerald-green dress and the celebrated dark curls, aware that Dora, with her haunted, faraway gaze of late, would not look out of place in one of these paintings. As Marianne has often commented, Dora could be one of Rossetti's "stunners."

Henry Hadley appears beside her and delivers a discreet message from Marianne that the others are gathered near the piano and would she come. Beatrice wonders how much he knows and allows herself a wry smile. If Marianne trusts him, then Henry must indeed be saintly.

As she descends the stairs, hand running down the thick oak balustrade, she sees Dora sitting on a velvet couch below her with her back to the wall. Even from a distance, she can tell something is wrong. Dora is so stiff, her face so chalky and un-animated, that she could have stepped straight from one of the huge portraits nearby with a chubby baby Jesus in her arms. Otto motions to Beatrice that they have to leave. And then Beatrice sees the problem. Charles Baker and friends are gathered around the piano, demanding the pianist play Gershwin. They are reeling, the air about them rank with cigar smoke and arrogance. The worst kind of Oxford student, in her opinion, on whom this most hallowed of institutions is utterly wasted.

As Beatrice reaches the couch, she recognizes the sensation she had all those years ago at the suffrage rally: the twisting and tightening in her gut that signals trouble is coming. Otto, angular face blanched with fury, hands Dora a glass of champagne and tells her to drink it.

One of the men begins to sing in the style of Al Jolson:

I've been away from you a long time
I never thought I'd miss you so
Somehow, I feel
Your love is real
Near you, I wanna be . . .

Baker joins him in full voice, arms around his companion's shoulders.

"We need to get her out of here, now. Where is Jourdain?" Otto hisses.

But Dora has risen from her seat and circled behind her friends. She is standing unsteadily at the far end of the piano from Baker. She looks magnificent, her vibrant-green dress against the crimson rug, the black piano. It is like a scene from a crime novel and for a moment Beatrice thinks Dora might pull out a miniature revolver and shoot Baker in the chest, but of course she does not. Instead she hesitates, as if she might throw the drink in Baker's face, and then she gulps down the contents of the glass and taps the arm of the singer next to her. When he turns, she puts her hands on his cheeks and kisses him hard on the mouth. Charles Baker stumbles over the lyrics, and stares transfixed.

When Dora finally releases the man, he has lipstick smudged around his sweaty pink face. There are cheers and shouts as Dora drags her hand across the back of her mouth and staggers out of the room. Beatrice and the others hurry after her.

"Bravo, Dora," says Otto, looking over her shoulder at Charles Baker. He stands motionless as his friends pitch and roll around him. Otto catches his eye and smirks, but he quickly turns away. Beatrice is surprised by how thoroughly miserable he looks. She can see now, he has charcoal-colored rings under his eyes and a sore on his bottom lip.

By the time they reach the foyer, Dora is sobbing and wiping her mouth in disgust. She flops onto a bench on the terrace outside. "I knew he'd be here. I knew it. I hate him. I really do." An elderly couple nearby move off, muttering in disapproval.

"We know you do, but calm down until we get out of here," says Otto. Then she turns to Marianne. "Jourdain is still here. You get the coats, I'll find a cab."

Beatrice sits down on the bench and Dora continues to rub at her lips. Her fingers are stained red with lipstick.

"At first, I was so happy he was alive, and now—now I wish he really was dead. It's my life that was a lie, not his. Dumb, dumb, dumb Dora." She waves her hand toward the Randolph Hotel, on the other side of the street. "Do you know, I stayed there once, when I was fifteen, in that room right there?"

Beatrice turns to look but she cannot make out the window. She has her own memories of that hotel as a girl that, after the ferocity of the kiss at the piano, are horribly vivid.

"I wanted to come here and visit the treasures, but they wouldn't let me." Dora continues to sob. "All the time I should've been thinking about my brother, I was crying over *him*. I'm a bloody fool."

Eventually, they bundle her into a cab, and as they return to St. Hugh's, Beatrice cannot bring herself to reveal that Miss Jourdain, standing with her arms folded at the top of the crimson-carpeted staircase, watched the entire sorry scene at the piano unfold.

22

Thursday, March 10, 1921 (8th Week)

On the penultimate evening of term, Dora is summoned by Miss Jourdain to discuss the second failed Responsion.

The principal's study, overlooking the lawn, is surprisingly spacious and the walls are hung with gilt frames featuring Miss Jourdain's own work: subdued watercolors of glassy lakes and avenues of poplar trees. Embroidered cushions are propped squarely on the armchairs, and a huge fern explodes from a beaten brass pot. It is how Dora imagines a Mediterranean home might look and smell—citrus scents, natural sunfaded hues. Nothing gaudy, nothing too new. Dora has never been invited in before, although she knows Miss Jourdain often entertains devoted third-years with piano recitals and hymn singing.

She is instructed to sit and nudges her way onto one of the armchairs, wary of denting the cushion. There is something a little too controlled about the principal today, as if the graceful movements and girlish voice are struggling to subdue the autocrat within.

"I will get straight to the point, Miss Greenwood," she says, with a brief smile that does not extend to the creases of her eyes. Dora has never seen irises the color of dried lavender before.

There is to be no preamble. Miss Jourdain proceeds to list a series of complaints against Dora, the first being the Responsion. The second that she has missed half of the Divvers coaching classes this term and has consequently failed that too.

"In addition to that, I witnessed your appalling behavior at the Ashmolean last week. If that were not enough, Miss Turbott tells me you acted in a highly unorthodox manner at a lecture at the Sheldonian Theatre. You have been seen by a member of staff coming out of the Covered Market after dark, an outing that was made without my permission, unaccompanied and without wearing a cap and gown. And—excuse me." The principal stops and draws a lace-edged handkerchief from her sleeve into which she sneezes. "I have reason to believe you have consumed alcohol on college premises on more than one occasion. Miss Greenwood, these are serious allegations."

Dora is stunned. Her first thought is that she has been confused with Otto. Her behavior has never been a topic of scrutiny before.

"Do you wish to say anything in your defense?" says Miss Jourdain, knotting her hands in her lap. All of her slender fingernails are filed to exactly the same length.

"I—" Dora's throat aches as if she has swallowed a stone. She shakes her head.

"When older students arrive at university having not been in school for some time, they struggle if they have not maintained a personal study habit. It is curiosity that is the key to academic success, Miss Greenwood, natural raw curiosity, and a fervent desire to learn.

"As you know, undergraduates must pass Responsions, Divvers, and Mods to continue into the second year. And you are slipping dangerously behind."

"I am sorry, I've struggled with the mathematics." Dora puts her hand to her knee to suppress the jittering. "It's not my strong suit."

But she knows Miss Jourdain is right. She is not the same as the others; she *likes* to learn, yes, but she does not *yearn* for it. Perhaps she does not deserve to be here. After all, it was George who was meant to come, not her. Failing Divvers must run in the family.

And now that Charles is back, everything is tainted. She is tainted. It seems that she was wrong, she is not Oxford material or marriage material after all. Perhaps she never was.

Miss Jourdain leans forward in her chair. "Proving that women can compete at the highest level academically is key to the emancipation of all women. You understand, then, why I cannot take the easy line, otherwise we are feeding the wolves."

Dora nods miserably.

"I am aware that you have suffered bereavement and recent emotional—upheaval, shall we say."

Dora looks up. What does Miss Jourdain know?

"Your tutors are sympathetic. Miss Finch has spoken in your defense. She says you have performed well in Old English. However, grief and anger are emotions we all suffer in this current age. While we cannot change what has happened, we can change how we react to it. Oxford is no place for melodramas of the heart. You risk bringing college into disrepute with such behavior.

"I'm afraid I have no alternative but to rusticate you pending a resit of your Responsion. Rustication means that you are forbidden to enter university premises for the period of time that I dictate. This will begin when term ends tomorrow. You may return if you pass the Responsion, whereupon you may attempt Divvers one more time."

The clock on the mantelpiece strikes eight. Miss Jourdain gets to her feet. Dora's body does not feel quite like her own. There is a queer burrowing feeling in her gut.

"Your tutor will post you a final Responsion paper. Please complete it and return it by this time next week. Your performance will enable me to assess what action to take next. I will be writing to your parents to see if they wish you to return here in May. They may well decide otherwise and that, of course, is their privilege."

AS DORA MAKES HER WAY back to her room, the main hallway is deserted. She pauses at the end of Corridor Eight and looks through the window into the empty courtyard. Outside, the night sky is blank except for a slim comma of slate-gray moon.

Her parents. She knows exactly how they will react to her failure, to why her tutors think it has come about, to the news about Charles. They will blame her, pity her, worry about what people will say, and ban her from returning to St. Hugh's to avoid any scandal. They will not surprise her. She picks at the skin from the side of her thumbnail until it bleeds.

As she enters her room, it occurs to her that nobody is rusticating Charles Baker. Nobody is admonishing him. He is free to go about his business, and it is her reaction that is deemed unacceptable. Why is it that women must suppress the feelings that are inconvenient or threatening to men? Their natural anger, grief, and rage. Why in literature do they kill themselves or get locked in asylums, attics, prisons, hotel rooms? Why cannot a woman act out what is in her heart without punishment? Constraining, pulling, tightening, tying, controlling, pinning, belting. Is that really the lot of a woman?

She reaches into the back of her bedside drawer, hands shaking. Then she halts in front of the little mirror above the washstand and unpins her hair, placing each pin precisely in the Three Nuns cigarette tin Charles gave her the day he left.

Before she can change her mind, she takes a fist of waist-length hair and pulls it taut under her chin, thumb up as if holding an umbrella. With her other hand, she opens the mouth of the scissors and forces them to open and close, eating into the tube of dark hair. It is like cutting a tough sinew in a piece of meat. Long remnants of hair fall to the floor in coils and create a glossy pile of ropes over her stockinged feet.

It is done in a matter of minutes. The bob looks longer on one side and her hand is red and sore between thumb and forefinger. There is no accompanying sense of satisfaction, though, and she regrets it immediately. She is nothing more than a cliché. Her mother will be hurt and furious. Dora has given her something to store in her armory of disagreeable memories she can revisit for the rest of her days. What foolish, headstrong Dora did to her "crowning glory."

The hair is surprisingly easy to pick up, still in its spools, not yet chaotic and sprawling. How odd that it was once joined to her and now lies alien at her feet. She places it in the wastepaper basket and wonders if Maud will burn it or perhaps even sell it. There is a quiet vacancy, an absence of warmth at the back of her neck. She will not mourn it, though; there has been enough mourning already.

From the dresser and wardrobe, she pulls dresses, skirts, blouses, shoes, and undergarments to form a loose pile on the floor. She folds each item quickly and unceremoniously, bending and straightening and bending again. Whoever unpacks it can deal with the creases. As she drops the first garments into the base of the trunk, motes of displaced dust rush to escape. There seems less space than before—perhaps she is too careless with her folding, but she continues regardless. She had intended to make the unused corset look worn, but she simply cannot be bothered and puts it in, still wrapped in the tissue paper. At the bottom of the drawer sits the unread novel Frank gave her for Christmas. She will leave it in the JCR. Last of all is her commoners' gown and soft cap. She picks a couple of long hairs from the cap and lays it on top.

Down the left side, she stuffs books, magazines, tennis racket, hockey kit, and her flannel dressing gown from the back of the door. She squeezes the air from a tube of face cream, screws tight the lid, and puts it in the dressing-gown pocket. What should she do with the gilt hand mirror her mother gave her? She rolls it in a towel and wedges the bundle in the right-hand side of the trunk. Then she burrows down into the dresses, hollows out a space, and inserts the framed photograph of her brother inside.

She makes a pile of the items that are left over: a peacock feather (birthday gift from Otto), a bottle of ink, a map of Oxford. They will go to Marianne. The oat biscuits and tea caddy, she leaves for Beatrice. Hesitating over her essays and notes, she glances out the window at her bicycle leaning on the wall opposite, then tosses them on top and attempts to close the lid. Her monogrammed initials still look freshly painted.

On the inside, the layers of her life—the strata—start to compress into fossils.

She turns around, sits on the lid of the trunk, and forces it shut.

There is only one item left unaccounted for, a single photograph lying abandoned on the mantelpiece. She tosses it onto the dying embers of the fire and watches as, inch by inch, Charles shudders and curls into smoke.

23

Dora, Summer 1917

I t always takes Dora a few days to acclimatize to the machine-gun fire. She never gets used to night ops, though, waking with a jolt at the *clamp-clamp-clamp* of boots on the gravel road outside her window. She can barely recall a time when Berkhamsted was not occupied by cadets marching about the countryside digging trenches and mock-raiding villages. The men, embraced by the majority of townsfolk in lieu of their absent sons, are officers in training, staying put for only three or four months. In that time, they make their mark: writing magazines, putting on shows, befriending local children and dogs, and creating an economy all their own. Since Dora was last home, her favorite draper on Castle Street has converted into a gentlemen's outfitters and boot shop, which brings the total in the little market town to six.

Dora likes to think she has not been shielded from war. At Cheltenham Ladies' College all the girls have been taught to carry stretchers and administer first aid. Her old boarding-house has been converted into a hospital, with the art room serving as an operating theater. She tries not to think too hard about this, otherwise her brain willfully conjures a bloody hand or foot lying discarded on an easel shelf where there ought to be a paintbrush.

Whereas Cheltenham is somber in red crosses and hospital

blues, Berkhamsted is buzzing in khaki. Three hundred white tents in impossibly neat rows dominate the land above the castle, recently renamed "Kitchener's Field." In winter, the men billet with locals, and each year Dora's family hosts the same whiskery drill sergeant whose snoring is far more thunderous than any night maneuver. There has been a spate of hurried weddings between cadets and daughters of billeted households, leading her mother to vow that no cadets below forty will sleep under her roof.

Dora is aware of a shift in herself this summer, as if she is about to step through a doorway into a world hitherto inaccessible. Adults speak to her as if they expect more of her, and she is the object of stares and gallantry when she walks in town. None of this is unwelcome, but she often has the sense she cannot quite catch up with herself. She is to be head girl next year, and beyond that there is a blurry spot in her vision that she assumes will evaporate as soon as she reaches adulthood and her assigned future becomes clear. Now she is seventeen, her parents have agreed to her taking a job in the cadet library, run by volunteers in the town hall. The cadets are all linked with the Inns of Court in some way, and many will become barristers after the war. *The best sort of fellow we could wish for,* according to her mother.

She completes her training at the library after a fortnight and Miss Pinkney, the librarian, is delighted with her. Dora enjoys the labeling and stamping, filing and typing. There is satisfaction in finding the right place for a book on the shelf or answering a blushing cadet's inquiry.

"Our job is to give the troops reading material that will relax and entertain them; there will be too much awfulness to come," says diminutive Miss Pinkney, who scoots about like a dormouse and never goes anywhere without a planning notebook or a goal.

Having lost a nephew at the Somme, Miss Pinkney devotes her free time to sourcing the books that cadets request. There are waiting lists for Nat Gould's horse racing novels, Edgar Wallace's murder mysteries, H. G. Wells and R. L. Stevenson. Miss Pinkney writes weekly letters to the YMCA and the *Times* to remind them that libraries outside London are also in desperate need of donations. Sometimes Dora types the letters for her, but she is still learning and is painfully slow.

SHE MEETS CHARLES THE EVENING Gilbert is killed.

It is after seven on Midsummer Day and the twins are rolling about the lawn, encouraging Gilbert, their elderly and unprepossessing rabbit, to navigate a series of obstacles. Wood pigeons hoot in the silver birch trees and Dora swings on the love seat on the terrace, shoes off, pretending to read. In actuality, she is wondering whether she should accept any of the offers she has received from cadets to attend the opening of the new Court Theater and whether her mother will let her go. If she turns down the invitations, Dora assures herself, she can never be viewed as one of those girls who are seen with a different cadet every night. The reality is, she is terribly nervous around young men, even friends of George's. She is well aware that, despite being described as "frightfully good-looking" by her friends at school, she has a reputation for being too sensible among the other young women in the town.

She is roused by a feral squeal and the boys shouting her name in panic. She jumps to her feet and sees a wiry black-and-white dog looping about the garden like a Catherine wheel. It has a white fur rag clamped in its mouth that looks alarmingly like Gilbert.

"Boys, stand still," she shouts. She does not trust dogs. Or any animal, come to that.

A cadet wearing a pack and carrying a rifle erupts from the bracken, shouting. "Blaze, dammit, come! Come!" The dog pauses to shake its catch violently. Gilbert's head whips from side to side, crimson eyes bulging.

"Good God. Stop. Bloody hell," the man pleads, bending low and creeping up on the dog. The animal races toward him, repeatedly swerving at the last minute as if it is a game.

Dora's brothers stand transfixed, their mouths hanging open. Then one breaks into an agonized howl and the other follows suit.

"I'm so sorry," the cadet says to the boys as he finally retrieves the limp body from the dog's jaws. Gilbert's eyes are fixed, his mouth gaping.

"It's not even my dog. I mean, it follows us about, and I—" There is shouting from within the forest behind him.

The cadet notices Dora on the terrace and then cocks his head as if surprised. He has a dimple like a tire rut in his chin, and thick wavy brown hair and ears that stick out just enough to give his almost-too-symmetrical face character. He is on maneuvers, she realizes. She has heard that some of the local dogs have decamped to Kitchener's Field and follow the cadets all over the place.

"I really am sorry. I'll get you chaps another rabbit, I promise," the cadet says as the twins wail and snivel. "Two rabbits, then," he adds, saluting. At this unexpectedly welcome offer, they cease crying and resume staring at him, as if he is a *Boy's Own* adventurer come alive.

The man returns his attention to Dora. "Please don't report it. I'll get in an awful jam," he says, holding her gaze. "I'll make it up to them. I could call on you and your family next week?" he says, wiping sweat from his brow on his sleeve.

She nods. Before she can think of anything to say, he is already leaving.

"Thank you." His shoulders drop and he exhales in relief. "I'm sorry but I have to go. My friends are waiting for me."

He lays the body on the lawn and backs away. There are whistles and more shouting from behind him in the forest. The dog is at his heels as he darts back into the undergrowth.

"Hadley, where the devil are you?" she hears him yell as he

disappears. The bracken closes where he has parted it and, in the hush that descends, she hears the lonely rattle of a woodpecker. The boys begin squabbling over Gilbert's funeral.

THE FOLLOWING DAY, DORA'S SCHOOL friend Hilda Dodd comes to stay for the remainder of the holidays. Hilda's parents want her out of London, away from the Zeppelins. Dora wonders whether a town referred to in the press as "a small but impressive garrison" might not be the best bet, but her father insists they are quite safe. Berkhamsted is merely a dot on the flight path to London, he says, and anyway, they all adhere to the blackout. But a Zepp was shot down over Cuffley last year, Dora recalls, and that was only twenty-seven miles away.

Hilda has a figure to match her glasses, Mrs. Greenwood observes, unflattering and round. However, Dora admires Hilda's vivacity and lack of inhibition. Hilda, who is fearfully bright and intends to apply to Girton, is terribly confident with men, having two older brothers, one of whom is a conscientious objector and drives ambulances for the Red Cross. She has boundless energy and, wanting to understand everything about the garrison town, interrogates everyone she meets. Friendship with Hilda is the equivalent of traveling to a foreign land: tremendous fun but also unsettling as one notices the limitations of one's own life that were never visible before.

When the cadet calls at Fairview a few days later, Dora is at the library showing Hilda the ropes. He brings two baby rabbits for the boys and buttery-yellow roses for her mother. He is a huge hit, and even accepts a cup of tea. Dora's only consolation for missing the visit is that she discovers his name is Charles Baker.

Over the next two weeks, Dora spots Baker about the town: winking at the twins whilst on parade at St. Peter's, unloading equipment at the station, coming out of the Crown laughing with his hand on the shoulder of a companion. He has a glorious baritone and sings at the theater opening, which she attends with Hilda. Baker's rendition of "Keep the Home Fires Burning" reduces the entire audience to tears. Hilda, already friendly with a number of cadets, discovers that Baker is known as "Buns" to his fellow trainees and his father was recently knighted.

"Johnny Thwaite knows him," says Hilda. "Apparently, he got up to a lot of mischief at Rugby, but always managed to charm his way out of it."

"He does seem the sort," says Dora, although she does not mean it.

One stuffy Monday in the middle of July, Dora is running the library desk alone while Miss Pinkney is making a telephone call and Hilda is late back from lunch. A new batch of cadets have arrived and there is a rowdy queue waiting to register. As Dora bends over the card box, her head is pounding. The rule is she must file the last application before she can accept the next, otherwise there will be chaos. But the letters are blurring, and her fingers are clumsy.

The next man in line taps his fingertips on the edge of the desk impatiently. "I say, miss, do you have a copy of *Mr. Britling Sees It Through?*"

"There's a long waiting list, I'm afraid," she says, without looking up.

"And how are the bunnies doing?"

Her chest contracts and her first thought is that she was an idiot not to wash her hair the night before. He is three feet from her, perhaps less. Raising her eyes, she notices that Charles Baker is too young to be a lawyer. He is eighteen or nineteen, she estimates. She knows the Inns of Court have stretched their nets more widely for recruits of late. He is probably a student.

"Oh. Um. They are fine," she says, cheeks flaming, scalp itching. "Thank you very much," she adds, busying herself by rubbing pencil marks off the blank card that awaits his details.

"It's the least I could do, Miss Greenwood. I was sorry not to see you when I visited," he says.

"You know my name," she says, flustered. Instantly, she berates herself. What an idiotic thing to say. He has called at the house.

"I do," he replies. "I'm a veritable Sherlock Holmes, ask anyone."

She laughs. There is a grumbling in the queue behind him.

"I already have a card," he says, waving a slip at her. "I'll take this." They touch fingertips under a battered copy of *Kidnapped*, and it is like flint sparking.

When Dora and Hilda leave the library at five p.m., he is waiting outside, holding the novel under one arm and picking fluff off his sleeve. His uniform is pristine, she notes, with its shiny brass buttons, each featuring a smirking winged devil holding a trident.

"I happen to be walking to camp, it's in your direction. May I join you both—if you are going home, that is?" he asks.

"That's all right with us, isn't it, Dora?" replies Hilda, nudging Dora, whose heart is thumping wildly in her chest.

He bows theatrically. "Then I will be the envy of the corps."

"Well, Dora *is* the prettiest girl in Berkhamsted," says Hilda. "Don't you agree?"

"Hilda!" says Dora, cheeks puce.

Charles Baker laughs, delighted. "That, I cannot deny."

It takes longer than usual to walk home. He tells them stories of cadets reading compasses wrong and losing their way in the forest at night, of trainee barristers getting out of disciplinary action by arguing their way out of trouble, of how he paid a local boy a shilling to find two baby rabbits. His mother is a snob, he says, and not at all charming like Mrs. Greenwood, but she has just sent him new boots and khakis, so he cannot complain. He is going up to Queen's College, Oxford, to read Law after the war and is in favor of women attending university. He is off hunting next week. He knows he might cop it in France, but we must all do our bit, mustn't we?

At the end of the walk up the hill to Fairview, he parts by shaking their hands and asking to accompany them the next day.

"I know it's you he admires, and he's a little bit vain, but I think he's heavenly," says Hilda, pushing her glasses back up the sweaty bridge of her nose.

Dora sends up a grateful prayer of thanks to Gilbert for his sacrifice.

THE REMAINDER OF JULY PASSES in a haze of library days and evening outings. Charles accompanies the two girls whenever he is free, sometimes bringing a campmate to make up a foursome. They spectate at the corps sports day, where he wins the sack race and falls on his face in the tug-of-war. Other days, they cycle around the countryside, go for a picnic or to the pictures. Dora observes how easy Charles seems to find life, brushing off failure or regret as if it were a fly, always looking for the next game or source of entertainment. He is neither terribly punctual nor organized, but his spontaneity is infectious. At first, Dora fears that she is too serious, too ordinary, to maintain his interest, but he keeps coming back. To her surprise and disappointment, he is a perfect gentleman.

In early August, Hilda asks Charles if he will show her the trenches the men have been digging on Berkhamsted Common. She would like to be able to imagine where her brothers are. Dora expresses a similar desire, privately ashamed for not having thought of it earlier. George ought to have been more on her mind this summer, but he hardly ever writes and never to her. When he did come home on leave last year, he spent most of the time asleep or in the Crown. He was distant and irritable, seeming to prefer the company of transient cadets to that of his own family.

Although the common is off limits to locals, Charles leads them over one evening after scouting it out. The trenches begin half a mile from Fairview on the other side of the road that leads up from the town. Once they cross the road, a dusty track twists through a curtain of trees onto a sloped clearing. The ground is littered with holes and heaps of dull clods. It reminds Dora of the half-dug foundations of a huge building.

After a few minutes, she is able to distinguish a zigzag system of trenches snaking all across this section of the common, some narrow, some wide. Most of the vegetation has been trampled, but there is a sense of orderliness and calm. She can hear cuckoos calling softly to one another. At the edge of the clearing sit neat piles of flint, boards, sandbags, carts, and tents. Behind them, nestled in the shade of hawthorn, oak, and beech trees, are gun carriages with bright red wheels.

"Can you imagine?" whispers Hilda. "Living in this."

Dora shakes her head imperceptibly at Hilda. She does not want the moment spoiled.

"So, ladies, there are three ways to dig a trench," Charles says, hands on hips. "In from the top as fast as you can before you're a goner. Or dig a tunnel and collapse the top. Or work sideways."

He jumps down into the closest trench.

"The clay and flint make it hard going, but we are very proud of these old girls. There's at least six miles of them now." Charles pats a wall of sandbags fondly. "Sweaty work in August. And if you lose your shovel the QMS will make sure you're cleaning the latrines for a week."

He motions to Dora to jump down into his open arms. She lands with a sway on the duckboards, and he steadies her. Hilda follows, tactfully walking away along the trench to the right.

"This is the start of the front line and those are support trenches." He steers Dora left toward a small turret and a series of gaps in the sandbags. "That's a machine-gun placement— and those are loopholes for popping your rifle through."

The trench is deeper than Dora imagined, with little ability to see beyond the walls, which she thinks would drive her mad. There is an earthy smell, mixed with urine and cigarette ends. It doesn't seem so bad, she thinks, although George complained about nibbling rats and freezing-cold mud when he was back last year. She closes her eyes trying to imagine the scene, the Germans just one hundred yards away doing their best not to die too. George says you can hear their voices sometimes and smell their burning cigarettes. It is unexpectedly cold in the trench in her blush silk. As she draws her arms to her sides in a shiver, warm hands snake about the sash around her waist and even warmer lips brush the back of her neck.

"God, Dora, you are irresistible, you know," Charles murmurs in her ear, and when she turns to face him, he presses his mouth over hers for the first time. What surprises her, more than the sweet appley taste of his tongue, is how close he is, with his thigh nudging thrillingly into the soft pleats of her dress. The ridges of his pockets press so hard into her chest she imagines her breasts are now imprinted with winged devils.

"Why the devils?" she asks, fingering the little brass buttons when he releases her.

"George III loathed lawyers and hated the idea of giving them guns," he says, kissing her earlobe. "He said they must be the devil's own army."

It is intoxicating to her that when she speaks, he responds as if she is the most important person on earth. He likes to explain things to her, and so she often questions him, even when she knows the answer perfectly well.

Charles begins to take evening walks in the forest next to Fairview, retrieving lost tennis balls from the bracken that Dora has tossed over the fence for him earlier in the day. It becomes a game. If she steps into the bracken to help him find them, he will take her hand. She has determined that she will be guarded but playful. Sometimes he catches her, gripping her arms behind her and kissing her urgently on the mouth, leaving her agitated later when she recalls the scent of soap on his cheek and coffee on his lips. Other times, he picks oxeye daisies and pokes them into her hair.

"Promise me you'll never cut it," he says, nuzzling her scalp. "Because one day, I want to undo it myself, pin by pin, and on that occasion, you won't be wearing any clothes."

She leans back into him experimentally and he groans. "Promise me."

"I promise," she says, but she cannot look at him.

She tries to memorize every detail of his body: the downy hair on his earlobes, the oval mole on his temple, the bony mounds on his wrists where his cuffs end. When she is with him, her senses are heightened, energy fizzes in her fingertips. When she is without him, she replays each word and action that has passed between them, frustrated that she cannot recall them perfectly. Strangely confident of his feelings, she is tortured by the thought of him going to France and prays at night for an immediate end to the war. Her mother, encouraged by Hilda, invites him to tea. He teaches the twins to sing and march to "It's a Long Way to Tipperary." They play cards on the terrace and Mrs. Greenwood, charmed, issues an open invitation for him to use the tennis court. Dora plays well, and Charles invites other cadets up for doubles. By mid-August, he is visiting Fairview most days. They are officially walking out. Her father offers him nightcaps, calls him "an absolute rogue," and pats him on the back.

The night before Charles leaves Berkhamsted to take up his commission with the Fifth Battalion of the Royal Berkshire Regiment, he asks Dora to marry him. There is no ceremony; he pulls her out into the hallway after tea and plunges so quickly to one knee she thinks he has tripped. Usually so ebullient, he is jittery and tearful.

"I'm madly in love with you, you must know that. Marry me, Dora. Be my good-luck charm in France."

He does not wait for her reply but that does not matter, because they both know he does not need it. Dora has been remolding herself around Charles Baker for two months, and now her future is no longer blurry but in sharp relief.

There is no time for a ring or an announcement, he says. He wants to do it properly, ask her father and so on. All that will come on his first leave when he will tell his parents, and it is most important that he does this in person. His hints that his mother might be difficult are based, she assumes, on the fact that her father is self-made, their family wealth and home merely a decade old.

"This is in lieu of a ring. Use it for your hairpins and think of me," he says with a wink, tipping out the last few cigarettes into his hand from a battered Three Nuns cigarette tin. The primrose-yellow lid features a suave young man in a navy suit smoking in an armchair.

She kisses away his tears, and in those kisses, she begs him to cling to life, to beat the terrible odds the newspapers give new officers at the front. To be jubilant and terrified at the same time is the strangest feeling. "I can wait," she says. "However long it takes."

THREE MONTHS LATER, WHEN SHE is the one to fall to her knees in the hallway, her parents assume it is George and her mother faints.

But George, advancing on Cambrai from the south, is safe for two weeks yet.

24

Sheldonian Theatre
March 11, 1921

• • •

VISIT OF HER MAJESTY
The Queen
to receive the degree of DCL

• • •

THE CHANCELLOR
PRESIDING
Program

T he queen is to visit Oxford on the last day of term to re- ceive an honorary degree. Despite the flurry of packing, postponed tutorials, borrowed books, and lost train timetables, Beatrice comes up trumps again with tickets. She suspects that as a socialist she should not support this royal visit, but the queen receiving a degree is a moment of enormous signifi- cance to all women, not just at Oxford. Causes need figure- heads, as Miss Davison demonstrated when she died a martyr under the hooves of the king's racehorse. Although the new Education Act requires children to remain in school from five to fourteen, there is little extra money behind it, and too many institutions still rely on slates. Beatrice agrees with her mother; education reform needs all the publicity it can get.

The thought of being back in Bloomsbury next week fills her with trepidation and, not for the first time, she wishes she could spend the Easter vacation in Oxford. Her mother has become increasingly volatile since the WSPU was dissolved at the end of the war and now claims to be writing her memoirs. When Edith is not overseas, she entertains struggling artists and mournful émigrés, often for weeks on end. Mother and daughter barely correspond during term time, and Beatrice cannot imagine that a month together will improve matters. When in London, she plans to have lunch with Otto, who has an equally problematic mother by all accounts. And with any luck, she will see Ursula too.

Knowing the Bodleian Library will be quiet today, Beatrice has put in a request for A. D. Lindsay's new book on Immanuel Kant, which has been proving hard to procure. She cycles down after breakfast, collects the slim volume, and makes notes for a couple of hours in the antiquated bays of the Duke Humfrey section. It is hard not to be thrilled by the leather-bound volumes chained to the shelves, or the medieval paneled ceiling with its intricately painted coats of arms overhead. In most other countries, the Bodder would have become a museum by now.

Beatrice thinks back to her first lecture in October, where Mr. Cowley explained that the library holds over a million books—with miles of shelving snaking under the Radcliffe Camera. The rarest books—hand-illustrated tomes on animal skins—were hidden during the war, in case Oxford was bombed. But it never happened. Now she hears the staff complaining about how the library is struggling to keep up as printing businesses like the Oxford University Press expand. Beatrice has taken to reading the many job advertisements displayed on noticeboards throughout the various buildings. It is something she can imagine herself doing after she graduates: making the Bodder and Oxford her home. Education is politics, after all. She is sorely tempted to rip down the advertisements and stash them in her briefcase until she is ready to apply.

———— ◇ ————

BEFORE SHE CAN LEAVE FOR the ceremony, Marianne must complete her essay on *Sir Gawain and the Green Knight*.

Of the Early and Middle English texts she has studied in her tutes with Miss Finch, it is *Sir Gawain* that has caught her imagination the most, particularly its magical green knight strolling nonchalantly out of King Arthur's court carrying his own severed head. Miss Finch keeps abreast of the latest thinking in her field, and their discussions are pleasantly challenging. Most recently, they have explored the symmetry and number patterning in *Sir Gawain* (something that Otto would adore), and Marianne is keenly aware that the symbolism of the green sash the eponymous hero wears at the end of the poem is not a million miles away from that of her silver locket.

She has borrowed Beatrice's typewriter for the essay, and although she suspects she could probably write faster with a fountain pen, there is a poetry in the way the machine stamps out thoughts into letters—into words—into sentences—into essays. Marianne loves the *coggle-strug* of the paper winding on. The surety of the *clunch-snap* as each spindly metal arm throws itself headlong into the paper. Little metal teeth competing at a tiny mouth, gnashing away at the ribbon. It is almost cruel.

DORA MISSES BREAKFAST AND DOES not turn up for the eleven a.m. rendezvous outside the Sheldonian Theatre. The other Eights cannot locate her among the crowds gathering on Broad

Street. Marianne, uneasy, wants to wait longer, but the royal party has already left Balliol and is processing slowly up the road.

Beatrice tugs at her sleeve. "We'd better go. She could be inside. She has her ticket."

The Sheldonian looks exactly as it did seven weeks ago, and Marianne wonders if perhaps Dora cannot face entering the building. Glancing up, she notes that the fat babies are still frolicking on the ceiling and finds herself thinking about Henry Hadley. She looks over to the seats they occupied together that day and is disappointed to see them filled by a row of flag-waving women from Lady Margaret Hall. She sees other familiar faces about the room: Josephine, Patricia, Miss Jourdain, Miss Kirby the vice principal, and at least five tutors from college. A trumpet sounds, and the queen enters dressed in academic robes, followed by her daughter, the Princess Mary, alongside the chancellor and proctors. It is hard not to be swept up in the occasion, knowing that Queen Mary is there to endorse them. She is the first queen to receive an honorary degree from Oxford, and photographs of her doing so will be on the front page of every newspaper in England tomorrow.

"She's wearing a bloody mortarboard," says Otto. "Why don't we get mortarboards?"

"Because you're not a bloody Doctor of Civil Law," whispers Beatrice.

"Well, I have to say, she has a formidable bust," says Otto, lighting a cigarette.

A goggle-eyed tutor on the row in front turns around and glares at them.

The queen is taller than Marianne imagined. She looks rather like Miss Jourdain, in that she is smart and dignified but with a smile that does not invite intimacy. Her movements are slow, in a bovine sort of way. At her elbow hovers Lord Curzon, Home Secretary, former Viceroy of India, and chancellor of the university.

Curzon's speech is rather witty, drawing on other queens who have visited Oxford, including Catherine of Aragon, who was accompanied by Wolsey ("unconscious partners in an impending doom"), and Queen Elizabeth, who was presented with a cup of gold and six pairs of gloves. He even makes a dig at Cambridge for not following Oxford's wise example to admit women to "her innermost sanctuary." Today, he says, is a milestone in womanhood and in British education. The room bursts into rapturous applause.

"What utter tripe!" whispers Beatrice, her face twisted in disgust. "He's making sixty years of struggle by women sound like a victory for men."

"Look at all these adoring faces," says Otto. "Everybody is lapping it up. Papa says he is thoroughly disliked in the Commons, despite being tapped for PM. But he certainly has the gift of the gab."

"I think he's rather handsome," says Marianne. "And he's done some good in India, even Ursula says so."

Beatrice winces. "Ursula would shoot him if she could, which is why she's not here."

The chancellor continues in praise of the queen, his voice echoing about the theater. Her Majesty, he says, reconciles the highest ideals of feminine progress and feminine emancipation with old-fashioned traditions of womanly reserve. She has raised the status of womanhood in this country, he concludes with a bow.

"I don't dispute what he is saying about her merits, but what does he know of feminine emancipation?" hisses Beatrice. "He was president of the National League for Opposing Woman Suffrage. Unbelievable hypocrite."

"I can't believe Dora has missed this, she would be cheering herself hoarse by now," says Otto.

It is true, Dora loves to read about the royal family in Otto's magazines, and often cuts clippings and photographs from the newspaper.

There is a hush while Lord Curzon prepares to read the queen's reply.

Beatrice is now leaning so far forward that her chin almost rests on the cap in front. "I do wish she'd speak for herself," she says. "It rather misses the point."

"Perhaps she's too vain to put on her spectacles," says Otto.

The chancellor clears his throat. "Her Majesty is confident that Oxford's daughters will show themselves worthy of the great victory they have won, and from the doors of this university will pour forth a fruitful stream of feminine ability and feminine enthusiasm that will exercise an uplifting and ennobling influence on the life of the nation." Hundreds of feet drum the floor in unison.

"The queen hopes for a generous response to the appeals of colleges for charitable donations so that an Oxford education will continue to be available to all women who deserve it," he concludes. More applause. Even Beatrice joins in this time.

Then the choir sings the first verse of a new hymn called "Jerusalem" featuring words by William Blake set to music by Sir Hubert Parry. The congregation joins to sing the second verse and the benches vibrate with fervor.

Beatrice is delighted. "Oh, the delicious irony. This is called the 'Women Voters' Hymn.' The Union of Women's Suffrage Societies owns the copyright, Parry gave it to them."

"Blake's original poem wasn't pro-war or pro-Empire," says Marianne with a wry smile, "but everywhere I go I hear this hymn, even in my father's services."

"We really should come along to Culham one Sunday for the morning service," says Beatrice. "Don't you think, Otto?"

"Hmm. It depends what time it is."

"Far too early for you," says Marianne, placing her program carefully in her bag.

"Let's take a program back for Dora," says Beatrice.

Afterward, they mill out on the street with the crowds, with no sense of what to do or where to go. The triumph and irony need a moment to sink in.

"The queen's reply was spot on, wasn't it? We'll never get equality of opportunity without donations. Some of the men's colleges are rich beyond belief, way richer than the king even," says Beatrice as they look around for their bicycles.

"Really? Let me guess, Christ Church?" says Marianne.

"Second. St. John's is the richest. They could fund all the women's colleges on a sliver of their endowments."

"All very well, but can we go for lunch now?" says Otto, prodding them both in the small of the back. "This morning was actually rather good."

———◇———

MISS ROGERS HAS ARRANGED FOR Otto to attend a reception for the queen at Somerville that afternoon in recognition of her war work. Over a disappointing lunch of mutton chops in the Good Luck Tea Rooms, Marianne and Beatrice insist she would be mad not to go.

"We'll be in the Bod making a start on vac work," says Beatrice, picking at the bone on her plate. "I'd go to the reception if I were you. You'll see the queen close up."

Otto pulls a tiny thread of tobacco from her lips. "Something to tell the nieces and nephews, I suppose," she says. "But you know how much I detest Somerville. I'm not sure I want to go back."

"Understandable," says Beatrice.

"If you decide to go and don't feel comfortable, you can just leave," suggests Marianne.

Marianne, of course, is right. Otto is free to do exactly as she likes. Why should she not attend? What can Somerville possibly do to her now? She won't be emptying bedpans or scrubbing floors. As she muses, Betty lays the luncheon bill on the table and quietly removes the teaspoons.

"Did you see that?" laughs Beatrice. "She's on to you. Touché, Betty, touché."

Before she sets off, Otto adjusts her cap in the mirror of the WC and reapplies her lipstick. Behind her, the familiar watercolor of distant Oxford spires is reflected in the glass, flipped a hundred and eighty degrees from left to right. Her hair is a mess. Dora had promised to wave it that morning, but Otto was forced to use the curling irons alone and now there is an ugly burn smarting on the side of her neck. Otto is becoming increasingly frustrated with Dora's unrelenting melancholy, mainly because she cannot work out how to fix her.

St. Giles' and Little Clarendon Street are lined with crowds, and it is more of a battle to reach Somerville than Otto has anticipated. The reception is to take place in the main quad, and Otto has been allocated a spot in the loggia that opens out from the library. As she is led there by a porter, she notices that the makeshift hole in the wall linking Somerville to the Radcliffe Infirmary has been bricked up. The college looks green and airy without tents and guy ropes crisscrossing the lawns, and the magnolias are opening up their pink fists. The last time she saw the loggia, it was occupied by convalescing soldiers playing cards or dozing in wheelchairs under blankets. Today, the stone pillars are punctuated by excitable children and a pack of conscientious-looking Girl Guides.

Although she feels a tad nauseous, it is not so terrible being back; the place has changed so much. The thought of it was far more terrifying than the reality, as is so often the case. Plus, her old ward—and the sluice—are nowhere near the library.

She finds a spot at the back of the loggia behind a pair of plain-looking women clutching uninspiring handbags, who are not in academic gowns. From their loud and incessant conversation, it appears that they worked together as nurses at Somerville during the war, but she does not recognize them. The quad is lined with students and staff and there is a good deal of cheering and flag-waving when the royal party enters.

The children throw their hats in the air and there is consternation as one hits the queen on the arm, but she takes it in good humor and bends down to address the culprit, smiling. She is mannish compared to her daughter and sports a peculiar hat that looks as if it has been cobbled together from a pair of cabbages. However, her moleskin coat is stunning. Princess Mary, in fox fur, is prettier than she appears in the newspaper and does not seem at all bored at the endless speeches and presentations, an impressive feat indeed. Vera Brittain and Winifred Holtby are presented to the queen as the only Somervillians to return to the college after nursing in France. Ursula is in the receiving line too. Otto sometimes wonders if Beatrice would be better suited to Somerville than St. Hugh's, and this is possibly why she finds Ursula so irritating. To be proprietorial about a person is a new experience for her.

The queen takes an interminable amount of time inspecting the architecture of the loggia, the flower beds, and even the badges on the Girl Guides. Otto has read the scandal sheets describing her as a kleptomaniac obsessed with acquiring antiques, jewelry, and artwork for the Royal Collection. But what is patently clear to Otto today is that the queen is very observant of small details and is genuinely interested, despite having been dragged around six locations in six hours. It seems the poor woman's job is to make everyone else feel better about themselves, and she does it very well.

Throughout the visit, the women in front of Otto have continued whispering and gossiping. There is a lull in the proceedings and Otto finds herself engaging with their conversation.

"I still laugh when I think of Matron slapping that Welsh captain when he tried to kiss her," says one of the women. She is wearing a cheap-looking crimson coat that she has boasted to her friend is new.

"Well, she didn't suffer fools gladly," replies her stout companion. "I was bloody terrified of her."

Otto allows herself a smile; she remembers that feeling well.

"Do you remember the MP's daughter—the little flapper with the German name?" says the one in the crimson coat. Otto, standing right behind her, freezes. There is a sudden whooshing in her ears.

"The one they threw out?" her friend replies. "Oh, I remember her. Arrogant. Thought she was a cut above."

"She was sent to us for an easy time, but Matron wasn't having it."

"Useless, wasn't she? The lipstick!"

"Couldn't even mop a floor."

As the women titter, a flush sweeps up Otto's neck to her forehead. *Who do they think they are?*

With a trembling hand, she presses her cigarette into the back of the nasty crimson coat until it has burned a hole. As she presses again and again, her hand steadies. She is immensely satisfied, even ecstatic. The wool smokes a little and there is the meaty aroma of burning hair. The four singed craters are works of art.

The woman in the coat gestures at the royal party. "I think they're leaving." She scratches idly at her neck. "I wonder what happened to Matron after the hospital closed?"

"No idea. Look, they're serving now. Shall we have some tea?"

"What's that smell?" says the coat-wearer, turning round.

But Otto is already sidestepping away. She descends the loggia and strides breezily across the lawn, out of the lodge, and into the crowds without a backward glance.

———◇———

WHEN MARIANNE AND BEATRICE RETURN to Corridor Eight from the Bodder it is almost six p.m. Maud peers out of the scullery door, scowling.

"Miss Wallace-Kerr just left. Said to tell you to meet her at Queen's College and to hurry," she says, with a snort.

"What on earth's the matter?" says Beatrice, aghast. She is exhausted from the long day and has been planning to lie down on her bed for an hour before supper.

"What I told Miss Wallace-Kerr," says Maud, shrugging. "I found Miss Greenwood's hair in the wastepaper basket. Miss Jenkins saw her go out of the gates without a hat or coat. She said she was going to see the queen."

"That can't be right," says Beatrice. "Dora would never cut her hair."

Maud sucks on her bottom lip. Then it dawns on Beatrice and she turns to look at Marianne. "Isn't the queen having tea at Queen's College before she leaves?"

"Oh, Dora," says Marianne, rubbing her temples.

Beatrice stuffs her key back in her pocket and sighs. "Let's go."

BUT BEATRICE AND MARIANNE NEVER reach the entrance to the college. On Queen's Lane, they encounter Otto leading a furious-looking Dora up the narrow road toward them.

"I want to see the queen. To tell her that one of the men at her college is a liar and a coward," says Dora, raising her voice. "His name is Charles Baker."

A policeman guarding a side door to the college raises an eyebrow at Beatrice and Marianne as they hurry past him toward their friend.

"Dora, come on, you'll be sent down if you don't stop," says Otto, trying to grasp Dora's wrist. "Don't let this destroy you."

"Too late for that on both counts," Dora laughs. "Oh, the cavalry is here, I see."

Marianne rushes over and embraces her. Dora begins to sob.

"Is she drunk?" Beatrice whispers to Otto.

"Don't think so. Just furious as far as I can tell. Did you hear? Rusticated until she passes. Bloody Jourdain."

When she looks at Dora, Beatrice feels a stab of shame that

she has not noticed how much weight Dora has lost; her healthy outdoor glow has been replaced by the streaky gray pallor of marble. How many meals has she missed?

The lane is choked with crowds moving south to catch the queen's departure.

A passing woman with bunting draped around her shoulders thrusts her face into Dora's. "Cheer up, love," she says.

"Break your heart, did he?" her friend adds, and they march off laughing.

At Beatrice's suggestion, they take refuge in the graveyard of St. Peter-in-the-East and force Dora to sit on a low tomb by the gate. It is the oldest church in the city, and every stone looks as if it might crumble at the touch. Beatrice fights the temptation to search for interesting graves.

"Are you all right?" says Marianne, taking off her coat and draping it over Dora's shoulders.

Dora pauses for a moment, then shrugs, putting a hand up to her bare neck.

She looks up at them like a disappointed child, face wet and smeared. She begins to sob again. "I cut my hair."

"Oh my goodness, so you did, I hadn't noticed," says Otto, putting her arms around her. "You are quite a talent. You must do Beatrice's next."

Dora laughs feebly.

Behind them, a chorus of male voices can be heard. "*Vivat Regina*," they shout over and over again. The words flit like bats up into the darkening sky.

"Can I go home now?" says Dora.

TRINITY TERM

25

St. Hugh's College
Oxford

Thursday, April 28

Dear Greenwood,
Well, it has been an interesting week. The dreaded dance took
place in the dining hall on Tuesday evening. No men
permitted, despite the JCR submitting a last-minute plea to
Miss Jourdain. Instead, we were subject to a fruit punch
decidedly lacking a punch, the tiresome company of women
from other colleges, and the stimulating conversation of Miss
Turbott, Miss Cox, and Miss Stroud. I've had better
nightmares and that is the truth of the matter.

We heard from Miss Finch that you passed the Responsion
and may return to college. Bravo! Does that mean we will see
you at the weekend? Please come soon because Marianne
refuses to wave my hair. Sparks would do it if I asked her, but
thankfully I am not that desperate.

Temperance Underhill has broken up with her chap from
Keble, so you can imagine the drama. No need for us to go to
the Scala this week, we just stroll along to the JCR for the
performance.

Miss Jourdain is rather perturbed about May Morning, but
it seems we can attend "under certain conditions." It won't be

the same without you. If you don't return soon, I shall have to send for another Ouija board to conjure you up, and we all know how that turned out last time.

Yours in desperation,
Otto xxx

Dear Dora,
Just a quick note as we are adding these to Otto's envelope.

This week in Pass Mods class we translated extracts from Livy's History of Rome. I have copied out my notes for you. Next week is the Aeneid—hopefully, you will be back by then. In my first tute of the term with Miss Finch, we began The Canterbury Tales. I'm not sure if you are up to the same point. She says we need not write essays for her this term as we must focus on Pass Mods, which I thought was jolly decent of her. Anglo-Saxon classes have moved to 11 a.m. on Thursdays.

Last night, we went to see an OUDS performance of Julius Caesar. It went on so long that we had to leave before the end to get back for eleven. At least thirty women stood up and left at the same time, all of us treading on hats and feet as we made our way along the rows. It was awfully embarrassing but also rather funny. The audience started to laugh, and the poor actors had to stop.

Please come back soon, we miss you awfully. The Armistice Magnolia is in bloom and the cherry blossom on Banbury Road is worth the journey alone. To quote Mr. Coleridge, do let us be your "sheltering tree."

Yours affectionately,
Marianne X

PS We saw Frank at the theater. He was crestfallen when he realized you were not with us. He says he will write.

Dear D,

I hope this finds you well. The others have stolen all the best news.

I am so glad I decided to sit Pass Mods rather than Jurisprudence Prelims. It turns out the Logic tutor, Mr. Andrews, is splendidly bright. He has a tiny office at the top of the Clarendon Building into which the five of us must squeeze at 5 p.m. He is terribly witty, acting out all the scenarios with grand hand gestures, and even offers us sherry, which of course we do not refuse. You are going to enjoy it very much.

The remaining Eights sat up late last night arguing about the essay question we were set in our entrance examination—do you remember it? "The true tragic conflict is not between wrong and right, but between right and right." Hegel, of course.

Otto said she took umbrage at the adjective "true" in her answer and never got beyond that. Marianne used Antigone and Creon as an example of Greek tragedy where the state and the personal clash. I wrote about the same sort of thing but in the context of conscientious objectors and militant suffrage. Justified civil disobedience and whatnot. We wondered what you had put. Do let us know.

Your friend,
B. S. x

26

Sunday, May 1, 1921 (2nd Week)

NOTICE

Students are reminded that permission is required to attend May Morning, and that groups may not depart college until 4:30 a.m.

Students must walk directly to and from Magdalen Bridge in groups of three or more.

Conversation between men and women undergraduates should be avoided.

All students must sign in and out at the lodge.

Please note, attendance at morning chapel is still compulsory.

MISS E. F. JOURDAIN
Principal

O n May Morning, according to hundreds of years of tradition, the choir of Magdalen College ascend Magdalen Tower at dawn to sing the *Hymnus Eucharisticus*. Beatrice, Otto, Marianne, and a thousand other spectators gather on the bridge below, necks craned, to hear the choir welcome in the spring.

With the crowd pressed shoulder to shoulder, hands stuffed in pockets, the early-morning chill is less biting. Some revelers, old and young, wear pagan crowns of foliage and blossom. Others, in black tie, look as if they have been drinking all night. The odd bell clinks among a group of Morris dancers but the choir's song is so delicate and faint there is hardly a murmur or cough from the spectators. The police patrol the bridge and riverbank, ready to pull foolhardy jumpers from the River Cherwell; it is well known that to swallow the water is to court a visit to the Radcliffe Infirmary. Some students bob in punts, covered with blankets, eating and drinking from hampers; others sit on the banks below Magdalen Bridge or hang from windows.

"Is this *it*?" whispers Otto as the choir's voices—distant, hopeful, sweet—are carried out of earshot by the breeze.

Beatrice ignores her. She has long imagined herself part of this May Day ritual, and this morning she is enjoying the convivial university spirit that so often eludes her. She takes pride in having stayed up all night in Otto's room to wait for sunrise, even though there have been no dazzling rays to speak of; only the gradual and pedestrian lightening of the bleak gray sky indicates that April has transitioned into May. When they set out from college Beatrice had hoped to bump into Ursula, and remains alert for her distinctive yellow beret, but there is no sign of her. Occasionally, she imagines she sees the graceful and athletic silhouette of Dora and wants to wave and call out. But Dora has not returned to St. Hugh's this term, nor has she replied to their letters or telephone calls. Without Dora, there is an awkwardness in the balance of the group, as if each must work harder to bridge the gap, repurposing themselves for the stretch. According to Miss Finch, Dora can return. She took her third mathematics Responsion by post, and has passed, which leaves Beatrice mystified. No man is worth losing a place at Oxford whether he has returned from the dead or not. But more than that, Beatrice misses her. Dora is a vital part of the Eights, with her wit and energy, her good sense, and her fragile dignity.

When the hymn has ended, the three women turn back toward college, the waning crowd noticeably less buoyant than an hour ago. They collect their bicycles from outside New College and stroll up toward Broad Street. The King's Arms is selling hot toddies in tin cups from a table outside, and Otto buys three.

"Oh, don't look at me like that. It'll help us sleep," she says to the others.

"And fall off our bicycles," says Beatrice. She is not a fan of whiskey, but Oxford is notoriously chilly in spring, and it does seem like a good idea. She swallows the warm liquid in a couple of gulps and feels its abrasive heat travel down her gullet.

Marianne, more cautious, takes a sniff. "What's this?" she says, peering into the cup.

"Oh, just watered-down whiskey, honey, lemon. Good for you. Like medicine for a sore throat," says Otto. She and Beatrice exchange a smile. "Drink up, I'm getting us another."

As she queues at the stall, Henry Hadley and two other Christ Church men appear from the direction of Catte Street. The Eights have met Henry many times since the night at the Ashmolean, including having tea (Miss Stroud in tow) with his friends at Fuller's, the new café on Cornmarket, and attending Sunday service with him at the cathedral. Beatrice scoffed at the idea of Christ Church having its own art gallery and cathedral, and told him so, but was secretly thrilled to visit the college where Charles I held his Civil War parliament and Peel and Gladstone studied.

Henry and his friends buy themselves a toddy each too. The publican simply refills cups returned by other customers, but nobody seems bothered. They decamp together to the steps of the Clarendon Building, leaving their bicycles propped against the pub. Downing the second toddy, Beatrice is left with a leathery taste in her mouth and the repeated need to yawn so widely that her jaw clicks. Tiredness draws over her like a heavy blanket. And that is the moment the outing ceases to be fun for her anymore: when the distance between the cold stone steps and her warm bed suddenly seems insurmountable.

———◇———

ONCE THE MEN JOIN THEM, the conversation becomes loud and frenetic. Marianne rubs at a knot between her eyes and puts her growing sense of agitation down to the hot toddies, lack of sleep, and the fact that Henry Hadley has vigorously shaken her hand and extended his long legs out on the steps to her left. She should be at home today but has skipped a week to experience May Day morning. It is hardly responsible of her, and if she thinks too hard about it, she feels sick, even though her father encouraged it. He sent her a postcard of Magdalen Bridge describing May Morning as one of his fondest memories of Oxford and insisting she attend. He quoted the Song of Solomon: *For behold, the winter is past; the rain is over and gone. The flowers appear on the earth, the time of singing has come, and the voice of the turtledove is heard in our land.*

Still, she should be waking up in Culham right now.

On the steps below her, the others are sharing plans for the term: Summer Eights, picnics, punting, and such. Henry yawns beside her. He looks drunk on lack of sleep.

"God, I'm tired." He smiles. "Reminds me of France."

She nods and inspects the bottom of her cup.

"Where is Dora today? You're always together."

"She hasn't returned yet," she replies quietly. "We hope she will."

Marianne is aware that Henry witnessed Dora's strange behavior at both the lecture and the private view, but he has proved himself tactful and discreet.

"I can only surmise she has a past with Baker?" he says. His voice is low but sounds concerned rather than merely curious. "He was a bit of a rogue at training camp, but good-hearted, I always thought. Toward the end, he spent all his free time with his sweetheart and her family. Dora, I presume. I was never introduced. There was also a dog. Always trailing round after him—"

"She thought he was dead," she says. "Until the lecture."

Henry stares at her. "What?"

"I shouldn't talk about it," she says, looking into his eyes. "It's Dora's business."

She thinks how nice it would be to be kissed by him. She is tired and a little drunk and he is solid and real and smells of whiskey. She remembers a time—on Armistice Day—when she experienced that same combination, and look where that got her. But his scars comfort her, make her trust him, which is nonsensical. Yet it is as if he, like her, has a piece missing. She is not attracted to wholeness or perfection in others, quite the opposite. She does not want it, does not deserve it. What a pity he can never know who she really is.

"Don't say anything, will you?" she adds. "I shouldn't have told you, I don't know why I did. I'm just sad she isn't here."

"I won't," he says, shaking his head. His hair flops over one eye. "For what it's worth, I'm sorry to hear it."

"HENRY HADLEY IS TERRIBLY KEEN on you, Marianne," says Otto, after they say goodbye to the men. "I've invited him and his sister to tea when she comes to visit."

Marianne wonders if there is a hint of annoyance in her tone, then decides, no, that is just for women in books. Otto is not jealous, she is relishing this information, rolling it out like dough and stretching it as if to form a lid over a pie.

"Have you ever made pastry, Otto?" she asks.

"Lord no, that's what cooks are for. To ensure I don't poison anybody, I'll stick to equations."

By the time they return to college they are yawning and exhausted, dragging their bicycles past the lodge and ditching them carelessly in the racks. Nobody remembers to sign in and

Marianne forces herself to attend chapel with Beatrice while Otto goes straight to bed. Marianne nods off during prayers and has a disconcerting image of Henry kissing her forehead. When she returns to her room, Maud is making up the fireplace but does not turn her head in greeting. Although Marianne knows she ought to write again to Dora, she has never felt so leaden. As she pulls on her nightgown, a Herculean task, her eyes are already closed.

HAVING SLEPT ALL DAY, MARIANNE wakes in the evening and wonders where she is. Neck stiff, limbs heavy, temples throbbing. She stands shakily and vomits bile neatly into her hand. Leaning on the wall, she wants to turn on the light, but the effort would be akin to scaling a mountain. She is afraid of the weakness in her legs and prepares to retreat backward onto the bed. She considers dropping to the floor so that she can crawl—the ground has appeal, the more she can touch the more real she must be—but she inches her way toward the mattress and flops sideways onto it. The effort is exhausting. Time passes. She wants water, but it is too hard. More time passes. The bell rings in the distance, footsteps wax and wane on the pavement outside, light moves across the room, although she still cannot move her head without retching. She is wet. Nightgown, hair, sheets blend into a damp film that clings to her. *What is happening?* she asks her mother, whom she has never met, who died at her age in a pool of uterine blood while Marianne mewled in the arms of a wet nurse. Then she sees a young man in khaki in the corner of the room. He is holding a baby. She asks to see the baby, but he shakes his head and then Marianne is lying on the floor, and it is very cold. The contents of the chamber pot are pooled on the floor. The smell of feces and vomit and urine makes it bothersome to sleep. Even worse is the interminable banging and moaning. She would call out, but her mouth is full of something strange, and someone has tied her down by the hands.

27

Tuesday, May 2, 1921 (2nd Week)

While the British government is partitioning six Irish counties and naming it Northern Ireland, influenza infiltrates college with alarming efficiency. A mild but feisty strain of "Spanish flu," it comes up to Oxford with a bearded Brasenose student from Kent who unwittingly gifts it to his violinist friend during a recital in the chapel. A few days later, the violinist attends the May Day celebrations on Magdalen Bridge, where he coughs on many people, including a long-necked first-year from St. Hugh's who is standing between a very tall and a very short companion. From then on, it is only a matter of time.

When Marianne does not appear for breakfast the next day, and Maud complains that Miss Grey's door is bolted from the inside and she cannot get in, Otto and Beatrice climb in through the unlocked window. The smell of ammonia, sweat, and diarrhea is overwhelming, and for a moment Otto is back in the sluice at Somerville.

Marianne is lying in her own filth on the bedsitter floor.

"Oh my God, oh my God," says Beatrice. "Is she dead?"

"No, she is not dead. For goodness' sake," says Otto, dropping to her knees next to Marianne. "The most important thing is to get her temperature down. Prop the window open."

Beatrice, ashen, does not move.

"Well, go on!" says Otto, aware of a foul wetness creeping

through her skirt and up her shins. She grabs a pillow from the bed and slides it under Marianne's head.

"If you think you might be susceptible, then keep away," says Otto. "I took care of influenza patients at Somerville. I'll be fine."

"Influenza?"

"I think so."

"There was something about it in the *Oxford Times* yesterday. Brasenose is bad, I think."

Marianne's pulse is fast but strong. She moans a slurred apology.

"Don't waste your breath, Marianne, it's all right," Otto replies, suppressing the urge to retch that is building in her throat.

"Pass me a glass of water. No—half-full. God, Beatrice, for a very clever woman you are an utter shambles in an emergency."

Otto puts the glass to Marianne's mouth. She tries to swallow, but the liquid skims off her lips and slides down her face into the pillow. The stuff of nightmares.

"This is not good. I don't know what to do, Otto. Tell me what to do," whimpers Beatrice.

"Go to the bursar and see what's going on. If Marianne's not the only one, then tell her to ring the Radcliffe Infirmary, ask for masks and bedpans and any Bayer aspirin tablets they can spare. They should have tons of the stuff since they closed the military wards. If it's really bad, suggest to the bursar that someone draw up notices and post them around college. Miss Brockett has nursed; she'll know what to write."

Beatrice turns to go.

"Wait. Help me move her first," Otto says. "Marianne, we're going to clean you up and move you into the hall while we sort out your floor." She gets to her feet. "Sparks, help me with the mattress."

They lift the thin mattress off the bed, sheets intact, over

Marianne and push it through the doorway into the corridor. Otto has forgotten how strong Beatrice is. It folds as easily as a piece of paper and springs back open, causing them to gasp and laugh at the awkwardness of it. Otto lays a towel over it.

They lift Marianne off the floor by the armpits. The soft hairs catch between Otto's fingers. The heat of her skin is strange, as if there is a furnace inside her, running out of control. Marianne's legs are weak, her head flops, but her eyes flicker open. They sit her down on the towel and drag the sodden nightdress over her head.

"No, no, no," moans Marianne, grasping the nightdress.

"Hush now, it's time to rest," says Otto.

Marianne flops back naked on the mattress, face flushed and feverish, lips pale. Beatrice busies herself shutting the curtains of the hall window.

Otto grabs the water jug from Marianne's room and instructs Beatrice to find Maud.

"Tell her to bring clean sheets and a new pillow. The floor needs to be mopped. The room stinks," she calls as Beatrice goes down the corridor. "She'll be in the kitchens."

She looks in the cupboard over the washstand that houses Marianne's toothbrush and finds a cotton sanitary napkin. Dipping it into the jug, she kneels beside Marianne on the corridor floor and sponges her face and neck, wetting her hair. Heat rises into the cloth as her friend's sour breath brushes her cheek. From the open window she hears indistinct male voices and the sound of crates slamming onto the pavement. She rinses and squeezes the cloth and says, "It's going to be fine, Marianne. I just need to wash you. You won't remember this and that's probably just as well for both of us."

She wipes across Marianne's collarbones, which stand proud, little valleys of dark skin pouching beneath them, and then works her way down from the nape of her neck to her sternum. Bending over her friend's body as if laying her out for burial, Otto cannot help but notice how it differs from her own: areolas darker, breasts looser, skin freckled and more yellow in hue. And then she notices an odd patterning that makes her lift her hand and inspect the cloth for sharp edges. But these are not scratches, they are ladders. Some silvery-blue, shiny, flat; others small white zigzags. They cluster at the base of Marianne's belly like forest bracken, tips pointy and unfurled. On her breasts they look more like the scratchings of a cat: irregular, narrow, deliberate. An unmistakable story written on her body in hieroglyphics. Otto has been shown these patterns by Gertie, who is keen to ensure her sisters know a lot more about the perils of married life than she did.

Has Marianne been pregnant, carried a baby? Marianne? She can hardly believe it, wonders if she is the one who is sick and hallucinating.

Barely registering the filth and the stench around Marianne's thighs, she washes her gently, wiping brown smears from her legs, and rolling her to clean her backside. She is party to something far more intimate than seeing Marianne naked. A secret she is not meant to share. She fetches a jug and cloth from her own room and begins again around the face, moisture evaporating from the blushing skin immediately. Marianne murmurs a few lucid words of apology but trails off into strange utterings that Otto cannot make out. She finds a simple shift nightdress in the bottom drawer of the dresser and works it down over Marianne's abdomen.

After a while, she hears Beatrice return with Maud, who ties a rag around her face and sets to with Lysol, mopping the floorboards and emptying the chamber pot.

"At least a dozen people are ill," pants Beatrice. "The twins, Norah, Ivy, Miss Jourdain, Miss Cox. How is Marianne?"

"Calm. Cooler. I could do with that aspirin, though."

"I'll telephone now." Beatrice pauses beside her. "Otto, you've been—I mean, you are—"

"Get out of here, Sparks," says Otto. Then, without looking

up, she holds out her hand to Beatrice, who takes it in hers and squeezes it. "Now wash your hands," she adds.

Once Maud has finished and Marianne is back in her bed, Otto strips off her own filthy blouse and skirt and curls up in an armchair next to her. Her hands are shaking, and she wants a cigarette desperately but has none with her, so she resorts to counting prime numbers until her pulse stops pounding so emphatically in her ears.

———◇———

BEATRICE FOLLOWS OTTO'S INSTRUCTIONS TO the letter, ringing the Radcliffe Infirmary herself and typing out Miss Brockett's advice for those who feel unwell, posting the notices on the doors of every WC and corridor. She is Otto's foot soldier.

By dinner that evening, she is ravenous, but all that is provided is a makeshift offering of minestrone soup and sandwiches. The events of the day have taken their toll on the whole college.

"Maud says around fifteen women are in bed, including four tutors," she reports, sliding into the seat next to Otto. "The scouts have been told not to go in."

"How on earth are they supposed to look after themselves?" Otto says, chin propped on her hand. She hasn't touched her sandwich and looks utterly exhausted. "The bursar needs to step up."

Ada Bird, a stoutly built third-year sitting opposite, glances up. "We're looking after our friend on a rota. We both had flu last year and it was jolly awful. I've asked the bursar to telephone her parents. I think she would be better at home."

"Miss Jourdain is very bad," ventures Patricia Clough from the end of the table, still reticent around Otto and seated as far away from her as possible. "I heard she's in hospital."

The women chew on in glum silence. Someone at another

table has a prolonged coughing bout and leaves the room, hunched over cupped hands.

"Two students at Lady Margaret Hall died in 1918," says Ada Bird, filling Beatrice's glass with water. "It was much nastier then. We're lucky it isn't worse."

"Are we lucky, though?" says Otto, though not unkindly. "Because I don't feel lucky at all. I feel like we've been through enough already."

The table nods because it is true. It occurs to Beatrice that she has been in the midst of some battle or another for at least ten years.

Otto pushes her plate toward Beatrice and gets to her feet. "I'm going to check on Marianne."

As she eats Otto's sandwich, Beatrice recalls her time at the WVR and how she did not get the job that she wanted as a motorbike messenger (probably just as well), but she got the one she was best suited for, administration. She must work to her strengths. At this thought, she rallies. She will read a book about first aid. Then she can be more use next time. She goes to the JCR and writes a letter to Dora, certain she will want to know that Marianne is ill. She dashes off a quick note to Henry at Christ Church, remembering how closely he was talking to Marianne on May Day. Then, one to Ursula, canceling their luncheon tomorrow and to check whether the flu has reached Somerville. She drops both notes into pigeon post and takes Dora's to the post office on North Parade in time for the last collection.

Thankfully, their fears of an escalation in the flu prove unfounded, leading Beatrice to wonder if it is an immutable legacy of war that her generation will always expect the worst of any situation. The outbreak recedes swiftly and, apart from Miss Jourdain, there are no prolonged cases. Marianne wakes the next morning with a lower temperature, although she says her head pounds, which makes her want to retch. She has no recollection of being found on the floor in such a state and asks

Beatrice for her locket, which lies coiled on her bedside table. Otto says the room smells like a hospital ward, but Marianne is oblivious. When she falls asleep again, Beatrice returns to her own room and weeps furiously into a cushion until she is spent.

The next day, Marianne eats a little toast and Maud fills the metal bath for her. Henry has sent a bunch of lilacs and a note to say he is quite well and that he wishes Marianne a speedy recovery. Marianne looks a little flustered and Otto administers the usual teasing. Later, when she is able to sit up in bed, Beatrice reads to her from a new political weekly called *Time and Tide*. Otto says it is guaranteed to put anyone in a stupor and disappears to get the gramophone.

Marianne asks Beatrice to pass her hairbrush. "Did I say anything odd when I was ill?" she asks, tugging the brush through her hair, leaving red scratches on the pale skin of her neck.

"You mentioned your mama," says Beatrice. "But it was Otto who was with you most of the time."

But Marianne does not ask Otto. Instead, they argue in the cramped little room about whether Marianne should go home to Culham to recuperate.

"I'll borrow my aunt's motorcar and drive you," says Otto. "You were meant to go home this weekend anyway."

Marianne looks past Otto and out the window. "I can't risk it. I might infect them."

Beatrice thinks of her own bed in Bloomsbury, of Cook's broths and milk puddings when she is poorly. "You'll be better looked after at home," she says.

Marianne's gray eyes shine. "I'm sorry I've been a bind."

"Don't be silly," says Otto, adjusting her hair in the mirror above the fireplace. "Stay if you want, but I'm determined to get out of here." As she opens the door and steps into the corridor, she calls over her shoulder. "In fact, I might pay a visit to Dora."

28

Marianne, November 1918

The day the Armistice is signed, the bells of St. Mary's ring all day across Culham and the neighboring fields. Marianne walks up the gravel path from the rectory to the tower doorway to watch the ringers at work; she has always enjoyed the rhythmical pull and release of the ropes. Today it does not look like an onerous task but a welcome one, and the men take turns, fueled by sandwiches and bottles of beer. They wave at her, as they have been doing for the last eighteen years. The rector's motherless daughter. One blows her a kiss. It is as if it is Christmas morning rather than an overcast Monday afternoon. Normal rules of etiquette do not seem to apply at the end of the war to end all wars.

It reminds her of how the aristocrats leave the court in *As You Like It*. Treating their exile like a holiday jaunt, they insist that there is *no clock in the forest,* and nobody minds *the churlish chiding of the winter's wind.* It is preferable to politics and conflict, Duke Senior argues, yet he returns to the court as soon as he gets the chance. He cannot resist the opportunity to lead, to control. There will be other wars someday, Marianne suspects.

Later, her father visits their neighbor's house for dinner, an invitation she has declined for herself, the company of two pipe-smoking widowers being more a punishment than a celebration.

Her closest friends, two cheerful sisters in their thirties who live together, are busy with visiting nieces and nephews. The half-moon is bright and the sky clear, so she takes the opportunity to wander along the lanes of the village, wrapped up in her father's greatcoat and felt hat. She imagines that even the burrowing creatures dwelling in the stone walls and hawthorn hedgerows must be awake, alert to the strange behavior of the human world around them. Treacly light glows through the windows of houses that are usually dim and she imagines there is dancing inside. Farther down the street, the Nag's Head rattles with glass and piano chords. Locals in caps and gloves have taken their drinks onto the village green and huddle around a bonfire, rusty flecks of ash dancing into the night sky. Fireworks burst into short-lived stars in the direction of Abingdon. She stops to look up, trying to remember all she sees for posterity but somehow unable to retain any of it.

On a whim, she walks down the side of the green and takes the old footpath that snakes through decaying bracken and skirts the riverbank toward the medieval bridge. She is not afraid on a night like this. She enjoys the swish of the wet grass against the hem of her coat, inhaling damp loam and the fecund smell of the River Thames. She cannot see much by moonlight, but she can hear a nighttime world of activity. Owls hoot as if they are signaling her arrival. Small creatures—rats or mice, she supposes—scurry through the undergrowth at ground level. The river maintains its constant lapping and babbling. It will meander through fields and villages, over pebbles and weeds and weirs on its journey across London and out to the sea. Masses of tributaries joining together, each drop contributing to an unstoppable force, as soldiers compose an army, or words a book. What does she contribute to? she wonders. A family of two, a village, a parish? She believes in belonging. After all, it is so much easier to swim with the current.

Eventually, she arrives at a small clearing beneath a willow tree where the path broadens, and lovers come in summer to picnic in the shade of the overhanging boughs. Marsh orchids fan out their tiny purple wings there in June and July, and she remembers sketching them as a child, swatting midges angrily and rubbing at nettle stings on her shins. But this evening, in the darkness, the rush of the water seems unusually loud. It is tempting to wish it away, but the sound is as inevitable as time, as aging, as the movement of blood around the body. Absence of motion, and the silence that accompanies it, is what she fears.

Now that the war is over, and she is eighteen, she has plans to follow this river upstream. Her father is tutoring her in Classics, and she will sit the examinations for Oxford women's colleges next year. Somerville is the best, it is said, but her godmother has sway at one of the others. Times are changing. Women over thirty with property have gained the vote and will exercise that right in only a few weeks. And now that the war is over, the world will surely be open to healing and regeneration.

Out of the darkness, a stumbling figure appears on the footpath from the other direction and steps into the clearing. She is startled but not afraid. It is obvious he has not sought her out. A bat swoops across the path between them. He is young, unshaven, slightly disheveled, with unhappy black eyes. They nod vaguely at each other in the moonlight, and he stands next to her looking out onto the water. He is in khaki, she can see that, and smells of tobacco and sweat. She thinks perhaps they attended the village school together. He swigs from a glass bottle for a few minutes, then offers it to her with an outstretched arm. It seems rude not to celebrate with a soldier on a day like today, so she puts her mouth to the cold glass rim and swallows. It burns, which makes her want to spit it out, but she does not. Perhaps it is brandy or whiskey, she would not know. She drinks again, coughs, and hands it back. She remembers his name is Tom and that he was once caned by the teacher. They stand for a while longer listening to the bells ringing and ringing, fingertips touching as the bottle passes to and fro between them. It could be three or thirty minutes; she is not sure. No words are exchanged between them, but she can tell that Tom is crying. She can feel his sobs in her own chest, feels the rawness of his throat in hers, the heave of his shoulders in her shoulders. It goes on and on, compounding with the cacophony of the river, until she cannot bear it any longer.

"It's over," she says, stepping to face him and putting her hands on his forearms like her father does if he needs to tell her something important. He moves closer and presses his cheek into her coat so that she takes the weight of it on her collarbones. She strokes his hair as if he is a baby, murmuring comforting nothings. They lean against each other in the darkness, the bells pealing, the river slapping, hearts pumping urgently as if they have discovered they are the only people alive on the earth. He lifts his mouth to her face and searches for her mouth. His wet lips drag over her chin, searching. He kisses her gently at first, then more urgently. His tongue pushes against hers and moves in time with the song of the river. Marianne finds that her body knows how to respond; the alcohol has unlocked her. They bend and coil into the earth, and she unpeels layers of herself, as if it were the most natural thing in the world to lie there among the leaves and twigs and beetles, finding the way together.

The next day it is as if it never happened: Tuesday is an ordinary Tuesday. Bells ring on the hour; the village is quiet, tired. Her father returns to counseling mourning mothers and she to her studies. She tries to revisit what happened moment by moment but can recall only flashes of it with a twinge of desire and nausea. She cannot recall the walk home—was it alone or accompanied? There is blood in her drawers, so she rinses them out in the scullery sink. At lunchtime, she thinks she sees him loitering at the gate of the churchyard and hides upstairs in her room for the rest of the day, but she knows that no soldiers have been demobilized yet. He must be on leave and will be gone soon.

A few weeks before Christmas, she hears that Tom has been admitted to hospital in Oxford with pneumonia. Busy with Advent services and preparations for Christmas at the rectory, she tries to forget what happened on Armistice night. On the first day of 1919, she begins a new diary and is about to count ahead to her next monthly cycle when she realizes that she has not bled since October. She knows what this means. There is a parasite inside her, sapping her energy and self-respect, destroying her plans to study at Oxford. Yet at the same time, she feels relief that she and her father will no longer have to be everything to each other. It is as if she has joined an orchestra, picked up a piece of sheet music, and realized she knows the melody. She is part of "something larger" after all.

Under a white January sky, Marianne takes the train to Oxford and visits the various military hospitals asking after him. He is not in Somerville College—that is for officers—nor New College or the Examination Schools. She locates him in the Radcliffe Infirmary, where he lies dangerously ill with complications, his heart weak, his prognosis poor. His bewildered mother allows the rector's daughter to join her at the bedside, hears a strange, bookish, motherless girl tell her that she wants to marry her son, wonders what an educated woman wants from a farm laborer who is unlikely to live out the month, and fears that her son, so angry on his last visit home, has forced himself on Marianne.

"Please know, he has done nothing wrong," says Marianne. "But the proper thing must be done for the sake of the child. For all our sakes. If there is a chaplain here, I'll ask him to get a special license."

"Do you want to marry Miss Grey, Tom?" the mother asks her son when he wakes for a short time.

"What?" he says, confused. His cheeks are hollow but he is broader than Marianne remembers, with the same sad, dark eyes. He does not register her presence at all.

"Miss Grey says there is a baby. That you should marry as soon as possible."

He nods, avoiding his mother's gaze. "I don't know. Whatever you think."

"Then I can see the child and watch over it until you are better."

Telling her father is the worst moment of Marianne's life. Her father has been her champion in all things. He has shared her dreams of reading English at Oxford, to study the classic works of literature in the footsteps of the greats. He asks God for direction and what he learns is that whatever happened to her on Armistice night—and he does not know—is the collective responsibility of them all. He is terrified that he will lose her in childbirth, as he did his wife, but it is too late to prevent that now. He blames himself for keeping her ignorant of the facts of planning a family, or of men's capacity to take what they want. But Marianne already knows disappointment, embarrassment, disgust, and anger—she carries enough for the both of them. He does not need to add to her shame.

On January 18, 1919, as the Paris Peace Conference formally opens at Quai d'Orsay, Miss Marianne Grey becomes Mrs. Thomas Ward. The couple are married at the groom's hospital bedside in the company of both parents. The bride wears her Sunday best and her mother's narrow gold ring.

Two days later Marianne Ward is a widow.

29

POST OFFICE
Telegram

FROM OXFORD 11AM TUESDAY MAY 10, 1921
TO MISS D GREENWOOD FAIRVIEW BERKHAMSTED

COMING TO RESCUE YOU SATURDAY DASH WONT
TAKE NO FOR AN ANSWER STOP MEN
OF OXFORD BEREFT WITHOUT YOU STOP
THE EIGHTS ALMOST AS BEREFT STOP

The drive to Berkhamsted is forty miles via Wheatley, Thame, and the Chiltern Hills. Beatrice has never spent so long in a motor vehicle and finds that if she looks at the view and tries not to inhale the hot fumes rising from around her cramped legs, she can just about manage the queasiness. She was seasick once, on a ferry to Calais, and the sour lurching stomach felt just the same.

"Chequers Court is up there." Otto waves her arm toward a sharp green ridge with a slender white monument on top. The car, a brand-new Crossley, dazzling in the sun, lurches to the left. "Lady Lee is a friend of Mother's."

Beatrice has heard of Chequers. It has been splashed all over the *Times*, this gift to the nation. Thanks to the Lees' bequest, prime ministers like Lloyd George who do not have estates of their own have a house in which they can entertain the likes of Woodrow Wilson.

"No children to inherit," shouts Otto over the engine.

Beatrice wonders if Chequers is symbolic of the demise of the "ruling classes" but does not like to mention it. Otto inhabits a world that she believes is quite ordinary, a world that suffers vastly different crises from the rest of the population. When they had luncheon together at the Ritz during the Easter vac, it felt as if Beatrice was undertaking an expedition to a foreign country. Otto introduced her to so many honorables and earls that Beatrice felt compelled to drink five glasses of champagne and staggered straight to bed when she got home. Today, glamorous in dark glasses and sheer cream scarf, Otto looks entirely comfortable at the wheel of her aunt's car. Beatrice wonders if she feels the Crossley's constant jolting and jerking at all.

A few miles on, there is another long drive, half-concealed by trees. "Halton House," shouts Otto, smiling and waving at the guards at the sentry box. "Sold to the RAF at the end of the war by the nephew who inherited."

Beatrice nods. Her backside is partly numb, partly agonizingly sore. By the time they enter Hertfordshire, she is planning how to pad it for the return journey. She tries to focus on the landscape: rolling chalk hills dotted with quaint villages and market towns. A group of little boys with sticks for guns run whooping alongside them as they enter Tring. The town center comprises a row of shops and a church that appears to be entirely made of flint.

"This is the entrance to Tring Park, Rothschild's place." Otto gestures across the road.

The Crossley rattles over a series of potholes.

"I can't hear you, who?"

"Walter Rothschild," shouts Otto. "He keeps emus and kangaroos in the park and drives a carriage pulled by zebras."

"As in Lord Rothschild of the Balfour Declaration? Working to establish a Jewish homeland?"

Otto looks blank. "If you say so. I heard he rides about on giant turtles." She lets go of the wheel and makes horse-riding motions with her hands.

Beatrice laughs, despite her aching rump. "You really should sell tickets for this tour, Otto," she says, turning her face to the vast cerulean sky.

ARRIVING IN BERKHAMSTED IN THE late afternoon, they encounter a wide high street with few pedestrians or motorcars. Signs to the station take them past a school with what looks like a Tudor chapel and over a glittering canal. Beatrice hops out to get directions from the stationmaster. Their journey continues around the ruins of a motte-and-bailey castle and up the hill toward the common. Dora lives in a house called Fairview on the edge of the Ashridge estate. After a few dead ends, they locate the house and pull up on the gravel drive. It looks as if it has been built in the last decade, with low tiled roofs, huge redbrick chimneys, black-latticed windows, and faux-Tudor beams.

Dora steps out of the shadowy doorway to embrace them.

"You got the telegram, then?" says Otto, stretching out her arms. "We're here to take you back."

"Miss Finch told us you passed your examination," says Beatrice, glancing around as she hobbles to the door. "It's very *green* here."

Dora smiles. She looks better than when they last saw her: fresher, pinker. "Come in, let me get you some tea," she says. "Tell me, how is Marianne?"

"She's fine, absolutely fine. She's sorry she couldn't come, but she had to visit the rectory." Otto takes Dora's arm. "Now, tell me, what do you think of Beatrice's new look? We went shopping in London. Doesn't she remind you of Radclyffe Hall?"

Beatrice straightens with pride as Dora admires her new ensemble: cropped hair, straight black skirt, plain white blouse, and a man's tweed jacket.

THEY SIT OUTSIDE ON THE brick terrace watching squirrels chase each other up and down an enormous willow tree.

"*Under the Greenwood Tree*," says Beatrice, pleased with herself.

Dora laughs. "I knew one of you would say that."

"Where are the dreaded parents?" asks Otto.

"Father will be at his club for hours yet, and Mother is visiting friends with the boys. We're safe for a bit."

The housekeeper brings tea and fresh scones. The garden is dominated by robust borders of lupins, delphinium, and agapanthus. Wisteria snakes along the stone balustrade. Dora's home is so immaculately presented that Beatrice is almost afraid to touch anything, although she is surprised to see the influence of the Arts and Crafts movement on the design of new homes so far from London. Beatrice thinks of the chaos of her parents' narrow Victorian town house in Bloomsbury and wonders what they are doing right now. She cannot imagine living in a forest, where the predominant sounds are birds and the earth gives off an ancient, prehistoric scent. The squirrels at play remind her of the kittens. She must tell Marianne, she thinks.

Overhead, an airship, a giant white seed, crosses the cloudless sky.

"I haven't seen one of those for months," says Beatrice.

They stare upward, heads lolling back.

"It's on the way to the station at Cardington. It's closing down soon. Not enough demand," says Dora. "A soldier shot a

Zepp down not far from here and they gave him the Victoria Cross. We're on the flight path from the North Sea. They used to follow the railway line carrying bombs for London. I still feel an awful churning when I see one."

Beatrice rubs her neck. "I'm the same, although it was the Gothas that were the real problem in London."

"Papa flew to Paris in an airship once," says Otto. "He described it as the most terrifying thing he's ever done, after marrying my mother."

A wasp buzzes over the table. Otto pulls the chiffon scarf from around her neck and waves it about impatiently. There is a lull when no one says anything.

Otto is the one who breaks the silence. "Oh, come on, Dora, what's going on? Why haven't you come back? Is it your parents?"

Dora sighs, twisting and folding her earlobe. "I can hardly believe I'm saying this, but it's not them. Obviously, they were disappointed about the letter from Miss Jourdain, but they won't stop me from returning." She organizes the china and pours them each a cup of tea. "Mother has been remarkably understanding. She's not a great believer in the female intellect, so me failing an examination was of little consequence to her." She lets out a long sigh. "She persuaded Father that I might as well see it through just in case Frank makes me an offer. The fact he was George's friend has made her doubly keen."

"Gosh," says Beatrice.

"Miss Jourdain was very generous in her letter and didn't dwell on the rule-breaking. Father received several letters from Jesus about George in the same vein, so he wasn't terribly cross. Seems to see it as a rite of passage at Oxford. And he isn't as quick to anger as before the war. In fact, he's become really rather indulgent and sentimental since George . . ." She interlinks her fingers at the back of her neck. "Before you ask, they don't know about Charles."

Otto waves a scone in the air. "Can I eat this? I'm starving. Go on."

"Miss Jourdain didn't mention it in the letter, which was jolly decent of her. And what would be the point in telling them? Nothing helpful could be achieved from it." She takes two gulps of tea and looks across the garden. "It's more that Oxford has lost its shine for me."

"Oh, what a shame," offers Beatrice, not able to imagine it at all.

Dora pours more tea, and they drink in silence. There is rustling and cooing in the trees beyond the garden. "It's not just Charles. I feel as if I've made an enormous fool of myself. I don't think I was there for the right reasons. I'm the sort of girl Miss Jourdain hates. The one who sees Oxford as a finishing school. I don't feel as if I am wanted by the college."

Beatrice bites into a doughy scone slathered in jam and cream. The wasp returns and doubles its efforts to disrupt them and she bats it away with her napkin. "We miss you and want you and we *are* the college. There isn't a college without students. Miss Finch keeps asking after you too."

"Oh, come on, Greenwood," says Otto, licking crumbs off her wrist.

Dora looks between them both. "I do want to come back and try again, but Charles is everywhere," she says. "It's as if he's tarnished it for me." She looks away. A magpie swoops over the lawn and disappears into the trees. "Also, it seems he's had some kind of change of heart."

Otto's head jerks up. "What?"

"He's written to say he wants to see me, to talk."

Beatrice can hardly believe it. "Golly. What will you do?"

"I don't know."

A heavy door slams from inside the house. The yelps and footsteps of children reverberate down the long central hallway.

"Let's go for a walk," says Dora, rising briskly. "Drink up. If the twins see us, they won't leave us alone."

Dora leads them down the wide stone steps and over the lawn and into a series of narrow pathways edged by walls of towering bracken. The children's high voices soon become muffled as their sister strides ahead on the dry dirt path.

———◇———

FAIRVIEW SITS ON THE BROW of a hill. Half a mile below, Otto can see tiny red canal boats on a strip of sludge-colored water, some puffing smoke, others towed by giant horses. Berkhamsted is a quaint sort of place, with its medieval castle, golf course, and school, but she cannot identify much else to recommend it. Apparently, Dora's father owns a factory in the next town. What sort of factory, she has no idea, and having known Dora for nearly eight months, she really ought to. She must ask Beatrice.

Dora leads them away from Fairview via a woodland path that crosses the road before opening into a chalk hillside. The land is grassy, crisscrossed with shallow ditches. There are piles of stones, sandbags, and broken barrels dotted under the trees.

"What happened here?" asks Beatrice.

"Practice trenches. They filled most of them in," says Dora. "But they left this section of the front line for posterity. We're going to walk along it."

Otto recalls that Berkhamsted was a garrison for the duration of the war. So Dora lived among healthy officers before they went to France, and she lived among broken ones on their return. She has never thought about it like that.

The women help each other down a set of collapsing sandbags into the trench.

"This is where I first kissed Charles," says Dora, leading the way along the creaking duckboards. "I thought my life was about to start and that what I wore and how people looked and getting married was everything. What a fool. I was *grateful* for the war bringing him to my doorstep, you know. Isn't that awful?"

Beatrice, behind her, says, "You're being terribly tough on yourself, old girl."

All Otto can see in front of her are Beatrice's broad shoulders, but she pokes her head to the side and shouts up the line to Dora. "It's what you do now that matters."

Otto wonders how this might apply to Marianne. She has not spoken to her about the scars on her abdomen yet, although she feels she must. There has been an awkwardness between them ever since. It never ceases to amaze Otto how the most unlikely people live with whopping secrets every day of their lives. Truth is merely an abstract concept, after all, she muses. Everyone has a different version of it.

Weeds poke up between the boards and drag at their skirts, but they walk on in single file. Occasionally, they pass a dugout that is overgrown or used as a camp by local children. In places the trench is wide and high enough to accommodate a horse; other times it is narrow, and the sides rear toward them. It is impossible not to feel somber after all that has happened in France, and they continue for five or ten minutes without speaking at all. The boards ping up as they walk, gray with dried muddy footprints. At last, they reach the end of the main trench and clamber out onto the edge of what appears to be a golf course.

Otto lights two cigarettes, handing one to Dora. "I can't see how you would want to sit in a drawing room pouring tea for guests when you could be riding a bicycle around Oxford in the rain wearing a daft woolen cap."

Dora inhales deeply. "I do miss it," she replies.

They stand in the shade of a silver birch tree, its bark peeling off into pieces of charred paper.

Otto feels a wave of tiredness. "God, I'm sweaty. How can you stand to wear that heavy jacket, Sparks?"

Beatrice, in her tweed jacket, is heavily flushed. "You should know things are improving, Dora," she says. "The men are getting used to us. Chap rules are less strict. Miss Jourdain's not about and Kirby's doing a terrific job standing in. The women's colleges are working together on funding. We are getting there, we really are."

"And," says Otto with a grin, "guess who's standing for JCR president."

Dora turns to Beatrice. "Good for you."

"I might stand myself, just to make it exciting," says Otto. "Oh, and some idiot from Somerville got caught climbing back in at three a.m. The chap was giving her a leg up, can you imagine? It got into the *Daily Mail* and now she's been rusticated for two terms for 'tarnishing the reputation' of the college. Of course, some might say that two terms off Somerville is a reward, not a punishment."

"You'd better watch out, Otto," says Dora, smiling.

Beatrice looks smug. "You'll be glad to know, she hasn't sneaked out for ages."

"I've come to the conclusion I rather like my life at St. Hugh's," says Otto. "And I refuse to give Jourdain or Kirby the pleasure of curtailing it."

They stand for a moment watching a pair of wood pigeons wrestling in the trees.

Otto elbows Dora in the ribs. "How did you pass that bloody Responsion anyway?"

Dora shakes the dust from her skirt. "Oh, I rowed with my mother about my hair. Shut myself in my room for five days. Nothing else to do but find my old school notes and practice quadratic equations."

"Bravo, you," says Beatrice, slipping off her jacket and folding it awkwardly over her arm.

"Your hair is certainly less lopsided than when we last met," observes Otto.

"Mother cried about it, and it's not even her hair. I had to go and get it fixed."

"Nice shingle, though." Otto blows a smoke ring into another smoke ring. A trickle of sweat runs down her back. "Can we go and finish tea now? Sparks needs to be fed every hour, as you know, and my feet are killing me."

Dora grinds her cigarette end inexpertly into the grass. "I'm surprised I got you this far," she laughs. "On the way back, I want to show you something."

THEY SKIRT AROUND THE EDGE of the golf course back toward the house, pausing to watch the skylarks that swoop and circle over nests hidden in the hollows of a clearing. The path is bleached white, cut into a bank of chalk covered with tall grasses and low spiky bushes that seem intent on laddering Otto's stockings. She follows Dora's careful steps through a swathe of crêpe-paper poppies, oxeye daisies, and wild strawberries that cling to the meadow floor. Every so often, the long grasses are bowed by dragonflies with turquoise thoraxes that look like threaded glass beads.

"It's beautiful," says Beatrice. To her surprise, Otto cannot contradict her.

"The owner died in March with no heir, so it's to be broken up and sold," says Dora. "There could be houses here next year."

Eventually, Dora stops at the base of a chalky slope. "Round about here," she says to herself, staring intently at the ground. Then she stoops and peers at a stout stem around five inches tall. "There!"

The stem supports two tiny lilac flowers and a bud at the tip. The plant is stiffer than the silky grasses around it and does not bend in the wind.

"Is that what I think it is?" asks Beatrice, carefully lowering herself to her knees. "Oh, Dora, it's much smaller than I thought. So delicate. See, Otto, the brown furry lip looks just like a bee and the three purple sepals are its wings."

"Jolly good," says Otto, inspecting her fingernails.

Dora crouches down. The sun has browned her cheeks with freckles. It suits her. "It's almost ready. Another week or so and it will be fully out," she says.

"And why are we excited?" asks Otto, getting out her cigarette case.

"Because bee orchids are clever and rare," answers Beatrice. "Male bees are tricked into calling and bring pollen with them. It's a form of sexual deception."

The crown of Otto's head begins to warm in the early-evening sun. There is an apricot glow to the scene that reminds her of the South of France. Beatrice takes out a notebook from her pocket and starts to sketch.

Dora gets back to her feet. "The best bit is that in England, our bees don't want to woo the flower, so the plant has evolved to self-pollinate. No need to attract the male bee anymore."

"So bee orchids are independent women," says Otto.

"Exactly," laughs Dora.

"Did you know, the word 'orchid' comes from *testes* in Greek because the tubers look like you know what?" says Beatrice, with a giggle. "That's why the surgery to remove testes is called an orchidectomy."

"And in Old English orchids are referred to as 'ballock-wart'!" adds Dora.

Beatrice snorts inelegantly.

"Thank you both awfully," says Otto, rolling her eyes. "But if I'd wanted an etymology lecture, I'd have applied for English. It's time to get Dora packed."

Dora sighs. "I'll still have to get through Divvers and Pass Mods to stay next year. I've missed an awful lot."

"You've got four weeks," says Beatrice. "And we'll help."

30

Tuesday, May 17, 1921 (4th Week)

When Dora returns to her studies, she has missed the much-anticipated display of cherry blossoms on Banbury Road. Brown-tinged confetti now skitters along the gutters and pavements of North Oxford.

The week begins with a Pass Mods class taught by Miss Rogers, where they translate passages from Virgil's *Aeneid*. Dora knows the story well. Dido gives herself to Aeneas, believing they are as good as married, but Aeneas deserts her at the command of Jupiter and leaves to do his duty. Dishonored and driven to desperation, she burns their bed and falls on his sword. Dora has no intention of sacrificing herself while Charles sails away. Not anymore.

Each evening, she catches up on the classes she has missed, alternating between Latin and Divvers revision with Marianne, and Logic with Beatrice. Otto toasts tea cakes and types up past questions. Determined not to get behind in English, Dora reads for two hours each day in the garden, plowing through *The Canterbury Tales*. A few pale students, still recovering from influenza, sit under blankets on the terrace, faces lifted to the sun. Miss Jourdain has been discharged from the infirmary but appears only as a shadowy figure at the window of her study. There are rumors in the JCR that she is not herself and may never fully recover. Thankfully, Marianne is almost back to full strength, or so she says. One never quite knows with Marianne.

Dora has not replied to Charles's letter requesting to meet but still finds herself checking her pigeonhole three or four times a day. This morning, she received a "welcome back" note from Frank Collingham in his familiar looping script, along with a dozen irises from the Covered Market. He is nothing if not persistent, and Dora is growing to appreciate his unexciting blend of generosity and tact. His respect for the memory of George lends heft to his courtship of her—for courtship it undeniably is. She has not been alone with him as such, thank goodness, but he did clumsily grasp her hand and kiss it when they bumped into each other outside the Radder yesterday afternoon. He bowed and flushed scarlet. She felt a little sorry for him, inviting him to the tea party today that the Eights are holding for Henry Hadley and his sister Lavinia, who is coming up in October.

After lunch, she makes a detour to her pigeonhole on the pretext of borrowing a bicycle pump from the lodge and, reaching inside, finds a scruffy envelope addressed to her in spiky left-handed scrawl. She stuffs it into her jacket pocket and dashes back to Corridor Eight, locking the door of her room hurriedly behind her. Hands trembling, she rips the top from the long-awaited missive and pulls out four creased sheets, each smudged with crossings-out and wonky lines that veer up the page. For a moment she imagines his hand—his left hand with the slightly crooked little finger—brushing over the paper and she has to sit down to catch her breath.

Queen's College
Monday, May 16, 1921

Dora,
Hadley tells me you have come up. You may not believe me, but I am glad to hear it.
From his glowering expression, I assume he knows a little

of what has occurred between us. Either that or he is in love with you. Thankfully, he is a decent sort and not at all the type to spread idle rumors.

Having not had a reply from you, I can only assume that you do not want to see me. I do not blame you for that.

I am no letter writer, as you may recall, but I feel compelled to explain myself (as far as I can) and attempt to answer your question as to why I allowed you to believe I was dead.

Please know, our time in Berkhamsted was the happiest of my life. I would give anything to be the boy I was then.

In France, many chaps became sentimental. They were buoyed up by thoughts of their sweetheart or family. They wrote letters constantly and dreamed of home in every idle moment. Others found succor in camaraderie, poetry, and religion, but I found no such comfort anywhere.

My view of life in England was, for some reason I cannot fathom, obscured by an impenetrable veil of misery. What filled my every waking thought was quite the opposite of you, my family, or friends. I thought only of myself. Of survival. Death held no glory for me, but I thought of it constantly. My mind was consumed with how not to be shot, gassed, or blown to bits, the thoughts unwanted and unending. I brooded about how not to catch influenza. I was careful. I took the pick of equipment, medicines, and food. I avoided getting too drunk. I planned. I was cunning. I lived on what wits I had left. I learned that to be distracted was dangerous, to be loyal was a death sentence, and that not to be constantly focused on my own survival would be fatal. So, when I got stuck in a crater overnight after a failed advance and my pal joked that he'd been about to start writing letters, I suggested that he should go ahead and write one to you.

In my mind, I was taking another precaution to stay alive. One less distraction, one less responsibility, is what it felt like. A lifeline. And afterward, I'm ashamed to say, I felt lighter.

In a way, I am sorry to say, my behavior had nothing to do with you whatsoever. In my darkest moments, I could barely remember who you were. If anything, I was angry with you. Why should I cower in a trench in France while you drank tea on the terrace and stamped books for cadets in your pink silk? I burned your photograph and your letters. They appalled me. I'm sorry, but this is the truth that you asked for. I am no hero, Dora.

By closing myself off to feeling, I lived. At least a different version of me lived, not the eager cadet who fancied himself in love. You could say that Charles Baker really did die, and you really did lose him in battle. I mourn him myself. That's why the parents packed me off to Italy to recuperate. The doctors say I have a nervous affliction and, judging from the raving I hear at night in the staircases of Queen's, I am not the only one.

When we were reunited in the Botanic Garden, I was unprepared. You looked more beautiful than I remembered, and it unmanned me. But I also felt ambushed. My instinct was to run. I was so angry with you for finding me, isn't that absurd? Angry and terrified and ashamed. Please forgive me for my cruelty. Whatever I said on that day, my deception was never to do with my parents' disapproval. It was all my own folly.

The night I saw you kiss Harris at the piano in the Ashmolean, I wanted to knock him down. Since then, I have not stopped thinking about you in that bottle-green dress, your mouth painted scarlet. I heard a chap at the pub describe you the other day as the most beautiful woman at St. Hugh's. Somehow, I resisted the urge to punch him too. Your legend precedes you, Dora, as I knew it always would. And you have conquered Oxford.

So, you are right, I am a coward. To that end, I am planning to leave for Cambridge at the end of the year, before this whole sorry tale ruins us both.

*One final thing I want to say is thank you for loving me
and for mourning me. I deserved neither but I am grateful.
Please accept my profoundest apologies, Dora, and my
sincere wishes for your health and future happiness. I have
been a fool and a cad and a lunatic to give you up. I wish we
could have remained in the forest.*

*Yours most sincerely,
Charles*

———◇———

WITH DORA INDISPOSED WITH A headache in her room despite
inviting Frank herself, Marianne arranges for tea to be served
on the terrace. She has been curious to meet Henry's sister
for some time. Apparently, she is to study Natural Sciences
at St. Hilda's. A first glance at Lavinia Hadley reveals she is
willowy like her brother, with dense sandy hair cut into a severe bob. Lavinia has the shortest fringe Marianne has ever
seen on a woman; her vast forehead rises from her brows like
a cliff face.

"The thing about Irish terriers," Lavinia says, piling her plate
with sandwiches, "is that they are terribly loyal. I have three
bitches at home. The youngest is pregnant, due in a month. Has
the reddest coat. The litter will be worth a fortune."

Mouth full, Lavinia continues to regale the table about the
gestation of Irish terrier puppies. Otto picks at a stain on her
sleeve, Frank nods politely, and Henry smiles apologetically at
Marianne over his tea. He always looks so composed, she
thinks, so approachable.

Only Beatrice is fascinated. "Do you use a stud dog? How do
you find them? How can you tell if it's, you know, been suc-
cessful?"

As Lavinia opens her mouth to answer, Otto stands up. "Oh
my goodness, what a clot I am. I'm horribly late," she says,

grabbing a couple of egg sandwiches. "Completely forgot I had a tute."

Otto is lying, of course; Marianne knows she had a tutorial that morning. She grasps at Otto's free hand under the table to pull her back down, but Otto dodges her attempts. "Save me one of those peculiar-looking scones, won't you, Marianne, I could do with a new paperweight. *À tout à l'heure.*" She strolls off humming to herself.

It is a strange little tea party. Rules decree it must be held between two p.m. and five thirty p.m. because it is mixed, and the food, provided by the kitchens, is dreadful. Thankfully, Miss Kirby does not insist on a chaperone and Henry and Frank are getting along famously. One can always trust Henry. Two eligible young men do not go unnoticed in a women's college for long, and to Marianne's amusement, Norah Spurling and Josephine Bostwick suddenly find it necessary to hover about the herbaceous borders. If the men notice the flurry of feminine activity, they are polite enough not to acknowledge it.

After battling nobly with one of the dusty gray scones, Henry reveals that the Oxford Union is to host a debate about the admission of women to the university. "I wasn't sure if you knew. It's a dreadful motion, I'm afraid. Some idiot at Magdalen is responsible."

"It's appalling," bursts out Lavinia. "*This House believes women have no place at Oxford University.*"

Beatrice almost chokes on her scone. "What?"

"How awful," Marianne says, but she is not in the least surprised. Nobody is.

Lavinia beams. "Henry is going to oppose it."

"G-g-good for you, old chap," says Frank, shaking Henry's hand.

"You must let us help you," says Beatrice. "The Women's Debating Society will want to contribute. I'll send a note to Ursula."

"I was hoping you would say that. We only have a few weeks.

The flu delayed the announcement." Henry waits until he has eye contact with Beatrice. "Do you think your mother would agree to be a speaker?" he says.

"Oh yes, I'm sure she would," replies Beatrice.

"I was thinking Miss Brittain from Somerville too," he adds carefully.

There is an awkward pause. On the other side of the garden fence, an omnibus clatters down Banbury Road. Marianne knows Beatrice would have dearly loved this opportunity.

"Oh, Brittain's the best person for the job, absolutely," says Beatrice brightly. "And I'll write to Mother tonight. Bravo, Henry, we are so proud of you."

Lavinia is all smiles. "He'll get us tickets, won't you, Henry?"

AFTER TEA, FRANK SENDS HIS regards to Dora and departs for rowing practice. While Beatrice and Henry discuss tactics for the debate, Marianne gives Lavinia a tour of the college. The redbrick building looks its best today, swathed in sunshine. Windows are open now that summer is a promise, and somewhere above them a halting soprano competes with a wavering flute.

"Your brother has been very encouraging about women at Oxford, which, I'm sorry to say, not every man is," says Marianne, opening a door off the main corridor. "This is the Junior Common Room, where we come to talk or have a meeting. Beatrice has just been voted JCR president. She did awfully well and starts next week. We pay a membership subscription of one pound a year. The newspapers are delivered daily, though you have to be early or the best articles get cut out, and lots of us come here to write letters at the weekend. With Mods and finals coming up, it's less busy than usual."

They continue down the main corridor past the principal's office, which is eerily quiet and devoid of its usual queue of students outside.

Lavinia tucks a dense block of hair behind her ear, only for it to spring out again. "Is there really so much resistance to women, even now?"

"Not all the time, but on occasion we are made to feel like unwelcome houseguests. Your brother is nothing like that, and that is why we enjoy his company. Would you care to see my room so that you'll have an idea of what to pack?"

What Marianne really wants to say is that misogyny is like the mice under the floorboards at the rectory, scuttling about unseen but never far away. The forthcoming debate is evidence enough, and just last week in the *Isis* there was a cartoon of a JCR full of babies, prams, and children's toys titled "The Future." The *Isis* and student publications like it lambast Oxford's women for being prudish old maids one week and frivolous husband-hunters the next. Women are mocked for being too dowdy or too attractive, too feeble-minded or too diligent. They are criticized for breaking rules, for slavishly adhering to rules, for using the university's resources lavishly, for operating on a shoestring. For encouraging the "wrong sort" to apply to Oxford and for driving the "right sort" to Cambridge. The truth of the matter is that with some men they can never win. However, it would be very unfair of Marianne to vent her frustration in front of poor Lavinia just now.

They enter the west wing and turn right into Corridor Eight. As they reach Otto's door, it swings shut as if kicked and Ivor Novello begins to warble at full volume. In some ways, it is a relief not to be around Otto this afternoon, thinks Marianne. Since the business with the influenza, she often looks up to find Otto observing her, head cocked, expression bemused.

Outside her door, Marianne explains to Lavinia that some students bring a lot of furnishings and others do not. "The main thing is to keep warm. To pack for bicycling in poor weather. Bring a good pair of boots."

"Righto," says Lavinia when she steps inside.

Marianne wonders if she should have shown her Dora's or

Beatrice's bedsitter instead. Hers is very sparse indeed. Tidy, but sparse.

After a brief glance around the room, they make their way back along the corridor toward the dining hall, and Lavinia stops to inspect the photographs of previous students. "That's Edith Sparks," she says in a reverential tone, pointing at the youthful image of Beatrice's mother. "And Elizabeth Rix. Look, and Emily Davison."

"Beatrice can tell you all about them," said Marianne, smiling. "You know, you'll have more freedom here than us, with a brother to escort you to events," she says.

Lavinia straightens up. "I do worry about Henry. I'll be glad to see more of him. He gets rather down about things at times. Thinks nothing good can last, you know."

"It must be hard."

"He says coming up is like being forced back to boarding school as an adult. That he feels too tired and old for it all."

"I can understand that," Marianne says as they turn out of the dining hall. She glances around and lowers her voice. "There are several women here who worked as VADs. Some of them feel doubly alienated at Oxford, both as women and as veterans."

"I expect he's told you, but my brother had rather a difficult time," says Lavinia. "He's never been vain, but he is self-conscious about his ear. I tell him there's tons of surplus wives out there now, he won't have a problem finding one."

"I doubt he will."

"He doesn't like talking about that sort of thing. So, when I try, he pretends he can't hear, but I know he can." She laughs with Henry's familiar hoot-hoot-honk. "He has mentioned you a few times, said you were unwell. I hope you are better."

"A dose of influenza," says Marianne, blushing. "I'm fine." It occurs to her that the sister might be inquiring after her on behalf of the brother, but she's not terribly experienced in these matters. She turns away to hide a smile. The sun is warm on her back as they proceed upstairs to the library.

"I wanted to ask you," says Miss Hadley, picking up a book from the shelf and inspecting the spine, "about his chances."

Marianne's hand flies to her chest. "His chances?"

"With Miss Greenwood. I hear she's awfully pretty. Henry mentions her a lot. He'd absolutely kill me for interfering, but might she be interested?"

The library swims about Marianne and she reaches out a hand to lean on the wall. Of course Henry is attracted to Dora! Why would he not be? He often asks Marianne about her. And what of it? It is not as if Marianne is free to pursue a relationship. Not now, not ever. How could she ever explain herself to him? A widow who has given birth to a child and lied about it. He does not even know her real name.

She looks out of the window at Henry seated on the terrace and reflects that it would be better to focus on Pass Mods and the scholarship that will lead to the job, the job that will provide the security, the security that will lead to the retirement, the retirement that will lead to old age and then—

She looks straight at Lavinia. "Dora and Henry would be lucky to have each other," she says, with a horrid pitching in her stomach.

Lavinia claps her hands. "I knew it!"

———◇———

THE FORTHCOMING DEBATE THROWS BEATRICE into a bout of nervous activity. The next three days are a blur of Pass Mods classes, essays, letter-writing, and preparations for her first JCR meeting. On Friday night, by the time the electricity goes off, she is exhausted. Just as she is clambering into bed, a familiar head appears around the door.

"I'm stuck," says Otto. In the dim light, she looks like a child, her tiny face wiped clean of its color and angles. "Have you done the final Logic question? It's a real tough nut. Can you give me a clue where to start?" She pauses and squints at Beatrice. "Why are you in bed? Are you ill? Oh God, don't tell me after all that window-smashing women went and lost the vote."

"Ha ha. I'm tired."

"Hmm. I know that face. What is it?"

Beatrice sits up in bed. "It's the debate. The motion is so infuriating. To claim that women have no place at Oxford? It's cruel and unnecessary and is going to get a huge amount of attention in the press."

Otto observes her quizzically. "But you've dealt with worse than this." She steps inside the door, wrapping her kimono tightly around her. "Come on, there's more to it, I can tell."

Beatrice looks about the room.

"Spit it out," says Otto.

"It's my mother."

"What do you mean?"

"She's written me the most awful letter; I wish she hadn't bothered." Beatrice holds up a page of spiky scrawl. "Mother believes in being candid. She prides herself on it, even if it seems unkind. She says I will never be chosen for events like the Union debate because I talk too much. That nobody will take me seriously because of my height and the way I dress."

"But that's not true," says Otto flatly. "The fact that you are JCR president shows how wrong she is."

"I know," replies Beatrice. "I used to believe those things about myself, but I don't now, not since Oxford. But it's still upsetting."

Otto sighs and sits down on the bed. "My mother won't speak to me at all." She shrugs. "I pretend I don't mind, but I do." She picks at a loose thread on the bedcovers for a moment, then says, "It seems to me that our mothers are disappointed because we haven't turned out to be just like them. And thank God, I say."

Beatrice nods.

Then Otto turns to face her. "When I look at you, I see a woman with a big brain and an even bigger heart, a woman whose company I can bear—and we both know that is very few people—and someone who cares about making this damaged world a better place." She gropes about for Beatrice's hand and gives it a squeeze.

Beatrice cannot speak at first, her throat is so tight. She wonders how on earth her mother coped with the loss of Miss Davison, because right now the thought of losing Otto or Dora or Marianne is agonizing. Eventually, she says, "I never had friends like the Eights before. It means such a lot to me that none of you expect me to change."

"As Sophocles said: one loyal friend is worth ten thousand relatives," says Otto.

"I think you'll find it was Euripides."

"I know, I was testing you."

Beatrice gives a sniffly laugh. "Can I ask you a question?"

"I would expect nothing less."

"I do wonder if I am any good at it—friendship, I mean. It seems to come so easily to the rest of you. Sometimes I have to hide away in my room because I need to be quiet. As if I've eaten too much and feel uncomfortable and have to sleep it off. Is that very odd?"

Otto groans. "I do that all the time, you idiot. Friendship is like this quilt—cozy mainly, but it can also be utterly stifling. I can assure you, the need to escape is entirely normal."

"Oh."

"And for the record, you are very good at it—friendship." Otto takes a lace-edged handkerchief from her pocket and tosses it at Beatrice. "Now buck up and stop fishing for compliments."

Beatrice laughs and blows her nose.

The clock ticks steadily on the mantelpiece and through the open window they hear the squeals of a distant catfight.

"Don't tell anyone I made mawkish remarks about friendship tonight," says Otto.

"They wouldn't believe me," says Beatrice, smiling.

"No, I daresay they wouldn't," says Otto, and she curls up on the end of the bed.

31

Through the binoculars, Marianne imagines she can see thirteen boats lined up along the banks of the Thames, coxes gripping bunglines tightly to ensure that there is the regulation one and a half boat lengths between each "eight." The boats remind her of water insects—pond skaters with fat needle bodies and eight long legs half-submerged on the surface. Ready to fly.

In fact, the boats are a mile away and hidden by a bend in the river called the Gut and must race upstream from Iffley Lock for at least half a mile before they are visible to the crowds, but the anticipation is contagious. It is Summer Eights, the university rowing event of the year, traditionally held from Wednesday to Saturday of fifth week. Together with Miss Stroud, the Eights are spectating from the top deck of the Jesus College barge as guests of Frank Collingham, who will be racing later that afternoon. Frank has lent Marianne his leather-and-brass army-issue binoculars. It is strange to think they have been used in a trench in France, that the seams may contain tiny fragments of French soil, or microscopic particles of English blood perhaps, which have made it home against the odds.

"The idea is to c-c-catch the boat in front of you and bump them. Then you both retire. The next day you start farther up the field, so the winner of Division One after four days is 'Head of the River.' If the two b-b-boats in front of you pull out first and you can catch the next one, you can double-bump."

"So a boat can go from thirteenth place to Head of the River if they double-bump every day? I like that," says Otto, draining her glass. "All the men are so terribly handsome and physical. I do love a regatta."

"New C-C-College won last year. Along with Univ, Christ Church, and Magdalen, they have dominated the last thirty years," says Collingham, smiling. He is more relaxed than Marianne has seen him before. His natural habitat becomes him.

"Do those colleges always win because they have more undergraduates and more money?" asks Beatrice.

"A proud rowing tradition, I'd say. A decent c-c-coach helps."

"So the St. Hilda's boat doesn't stand a chance?" Beatrice asks.

Otto blinks. "St. Hilda's are racing?"

"When the rules were c-c-compiled all those years ago, nobody dreamed women would form an eight, so they never thought to exclude them," says Frank. "It is the most splendid loophole."

"This I have to see," says Otto, opening her compact and rubbing at the lipstick on her teeth.

Frank laughs and offers around a plate of sandwiches. "St. Hilda's have worked terribly hard and have an experienced c-c-coach. I'm sure they will do brilliantly against the chaps this afternoon."

"If they aren't disqualified for some spurious reason, which we all know is very likely," says Beatrice, taking three sandwiches. "Are you trying to bribe us with delicious food just in case, Frank?"

"You have seen right through me, Beatrice." He bows, then turns to the chaperone. "C-c-can I get you another drink, Miss Stroud?"

He knows whom to butter up, thinks Marianne. She likes him. He is considerate without being toady, and there is an unworldliness about him that is out of place in someone who has been to war. But she can also see that Dora is edgy, snappy, and not at all interested in Frank Collingham's attentions today. Scanning the crowd and smoking in public.

Marianne takes a seat at the railing as Beatrice entertains Frank and his friends with the story of the arson attack by suffragettes on Rough's boatyard. They laugh riotously as she relates how furious undergraduates took revenge by ransacking the wrong offices. Dear Beatrice, who in her first weeks at Oxford nervously repeated facts and quoted her mother, now holds court as confidently as Otto.

From her position, Marianne can see at least twenty college barges moored on the little island formed by two narrow tributaries of the Cherwell that divide to meet the Thames on the other side. Behind the triangle of land, giant horse chestnut trees rise, dwarfing the row of white masts from which the college flags wilt and revive in unison.

The barges belong to another time. Built for Lord Mayor's ceremonies, most incorporate ornate wood carvings and latticed window designs and have been towed to Oxford and refitted as pavilions and function rooms. Today, each barge is crammed with so many spectators on the upper deck, Marianne wonders why they do not sink. Despite the fact that it is moored and at least sixty feet long, she can feel the Jesus barge list and creak beneath her.

Avoiding Otto has been easy today. They have been dodging around each other for weeks; Otto is clearly working herself up to some kind of discussion about something Marianne said—or did—while ill. Perhaps Otto phoned the rectory, and somebody gave her away; perhaps she raved about it in her delirium or Otto looked through her bedside drawer. Marianne will have to find out what Otto knows at some point, but there is no sense rushing into giving away the truth (or partial truths) when she does not need to. Her bones ache and since the tea party last week with the Hadleys she has found it hard to muster any enthusiasm about leaving her room. The news that Henry is interested in Dora has set her back, although it has no right to, no right at all. She has woken in the night gulping for breath again, terrified, although of what she could not say. Frightened of fear itself, perhaps. Of that looming sensation that the world about her is not real.

It is hot and the midges make her head itch maddeningly. The motion of the water is barely audible over the human clatter. Despite being continually plowed through by the hulls of boats, the river looks desperate to return to its natural surface of bottle-green bark flecked with silver. It brings to mind how she conceived a child on a dark and thronging riverbank, nine miles downstream from here. By comparison, this stretch of the river is urbane, tame. To look at it now, one could not even tell which way is upstream. It has lost its instinct to fight back.

Below her, Otto steps off the Jesus barge and enters the next one along. It is crammed with women in pastel-colored hats and men sporting striped boaters and cable-knit sweaters. On the towpath, umpires with gold buttons and Admiralty-style caps stride about looking severe. Between the barges, boat-club officials chalk results on huge blackboards and ferrymen row cyclists to the far bank to save them from going over Folly Bridge. Older women sit along the towpath beneath lace parasols and students roll out picnic blankets on Christ Church Meadow, just visible through the trees. Dogs bark, babies cry, small children coax the geese with crusts.

Every time the cannon goes off to start a race, she cannot help but watch for the men who wince or shudder, the summer bloom fading from their cheeks to leave a drained gray. She wonders how Henry reacts when he hears it. Henry who can never belong to her, even if he wanted to.

OTTO ADORES THE FRISSON OF excitement that accompanies the cannon fire. The craning forward to catch sight of the boats coming around the corner. The thunderous clamor of the spectators shouting wildly for their colleges. The coxes yelling until they are hoarse, "full pressure," "hard for ten," in a last-ditch attempt to bump or not be bumped before the finish line. The coaches tear down the towpath, barking into cones held in one hand while the other hand wobbles on the handlebars. At least one cyclist has fallen in the river today, much to the delight of the crowd. And of course, Miss Stroud is unable to keep track of them all. This is the closest to a night out in London she has had for some time, even though it is two p.m. on a Wednesday afternoon. To cap it all, the crew from St. Hilda's are the toast of the river. To the crowd's astonishment, they bump several of the men's eights; the races are a sensation and even Otto shouts herself hoarse.

She adores the mathematical aspect of the occasion. The bump charts, the distances, the times, the weights. And eight is her favorite number, of course! Beatrice loves to interrogate her over the reasons why. Because, Beatrice old girl, it's an even number, a cube, and a Fibonacci number. Because it has the most recognizable Greek root in English, one that gives rise to splendid words like *octopus* and *octave*, *octameter* and *octagon*. It is the number of squares on one side of a chessboard, the periodic number of oxygen, the indicator of a gale on the Beaufort scale, the number of furlongs in a mile. It is the most interesting shape of any of the digits with its infinite symmetry. It's an egg timer, a snowman, a knot, a belt buckle. And she was born on the eighth day of the eighth month, the youngest of four sisters. Eight legs, eight feet, eight hands, eight eyes, eight ears, eight breasts. All intact in 1918.

She's rather drunk by the time she gets back to St. Hugh's, and, not being able to face prunes and custard, she skips out of dinner early to lie on the grass smoking a cigarette.

Marianne pads across the neat lawn and sits down beside her, hugging knees to chin. Behind them, women spill out onto the terrace with cups of weak, milky coffee.

"Do you want to talk about it?" says Otto to the sky, feeling the sharp edge of a headache.

"Yes, I think perhaps I do," replies Marianne, selecting each word carefully. "I need to get it out of the way. I'm fed up with avoiding you, so I've decided to trust you." She pauses for a moment. "What do you know?"

Otto breathes deeply into her nostrils. "I know you had—gave birth to—a child at some point. I saw the marks when I washed you."

"Oh yes," says Marianne quietly. "I should have realized."

"These things happen, and it really isn't any of my business except I can see it causes you pain. And that makes it my business as your friend." She rolls onto her side, to face Marianne. "I'm quite good at secrets, you know."

"Have you read *Tess of the d'Urbervilles*?" asks Marianne, picking at the grass with one hand.

"I started it."

"Well, the story is a little like that one. Except without the murder. I had an encounter on Armistice night with a man from the village. He was terribly sad. He'd been at Passchendaele. I think he had the shell shock. He gave me whiskey and cried, so I held him. I don't know what I was thinking, it seemed like the point of living was for just that moment. Carpe diem and all that." She shivers a little. "It was only the one time."

"Did he—hurt you?"

"No, no, not at all. Gosh, no. When I realized I was pregnant, I found him, and I married him. But he died. Pneumonia. We never lived as man and wife."

"What was his name?"

"Thomas Ward," says Marianne, looking up at the tips of the trees waving around above them.

Otto grins. "Hello, Mrs. Ward."

The college cat sidles over to Marianne and weaves in and out of her legs.

"So, you had a baby two years ago," Otto muses, thinking of the locket, the spiritualism, the desperation to save the kittens, the quiet resolve, "and then applied to Oxford as an unmarried woman."

"You know how much Miss Jourdain fears scandal. It would have been a talking point, a widow at Oxford. My father insisted it was best to omit some of the facts. I would never have got the exhibition otherwise, and I needed the money."

The sky grows dimmer and the shadows of the cherry trees creep over their feet and up their legs.

"Marianne, can I ask—what happened to your baby? Obviously, you don't have to tell me."

"She was born on the eighth of August 1919 at the rectory."

"The eighth?"

"I know, I know, your birthday. My mother-in-law was there. It was terrible. I thought I was going to die like my mother. It was so hot, but Mrs. Ward wouldn't open the windows. She said my father shouldn't hear. Can you imagine giving birth next to a graveyard? All those tiny headstones.

"It took an awfully long time. All that pain, and then she sort of slithered out. She was red, white, and blue. I remember thinking she looked like a painting of a Union flag where the colors had run. She had lots of dark hair stuck to her head. Mrs. Ward—Olive—wanted to take her away but I wouldn't let her.

"It felt like she was a part of me. Like she was me and I was her. A kind of psychic connection. She wasn't ready to be born.

"She wouldn't suck. They took her away in the end. We were both ill. I don't remember much of it. Slept a lot."

Tables and chairs scrape on the terrace. Out of the corner of her eye, Otto sees Beatrice walking over the lawn toward them.

"I'm her mother. I miss her every day." Marianne reaches out for Otto's hand. "I know this sounds mad, but I think my daughter spoke to me through the Ouija board. Our psychic connection is still there, I'm sure of it."

"What do you mean she spoke to you?" Otto says. She cannot fathom how a dead baby could possibly be a coward.

Marianne's hand squeezes hers more tightly. Beatrice is almost upon them, calling out something about coffee and cocoa.

"I named her after our mothers." Marianne lowers her mouth to Otto's ear. "Constance Olive Ward."

32

Otto, August 1919

Caro is married on a warm summer's morning in 1919. It is also the anniversary of the day Caro saved Otto's life.

Otto has heard the story a thousand times. How, an hour after she was born, she quietly ripened like a peach from pink to purple to blue and Caro was the only one to notice. It was Caro who asked the question that brought the adults running to the cradle. *Why is the baby blue?* It was thanks to Caro that the mucus blocking Otto's windpipe was sucked out by a midwife through a straw. And so, it became legend: four-year-old Caro saved her baby sister Ottoline's life.

This is why she must always be grateful to Caro, because without her, Otto would not exist. Plus, Caro is the eldest, the most beautiful, and their mother's undisguised favorite. Hence, when Caro announces she is getting married on Otto's twenty-third birthday to wealthy American Warren Powell II, nobody gives the date a second thought. But Otto understands exactly what Caro means to do by selecting it. Caro wants the eighth day of the eighth month for herself because she knows it is special and therefore, by rights, it ought to be hers.

St. Margaret's Church, Westminster, is deemed similarly special. Squatting in the shadow of the abbey and Big Ben, it is a desirable venue for weddings, and Otto has attended three ceremonies there this year. Weddings are all the rage in 1919.

When Caro takes Warren's arm and they squeeze down the narrow aisle, Otto suppresses the urge to clap and whistle. Caro sails for America in a month and this marriage stamps her ticket. Presumably, she will have children of her own to torture soon, and as long as they are boys, they may stand a fighting chance. Out in the sunshine, as the guests mingle, the photographer's assistant flutters about the courtyard, arranging the acres of diaphanous veil that appear to sprout from Caro's temples. Caro hisses instructions from the corner of her smile. The gown is a Reville & Rossiter design, resembling the one Princess Patricia wore in February. It is undeniably beautiful, but Otto is heartened that Caro's long pearls (once their mother's) have been hooking onto the corsage at her waist all day.

If Otto ever marries—the idea of which is becoming increasingly unlikely—she will design her own dress like Lady Diana Manners. Two months ago, Manners and Duff Cooper posed on the same spot where Caro is standing now. The image was featured in every paper and magazine on the stands, Manners elegant in a homemade gown of gold tissue and lace with a simple round neckline. Caro was furious that she had already committed to a plunging V-neck. For the rest of the day, she made caustic comparisons between Manners's checkered VAD work and Otto's.

"If you can't stick at things, then you have no backbone."

Caro sticks at being a bitch, thinks Otto.

AT LAST, THE THREE BRIDESMAIDS are inside a motorcar en route to the Savoy. Otto drops the heavy bouquet at her feet, peeling off the wide-brimmed hat that is making the base of her scalp sweat and itch.

"We look absurd," she says. Opposite her sit Gertie and Vita, wearing the same pastel-blue shift dresses, pearly gray slippers, and matching gloves.

"The whole thing is absurd," Vita replies, piling her bouquet on top of Otto's and rummaging in her stockings. "Cigarette? Bit crumpled, ha ha."

The car circles Parliament Square and sets off up Whitehall, where black-clad women mill around the new memorial. Otto pulls down the window. The wet scent of decaying flowers hits the back of her throat. For a moment she is emptying vases in the sluice.

"Well, she's done it now. Off our hands," says Gertie.

"She hasn't spoken a word to me today." Otto takes a deep drag of her cigarette. "Warren is a pig."

Vita stamps her feet on the floor in delight, causing the driver to turn his head.

"Oh, he's not that bad," replies Gertie airily, waving at the driver to carry on. She leans over and takes Otto's cigarette.

"He offered me a lift into town last week, then tried to put his hand down my shirt," says Otto. Men take liberties with her all the time, and usually fighting them off is a game, but there is something proprietorial about Warren that makes her skin crawl. He is a large man, muscular, and must weigh twice as much as she does.

"He was so eager, poor thing, I let him put his hand up my dress last night," says Vita, smirking. "Just to see what all the fuss was about."

"You did not!" says Gertie, looking to Otto for support.

"You didn't miss much, Otto," Vita adds. "He might be handsome, but he has fat, fumbling fingers, and no technique to speak of."

Otto and Gertie shriek with laughter.

"You are terrible, Vita," says Gertie, shaking her head.

As the car turns into Trafalgar Square, an enormous bronze lion peers down at them from a plinth at the base of Nelson's Column.

Four lions. Eight eyes, eight ears. Eight kidneys, eight lungs, eight testicles.

"Do you think Caro knows?" says Otto. "About what he does?"

"Of course she knows. Happiness in marriage is entirely a matter of pretending one has not noticed," scoffs Vita. "Isn't it, Gertie?"

"Men are"—Gertie looks pained for a moment as if she needs to burp—"different animals."

"When you make a deal with the devil, there is always a price to pay," says Vita. The car pulls up outside the entrance to the Savoy, where Caro and Warren are posing for yet more photographs. "Ah, here we are. What fun."

TO OTTO'S RELIEF, TEDDY IS waving at her from one of the tables at the rear of the Lancaster Ballroom. The room is decorated tastelessly to resemble a jungle. The white pillars are festooned with vines fashioned from crêpe paper and wire and there is a cage of cowering parrots on the stage, surrounded by painted fruit. She walks between the tables, greeting friends and relatives on the way, using her bouquet like a shield to forge a path to Teddy.

"Welcome to the part of the tropics where the cripples and eunuchs reside," he says, above the scraping of the string quartet. "My own little club of one."

He is in the chair today, which means either the pain in his groin is too much to bear or the prosthetic leg is irritating his stump again. He is beautifully turned out in frock coat with matching gloves and spats. She kisses his head, which smells of citrus pomade, and takes the seat next to him.

"I thought you'd never come," he says. Then he pats his jacket pocket and smiles conspiratorially. "Got you a teaspoon."

He looks tired. Since the end of her VAD work in Oxford last summer, they have become firm friends. Teddy was one of Vita's set before the war, but he was so badly wounded he never made it back to midnight gallivanting, nor to Oxford. The first time they met, Otto was not at all fazed by Teddy's chair or his injuries, and that is why, she suspects, she is one of the few people he can bear.

"When we get married, it'll be much grander than this. Caro will be spitting." He signals to a waiter with a tray of champagne. "Just don't expect to bounce on a Savoy mattress with me afterward."

Teddy came up with his grand plan a month ago. They will marry, and she will provide an heir to prevent his estate from going to his cousin. How she begets that heir will be entirely her own choice, his penis having been slashed in half by flying shrapnel in 1915.

He takes two glasses for each of them. Unlike her own scarred digits and flayed cuticles, he has pianist's fingers with perfectly manicured nails. From his hands, you would never expect he has been to war.

"Oh, come on, old girl, we're both alone, we like each other. And our mothers are frantic for it. All the money and freedom and lovers you want."

"I told you. I'm going to Oxford."

"If you get in." He leans over gingerly and pokes her in the ribs. "You might not be bright enough."

"I will get in, Teddy. And what if I don't want to make babies?" She wonders why the people who know her best assume her goal in life is marriage and children. Even Gertie.

"Well, technically, that would be breach of contract, old girl."

From the swinging kitchen door, waiting staff process with loaded trays and trolleys. Luncheon is served. Gertie and her husband Harry weave their way over to the table. There is a swelling in Gertie's abdomen that the shift dress cannot quite hide.

"I couldn't bear to live with any woman but you." Around his slate-gray eyes and dark lashes there is tension. He is in pain, she thinks, but knows better than to ask.

"You could live with whomever you want," she replies. "Sell up. Go abroad."

"No succulent young men are going to want to tangle with my body. Only my wallet." He laughs, but he is brittle and desperate, and they both know it. "You would make me happy."

"We would hate each other in a year, I promise you."

"As soon as you leave Oxford, then," he says, grabbing her hand triumphantly and kissing it. "That's settled."

"Oh, do shut up or I'll wheel you onto the Strand and leave you there."

AS CARO GIGGLES AND SIMPERS behind the absurdly high wedding cake, Otto watches from her parents' table.

"Try not to look so bored, Ottoline," says her mother, elegant in cream silk couture. "Why are your gloves so filthy?"

Otto exchanges her empty glass for a fresh one as a waiter glides by.

"And do try to look happy for your sister."

"She returned my wedding present to the shop," says Otto. "Exchanged it for God knows what." She had taken ages to select the right gift, settling on a smoky glass vase etched with a lithe female archer—Diana—taking aim at a giant eagle. She thought it was a witty representation of Caro having got her American, but clearly the joke was on her.

"The Lalique? She showed me. Perhaps you shouldn't have tried to be funny."

"I was trying to be thoughtful," she lies.

"I despair of you."

"Not now, Mother, please."

Caro and Warren are forcing a sword into the bottom tier of the cake. There is applause. She waits for what must surely come next.

"Lady Holbrook just told me that Teddy proposed and you turned him down."

Otto empties her glass.

"Are you such an idiot that you are going to refuse him in order to go to—university? Are you completely mad?"

"It's important to me."

"You're not a man, and you're not going to run the country. What on earth is the point?"

"Papa says I can go."

"Because he knows you won't see it through. For someone who is very good at figures, you really can be very stupid."

Her mother takes Otto's hand and squeezes it so tightly her knuckles grind together. "Caro is right. You won't ever get an offer as good as this."

"You're hurting me."

"Just as you are hurting me, dearest," she says between her teeth, smiling brightly and waving at a friend. "You'll be regarded as a spinster. It's hard enough being your mother as it is."

Otto shrugs. She will not cry.

"I expect you to fix this when I'm in America," says her mother, getting to her feet. "Do you understand me, Ottoline?"

WHEN HER MOTHER SAILS TO America with Caro and Warren in September, Otto goes out with Teddy to celebrate.

Their first stop is Liberty of London, where she repurchases the Lalique vase.

33

Thursday, June 2, 1921 (6th Week)

———◦•◦•◦———

OXFORD UNION SOCIETY

Thursday, June 2, 1921

at 8 p.m.

QUESTION FOR DEBATE

"This House believes women have no place
at the University of Oxford"

Moved by MR. G. C. HOLLAND, Magdalen

Opposed by MR. H. J. HADLEY, Christ Church

THE RT. HON. G. S. BOTTOMLY, Oriel, will speak third.

MRS. E. V. SPARKS, St. Hugh's, will speak fourth.

PROFESSOR J. E. ENTWISTLE, St. John's, will speak fifth.

MISS V. M. BRITTAIN, Somerville, will speak sixth.

TELLERS

For the ayes

Mr. R. G. Ratcliffe, Exeter

For the noes

Mr. B. F. Dickens, Balliol

PRESIDENT

Mr. C. B. Ramage, Pembroke

B eatrice's first meeting as JCR president has record attendance. At least fifty women are crammed into the room,
some sitting on the floor, others hovering at the back, necks
craned. It reminds Beatrice of the gatherings she attended as a
child at the WSPU office—only this time she is standing at the
front rather than folding piles of leaflets in a corner. She was
thrilled to win the election against two strong second-year
candidates and now she holds the most important undergraduate position at St. Hugh's. Otto, whose father is an MP, insisted
on running her campaign. *You stand out,* she said. *It isn't always a disadvantage.*

"I propose we write to Miss Brittain to offer our support
and congratulations," third-year Ada Bird is saying. "It's a huge
responsibility to be the first woman undergraduate to speak at
the Union. What do you think, Miss President?"

Beatrice nods. Although the honor is one she would have
dearly relished, she suspects Vera Brittain is both a better
speaker and more pleasing to look at than her. Perhaps one day
a woman's appearance or class will not matter so much in politics, she muses, but right now it is the votes that count, and they
must be tactical. Women must fight with the weapons they have,
and Beatrice made peace with her height a long time ago. Persistence and ingenuity, as Miss Rix put it. Her turn will come.

Norah Spurling is red-faced and furious. "Most men find the
motion hilarious. You only have to look at this week's *Isis.*"

"The majority still believe this is a man's university," says
Temperance Underhill, "and that's a fact. At St. Peter's, the JCR
just passed a motion declaring that members have a right not
to be taught by women."

Grumbles of discontent evolve into heated debate.

Beatrice is in her element.

ON THE NIGHT ITSELF, THE evening is balmy, and St. Michael's
Street is crammed with nonchalant young men queuing at the

narrow gateway to the grounds of the Union. They have nothing to lose, even the ones who support the admission of women, thinks Beatrice, and the injustice of it makes her want to scream. They have no idea how it feels to be powerless, to be subject to others' choices and whims, to be considered a lesser human being because of one's sex. Some of the JCR had wanted to protest outside the Union, but Beatrice discouraged it, on the grounds that any disturbance might be used in the debate to demonstrate female irrationality and hysteria. She was also summoned by Miss Jourdain and, shocked by her fragility, promised not to encourage any behavior that might catch the attention of the proctors, who will no doubt be lurking about to maintain order.

Beatrice has a ticket to the debate as her mother's guest, although she has no idea where Edith Sparks is or what she is going to say. Henry and his Christ Church friends have organized four more tickets, including one for Henry's sister Lavinia. The Union debating chamber, like its library, is separate from the main building and resembles a Baptist church from the outside. As guests, they are directed up the curved stone staircase to watch from above.

The gallery is already rammed with spectators. Beatrice, along with Marianne, Otto, and Dora, joins Lavinia on a row of narrow folding chairs by the brass railings. To their left are a group of first-years, including Norah, Josephine, Temperance, Patricia, and Ivy. Beatrice spots Miss Rogers sitting on a wooden bench against the wall, alongside Miss Finch, Miss Lumb, Miss Kirby, and Miss Brockett. On the opposite side of the balcony, Ursula is seated with a distinguished-looking Sikh gentleman with a curled mustache and fashionable baggy trousers. Brittain's friend Holtby sits next to him looking grave and clutching a notebook. There are a few women Beatrice recognizes from other colleges sitting with brothers, or simpering with lovers, plus a woman in large diamond earrings who looks like she might be lost and turns out to be a researching novelist doubling as the correspondent for the *Times*. Beatrice is uncomfortable on the rickety little chair, the leather seat pad squeaking beneath her, the late-evening sun pressing between her shoulder blades. Her discomfort eases when she spots her father, waving and smiling at her from the other side of the chamber, a chasm of thirty feet between them. Taller than anyone in the seats around him, he is wearing a pair of wire-rim spectacles. She has never seen him in glasses before and laughs as he waggles them at her and grimaces.

Down below, her mother, squeezed into a magenta evening gown, is talking animatedly with Henry and flapping her papers about. Henry looks up, scanning the gallery until he locates Beatrice, and says something to her mother, who then looks up too and gives a little wave. Beatrice has no idea what they are saying about her—something awful, no doubt—but she refuses to dwell on it. Since arriving at Oxford, she has sought her mother's approbation less and less. The Eights listen to her and the JCR trusts her judgment and that is what counts.

Below her, the chamber floor is filled with at least four hundred young men on wooden benches. The lower part of the room is covered with dark wood paneling and decorated with prints, paintings, and marble busts of old men. At the far end, where the benches are perpendicular to the rest, the "ayes" sit on the left and the "noes" on the right. The debate takes place right here on the wooden floor, in front of the dais where the president and committee sit waiting.

Eventually, the president stands to introduce the motion and the proposer, Geoffrey Holland, who in turn introduces the opposition speakers and launches into his argument that Cambridge is capitalizing on the admission of women at Oxford.

"My friends, our rivals at Cambridge are spreading the idea that Oxford has become overrun with socialists," he says. "We risk becoming a mockery! Parents are afraid that at Oxford, their sons will be tempted to marry early or become distracted from their studies. Many mothers consider it an insult that their sons are being taught by women. I have heard of at least three undergraduates who recently left us for Cambridge, one of whom was a foolhardy Romeo rusticated after being caught atop the wall of a certain ladies' college."

The chamber is amused by Holland's drawling and sardonic arguments. Beatrice and Ursula wave and mouth greetings across the gallery. They have not seen much of each other since Ursula began revising for her finals, although Beatrice has heard a rumor that Ursula helped Miss Brittain write her speech.

Henry is next, handsome in black tie. Beatrice casts a glance at Marianne, who is leaning over the metal rail in concentration. Henry's battle scars are obvious even from above and command the immediate respect of the floor.

He argues that women bring a new dimension to the university—not undermining it but enhancing it. He is fluent and convincing, stating that Cambridge will be the subject of scorn in the future for not admitting women sooner. He argues that the hurdles women must overcome to get into Oxford prove their determination and commitment, especially since there is such a poor tradition of teaching Classics at girls' schools, and that their academic performance will challenge men to better results.

"Surely Oxford men are not such beasts that they cannot control themselves in the presence of women. If they are so easily distracted, then perhaps they shouldn't be here at all." He stops to take a sip of water. "The presence of women has enhanced my own experience of Oxford. I have been challenged intellectually and had my outlook expanded particularly in terms of art and poetry. I look forward to my own sister coming up in October." His eyes flit up to the gallery, where Lavinia sits next to Marianne.

"Hasn't he done a marvelous job?" says Lavinia, hanging over the balcony, hat off, flushed with clapping.

The MP who follows is clearly fond of the sound of his own voice, which is decidedly whining and nasal. He uses the emotive argument that women are consuming valuable resources owed to the generation of young men who fought and died in the war. "I am talking about accommodation, library space, books, seats in lectures. The introduction of women has caused extra work and expense that Oxford can ill afford at this perilous economic time." His speech receives thunderous applause. There is even stamping on the floor.

Beatrice's mother responds with the argument that women educate others and therefore it is important to society that they get the best education possible. "I put it to you that more women than ever will be unmarried as a result of losses in the war. They must be able to find meaning and to earn a living in these changing times.

"Over the last two years, we have won the right to vote, to study medicine, work in the law and civil service. We have female members of Parliament and a Nobel Prize winner in Marie Curie. Our queen has led the way by accepting an honorary degree here at the university, only a few months ago. Times are changing and the Sex Disqualification (Removal) Act of 1919 requires that a university may regulate but not preclude the admission of women for degrees. Ladies and gentlemen, the law says women may have a place at Oxford, but I ask, is Oxford worthy of its women?"

Again, there is thunderous applause, this time from the gallery. Beatrice is stunned to see her mother pointing up to her and adding, "Women like my daughter, JCR president of St. Hugh's." Hundreds of faces turn upward and, despite herself, Beatrice's eyes fill. Her mother has never acknowledged her publicly before. Henry must have told her about the presidency; she has been too busy to tell either of her parents yet. Hands pat her on the back, and across the room she sees her father applauding. Beatrice smiles bashfully at her mother, who nods briskly and takes her seat on the opposition bench.

The don is next, but after her mother's invocation of the law, some of his arguments lose their sting. "I am certain that, as in America, women would be happier in an all-female institution where the courses are designed to suit them and their futures," he says.

"Women's colleges will never be well funded as they do not have a history of benefactors or endowments. There can be no income from land or investments. How can they ever compete with men's colleges on an equal footing? They will drag this university down.

"Gentlemen, would you like to see the Oxford Union Society taken over by women? Knitting in the chamber, having tea parties in the library? Because that is where the admission of women to Oxford will lead, I can assure you!"

There is a burst of laughter, applause, and shouting.

How dreadful for Vera Brittain, who must follow this, Beatrice thinks, although she does not look at all rattled. Brittain makes a restrained argument about how all-female colleges do not seek to undermine the ancient collegiate system; they serve to reinforce it and replicate it. She gives unthreatening examples of contributions and academic excellence, of the importance of attracting the brightest female minds to Oxford by voting against this potentially destructive motion. It is less a debate speech than a skillful management of male ego. Beatrice can tell she is holding back, playing to the undecided voters and their insecurities about women taking over. Beatrice could never have appeared so reasonable, charming, intelligent, and desirable. Brittain was the perfect choice.

———◇———

THERE IS SUCH A CRUSH of heads and tweedy shoulders around the exit, it is impossible to see which side of the door, Noes or Ayes, is the busiest. On the other side of the gallery, Winifred Holtby is hunched awkwardly over the railing, trying to make a tally. It is a relief to get out into the evening air after the humidity of the chamber, and when Marianne steps into the crowded courtyard, for a split second she has absolutely no idea where she is. Usually, she would panic and struggle to catch her breath, but tonight she feels strangely exhilarated. Her pulse thrums away in her fingertips on its singular mission to keep her alive, and she is grateful for it.

The speakers have their own special reception and only Union members may enter the bar, so the guests—mostly women—wait outside in the garden. Beatrice and Lavinia sit together excitedly rehashing the debate, while Dora and Otto smoke under the trees, and Frank fetches drinks for everyone. The result will not be announced for at least twenty minutes and, much as Marianne distrusts spontaneity, she cannot help but wonder if this is the best opportunity she will ever get to see the famous Pre-Raphaelite murals.

"I'm going to the library," she whispers to Dora, and slips away from her friends toward the octagonal building that was once the original debating chamber. The lights are on and the door creaks a little as she pulls it open and steps inside. It, too, has a narrow viewing gallery running the entire way around the upper level, now filled with bookshelves. In the center of the room sits an illogical-looking fireplace with no chimney. Despite the Gothic grandeur of the exterior, the library resembles a down-at-heel gentlemen's club, or what she imagines a down-at-heel gentlemen's club might look like. The air is thick with polish, leather, soot, and damp books. A few paces to her right there is a narrow stairwell, which she hesitates at, then darts into, panting lightly and laughing to herself. At the top of the steps, she glances into the Poetry Room on the left and turns right onto the gallery floor. Bare boards announce each footstep. Electric lamps hang level with her face, creating pools of creamy light on the leather chairs and polished walnut tables below. All about her are ornate touches: notches cut into the sides of shelves, leaves painted onto beams, wrought-iron lilies worked into the balcony, no opportunity wasted to decorate and inspire. She walks around the gallery to the other side and takes a preparatory breath as if she is about to dive underwater, then lifts her chin until her neck crunches at the top of her spine.

There they are. The greatest story a library could ever hold. Ten panels of Arthurian legend featuring Lancelot, Guinevere, Arthur, Merlin, knights, ladies, lakes, stags, and swinging swords, in muted shades of russet red, royal blue, and pond green, the original vibrancy having faded long ago. She imagines Ruskin trying to organize the inexperienced painters he later referred to as "the least bit crazy," how they spent a riotous summer drinking soda water and painting from dawn until dusk, how three of the ten panels had to be completed by local artists after Rossetti lost interest and wanted the project whitewashed. She sees for herself that the paintings by William Morris are indeed poor, but the ceiling, precursor to his later wallpaper designs, is marvelously intricate with its pattern of fruits and animals. Her eyes land on Guinevere in front of the archetypal apple tree, red-haired Lancelot slumped on the floor to her right, the Holy Grail being held by Christ on the left. It reminds her of Holland's arguments about women students tempting men from their great endeavors.

"Here you are," says Henry. "Dora insisted I fetch you."

"Oh. Hello," she says, feeling rather foolish that he is at least fifty feet below her, standing at the door. How long has he been watching?

"If I turn out the lights, you'll see them much better." He moves across the room and a moment later the only light is that of the summer sun, almost at its equinox, streaming through the rose-shaped windows that punctuate the murals. He is right. Suddenly, she sees the stag leaping toward her, an enormous white shield with a red cross, Lancelot's haunted expression and red beard.

"You did very well. In the debate," she calls out, embarrassed.

She cannot see him below. Then a creak announces his presence behind her at the top of the stairs.

"They are announcing the result," he says, and remains behind her. Cheers and applause echo from the courtyard. "We won by eight votes."

"We did? Really? Oh, how marvelous," she says. "Congratulations and thank you, Henry. Your sister must be so proud." She cannot turn around and look at him. Instead, she taps her fingertips to the motion of the wooden clock hanging on the railings. Slow ticks.

"What are you thinking?" he says eventually, his voice low and quite unlike the one he used in the debate. It makes her feel a little afraid.

"I'm wondering—how on earth does that strange fireplace work, if it does at all?"

"The flue is under the floor. It doesn't work well—the wind has to be blowing in the right direction or there's a bit of a drama."

There is more creaking behind her, a shifting of weight.

"I'd very much like to continue my education on the Pre-Raphaelites," he says. "What should I be looking for?"

"I'm not sure we should be here alone," says Marianne, attempting to sound jovial, heart beating like a river in her ears. He does not answer, but she can smell him—that now-familiar waft of beeswax that makes her so uncomfortable because she not only likes it but wants to rub it into her skin. "They are darker than I imagined," she begins. "Larger. This one—by Rossetti—is said to be superior in its portrayal of human emotion." She senses him moving closer to her. "I see a man in love with a woman he can never have because she is married. The battle between duty and passion has driven them both mad." She is gabbling now. "Rossetti is asking us to see beyond the myth. He wants us to connect with the real feeling, the suffering—"

Henry steps closer and strokes his fingers against hers. She feels the heat of his proximity and shudders, a soft moan escaping her lips. She has been an idiot. There never was any competition from Dora. With Henry she has a connection that has bound them since the day their knees pressed together at the Sheldonian. And once upon a time, such a connection would have been welcome. Because she could love him, wants to love him, perhaps does love him. But she cannot have him. Like Guinevere, she is not new and fresh, unsullied, innocent. She has eaten of the apple, and he deserves better than that.

Without turning, she takes his hand in hers and, looking at the stag and the shield, the grail and the knight, the tree and the wife, tells him she is not the woman he thinks she is. She tells him her story. The one where she is Marianne Ward the protagonist but nobody's romantic heroine.

34

Monday, June 6, 1921 (7th Week)

IMP-RESSIONS

There is a story doing the rounds that a certain red-headed student at this college was recently challenged by a proctor at Summer Eights. It is thought that the proctor had taken exception to the fact that the young lady was walking unchaperoned between college barges.

When challenged by the proctor in the customary way, "Are you a member of this university?" we understand that her reply, before walking away with head held high, was thus: "I never speak to strange men in the street."

If this is true, then the *Imp* applauds the lady in question! We hope our heroine will continue to entertain us with her quick wit.

IMP
TRINITY TERM 1921

The early morning grates on Otto: the grind of awnings being lowered; the rasp of wet brooms on flagstones; the metallic, earthy smells emitted from the various shop fronts on the High. Normally, it would be charming, but today she could easily dash her fist through one of the windows. It is the first day of Pass Mods.

The Examination Schools have finally reopened after their stint as a military hospital, looking much the same from the exterior, except the Red Cross and Union flags no longer flutter above the porch. Two familiar scenes remain carved above the door. Otto knows them by heart: eight figures in all, four dons and four students, the left scene featuring a student undergoing a viva voce, and on the right, degrees being conferred on kneeling undergraduates. All are men, of course. The building, with its enormous leaded windows spanning three floors, reminds her of grand Elizabethan houses like Hardwick or Hatfield. If the intention of the architect was to intimidate students, she thinks, then it was a job well done.

Otto has entered this building often, both through the porch and via the unexpectedly elegant quad on Merton Street. How many times has she run up these stairs, her hands glancing off the pink marble balustrade that looks as if it was made of coral? Delivering messages, collecting packages, waiting at the curb for a harassed doctor needing to get to another site. It was here that the orderlies nicknamed her the Red Baroness because of her cut-glass accent and the trail of smoke that lingered in her wake. She shuts her eyes and can still smell the Lysol, hear the echoing cries, the coughs, the shouts of *What do you have for me today, Baroness?*

Today, the Eights will sit the Latin translation paper, and the group is unusually subdued. Last week, Dora heard that she had passed Divvers, but if she fails Pass Mods she will not be allowed to return. Marianne needs to convert her exhibition into a scholarship to be able to afford to stay. Beatrice, clutching her suffragette penny, is determined to show that women can excel at Oxford. Otto's motivation comes from proving her mother wrong—that she can and will stick at this. There is a good deal at stake.

The crowd files up the stairs to the North School, which Otto remembers as a large L-shaped room. At least a hundred single wooden desks fill it now, the flimsy type that wobbles underneath the user in a premature attempt to fold up. Surprisingly, men and women are mixed together alphabetically—an oversight, very probably, for which someone will be reprimanded. The last time she was here, three years ago, there were metal bedsteads positioned back-to-back down the center of the room to make two aisles. It was an orthopedic ward then, with bedsheets tented over absent limbs, one's peace of mind dashed by the constant squeal of wheelchairs. God, she pushed her fair share of moaners and fools. She much preferred the men who could hobble about in hospital blues, trying to engage her in conversation or cadge a cigarette. Men with wounds like Teddy. He has not written or sent flowers this term and she wonders, with a pang of sadness, if he has found himself a wife.

If Teddy's proposal has taught her one thing, it is this: until she meets a man who makes her pulse jump like geometry, her breath catch like calculus, she will not marry. Convention can go to hell—and when she sees her mother next month for the first time in nearly two years, she will tell her so. Miss Brockett says she has the makings of an academic; and who knows, one day it could be Otto at the lectern while girls in cherry lipstick chew their pencils on the front row. Before Oxford, Otto used to fear being labeled *surplus*. Quite frankly, these days, it is a relief.

When she glances around the room to see where her friends are seated, she spots the redheaded student with the limp from her very first lecture, the mysterious man she has seen about Oxford all year, each time with that irritating inability to place him. He smiles at her and holds up a flat palm to his brow in salute. Then it comes to her. He was once sitting beside a bed in this very room, having had surgery on his foot. Her job was to collect him and drive him back to a convalescent ward at Somerville. Woozy on morphine, leg up on the back seat, he asked her to marry him, promising her "handsome redheaded babies." He sang "Mademoiselle from Armentières" all the way to Somerville and she had laughed, delighted. And here they are again three years later. He points at her, mouths the word *Baroness*, and smiles to himself.

Perhaps she did do some good, she thinks. Yes, she was lazy and afraid, antisocial and counting down the days, but it was better than doing nothing. She might wait for him outside. It might be fun to reminisce about old times and she could never give up flirtation—it is a habit as ingrained as cigarettes and coffee. A don at the front points at the clock and tells the examinees they have three hours. There is a squeak of chair legs, a flurry of paper, a brace of coughs. And then the music begins: the rhythmical scratch and pause of a fountain pen, the ding of nib on ink bottle, the stroke and tap of a pencil, and the *schwit schwit* of the sharpener.

———◇———

AFTER MODS, WHEN THERE IS nothing further she can do about the result, Marianne gives herself permission to relax. There are no more lectures or tutes this term. In a few days she will migrate downstream to her old life as Marianne Ward, and for three and a half months she will wake to the clang of a different bell. She cannot imagine asking her father to pay for two more years of tuition fees if she does not get a scholarship, but there is nothing to be done now. Just as there is nothing to be done about Henry. She can only hope he is as discreet as his word.

They celebrate the end of Mods with a picnic lunch of cold game pie, pickled eggs, and Pimm's on the Jesus barge with Frank and his friends. Miss Turbott neglects her knitting and dozes through the laughter and card games, waking only when the men begin jumping in the river.

"We should set up an eight at St. Hugh's: Dora as stroke, Otto as cox," says Beatrice as they walk home up Cornmarket, faces sunburnt, shoes dusted orange. "I'll coach."

"What do you know about rowing?" scoffs Otto.

"She'll read up on it, won't you, Beatrice?" says Marianne. "But we'd need a different cox. Otto would be far too terrifying."

Beatrice laughs and takes her arm. "I'm serious. I'm going to talk to the president of boating, Veronica, when we get back," she says. "If Hilda's can do it, so can we."

THE FOLLOWING DAY, A BALLOON appears on Christ Church Meadow, a great fat thing nestled amid the hummocks of long grass like a swollen mushroom. The Oxford Balloon Society, a group of decommissioned officers from the Royal Flying Corps, is charging customers sixpence to float one hundred fifty feet above the city in an observation balloon. Profits are to go to "war widows and orphans," although given the men's vagueness on the topic, Marianne is not entirely convinced this is the case.

"It doesn't look safe to me," whispers Dora. "I hate heights. Are we sure they know what they're doing?"

"I bloody hope they know what they're doing," says Otto, for the benefit of the queue. A party of male students behind them laugh and offer her a cigarette. Miss Cox, their chaperone for the evening, gives the men a tight smile and inserts herself between the groups.

Marianne is inclined to agree with Dora. The canvas is patched in at least four places, and though the balloon looks passive enough, she is keenly aware that the hydrogen inside is dangerously flammable. It resembles a rotund matron wearing a garter belt. Cables attached to the belt are winched up or down in unison to control the balloon's movements, but she can see that the ropes are taut and quivering. It is obvious that, allowed to whip about, they could be quite deadly.

The rides are only available three hours after sunrise and three hours before sunset, when the wind is low. As Otto refused to get up at dawn, they have been queuing from four p.m. for an evening ride. The flat expanse of Christ Church Meadow is the perfect spot to attract both tourists and students, and there is an animated line snaking back toward Christ Church and Merton.

"Do you realize how fitting it is? This is the location of the first ever balloon flight by an Englishman," says Beatrice. "1784, I think."

"Really?" replies Marianne.

"He was a celebrity in his day, but the university refused to acknowledge him because he was a pastry chef," Beatrice rushes on eagerly. "James Sadler was his name. He's buried in that little graveyard next to Queen's."

"St. Peter-in-the East," interjects Miss Cox. "Haunted."

Dora winks at Marianne.

"The basket takes eight plus the pilot," says Otto. "There's five of us. We'll have to share." She smiles at the men jostling behind them.

Beatrice looks down at Otto. "You are an incorrigible flirt."

"But I'm so good at it."

"Four," says Dora. "I'm not going." She hands the camera to Otto. "I'll wait here by the fence."

Miss Cox looks conflicted.

"I'll be fine," says Dora to Miss Cox. "Don't let me stop you going up."

So it is decided. Marianne, Otto, Beatrice, and Miss Cox wade through the tall grass and step into the basket as directed, alongside a nervous-looking father with three excited little boys. The basket is shabby close up, with what could be bullet holes through one panel, which has been reinforced with wire. Above them, the huge round envelope gives off the smell of damp tent. It is strange to think they will be lifted by a gas that is lighter than air. The basket door is closed, and a man begins counting time as the winches are cranked in unison, two men sweating at each one, shirtsleeves rolled up. The balloon rises in unsettling judders, and as Otto and Beatrice laugh, Marianne feels suddenly frightened and clutches on to the basket. Dora, waving at the fence, becomes smaller and smaller. Eventually, they draw level with the top of the University Church of St. Mary, the Radcliffe Camera, and Christ Church Cathedral. The pilot in the basket blows a whistle and the men below secure the winches and flop exhausted to the ground like toppled tin soldiers.

High above the city, it is strangely quiet. The women smile at each other and grasp hands in wonder, even Miss Cox, who has tears in her eyes. The horizon reminds Marianne of a model village she once visited, hills molded from paper and paste, rivers daubed in wiggly lines with a thick bristled brush. She fancies she can see far-off rivers collide and marry. Perhaps she can spy Abingdon in the distance beyond Boars Hill. And below her, the river is lined with barges and people as if someone has meticulously sculpted and painted each one. This must be how a bird lives its life, she thinks: *Ring'd with the azure world.*

From this perspective, some of the men's colleges look smaller than St. Hugh's. They reveal their hoarded treasures: lush green lawns, Gothic chapels, narrow passageways inaccessible to the average person. The huge walls no longer intimidate—that job is taken by the vast expanse of rooftops, the habitat not of students but of birds and bells and attic windows. Their landscape is one of sharp angles, ramparts, gargoyles, gutters, flagpoles, and spires. And below, bicycles, buses, trains, cabs, horses pulling carts, and canal boats. Passengers descend from an omnibus, fanning out like ginger beer spilled from a bottle. White-clad cricketers and tennis players dart in random directions on islands of green turf.

The pilot exchanges war stories with the father while the little boys point and chatter. Marianne imagines the soldiers who will have stood in this basket, eyes desperately scouting the ground for German artillery, ready to telephone command, behind them a colleague searching the sky with his machine gun for "balloon busters." Knowing if they are attacked, they will have to jump out in a hail of bullets. She cannot begin to imagine what strength of character it would take to get in the basket—and how much more would be required to refuse.

Thoughts of Henry come to her. She does not expect to hear from him again. He said very little after he stiffly gave her his condolences and they left the library to rejoin the others in the garden.

She can hear the pilot telling Miss Cox that when an observation balloon went up it was a sign that a battle was about to start. She forces herself to think about the letters she has to write, about the aspirin she needs to buy, the train times for going home. Grounds herself in the mundane.

Glancing idly at the path below, she can just about make out Dora at the fence. She is talking to someone. He leads her by the arm away from the queuing crowds and they disappear beneath a tree on the other side of the dusty path that leads down to the river.

Marianne cannot be sure, but the man looks a lot like Charles Baker.

WHEN CHARLES APPEARS AT HER side, Dora is alone at the fence staring at the sky, trying to identify which of the tiny figures inside the basket are her friends.

"Hello, Dora." The lids of his eyes hang heavy and pink, as if he has received terrible news. "Can we talk?"

She feels a rush of panic. All she can do is nod in return. She does not know what to say to him now that she has read his letter. She is not sure she can force out even one word. The letter's brutal honesty cut into her like a whip. She had believed for so long that she had wanted the truth, but it was nothing like the catharsis she had imagined. She has read the letter two dozen times, maybe more. It rained blows rather than offered resolution, left her appalled, shaken.

I wish we could have remained in the forest.

"Give me five minutes and then I'll leave you alone for good," he says, seeking out eye contact. "If that's what you want."

She glances about her. "Just until my friends get out of the balloon," she says.

"Thank you." He takes her gently by the arm and leads her to an empty bench on the other side of the path. His touch burns through her sleeve.

"I like your hair, by the way."

She puts her hand to her head almost apologetically, remembering her promise not to cut it. "I still have your cigarette tin."

He shakes his head at the memory. "The tin. I forgot all about the tin."

They are seated beneath a towering chestnut tree. Layers of dense foliage block the low creep of the sun, and she feels a sudden chill. A clock tower nearby strikes six.

"Old Tom," he says.

"Old Tom," she repeats.

The path in front of them swims with students in boat-club blazers pushing bicycles down to the barges. Men in shirt-sleeves and braces begin winching down the balloon, shouting "heave" in unison.

"Did you read my letter? The one I sent to your college."

"I did."

"And what—what did you think?"

"It made me very sad."

He does not say anything for a while, lights a cigarette. She steals a look at him. A vein pulses in his throat and short, blunt hairs are reasserting themselves after his morning shave.

"I went to St. Hugh's to find you, and someone told me you'd be here."

She imagines cupping his face with her palm and pulling his mouth to hers. How was that once so normal?

He turns to her. "I want you to know that I was only ever truly happy with you. With your family. In your garden. And however hard I try, I can't re-create that feeling."

"Are you really leaving?"

He sighs. "People are already talking about us, and I don't think I can bear seeing you around and not being able to take you in my arms." Then suddenly he is down on one knee in front of her, dust flying.

"Charles." She looks about frantically.

"Dora. Will you marry me?"

He pulls a velvet pouch from his jacket pocket and shakes a ring into his palm. It is set with an emerald the size and shape of a split pea. Two rows of tiny diamonds encircle it. "It was my mother's. She died last year."

"I'm sorry," she says.

He leans in until their heads almost touch. His hand is trembling. "Do you like it?"

"It's—beautiful." She thinks of the first time he proposed to her in the hallway, so sure of himself, so vibrant. The tin.

"We don't even need to do it until after Oxford if you don't want to."

"I don't understand," she says. She can see Marianne and Otto climbing down from the basket and Beatrice talking to the pilot as he waits for Miss Cox. "You want to marry me?"

"Yes," he says, laughing. As if it is obvious.

She wonders if she might be sick. "I wasn't expecting this."

"Dora," he says earnestly. "We can put this right."

"What?"

"We can start again. I still love you, and I think you still love me?"

Does she love him? And even if she did, how does one forget, how does one forgive? Whatever would she tell people? Her parents?

"I can't."

"Whyever not?"

"I just can't," she says. Coppery dust swirls about her feet. The others are only thirty yards away.

"Dora?"

I wish we could have remained in the forest.

"I can't marry you, Charles." She looks at him, sees the cleft in his chin, remembers the brush of his lips on her neck, feels a weight pressing her into the orange dirt, wonders if she is making a terrible mistake. "Because I'm already engaged to somebody else."

35

REPORT FROM ST. HUGH'S

It has been a busy term, notwithstanding the influenza that swept through college in second week.

We offer our heartfelt thanks to the debating team that did us all proud at the Oxford Union in sixth week, in particular St. Hugh's alumna Mrs. E. Sparks.

There was a small dance at the start of term that raised £23 4s 6d toward the Appeal Fund. A further £51 7s was donated by the JCR.

Miss B. Sparks has been appointed JCR president.

The Debating Club has run only one event this term due to Pass Mods and influenza afflicting most of the team. The debate, "In the opinion of this House bullfighting is a cruel custom and as such ought to be abolished," was held in first week.

The War and Peace Society met in May and was addressed by Mr. R. H. Tawney, Fellow of Balliol College, on the topic of "Christian Socialism."

The Literary Society was addressed by Mr. J. C. Squire, editor of the *London Mercury*, who was kind enough to read a paper titled "Some Women Poets."

In fourth week, the Dramatic Society performed *Rosencrantz and Guildenstern, A Tragic Episode* by W. S. Gilbert. The third year will perform *Twelfth Night* at the Leavers' Garden Party on June 13.

TENNIS
Captain: A. Prendergast
Secretary: E. Wells

Membership has increased and we are pleased to announce the opening of two new courts on the lawn.

The First VI have won matches against Oxford High School and Somerville, and particular mention should be made of Miss D. Greenwood, who has not dropped a game this season. In Cuppers, we lost against a strong LMH team in the first round.

We shall be losing most of our First VI at the end of term and hope the Second VI will rise to the challenge. To celebrate the end of term, we have organized a mixed doubles tournament with Balliol and Worcester, to be played here on the lawn. For more details, please contact Miss E. Wells.

BOATING
President: V. Clattersby
Captain: A. Bird
Secretary: M. Harrington

Due to the excellent weather, it has been a busy term. There has been a high demand for boats, which has resulted in a large number of private hires. As such, it has been decided that from next term we will no longer test new members for proficiency before allowing them to borrow punts or canoes. This is a great relief to our proficiency captains!

> We have two "fours" shaping up nicely for next year,
> with the help of newly appointed coach Mr. Lush. Our
> rowers are still learning the basic skills, but we do hope
> that, thanks to a surge of interest among the first year, a
> rowing tradition will be established here at St. Hugh's and
> that an eight may be possible by next summer.
>
> *FRITILLARY*
> June 1921

There is an air of nostalgia about the end of the academic year. Beatrice makes a list of suggestions as to how the Eights might spend their last few days together before the long vac, and to her surprise, Otto deems them perfectly acceptable.

The last week of term begins with the third-years performing the traditional "going-down play" on the lawn. Staff and students drag armchairs under the trees, drinking tall glasses of lemonade and fanning themselves with straw hats. *Twelfth Night* has been chosen, presumably so that the third-year twins can play Viola and Sebastian, whom they portray as penniless undergraduates. Olivia and Orsino are dressed comically as dons, and Ada Bird steals the show as Malvolio in the guise of a proctor waving a copy of the statute in everyone's faces. Beatrice laughs and applauds until her hands and throat ache. The chaos is infectious: forgotten lines, makeshift costumes, accidental moments of farce.

Miss Jourdain appears in a bath chair during the second half and is positioned under one of the cherry trees away from prying eyes. Marianne tiptoes over to her with a glass of lemonade.

Otto lowers her sunglasses in mock horror. "What on earth is Grey doing?"

"Being kind, I expect," says Dora.

But the principal merely waves Marianne away.

"She doesn't look at all well," says Marianne, on her return. "Very thin."

"It's gone to her heart. That's what I heard," whispers Dora.

They see no more of the principal for the remainder of term.

THE REST OF THE WEEK is spent playing the role of tourists: visiting colleges, climbing towers, and buying ha'penny ices from tricycles. *Women in Love* is finally published and Beatrice goes with Marianne to purchase it from Blackwell's. Friends from other colleges, men and women, drop in for tea. Miss Finch the English tutor announces she is engaged to be married to a don at Keble but will continue her role at St. Hugh's, and there are drinks after supper to celebrate. Ursula hires a seventy-foot pleasure boat from Salter's called the *Gaiety*, and they cruise up and down the Thames drinking cocktails, eating salmon mayonnaise and cold chicken, and sunbathing on the top deck. She promises to write to Beatrice when she is back in London looking for work. Although Beatrice would willingly have made a fool of herself over Ursula, she knows the opportunity has passed. The yearning she endures is not reciprocated, and the thought of it being returned is so fantastical—and terrifying—that she finds herself almost relieved. Ursula will be a good friend, she tells herself.

Having first thought to ask Ursula, she invites Dora to holiday in Barcelona with her family over the summer. Her parents are fascinated by the work of Gaudí and hope to meet him. The thought of spending time with her mother is a less daunting prospect for Beatrice since Edith's unexpected acknowledgment of her at the Union debate. Plus, Otto has shared her own thoughts—some more practical than others—on *dealing with difficult mothers*. Despite this, Beatrice requests permission from the bursar to stay into ninth week in order to make up work missed during the influenza outbreak. In truth, she is not behind at all but it is hard to relinquish the precious camaraderie just yet. Unfortunately, Marianne is needed at home and cannot afford to stay. She leaves on Saturday with a crowd of other women, riding off as if to the gallows on a hired cart overseen by Miss Cox and Miss Stroud.

After they have waved Marianne off with promises of letters and telephone calls, Dora disappears into the lodge to check her pigeonhole. Beatrice follows her in and roots idly through out-of-date flyers in the narrow little box marked *JCR President*.

"'Results are posted up in the lodge on Tuesday at eleven,'" reads Otto from the noticeboard. "I think we should go punting afterward to celebrate."

"If there is something to celebrate," says Dora miserably, accepting a bunch of wilting scabiosa from Miss Jenkins, who seems to keep a tin pail under her counter entirely for the purpose.

"Don't be a Dumb Dora," says Otto, grinning. "We'll take a picnic."

Beatrice nods, smiles, and says nothing. They all know that, having missed half the term, there is a very real chance that Dora has failed.

ON TUESDAY OF NINTH WEEK, an hour before results are posted, they cycle to the Covered Market to gather provisions for the punting trip. It is hard for Beatrice to think of anything but the results now, which are already decided, historic, unchangeable. She feels as if she has just hit the curb—even though she has not—and is flying untethered through the air toward the pavement.

Dora, riding ahead, pulls up beside the new city war memorial on St. Giles', forcing Otto and Beatrice to stop behind her. The memorial, due to be unveiled in a few weeks, is usually concealed by wooden panels and tarpaulin. Apart from an ornate stone cross peeking out of the top, nothing has been visible for weeks. Today, however, the fencing lies prostrate on the dusty ground and there is only one stonemason about. He is eating a sandwich on the low wall opposite them. The women are curious, having passed the site many times.

Otto skips up to the structure and counts the sides. "It's octagonal," she says, delighted. "I told you, Sparks."

"What does that mean?" asks Dora.

"Something to do with rebirth—I forget what, exactly. But it's why christening fonts have eight sides. Sparks will know. Sparks, are you listening?"

But Beatrice is thinking of an entirely different number. It is nine years ago today since a stranger groped and kissed her against her will at the suffrage rally at the other end of the street. Yet the memory is far less insidious than it used to be. She has forged dozens of new memories of Oxford, far more interesting and worthy of her attention than this one. She can afford to let it go.

"Can we take a closer look? It would mean an awful lot," says Dora as the stonemason gets to his feet.

"By all means, miss," he says, mouth half-full. "Just one panel to go." Ignoring their protestations, he drops his lunch back into a tin and secures the lid. Then he brushes off his apron and ambles over.

The memorial is composed from an octagonal plinth with five stepped layers; a middle section of eight panels, seven of which contain a symbol or coat of arms; and a spire topped with the cross.

"What's going on the final panel?" Beatrice asks.

"Well, see, that's what I'm starting on now." He turns away to cough. "They couldn't decide on the words, so we fitted the plaque blank. I suppose they had to get them right, seeing as they're the only words on here." The mason pulls a crumpled piece of paper from his pocket and holds it out to Dora.

IN

MEMORY

OF

THOSE WHO

FOUGHT AND

THOSE WHO

FELL

1914–1918

The man's eyes fill, and he turns away briefly to wipe them. "Excuse me," he says. "My son."

Dora pats him on the arm, whispering quietly about her brother. All Otto and Beatrice can do is mumble the usual words of condolence. Mean, learned phrases that lack authenticity. Dora, however, speaks the language of loss, a language one cannot be taught in the schoolroom or examined on. It is her native tongue now and she is more fluent in it than Beatrice could ever be.

As they cycle away toward the Covered Market, it strikes Beatrice that such an interaction is as commonplace as commenting on the weather or asking after somebody's health. Loss is everyday parlance, even in 1921.

———◇———

THE FOLLOWING CANDIDATES FROM
ST. HUGH'S COLLEGE HAVE ACHIEVED A PASS
IN THE FIRST PUBLIC EXAMINATIONS 1921

Miss Florence Alderman *Modern History*

Miss Josephine Bostwick *English*

Miss Patricia Clough *Modern Languages*

Miss Sylvia Dodds *Modern History*

Miss Joan Evans   *Modern Languages*

Miss Elizabeth Fullerton-Summers   *Modern History*

Miss Theodora Greenwood   *English*

Miss Marianne Grey   *English*

Miss Yvonne Houghton-Smith   *Jurisprudence*

Miss Esther Johnson   *Modern Languages*

Miss Phyllis Knight   *English*

Miss Katherine Lloyd   *Modern Languages*

Miss Ivy Nightingale   *Lit. Hum.*

Miss Rosalind Otley-Burrows   *Modern Languages*

Miss Beatrice Sparks   *PPE*

Miss Norah Spurling   *Modern History*

Miss Celia Thompson-Salt   *English*

Miss Temperance Underhill   *English*

Miss Ottoline Wallace-Kerr   *Mathematics*

Miss Ethel Wilkinson   *Modern History*

Award of Scholar: Miss Marianne Grey

MISS J. L. KIRBY

Acting Principal

AFTER AN HOUR OF MEANDERING up and down the Cherwell, Dora moors the punt behind the trailing curtain of a willow. They drink beer from bottles, which they hang in the water by Beatrice's bootlaces, and eat pork pies from paper bags, toasting themselves for passing Mods and the fact that they have no life-or-death examinations for two years.

As Dora leans back in the punt, fingers of sun caress her bare legs. She has slipped off her stockings and pulled up her skirt, the sleeves of her blouse still wet and clingy from the water that slid relentlessly down the punt pole. She was the only one who could get the hang of it and they left her to the job, her relief powering every plunge and lift. Now she dozes, feeling the bob of the water, watching leaves seesaw down from above and float off toward an uncertain future. She revisits the moment when she pushed through the crowd, ran her finger down the list of results, found her name, and discovered that she had passed. How she burst into tears, hugged the girl next to her, and danced a reel in the courtyard with Otto and Beatrice. She can stay for two more years. She supposes she should tell Frank.

His proposal, a few days ago, came sooner than she had expected. He took her—and Miss Cox—to tea at the Randolph, and afterward they walked in the Parks, where fielders with red noses crouched, ready to spring into action. His offer was delivered between innings with sincerity and consideration, although he could barely get his words out. Would she consider becoming a doctor's wife after Oxford? he asked. They could live in London, or even overseas if she wished. He would devote himself to her and any children they might have.

It is not an unhappy prospect.

Since the day of the balloon ride, she has believed that Charles leaving is for the best. Physical attraction renders her delirious in his presence, but she can never marry him. There can be no happy ending, whatever the circumstances. The truth would unravel like a bolt of cloth between them and she deserves better. That is why she felt justified in deceiving him. It was only a half lie anyway, for she knew Frank would propose. It was simply a matter of time.

She has not told her friends about Charles's proposal—or Frank's, come to that. There is a peculiar self-possession about her now, which she supposes is due to the fact that only she can decide what happens next. Stay, go, marry, don't marry. She has choices.

Nervous about traveling with the Sparks family to Spain, she wonders if she will be a disappointment to them when they expect her to be witty or informed at dinner. Perhaps she should swot up on the war in Morocco, read the paper. Had she discussed politics and "ideas" with her parents at home, perhaps it would have been easier. Greenwood family conversations tend to feature the unpicking of things: conversations, letters, meals, suitcases. When she is a parent, she will do better, she resolves; there will be lots of *ideas*—and laughter. She assumes Beatrice has invited her because Marianne cannot leave her father and Otto abhors the idea of sightseeing and would refuse to go out until sunset, but she is flattered nonetheless. Magdalen Tower rings the half hour and she exhales, long and loud.

"I might as well tell you, I've received a proposal of marriage," she says to the sky.

"I hate to be beastly, Dora, but who the hell from?" says Otto, swigging from her bottle.

"What do you mean?"

"There are two obvious candidates. Baker and Collingham. Or is there another one hiding in your closet with your corset?"

"Am I that dreadful?" says Dora.

"No, not dreadful, just the sort of girl a chap would be glad to marry. But after Oxford, I hope?"

"After Oxford. If I accept."

"I bet you do. So—who is it to be? Mrs. Baker or Mrs. Collingham? My money's on Baker. What about you, Beatrice?"

"I much prefer Frank," says Beatrice, her thick eyebrows nudging together into one. She looks as if she is about to comment further and thinks better of it.

"Well, I shan't tell you now, you don't deserve to know," says Dora, bored of the subject.

"Oh, go on, Greenwood," says Otto, tossing her empty bottle into the water with a *plunk*.

"Yes, tell us," adds Beatrice.

"Absolutely not. I'm going to keep you in suspense." She sits up, hands on the side of the punt as it rocks, head spinning. "I say, I've got a splendid idea, let's go and tell Marianne she's a scholar. It's only nine or ten miles away, isn't it? We can catch a train or borrow your aunt's car. We could be there in two hours."

THEY ARRIVE IN CULHAM AT four in the afternoon. Otto parks the Crossley beside the long stone boundary of the graveyard. The wall is bloated and bows outward into the road as if the burden of the dead is too much for it, but the church, with its Gothic Revival bell tower, would not look out of place in Oxford. It sits on a floodplain, within a deep fold of the Thames, a mile south of Abingdon. The air, damp with loam and heavy with the metallic tang of cow parsley, reminds Dora of Fairview. The graveyard is unremarkable except for a newly constructed war memorial positioned just inside the gate. The earth at the base has dried in lumps of dry, sandy clods, and an elderly woman in a faded brown hat is tidying the wilting floral tributes. She points them in the direction of the rectory, which is back down the road, the narrow entrance cut into a towering hedge and easily missed. As they open the wooden gate into the L-shaped garden, Marianne is right before them, standing on an upturned crate, washing a latticed window. She has a scarf wound about her head and is wearing an oversized pair of gardening gloves. She does not turn around.

"I hope this is good news," she says.

Dora can see Marianne's reflection repeating in the diamond-shaped panes of glass.

"Marianne, you passed and you're a scholar," says Beatrice, rushing toward her. "All your fees paid and a fancy gown *with sleeves*. We had to tell you."

Marianne turns and steps calmly off the crate, pulling off her gloves. "And the rest of you?" She embraces Beatrice. "You smell of beer."

Dora is barely able to contain herself. "I passed. We all passed. We had to come, I hope that's all right. You look well, by the way."

"And so do you," says Marianne, smiling and kissing her. "Well done, everyone, I'm so happy for you. For us all."

There is something odd about Marianne, although Dora cannot quite put her finger on it. A sort of satisfied confidence.

"Oh, and Dora's engaged to a mystery man," says Otto.

"Could we possibly have some tea?" asks Beatrice. "I'm parched."

Marianne laughs. "Well, you'd better come in. The parlor is first right. The lavatory is out the back, I'm afraid."

Beatrice and Otto go inside chattering noisily, but Dora stops in the doorway. "I'm not being mysterious," she says. "Frank Collingham proposed. He asked, I haven't answered. You know what they're like. They won't listen."

"Are you happy?" says Marianne, taking her hand but looking beyond Dora into the far reaches of the garden.

"Yes, I think I am. Even if I am still trying to bring George back a little. But at least I realize it now. I'm trying to be more honest with myself."

"I think you are being jolly tough on yourself. I don't think it's possible for us to do anything that isn't touched by the war. Once I worked that out, I was a lot happier." Marianne glances over Dora's shoulder again. "We don't have to prove we deserve to be here anymore. We just have to get on with living."

"You knew, didn't you, about your result?" says Dora.

"Henry telephoned me this morning."

"I'm so proud of you, Marianne." Dora cocks her head and smiles. "You could tell the others that you're in love with Henry, you know?"

"It's complicated—"

From the side of the house, a small girl appears, stumbling after a young black-and-white cat. The child is around two years old, with a snotty nose, filthy apron, and long dark-blond hair. She runs up to Marianne and rubs her face in her skirt. "Mama," she says, demanding to be picked up, her palms open to the sky. Marianne lifts the child to her hip, kisses her temple. The girl fishes below the V-shaped neckline of Marianne's blouse and retrieves the locket. She begins sucking on it.

"Connie, I want you to meet my friend Dora," says Marianne.

"Hello, Connie," says Dora, bewildered.

"Connie is my daughter."

Dora starts. She thinks she must have misheard. But the child looks like a darker version of Marianne and their physical bond is unmistakable. She becomes aware her mouth is hanging open. "Gosh, I—"

A tall redheaded man in shirtsleeves appears around the corner. "Connie, what about the gooseberries?" he calls, stopping suddenly in his tracks. "Oh, hello, Dora," says Henry. "What have I missed?"

36

Marianne, August 1919

———◦◆◦———

C onstance Olive Ward does not die at birth. Sinewy and lean, she enters the world to the beat of Culham: the bustle of the harvest coming in, the steady thrum of the river going about its business, the clumsy drone of the church organist at rehearsal.

The day Constance is born, Marianne is so depleted from blood loss and shock that her mother-in-law moves in to nurse them both. Thankfully, Olive Ward is the sort of person who sees what is to be done and does it. She is a pounder of dough, a beater of rugs, a silent, stoical woman who swings Constance about as if she were a church kneeler. The pockets of her apron are full of items she collects to show the baby: acorns, ribbons, a photograph of the king cut carefully from a newspaper. What Olive respects above all is what she was denied as a child: education. Occasionally, her tawny eyes fill at the knowledge that her precious granddaughter will *know her letters*.

It is a confusing time for Marianne, the family doubling in size overnight, footsteps bringing silent rooms in the rectory to life, this gruff stranger scooping them up in her stout arms and rescuing them. But Olive's presence is far from invasive, and soon it is hard to imagine life without her swatting at mice with her broom or pickling onions in the scullery. After a few weeks, Olive gives notice to her landlord. Her rent has gone up again and she is barely there anyway. And the village agrees, someone must take care of the rector.

At first, the responsibility of motherhood threatens to overwhelm Marianne. She spends the first three weeks in bed but insists she must feed Constance herself. She grieves for her own mother, who never held her, and obsesses about the nameless woman who wet-nursed her all those years ago. Her father, drowning in loss at the time, cannot recall the woman's name or anything about her.

The attachment Marianne has with her daughter is intense and bewildering. It is as if Constance is a spare organ or limb that has been removed from her, and for a few weeks it feels as if they are inhabiting the same consciousness. But this psychic connection, as Marianne likes to describe it, soon fades. It reminds her of plucking offspring from the spider plant in the hallway to grow in water. In the violence of an instant, they are irreparably severed.

By the time she is three months old, Constance has become Connie. Olive says she looks like Tom with his conker-brown eyes and wavy hair, but to Marianne, who barely exchanged a dozen words with her husband, Connie may as well have been a virgin birth. When she walks out into the village with the perambulator, Marianne is surprised to find herself addressed as *Mrs. Ward*. In church services, Connie is fascinated by her mother's singing and reaches vaguely toward her mouth. The fat little digits smell of milk and spittle and Marianne nibbles and kisses each one over and over. She has to resist the urge not to bite.

Apart from sleep, what Marianne misses most of all about her old life is reading. As the months progress, she nods off over novels that she might have devoured before, and those she manages to reread often reduce her to tears. The Oxford Senior has already come and gone, as does the Summer Meeting, a series of lectures in Oxford that she had hoped to attend over the long vac. One early morning in November, however, she attempts to translate a short passage of the *Iliad* after Connie's first feed, completing it between the bedtime and night feeds. And suddenly, the old thirst is back.

AT CHRISTMAS, HER GODMOTHER MAKES her annual visit with gifts of secondhand books and powdery Turkish delight. An old school friend of her mother, Eleanor is an expert in Dante and studied at the University of Paris. Although she is elegant, well traveled, and the principal of an Oxford college, society brands her first and foremost a spinster. Marianne has heard from her father that Eleanor was famous for attending suffrage rallies in her doctoral robes.

"It's wrong that a woman of your intelligence should miss out on a first-class education," Eleanor says. Dignified in her customary black, she accepts only tea and refuses to hold Connie. "There was a home student married with a stepchild once. She was viewed as a freak, I'm afraid, even by the other women. Only lasted a few weeks. The idea of a war widow leaving her child at home to be educated would be considered even more scandalous. No college would sanction it."

"What if Marianne applied in her maiden name?" says her father. "A clerical slip of some kind." He has mooted this before, but Marianne has always dismissed it as idle thought. She sits up like a hare sensing danger.

"Marianne could leave Connie here in term time and return at weekends," her father continues. "It's only twenty-four weeks of the year. If she got an exhibition, I'm sure we could manage." He runs his finger under his clerical collar, much cleaner since Olive arrived. "I'm thinking of her future security, you understand . . ." Marianne feels heat rising in her cheeks, her heart skittery like it was in the days after Connie was born.

Eleanor says nothing at first and sips her tea. Then she fixes her gaze on Marianne. "I remember Constance wearing that locket the day she was married."

"I carry a lock of Connie's hair in it now," Marianne replies.

Connie has woken and is making sucking motions with her lips. She will need feeding soon.

Eleanor puts down her cup. "If word got out, you would be sent down for using a false name and perhaps even accused of child neglect. You would need to be prepared for the consequences."

"I would. I am," says Marianne. She cannot countenance leaving Connie, but it is interesting to see where this fantastical conversation might lead.

"I would say, sit the examinations. See what happens. You're a bright young woman. If you get an exhibition, then I may back you—may—but you must prove you are worth the risk. Nothing less than top marks.

"And there could be no favoritism, and no one must know. When we came across each other, I could not acknowledge you and you could not acknowledge me."

"Indeed," says her father, nodding vigorously.

"That is the arrangement I would bind you to. I could not be seen to treat you differently. If you are discovered, I will deny all knowledge. I have enemies within the college and the university who want me out. It is a huge risk."

"I understand," says Marianne, not believing at all that this situation might ever come to fruition. "I won't let you down."

As she is leaving, Eleanor kisses Marianne on the cheek in a waft of freesia scent and murmurs enigmatically in her ear. "We all live with secrets, my dear. And when I'm dead you will know mine."

"She was in love with your mother at school," says her father, cheerfully, when he closes the front door. "Did you notice the color of her eyes? Violet, would you say, or mauve? I always underestimate how extraordinary they are."

MARIANNE COMES TOP IN THE county for the Oxford Senior the following July, receiving distinctions in all subjects, including

Latin and Greek, and receives an offer of an exhibition to St. Hugh's College. An arrangement is made with the college that Marianne will return to Culham every fortnight on the premise that her father is unwell. She removes her wedding ring but clings to her mother's locket containing Connie's dark curls. It is her talisman, her reminder of why she is doing this: to make a better life for them both.

When Marianne arrives at Oxford, Eleanor Jourdain is true to her word and ignores her. They speak alone only once during the entire first year, on the night of the Ouija session when the principal puts her to bed and tells her the spelling out of Connie's name on the board is a sign that they are both doing the right thing, that her mother approves. The agony of separation is terrible at first, but Marianne's fear and guilt diminish as Connie thrives. As each weekend at home passes, it becomes easier to return to Oxford. She panics less about bumping into locals who might address her as Mrs. Ward when she is with other people. The villagers assume she has a job at an Oxford college and nobody has contradicted them. She finds that living a lie—assuming a false identity—is not so hard when the identity is your own. Even lying to Otto, Dora, and Beatrice becomes a habit, though not one she is proud of. She has not expected to like them so much, to become so inextricably bound up in their joy and their struggles. The more solid the friendship, the more brittle the lies.

And then there is Henry.

TO HER SURPRISE AND MORTIFICATION, he is at the station on Saturday of eighth week, leaning against a pillar reading the newspaper. He stands out among the crowd of departing students, with the map of red etchings on his cheek, the lumpy contours of flesh and hair where his ear once was. Miss Stroud is busy remonstrating with the cart driver over who will unload the trunks, while Miss Cox supervises their charges in the long queues at the ticket booths. When Henry glances their way, he does not wave or acknowledge Marianne, and her throat constricts. She prays he has not seen her.

She is relieved when the two-fifteen to Didcot finally departs. With her trunk safely stowed in the guard's van, she settles into a seat by the window, ready to watch one half of her life recede into distant spires as the other comes into focus. The third-class carriage is almost full. She cannot be bothered to look at the other passengers and imagine, as she so often does, what character they would play in a Dickens novel. As the conductor blows his whistle and the final carriage door slams, a passenger lands heavily in the seat facing her. Glancing up, she sees a man with oxford brogues, long legs, and a map on his face to show her the way home. The train gathers speed at Hinksey, and as they pass the shimmering reservoir of the city waterworks, his foot nudges forward and presses against hers.

When the train draws into Culham, she jumps out quickly to claim her trunk. Henry is right behind her, still saying nothing, just looking at her and smiling. The porter calls for a boy to drive the trunk the mile to the rectory, and they set off walking behind him. To anyone watching they could be husband and wife. As soon as the station is no longer in sight, the road clear and the cart in the distance, Henry pulls her to him and kisses her gently on the mouth. Then he runs his lips over her neck, her chin, her eyelids.

"The thing is," he says into her ear, "I forgot to tell you that I love you."

He returns to Culham on his bicycle the next day and the next and the next.

37

After Henry cycles away from the rectory toward Oxford, they drink tea and watch Constance play with the kitten on the parlor floor. Unlike her mother, Constance has a tanned, fleshy build, but she has the same long neck and hooded eyes. Beatrice watches her with fascination, slowly digesting the news and replaying scenes from the last two terms that did not quite make sense at the time. How Marianne would return from a weekend home exhausted. And with very little reading done.

Otto pronounces herself excellent with children. "I shall be her unofficial aunt," she says, flashing her neat little teeth. "We will celebrate our birthdays together."

Constance leans into her shyly, enchanted by the long yellow beads that swing and click as Otto talks.

Otto ruffles Connie's hair. "She won't bite you, Sparks."

"I know," replies Beatrice, but the truth is, she is not entirely sure.

"She's rather spoiled by my father and mother-in-law, I'm afraid," says Marianne. "I spend my weekends trying to unpick the effects of too many late nights and too many jam tarts."

Dora shakes her head in wonder. "I don't know how you manage. I had no idea."

"None of us did," says Beatrice. Tea, cakes, pets, children in a neat little sitting room with an inglenook fireplace. Definitely not what she imagined when she woke up that morning.

"Olive lives here and takes care of things in term time. I'm hugely indebted to her. She could have made life very difficult, but she said that I must go. She said Thomas would have wanted it."

It is odd to think of Marianne as a widow, that her name is really Mrs. Thomas Ward. Beatrice can hardly believe it. It must have been exhausting keeping such a weighty secret.

"What will happen if Miss Jourdain finds out?" asks Dora.

"We have to make sure she doesn't," replies Otto darkly.

"Are there any rules forbidding widows or mothers enrolling?" asks Beatrice.

"That won't matter to her."

Marianne rubs at her temple. "Miss Jourdain has met Connie. She was at school with my mother."

The news that Miss Jourdain is involved surprises Beatrice far more than the news that Marianne is a widow with a daughter or that the Ouija board spelt out Connie's name. That Miss Jourdain, with all her rules and religious fervor, was party to this secret seems impossible.

"There are no rules against mothers attending as such, but it would be considered a bad show. Home-wrecking and that sort of thing. They might even threaten to take Constance away. She swore us to secrecy."

"You could have told us, perhaps we could have helped," says Beatrice. She shrinks back into the armchair as Constance veers toward her. "I'm so sorry, Marianne. All that fuss with the kittens, I should have realized. And now I think of how you cried at *The Kid*—"

"Even an enormous brain like yours misses things, Sparks," says Otto.

"I'm sorry I deceived you," says Marianne, wiping her eyes. "I was too ashamed to tell you and I promised Miss Jourdain I wouldn't.

"From the moment I got to Oxford, I was in a state of panic. I was counting down the days until I got home at the weekend. But I knew Connie and I would both have a better life if I could teach. The eight-week terms seemed bearable as long as I got to see her some weekends. I kept returning to the same question: is it so wrong to want something for myself?"

"It isn't wrong at all," says Dora, taking her hand.

Otto looks at Constance and then at Marianne. "We don't all go to Oxford to become Marie Curie. Most of us are ordinary people grasping the opportunity of an extraordinary education—and that goes for the men too."

And for once, there is nothing further to explain.

AFTER CONSTANCE GOES TO BED, they eat supper with Marianne's father. Having spent so long imagining him as infirm in some way, Beatrice is surprised to find that the Reverend Grey looks younger and more vital than her own father and is an expert on ancient Greek theater. He talks passionately of his time studying Greats at Magdalen and wants to hear all about the new school of PPE.

After helping Marianne's mother-in-law to clear up, they take the motorcar to Boars Hill to watch the sun set over Oxford. Home of poets and academics who prefer to live out of the city, Boars Hill unfolds into rolling pasture, the open heathland dotted with ancient oak and beech trees. Speckled kestrels hover and swoop with tails fanned. Bony cows stroll aimlessly, heads bowed.

"This is the view Arnold had in mind when he wrote about *that sweet city with her dreaming spires*," says Marianne, picking daisies from the grass beside her.

"'Thyrsis,' isn't it? The poem he wrote about Arthur Hugh Clough?" says Dora.

"This is the exact spot he was describing. Except they experienced it together in winter."

"I doubt it's changed much in eighty years."

"One day it will change, that's the number one rule of life, I'm afraid," says Beatrice, removing her hat. She feels the urge to capture the skyline and takes a notebook and pencil from her pocket and begins to sketch the individual spires and rooftops that can be discerned from the mass.

"It puts me in mind of a Turner painting," says Otto in an exaggerated drawl.

Beatrice looks up at her, incredulous. "Oh, really?"

"Don't look at me like that, Sparks, I am not a complete heathen."

"So, do you mean William Turner of Oxford, the watercolorist, or J. M. W. Turner? They're both in the Ashmolean and they both painted this scene," says Beatrice, smiling to herself. She begins to number the spires in her drawing in order to create a key.

"I mean the one on the wall in the WC at the Good Luck Tea Rooms." Otto sticks out her tongue. "I know that smelly little room inside out."

"Do orchids grow around here, Marianne? Is it chalk?" asks Dora.

"I don't think so, it's too sandy," replies Marianne.

"Henry says they found orchids in the meadow at Christ Church," says Beatrice. "They let the land go to seed after all the vegetable growing. Apparently, they've been dormant all this time. There's only one bee orchid, which they've cordoned off, but he thinks there may be more."

"It's incredible to think they were under our feet all that time," says Dora.

"Just like the cowpats," adds Otto, blowing a smoke ring.

From this vantage point, some four hundred feet above sea level, Oxford lies below them. Dwarfed by the sky, the city looks as if it is sinking into the surrounding hillsides, as if it is fleshy and yielding. It is easy to identify the rounded dome of the Radder, the matching turrets of All Souls, the spindly steeple of Exeter College chapel with its angled gray roof. The University Church, St. Mary of the Virgin, is the tallest building, and by locating it they recognize All Saints' Church tower at the end of Turl Street, Magdalen Tower to the right, and Tom Tower in the fore. At the back of the scene, the tiny white cupola of the Sheldonian Theater glints in the dimming evening light.

The sun, on its longest journey of the year, is descending in amber brushstrokes to their left. The city blushes as it sinks further into the shadows.

"The thing about Oxford is, you spend all this time fretting that you don't belong, but when you are apart from it, you feel as if you've left something precious behind," says Dora.

"In your case, two engagement rings," says Otto.

An affectionate scuffle ensues.

"On that note, we'd better get off," says Beatrice. "I promised Miss Kirby we'd be back by ten."

Marianne moves closer to the others and puts her arms out. They encircle her, heads pressed together, as if it were the most natural thing in the world.

And then they rise.

Author's Note

O ne of the joys of writing this novel has been the research and the way it helped to shape the characters and plot. It felt like a collaboration at times; whenever I was stuck, I went back to Oxford and she always provided the answer. Although I have woven fact and fiction, my aim has always been to re-create accurately the life of women at Oxford in 1920. However, I am no historian, and if I have made any irritating errors, I heartily apologize.

The idea for *The Eights* came from two sources. Firstly, my regular dog walks in Ashridge Forest, Berkhamsted, where a section of practice trenches has been preserved by local historians. Secondly, images shared by Oxford University on social media in 2020 to commemorate the centenary of women receiving degrees. I wondered: what might happen if a woman from Berkhamsted fell in love with a cadet and then met him a few years later at Oxford?

Apart from the main characters' homes, the locations used in the novel are all real, as is the history behind them, especially as regards the Great War. For example, Somerville College and the Examination Schools were indeed converted into military hospitals. I made a few small changes for the sake of the story, such as moving the position of the Good Luck Tea Rooms from Cornmarket to Broad Street. The church at Culham is actually called St. Paul's, which I thought had the potential to confuse the reader. For dramatic purposes, I chose to fictionalize the cold weather described in January 1921—according to the Met Office, it was actually "abnormally mild" that month.

Technically, the women's colleges were defined as halls or societies in 1920 (St. Hugh's was converted in 1926). However, archived letters and articles show that they were commonly referred to as colleges. The Society for Home Students later became St. Anne's College. (For those interested, the website of the Oxford University research project Education & Activism collates all manner of treasures related to the first women at Oxford, including how the women's colleges were established.)

Otto, Beatrice, Dora, and Marianne are drawn from my own imagination, as are all the students with the exception of Vera Brittain and Winifred Holtby. I borrowed surnames and first names from actual students listed in the *Fritillary*. The extracurricular activities the students undertake are factually based, and the St. Hugh's archive was especially helpful in this regard. Women really did leave the theater early en masse and sometimes had to climb through windows. The notorious "chap rules" are entirely factual. It is also true that a St. Hilda's boat competed at Summer Eights in 1921, bumping some of the male crews.

I could find only one instance of a "freakish" undergraduate being married with a young baby, and she was a home student rather than a college resident. Laura Schwartz, in her excellent book *A Serious Endeavor*, describes how this information appalled a St. Hugh's student when she was invited to tea.

I simplified the end-of-first-year examinations so that all the first-years at St. Hugh's sit Pass Mods (as described by Vera Brittain in *Testament of Youth*). In fact, a minority of women who wanted to gain honors degrees did sit Mods or Prelims in History, Law, Modern Languages, and Classics. It was possible to do Mods in subjects one was not studying and this was not unusual, some being considered easier than others. Later in the 1920s, the numbers of men and women doing Pass Mods decreased dramatically, but at the time the novel is set the majority of women studied History, Modern Languages, or English; sat Pass Mods; and left with a pass degree.

Miss Jourdain and Miss Rogers are based on real people, as are Lord Curzon, Mr. Cowley, Professor Elliott, and G. H. Hardy, but the remaining chaperones, tutors, and lecturers are fictional. The story of Annie Rogers coming top in the entrance exam and being given books as a consolation prize is true. I visited Oxford over fifty times in the course of writing the novel and decided to include Miss Rogers after spotting the blue plaque commemorating her life at 35 St. Giles'. Eleanor Jourdain led a fascinating life, deserving of a novel in itself, and was posthumously revealed to be the co-author of a best-selling book about seeing ghosts at Versailles. She died suddenly in 1924 after a scandal about her leadership. Queen Mary did visit Oxford as described in 1921, as did Thomas Hardy.

Regarding the Oxford Union Society, although there was no debate like the one I have imagined in 1921, there was a motion in 1926 that argued "Women's Colleges Should Be Razed to the Ground." The motion, reportedly lighthearted in nature, was passed. Women were admitted to full membership of the Union in 1963.

The balloon ride is also fictional, inspired by the true story of the first English aeronaut, James Sadler, who ascended from Christ Church Meadow in 1784. Similarly, the private view at the Ashmolean is imaginary but inspired by the Combe Collection, much of which is still on view today.

There was a suffrage rally in Oxford that ended in violence in 1912. Edith Sparks and Miss Rix are fictional characters, however, as are the other parents of the Eights. Emily Davison, who died under the king's racehorse at Epsom in 1913, did attend St. Hugh's for a term. Her attendance at the rally is fictional; she was still in prison at the time and attempted suicide the day after. The story of the Steamboat Ladies is true.

Berkhamsted was a garrison town for five years during the Great War, and the remains of the trenches can be seen on Berkhamsted Common, near the memorial to the Devil's Own Regiment. I imagine Fairview to be where the clubhouse of Berkhamsted Golf Club now sits. The Berkhamsted Local History & Museum Society describe the impact of the cadets on town life in their publication *Berkhamsted in WWI*.

Apart from the May Day notice that is fictional, the rules and notes sent out by Miss Jourdain are taken from real documents in the St. Hugh's archives. Some of them now hang framed on the walls in the corridors. The *Daily Mail* headline about "a million women too many" appeared in February 1920, not October, but it was too good not to use. The *Oxford Chronicle* article about Guy Fawkes Day was actually published on Friday, November 12, 1920, but for my purposes it needed to be a Monday. The *Daily Mail* article about "undergraduettes" was printed as it appears on the page, except that the author described the hats inaccurately as velvet! The other articles have been adapted or edited to different degrees. The *Isis* published a similar poem to the one I have written, and featured cartoons about women with children in the JCR as described. The *Imp* article about the proctor is based on a "legend" Vera Brittain describes in *The Women of Oxford*. The student from Somerville who made headlines in the *Daily Mail* for climbing a wall to see her fiancé was the film critic and journalist Dilys Powell.

The battle for equality and acceptance raged on after 1921. In 1927, the University Congregation passed a statute limiting the number of women at Oxford to a quarter of the men. This quota was finally abolished in 1957.

Readers might like to know that St. Hugh's admitted men for the first time in 1986, its centenary year. I understand they were welcomed with open arms.

Acknowledgments

I am hugely grateful to Marina de Pass for signing me on the basis of a half-finished manuscript. Marina, you are kindness and wisdom personified. Thank you also to the Soho Agency. I cannot imagine that a more welcoming agency exists, nor a more talented and lovely agent.

To my editor Helen Garnons-Williams and to assistant editor Ella Harold, thank you for your unwavering belief in *The Eights* and for your editing genius. It's an honor to have joined the list at Fig Tree. Thank you to Sarah-Jane Forder for the eagle-eyed copy-edits and to Olivia Mead for publicity—you had me at "Team Beatrice." Also to Emma Pidsley for the stunning UK cover and Mike Hall for the beautiful map.

To my American editor Tara Singh Carlson for her passion, determination, and vision. Thank you to the wonderfully supportive team at Putnam, especially assistant editors Aranya Jain and Molly Donovan, copy editor Amy J. Schneider, director of publicity Alexis Welby, assistant director of publicity Katie McKee, and marketing manager Shina Patel. Thank you, Sara Wood, for the elegant US cover.

To Nicky Kennedy and the team at ILA for championing *The Eights* in translation. Especial thanks to Cordelia Borchardt at S. Fischer Verlag and Katel le Fur at Robert Laffont. Their early interest in *The Eights* meant so much.

Thanks also to the Faber Academy and my tutor on the Write Your Novel course, Sabrina Broadbent. I am hugely indebted to my classmates, Hester, Lyndsey, Cathryn, Megan, Emma, Beena, Miriam, Jude, Vicki, Carina, Ali, Clara, and Connor.

To the National Center for Writing for its work supporting emerging writers, and for my place on the Escalator Talent Development Scheme. To my mentor Michael Donkor for his warmth, insight, and excellent jumpers. Thank you to my fellow mentees for their support: Melody, Ben, Shirley, Mark, Isabelle, Adam, Carrie, Rick, and Bang.

To the tutors on the Diploma of Creative Writing at Oxford's Department of Continuing Education. To my classmates, Claire-Louise, Helen, Sara, Ollie, Marianne, Ejaz, Olu, Edie, Esme, Cate, Fay, Felix, Emilie, Mark, Ellie, and Audrey, thank you for two years of sharing and camaraderie. I miss our Saturdays at Ewert Place.

To Thea Crapper at St. Hugh's College, thank you for the guided tour and for your invaluable notes on the manuscript. Thank you to the St. Hugh's College librarians for allowing me access to the archives. To read firsthand accounts of women's experiences at Oxford in the early 1920s was both a thrill and a privilege.

To the Bodleian Library for reactivating my Bod card after thirty years and to Elizabeth at the Oxford Union Society Library for the superb tour that inspired a whole chapter of the novel. Thank you to Exeter College for its continued support. *Floreat Exon!*

I am hugely grateful to the Berkhamsted Local History & Museum Society for fact-checking the two chapters set in Berkhamsted. Thank you, Mary Casserley, Linda Rollit, Richard North, and Bill Willett. Thanks to the Oxford Bus Museum for answering my questions about traffic in the 1920s.

To my colleagues Charlotte, Hannah, and Amelie at the Berkhamsted Bookshop for being flexible when edits got tough.

Thank you also to Our Bookshop Tring and BeaconLit Festival for bringing so many wonderful authors to our doorstep.

To the women who have kept me afloat at different stages in my life. The intensity of those friendships and how necessary they were to my survival and happiness at the time is, in part, what inspired this novel. Especial thanks to Yasmin Wilde, Tiffany Gaston, Emma Hall, Alison Wood, Natasha Gunning, Charlotte Woollett, Lucy Davies, Holly Green, Sarah Lever, Mich Lancaster, and Su Lawrence.

To Nina and James Anderton for your exceptional friendship and cooking.

To Mum and Dad, for encouraging my academic dreams. To Pat, Jo, Simon, Henry, and Nicholas, and my father-in-law David, who is much missed. To Annie, James, Rachel, and Lucy, and to my brother Chris, who would have been so proud of us all. To Rob, Raff, Sav, and Dooey for making Sydney feel like home.

To my sister and best friend, Ali Lowe. Thank you for sharing your agent with me, for the witty one-liners that inspired the character of Otto, and for telling me to *just get on with it*. I adore you.

To my children, Darcy, Jackson, and Archie. Thank you for the hugs, the bookish gifts, and for hunting bee orchids with me. I'm sorry for the times I was late picking you up because I got lost in my writing. *The Eights* is dedicated to you with all my love.

To my husband, Craig, for accompanying me on two-hour walks around Oxford every Sunday, for his unquestioning belief that this novel would be published (despite never reading it), and for always fetching the coffee.

And finally, to Dickens, who slept at my feet while this book was written and was the best boy that ever lived.

Glossary

Bodleian/Bodder/Bod—the university library

Bursar—responsible for finances and domestic issues within college

Chap rules—rules regarding chaperones

Collections—start-of-term examinations

Come up—arrive at the start of term

Commoner—student without exhibition or scholarship

Congregation—governing body of the university

Cuppers—intercollege competitions

Divvers or Divinity Moderations—compulsory scripture examination for first-years

Don—professor, lecturer, or fellow

Entrance examination—taken by all applicants to Oxford and followed up by interview

Exhibition—a small financial award for academic merit

Fellow—don who is a member of the governing body of a college

First—highest result possible in papers or examinations

Freshman/Fresher—first-year undergraduate

Fritillary—twice-yearly magazine of the women's colleges

Gated—confined to college premises as a punishment

Go down—leave at the end of term

Greats—an undergraduate degree in Classical Languages, History, and Philosophy

Hilary term—January to March

Imp—termly magazine of St. Hugh's

Isis—weekly university magazine

JCR—Junior Common Room (for undergraduates)

Lit. Hum.—Literae Humaniores, also known as Greats

LMH—Lady Margaret Hall (a women's college in 1920)

Long vac—summer vacation

Matriculation—enrollment ceremony

Michaelmas term—October to December

Mods/Prelims—end-of-first-year examinations (for those seeking honors)

Oxford Senior—end-of-school qualification; exempts students from Responsions

Oxford Union Society—private debating society

Pass Mods—Mods for arts students and linguists not seeking honors

Pigeon post—the university's internal postal system

PPE—an undergraduate degree in Philosophy, Politics, and Economics

Proctors—responsible for student discipline across the university

Quad—quadrangle, usually with a lawn and staircases on all sides

Radcliffe Camera/Radder/Rad—iconic dome-shaped library, part of the Bodleian

Rag—to joke or trick, a prank

Responsions—tests in math and Latin taken by undergraduates without the Oxford Senior

Rustication—temporary expulsion from the university

Scholar—recipient of a scholarship

Scout—cleaner or servant allocated to a group of rooms

SCR—Senior Common Room (for staff)

Sent down—permanent expulsion from the university

Set—pair of college rooms

Statute—rules of the university

Sub fusc—dark suit worn with gown on formal occasions

Summer Eights—rowing races in Trinity term

Summer Meeting—summer lectures and tutorials open to the public

Taylorian—the Taylor Institution (part of the Bodleian Library)

The High—High Street

Torpids—rowing races in Hilary term

Trinity term—April to June

Tute—tutorial

Tutor—teaches one-to-one or in small groups; could be a don or other academic

Univ—University College

VAD—the Voluntary Aid Detachment (civilian unit providing nursing care)

Viva voce—oral examinations for students

WSPU—the Women's Social and Political Union (members known as suffragettes)

WVR—the Women's Volunteer Reserve (established by members of the WSPU)

Key Dates

1873—Annie Rogers comes top in the Oxford Schools' examinations. "Lectures for Ladies" are provided by willing dons

1878—The Association for Promoting the Higher Education of Women in Oxford (AEW) is established. The first college for women, Lady Margaret Hall, is founded with nine students

1879—Somerville College and the Society of Home Students are founded

1886—St. Hugh's College is founded

1889—Cornelia Sorabji is the first Indian woman student, and the first woman to study Law

1893—St. Hilda's College is founded

1894—Women are able to sit the same final examinations as men but are still ineligible for degrees

1895—Oxford and Cambridge are now the only British universities not to award degrees to women

1906—Women are allowed to attend lectures, but dons can exclude them if they wish

1911—The Oxford Women Students' Society for Women's Suffrage is established

1912—A suffrage rally is held at Martyrs' Memorial and ends in violence

1913—Emily Wilding Davison dies under the king's horse at Epsom

1914—War is declared with Germany. The Women's Volunteer Reserve is founded by suffragettes. A garrison is established in Berkhamsted by the Inns of Court Officers' Training Corps. Women are permitted to attend lectures unchaperoned

1915—Somerville College becomes a military hospital. Miss Jourdain becomes principal of St. Hugh's. The first women are invited to lecture at the university

1916—Women are permitted to study Medicine at Oxford

1917—The Battle of Cambrai takes place in November and December

1918—The Representation of the People Act is passed in February and eight million women over thirty get the vote. War ends on November 11

1919—The Sex Disqualification (Removal) Act requires universities to admit women

1920—Oxford University Congregation votes to admit women. Women matriculate for the first time on October 7. The first degrees are awarded on October 14, and any woman who is eligible may apply retrospectively

1921—Queen Mary visits Oxford and is awarded an honorary degree

1926—Lady Margaret Hall, Somerville, St. Hugh's, and St. Hilda's are recognized as Oxford colleges. The Oxford Union debates whether women's colleges should be "razed to the ground"

1927—The university limits the number of women admitted to 840

1928—All British women over twenty-one get the vote, gaining the same rights as men

1932—Merze Tate becomes the first African American woman student at Oxford

1942—The Society for Home Students becomes St. Anne's

1948—Women are admitted as full students at Cambridge University

1957—The quota limiting the number of women undergraduates to a quarter of men is lifted

1959—The five women's colleges gain the full status of men's colleges

1963—Women are admitted to membership of the Oxford Union Society

1974—The first men's colleges admit women

1979—Lady Margaret Hall and St. Anne's are the first women's colleges to admit men

1986—St. Hugh's College admits men

1993—Professor Marilyn Butler becomes the first female head of a formerly all-male college

2008—Oxford University becomes fully coeducational

2016—Professor Louise Richardson is the first woman to become vice chancellor

2020—Baroness Valerie Amos becomes the first black woman to head an Oxford college

Bibliography

Berkhamsted in WWI by Berkhamsted Local History & Museum Society (2017)

Bluestockings: The Remarkable Story of the First Women to Fight for an Education by Jane Robinson (2009)

Britain in the 1920s by Fiona McDonald (2012)

Dangerous by Degrees: Women at Oxford and the Somerville College Novelists by Susan J. Leonardi (1989)

Degrees by Degrees by Annie Rogers (1938)

Education & Activism: Women at Oxford, 1878–1920, research project at the University of Oxford led by Professor Senia Paseta (2020)

Gaudy Night by Dorothy L. Sayers (1935)

The Great Silence: 1918–1920 Living in the Shadow of the Great War by Juliet Nicolson (2009)

The History of the University of Oxford: Volume VIII: The Twentieth Century by Brian Harrison (1994)

Not Far from Brideshead: Oxford between the Wars by Daisy Dunn (2022)

A Serious Endeavor: Gender, Education & Community at St. Hugh's, 1886–2011 by Laura Schwartz (2011)

Singled Out: How Two Million Women Survived without Men after the First World War by Virginia Nicholson (2007)

Suffragettes: The Fight for Votes for Women, edited by Joyce Marlow (2000)

Testament of Youth by Vera Brittain (1933)

The Virago Book of Women and the Great War, edited by Joyce Marlow (1998)

The Women at Oxford by Vera Brittain (1960)

About the Author

© Lucy Noble

Joanna Miller studied English at Exeter College, Oxford, and later returned to complete an English teaching degree at the Department of Educational Studies. After ten years as a teacher and literacy adviser, she set up an award-winning poetry gift business. Joanna's rhyming verse has been filmed twice by the BBC, and in 2015 she won the Poetry Prize, awarded by Bloomsbury Publishing and the National Literacy Trust. In 2021, Joanna graduated from the Faber Academy, after which she was accepted on the Escalator Talent Development Scheme at the National Center for Writing. She has recently returned to Oxford to study part-time for a diploma in creative writing.

Visit Joanna Miller Online

joannamillerauthor.com

JoannaMillerAuthor

JoannaMillerReader

X JoannaMAuthor